One Foot Out the Door
The Collected Stories of Lewis Warsh

PORTRAIT OF LEWIS WARSH BY PHONG BUI
2014. Pencil on tea-washed paper. 11" x 15"

ALSO BY LEWIS WARSH

FICTION

Agnes & Sally
A Free Man
Money Under the Table
Touch of the Whip
Ted's Favorite Skirt
A Place in the Sun

POETRY

The Suicide Rates
Highjacking
Moving Through Air
Chicago, with Tom Clark
Dreaming As One
Long Distance
Immediate Surrounding
Today
Blue Heaven
Hives
Methods of Birth Control
The Corset
Information From the Surface of Venus
Avenue of Escape
Private Agenda, with Pamela Lawton
The Origin of the World
Debtor's Prison, with Julie Harrison
Reported Missing
Flight Test
The Flea Market in Kiel
Inseparable: Poems 1995-2005

AUTOBIOGRAPHY

Part of My History
The Maharajah's Son
Bustin's Island, 1968

TRANSLATION

Night of Loveless Nights
  by Robert Desnos

EDITOR

The Angel Hair Anthology,
  with Anne Waldman

RECORDING

The Origin of the World

One Foot Out the Door

THE COLLECTED STORIES OF
LEWIS WARSH

SPUYTEN DUYVIL   *New York City*

Some of these stories first appeared in *2000 and What? Stories About the Turn of the Millenium* (Trip Street Press), *BOMB*, *The Brooklyn Rail*, *The Brooklyn Rail Fiction Anthologies* (#1 & #2), *Conjunctions*, *Lift Magazine*, *Mimeo Mimeo*, *Pequod*, and in the collections *Touch of the Whip* (Singing Horse, 2001) and *Money Under the Table* (Trip Street Press, 1997).

Thanks to Gil Ott, Karl Roeseler, Donald Breckenridge, Kyle Schlesinger, Jed Birmingham, Wang Ping, Barbara Henning, Nava Renek and Tod Thilleman. Thanks to Phong Bui for the portrait as fontispiece.

And to Marie Warsh, Sophia Warsh, Max Warsh, Alyssa Gorelick and Zola Ray Warsh.

ISBN 978-0-923389-93-2

Library of Congress Cataloging-in-Publication Data

Warsh, Lewis.
  [Short stories. Selections]
  One Foot Out The Door :
the collected stories of Lewis Warsh / [Lewis Warsh].
pages cm
  ISBN 978-0-923389-93-2
  I. Title.
  PS3573.A782A6 2014
  813'.54—dc23
2013021415

for Katt Lissard

TABLE OF CONTENTS

Working Late   1
G & A   35
Inner Circles   47
The Merit System   52
Crack   63
Sirocco   81
Pick Up On Tenth Street   85
The Rightful Heir   102
Special Friend   105
Money Under The Table   114
No Vacancy   167
Outside Boston   169
The Acting Lesson   175
Pedagogy Of The Oppressed   200
Dubrovnik   204
Midnight Sun   208
Sadness On Ludlow Street   213
Sweet Sixteen   220
Après Le Bain   232
Holy City   242

None Of The Above   252

She Was Working   302

Vicki   315

To Have And Have Not   321

Story Of The Kidnapping   329

Romance   337

Ralph   345

We Live   347

Lost Time   349

Without Speaking   357

Self-Portrait, San Francisco, 1971   386

One Foot Out The Door

Maybe life can be defined by the things
you didn't do. The days of amnesty, a pinup
on the door of the locker, the combination
safe and all the pleasure that comes from
staying indoors when the sun is shining.

"At its apex," you might say, describing nothing.
For once in your life you're at a loss for
words. There's a new library, named after yours
truly, at the dark end of the street. Located between
the dump and the cemetery, just so you know.

Working Late

I t was suddenly dark out, night time, but no one cared. We were all so immersed in our work, our deadlines, that we didn't even notice.

Eventually my coworkers began to leave. They had decided, I suppose, that whatever they hadn't finished could wait till tomorrow. I heard them sighing from across the office as they closed down their computers. The men loosened their ties. The women primped in front of hand mirrors and applied new coats of lipstick. Someone passed my desk and said, "Have a good night." I waved my hand in the direction of the voice and nodded without looking up.

Someone else said, with a trace of sarcasm, "Don't work too late." By then it was almost ten o'clock.

At some point I turned away from my computer and realized I was alone in the vast office space where everyone works except for the president and the vice-presidents of the company who have special offices down a secluded hallway. I stared out the window at the windows of the buildings across the street. Tonight all the offices were dark except the one facing mine. Like me, the occupants of the office, a man and a woman, were working late.

I didn't know who these people were, or what they did,

but I'd seen them before. Maybe one night a week I was the last one to leave work and invariably they were there, at facing desks, staring down their computer screens while the night went on without them.

Then it happened, I looked up, and the man was leaning over the woman's desk. He was saying something to her and then he put out his hand and touched her hair, gently, as if she was a child, but she pulled away. I wasn't close enough to see the expression on her face but I could imagine her surprise. Her bewilderment.

The entire office—desks, chairs, computers, potted plants, the Magritte print, fluorescent beams—was bigger than life, like a stage set or a diorama. I knew I should try to concentrate on my work—on finishing what I had to do so I could get home before midnight. But it was hard to peel my eyes away from the figures behind the glass. Something about the woman's attitude had changed and she tilted her face submissively for the man to kiss. She had decided, in the space of a moment, not to resist him. The last thing she cared about was whether anyone was watching. Her hair was straw-colored and tied back with a handkerchief. She wore a turquoise bracelet around her left wrist and a tiny crucifix around her neck. She was in her early twenties, like a Greek statue come to life, the last of her tribe. One could see her as a child, crossing her legs at the ankles, in the pew of a church. The man, in shirtsleeves, barrel-chested and chinless, was twice her age.

My work allows for moments of distraction when I can turn from my computer to the street, ten stories below, and to the people who occupy the offices in the building opposite. Everyone in my office takes frequent breaks, some more often than others. Like every other workplace there are over-achievers and there are slackers. I think I fall somewhere in between. I don't feel guilty when I go downstairs for a cigarette or into the lounge for a cup of coffee. Or, like now, if I simply stare into space. No one checks up on what I do during the day and as long as I finish my quota for the week no one complains. I've been working here for five years and no one has ever complained. It's obvious, even to the president and vice-presidents, that if you continued to work without taking a break you might go crazy. So it wasn't the first time I was working late and looked up from my computer and saw the woman with straw-colored hair and the older man in their office across the street. I envied them, actually—the conversation, the camaraderie. It made me look around and see how little I had.

Most often, I would watch them for a few minutes, and then I would go back to my work, and when I looked again they were gone. The screen of my computer stared back at me—yellow and blue. It was almost midnight. Why was I still here?

On this particular night things were different. I had done enough work and I was confident that I'd meet all my deadlines by the end of the week. I knew that I might as well return to my apartment but for some reason I lingered on. I was putting off the moment when I would slip my arms through the sleeves of my jacket and turn off my computer when I turned back to the window and saw the man reach out again and put his hand on the front of the woman's blouse. I could see her stiffen, recoil, lean back in her chair. I could feel what she was feeling, or thought I could, though I didn't even know her name, and no doubt, as on other occasions, my misguided sense of empathy was off the mark. Her blouse was white with little poodles on it and it was open halfway down her chest so that when she turned in my direction I could see the tops of her breasts. The poodles had their mouths open and looked like they were barking and they all wore little bells around their necks. I wondered whether she had unbuttoned her blouse as a way of tempting him, teasing him, that she wanted him to touch her but was playing hard to get. Then he actually reached out and ripped the buttons off the front of her blouse and pushed her chair so hard it swiveled backwards and hit the wall. I saw her lips move as if she was cursing him or crying out for help, but of course I couldn't hear what she was saying. Neither of them, as far as I knew, were aware that I was watching.

You could say that watching them was like listening to the words of a song on the radio. Then someone turned off the radio and you didn't realize how quiet it was. That you were singing the song on the radio in your head. The song was in your head whether you liked it or not.

That's what it was like to watch the couple in the office across the street. It reminded me of the time, in a darkened movie theater, when a man sat down beside me and put his hand on my knee. I looked back at my computer, as if there was something I had to do that I had forgotten about, but there was nothing, there was never anything, I could go home any time. Then I looked back at the office across the street and saw the man reach out again but this time she grabbed his hand and bit down hard. I could see the man's face as he pulled back his arm and it looked as if he was going to smack her across the side of her head. The woman had stood up by then, clutching her torn blouse to her breasts. She angled towards the door of the office but there was no escape.

It occurred to me, as the song in my head kept going around and around, that I should call the police, or that I could turn back to my computer and pretend I hadn't seen any of it. There are at least two dozen people working in my office on any given day and everyone stands at the window and makes up stories about the people in the offices across the street. Once I thought I saw the woman with the poodles on her blouse in a diner on the corner, but who could be sure?

The man had wrapped a towel around his hand while the woman cowered in a corner. He looked defeated, like a wounded dog. The whole scene resembled the cover of a cheap paperback from the 1950s, the lurid mysteries where a half-naked woman tries to avoid the advances of a man with a gun. The cover suggests that because the man has the gun the woman will be forced to submit to his will, to his desires. The woman in the office crossed her arms over her chest, but her breasts were still partially visible. The man was standing closer to the door of the office but he wasn't blocking it.

I pressed my forehead against the window until I

thought I could almost make out the streaks of mascara on her cheeks. She was crawling across the floor of the office, in her heels and stockings and in her short skirt, trying to get to the door. The man had turned his back to her, deliberately, as if he didn't care whether she escaped or not, but at the last second, just as it appeared that she was going to turn the knob of the door, he grabbed her wrist and dragged her back across the carpet.

The idea that she would try to escape enraged him. As if she really thought she could get away so easily. It was all in his head, of course, all the desire he felt for her after working in the same office for six months. She had been hired, initially, as a temp, but after a week or two he convinced his boss to hire her full time. And for doing this he expected something. Something. She was just a girl from the midwest, who had escaped small town life by going to school in Chicago. Her real dream was to come to New York and here she was. People had warned her about things like this: if the boss wants to fuck you you better do it or you'll get fired. Some days, when she wore a skirt that was too short or a blouse that was too tight, she would notice him watching her. She noticed everything. And now what everybody told her might happen was happening. She was learning her lesson the hard way. She should have listened to her friends and family, she should never have left the farm. But whom could she trust?

The man drew back his arm again as if he was going to punch her in the face but checked himself. Instead, he took an empty whiskey bottle from the drawer of his desk and swung it in her direction.

I wish there had been someone with me. It was hard to be the only witness. I felt a pain in my chest, like I had been holding my breath under water for a long time. Someone was pressing my head under water and I was trying to fight back, but couldn't.

I tried to imagine the first questions that the police would ask: why were you working so late? What were you doing looking out the window? They would think I was a kind of voyeur. They would think about the movie with James Stewart, and how no one believed he had seen a murder committed from his window. The police would probably think I was guilty since I was the only one who had seen anything. That there was a naked woman hidden in my closet.

The man stepped away from the woman's body. A pool of blood had formed on the rug near her head. He bent at the waist and stared directly into her face. He had hit her across the head more than once and she was no longer moving. He was standing over her, observing his work. Then he did something odd, though in retrospect it makes sense. "Odd" isn't the right word but that's what I felt at the time. He looked around him, around the office, then out the window. He looked right at me, or so I thought. Except for the light in my office the building where I worked was a wall of darkness. He could see me as well as I could see him.

I turned away from the window, trying to fade back into the shadows. Maybe he was simply looking out into the night and I was just inventing the part about him looking directly at me. Whenever someone directs their attention at me, I wonder whether I'm being paranoid, or whether they're really interested. It was after ten at night. The man at the window reached behind him and took a cigarette from a pack of Lucky Strikes on his desk, lit it with a disposable lighter even though it was forbidden to smoke in the building, while the woman died miserably behind him.

It was early winter and I thought I noticed some flakes of snow in the air. I realized that precious moments were slipping away. I knew what I should do was call the police. Some Helen Mirren type would push her way into my office and conclude that I was the prime suspect. I'd read enough novels and seen enough TV shows to realize that the witnesses are often considered suspects if they don't have alibis. And what was I doing anyway? If the man had seen me watching him and knew I had seen him murder the woman did that mean he'd try to hunt me down?

Only the night before I'd seen Jill with her new boyfriend. "Seen" is probably not the proper word. It had been a mistake to get involved with a next door neighbor but for the time that it lasted it had seemed like a convenient arrangement. It meant we could share everything with one another and still have our own space when we wanted it. We slept together every night, one night my apartment, the next night hers. It went on for over a year before she confessed that she had fallen in love with someone else. It was something I had not seen coming, so to speak. We just had sex the night before when she told me that in fact she had spent the afternoon at his apartment, the nameless lover's apartment, and I assumed that meant she had literally gone from my bed to his without even going to work, which is what she admitted, finally, annoyed that she had to spell it out for me in bright neon. That had been more than a year ago and since that night we had never spoken together except when we met by accident on the stairs or in the vestibule near the mailboxes. On those occasions both of us lowered our eyes and muttered the words "Hi" or "How're you doing" out of the corners of our mouths. It never occurred to me to find a new apartment, even after Jill started bringing her new boyfriend home, and I could hear them laughing as they climbed the steps, and then their voices as they removed one another's clothing and got into bed.

In the old days, when we ate dinner together every night, I would rush home from work, usually stopping to buy food along the way. Jill was the better cook so she tended to prepare the meals, something she said she didn't mind doing, even though she also worked a full day. But there she was, in her kitchen, as I let myself into her apartment, with food for salad and a bottle of wine. What we enjoyed most was staying home watching movies, eating popcorn or sharing an expensive bar of dark chocolate. Often I stopped at the local video store on Greenwich Avenue and picked up a movie before coming home.

In the first weeks of our relationship, when it seemed that we might be together for a long time, we would get into bed as soon as we returned home from work. Food could wait, obviously, as well as checking phone and e-mail messages. It was with a feeling of reassurance that we measured our time together against everything else in our life, and for awhile being together was the only thing that mattered to both of us. There's a feeling of bliss and serenity that comes with the permission to touch another person's body whenever you want. But that's all over.

Once I had a fantasy that Jill came to the door of my apartment in the middle of the night, that she woke me up hammering at my door, that she was in tears, her clothing was torn, her boyfriend had beat her up. I emptied my ice tray in a bucket, wrapped some cubes in a towel, and told her to hold it to the bump above her eye, something my mother had once done to stop the swelling when I fell off my bike. Then I went to the apartment next door where the drunk boyfriend was sitting in a lotus position on the living room rug. It had been awhile since I had been in the apartment but nothing had changed. There was the collection of framed photographs of Jill's family on the mantelpiece above the fake fireplace but I couldn't tell whether she had removed the photo of herself which I had taken one winter afternoon in Montauk when we rented a car and drove out to the lighthouse. I took a stool from the kitchen and hammered it over the boyfriend's head. Then I kicked him in the ribs a few times for good measure.

When I came to work the next day, a few minutes before nine, all my coworkers were standing at the window staring at the office directly opposite. I decided to act dumb and asked them what had happened and they told me, though it was too soon to know anything for sure, that someone had been killed in the office the night before. I leaned into the crowd at the window and saw that the office was occupied by three uniformed policemen and an older man in a tan raincoat who seemed to be giving orders to everyone else. The body of the woman with straw-colored hair was still there.

Later in the day, the man in the raincoat appeared in our office and asked if anyone had been working late the night before.

"Harkavy," someone said. "Weren't you here last night?"

The detective approached me. He was still wearing his raincoat over a jacket and a shirt. He had removed his tie and I could see a rivulet of sweat running down his neck when he swallowed. He had a long plain weather-beaten face, no forehead and a pointy chin, with deep pouches under his eyes.

"I'm Detective Bowman," he said. His eyes flickered over me with contempt as if he wasn't sure whether I was an object worthy of his time and attention. He was probably wondering why anyone would want to spend their life working in an office like this one. "Were you here when it happened?" he finally asked.

Everyone in the office stopped what they were doing.

"Yes, I was here," I said. "And yes, I saw the murder."

The detective's features sharpened when he heard my words and a muscle twitched like a stoplight beneath the flesh of his right cheek. He blinked rapidly and turned in a half-circle, not certain whether asking me these questions was appropriate in front of a large audience. It occurred to me, as well, that whatever I told him should be done in private.

"Is there a place where we can talk?" the detective asked, turning to the office manager, Ms. Kuten, an impatient blonde who was wearing a tight flannel skirt and a white round-neck blouse and who rumor had it was having an affair with Mr. Elkin, our boss. She led us down a corridor, her high heels making scraping noises on the tiles, and it was hard not to be aware of the movement of her hips, accentuated by the tightness of the skirt, as she bent at the waist to open the door of an office with a key. The key was one of several on a large silver ring and she had to try three of them before she found the one that worked.

I had never been in this room before. It was the conference room where the president and the vice-presidents met to make decisions and where they entertained guests. The walls were covered by a gallery of portraits—paintings of the founder of the company and his children. The detective and I sat at the end of a long narrow table and I told him everything I had seen the night before. He took out a pad and a ball-point pen and scribbled as I talked, occasionally asking me to backtrack and repeat something I had already said.

First, of course, he asked me my name and my address, and how long I had been working at the company. He asked me if I was married though I'm not sure why that was relevant. I was tempted to tell him about Jill, as if my relationship with her was the equivalent of being married, in which case we would be divorced by now, but

I didn't say anything, and I realized I was still clinging to some hope we'd get back together. I thought about her every day, often for long periods of time, and it was torture to lie awake every night and think of her sleeping with someone else behind the wall that separated our two apartments. One reason I didn't mind working late was because it was preferable to being in my apartment, where everything reminded me of her. It had been a year since we had broken up—since she knocked on my door late one evening and told me she was in love with someone else—and I hadn't slept with anyone else since. All my friends advised me to move out but it wasn't easy to find an apartment. And I knew that once I moved out it meant the end of everything.

The detective wasn't interested in any of this and I had the good sense not to mention it. For a moment I had the feeling we were like characters in a movie. In every movie there are scenes like this. The witness to a crime is questioned by a detective. Usually it takes place in a police station. Would you like some coffee? the detective asks. There's always a second detective present who leaves the room for a moment and then returns with the coffee in a styrofoam cup. The so-called witness takes a sip of black coffee and grimaces. "This tastes like shit," he says. In most cases, the person being interrogated is a suspect in the crime, but that wasn't true about me, at least as far as I know. The detective asked me questions and wrote down the answers. I noticed he was left-handed and I was tempted to say "My wife is left-handed" but I have no wife, even though when Jill and I were together we would occasionally argue in public and our friends would remark that we were like an old married couple, when in fact we'd only known each other a few months. Finally, after the detective was satisfied with my personal information, he asked me to tell him what happened that night. What I saw from the window when I was working late.

It must have been about nine o'clock, I said, when I looked up from my computer and stared at the building across the street, at the office directly opposite mine where two people, a man and a woman, were working. The detective looked up from his pad and asked if I had ever seen these people before and I said of course, on every night I worked late they seemed to work late as well. For all I know they worked late every night. Then the detective asked if we could smoke in the conference room and I told him not usually but since I wanted a cigarette as well we could make an exception—and I realized that when I said "we" I was talking for the whole company, the presidents and the vice-presidents and the founder whose dour face stared down at us from the wall. So I found a glass ashtray in the closet that looked like it had been stolen from the lobby of a hotel and we sat down again and lit cigarettes. He took off his raincoat and wiped his forehead and neck with a handkerchief.

"Tell me everything," he said. "From start to finish."

I said that I'd try, but that there wasn't really much to say, that it all happened very quickly. At one point he asked me whether I wore glasses or contact lenses and I smiled and told him that my eyesight was perfect, 20-20, that I'd recently had my eyes checked and that nothing had changed. You're lucky, the detective said, blowing smoke through his nostrils. There were no windows in the conference room, which resembled a kind of bunker, and the smoke drifted upwards to the ceiling and hovered in the air like a layer of fog.

I told him how the man had approached the woman's desk, how he leaned forward to kiss her and how receptive she had been at first, even going so far as to unbutton her blouse and reach behind her back to unfasten her bra so that in a matter of moments he had pressed his lips to her shoulders and breasts, while with his other hand he tried to reach under her skirt. It was she who seemed to be leading him on, whispering in his ear, though of course I couldn't tell. I didn't say that to the detective but it seemed like she was as interested in having sex as the man, and that it was only when they were on the floor of the office and he was on top of her and began to unfasten his pants that she seemed to have a change of heart and pushed him away. It was then that the trouble started: first she slapped his face, then he ripped off a strip of her blouse and gagged her and tied her up. Finally, when she tried to break free, he smashed her over the head with a lamp. I told the detective that after he had hit the woman several times the man looked around him as if he was suddenly aware of what he had done and that he seemed to be looking directly at me, from his window into mine. I told the detective that once he started beating up the woman I had the thought of turning off the light in my office so he couldn't see me, but that I was too mesmerized to do anything. The detective made me tell the story again and by the time I was through we had both smoked another cigarette.

There were certain things I remembered the second time around: how when the man tried to force her to have sex she had grabbed his hand and bitten into it. And how, on other nights, I had seen the same couple have sex leaning up against one of the desks. The detective put down his pen and looked directly at me when I told him this. You mean they fucked in the office? he said. He made me tell him about all the nights that I had watched the couple in the office. I told him I wasn't sure how many times I had seen this happen. Did it always happen? the detective wanted to know. He was giving me that weird look again and I knew what was coming: he was thinking that it was me, that I was making it all up, that somehow I had committed the murder, that he would get a subpoena to search my desk. What a joke, I thought. So what if the couple had sex in the office and so what if I watched? There were people who liked being watched when they were having sex. There were husbands who liked watching their wives have sex with other men. Who knows what people want? There was a rumor that Ms. Kuten, the office manager, and Mr. Elkin, the president, had sex in his office every morning. It was understandable. People who coexisted in a small space day after day invariably became attracted to one another. It made sense, especially if you were working late.

"And what happened when he persisted?" the detective asked.

"He tried to force her and she slapped his face. That's

how it all started."

When I finished telling the story the second time the detective stared at the words he had written on the pad and nodded in my direction. He looked like he was squinting and I wondered if he had gotten any sleep the night before. He put his hand in front of his face as if he was stifling a yawn.

"And then what?" he said.

I wasn't sure what he meant.

"What did you do after he killed the woman?"

"I went home," I said.

"Let me get this straight," the detective said. "You were working late, you looked up from your work, you saw this man and this woman having sex, you saw the man hit the woman over the head with a lamp, you saw the man leave the office, then you left your office and went home, and you didn't notify the police."

"That's right," I said.

"You didn't call up a friend and talk about what you had seen."

"I went home, I had a drink, I read a book, I went to sleep."

"You saw a crime committed and you didn't notify the police. Doesn't that seem odd to you?"

"It seemed like none of my business, that there was nothing I could do about it."

"But he's gone. The man who works in the office is gone. No one knows where he is. And the woman is dead."

"And if I had called the police last night they would have found him? Is that what you're saying?"

The detective stared at me as if I had committed a crime worse than the man in the office.

"We live in the world," the detective said, shaking his head. "We all live in the same world. If we see someone in danger we try to protect that person. If we can't do it by ourselves, we call the police. Since you weren't in the office with the woman there was nothing you could do to save her but you had to tell the police afterwards. It's your duty...."

Everything the detective said was true. I wanted to explain why I had never even thought of calling the police, but I couldn't. All I could say was that after the man left the office I closed down my computer and went home. I took the subway home, as always, the number 9 train to the west side. It's two blocks from the train station to my building and I didn't see anyone I knew; nor did I see any of my neighbors as I walked up the four flights of stairs. I do know, at that point, I was thinking about Jill, and it's true that if I had met Jill on the staircase or in the lobby I would have been tempted to tell her what I had seen. Just like in the old days when I returned home from work and we sat on the sofa in the living room and told each other everything we had done in the time we were apart. But that was over, all my so-called friends tell me I have to face the fact that my relationship with Jill is over. I always pause for a moment on the landing and listen for the sound of voices from behind Jill's door, or the sound of music, but last night I heard nothing. I opened the door of my apartment, went to the kitchen and poured myself a drink (Dewar's with ice) and went to the living room to check my phone messages.

There was a message from my father, who lives in San Francisco. He was calling to tell me that he was getting remarried in a few months to a woman named Diana Curley, whom he had mentioned on a previous phone call but whom I had never met. He gave me the exact date and time of the wedding, which was going to take place in the backyard of a friend's house in a town up the coast, and said he hoped I would be able to attend. "You'll like Diana a lot," he said, and hung up. My father is a painter and teaches painting and drawing at the San Francisco Art Institute and periodically he falls in love with one of his students. But this is the first time, as far as I know, that he was going to marry one of them. My parents split up when I was eight and my mother, who never remarried, lives alone in Florence. My mother is an art historian and an authority on 15th Century Italian Art, especially Fra Angelico, about whom she has written numerous articles and a monograph. She used to teach but now she spends most of her time writing and traveling. I see my parents whenever they're in New York and once a year I travel to San Francisco and Florence to visit with them. I'm not sure why my parents split up, since on the surface they have many interests in common, and like many children I somehow think my presence in their life was the cause of what happened, that somehow I altered the equilibrium of their lives in a way that made it impossible for them to go on. After they split up, I lived with my mother in New York and spent the summers in San Francisco with my father but that schedule ended once I entered college.

Then I saw them more sporadically as I tried to make a life of my own.

"I don't want you to leave town," the exhausted detective said. He stood up, carrying his raincoat over his arm. "I have a feeling we're going to want to talk to you again."

"I'm not going anywhere," I said. "You can call me any time."

It was only ten in the morning and there was a whole day of work up ahead. Everyone in the office looked up when I returned with the detective and after he left they surrounded my desk, anxious for a first hand report.

"They work at Jenson & Jenson," someone said.

"I once had lunch with that guy."

"How many times did he hit her?"

"They were having an affair, everyone knew it, it's been going on for years."

The conversation swirled around me. I had been working in the office for five years but I wasn't friends with any of my coworkers. I had no enemies either. I make a point of trying to get along with as many different types of people as possible. I try not to gossip, even though I know that gossip is the lifeblood of places like this. Can I say honestly that no one is working in this office because they want to? I think that must be correct. I know that Jill often admonished me for not working at a job that had some value in the world. She couldn't understand why I was wasting my life away. That I had settled for being a cog, an underling. I always had the thought that one of the reasons she ended the relationship is because she wanted to be with someone who was more ambitious, who made things happen. I could tell when she introduced me to her friends that she lowered her eyes as if she was embarrassed. She was a year or two away from getting her PhD and had already started teaching and a lot of our social life involved hanging around with her graduate school friends. I would sit for hours in restaurants and cafes listening to them talking about professors I didn't know and books I hadn't read. When Jill asked me, as she did on occasion, what I liked about her, what I said was that I liked the nights we spent alone, having sex, eating dinner, watching movies. Even more than doing these things was the pleasure of anticipating them. It made the day bearable, it made me smile to myself just thinking about things she did or said. Sometimes I would turn off my computer and stare at the screen but really I was in a different world. I would think of the times when I would open the door of her apartment with the key she had given me and she would be lying in bed naked. I would remember the expression on her face when we were having sex and how it seemed like she was about to burst into tears as she passed over the edge and then the expression of utter relief and contentment when she came back to life. The few hours we spent together every day made all the difference. The last few months we were together she often had to go to class at night and wouldn't get home till midnight or later. She would explain that she liked to hang out with her graduate school friends at a cafe near the campus but I know now it was because she was fucking someone else.

Shortly after noon Ms. Kuten called me into her office and asked me to tell her what I had seen the night before. I don't know why I had to repeat it all again but she said something about "company policy" and that we all had to be "on the same page." She was only a few years older than I was but she made me feel like a child. She reminded me of Ms. Brill, my teacher in third grade, who would lean very close to me so that it seemed like her perfumed breasts would swallow me up, that I could crawl between the buttons on the front of her blouse and disappear. There was something about being with Ms. Kuten, whose first name I knew was Linda, that blurred the boundaries between what might be permitted and what was forbidden. Maybe it had to do with the way she pushed the hair out of her eyes or crossed her legs and adjusted the hem of her skirt over her knees. She looked at me as if witnessing a murder made me more interesting because the details surrounding the murder itself were interesting. I knew that she wanted me to tell her about the sex part, the torn blouse, the way the man began unbuckling his pants and then the woman stopped him. Everything I told the detective twice I told her again until I got tired of hearing the sound of my own voice. What I noticed was her smile as the narrative unfolded. She never said anything, never prompted me when I lost the thread of what I was saying. Every time I paused to get my bearings her smile became brighter and more encouraging. I had the feeling that the words were titillating her in some way and when I came to the part about the torn blouse her eyes glazed over. I tried my best to keep it all to a minimum. She could add any embellishments she wanted on her own time for all I cared. She could think about it all in the privacy of her bedroom, if that's what she wanted. I let my eyes flicker over her body as I talked. We had never been together in an office before. We had never been alone. On the wall behind her desk there was a poster of a woman in a bikini emerging from the ocean and the words "Come To Maui" in big letters. There was a fishing boat on the horizon and a young man carrying a surfboard under his arm. The waves rolled peacefully into the shore. Jill and I had once talked about going to Hawaii for a vacation, but our schedules never coincided. She wanted to learn how to scuba dive and Maui was apparently as good a place as any.

I wonder if Ms. Kuten and the president of the company, Mr. Elkin, were still having an affair. Whether they met secretly in places like Maui or San Juan. He was an imposing figure, about six and a half feet tall, with long sideburns and thick rugged skin. It wasn't difficult to imagine her leaning over the desk in his office while the man lifted her skirt and came inside her. Jill and I once rented a porno movie where things like that happened. In the movie, which was not very well made, there was a secretary hiding beneath a desk giving her boss a blow job. This scene went on forever, long past the time when it might have provided any excitement. Someone came into the office to talk with the boss and the woman beneath the desk continued what she was doing. Then there was the conference room like the one I had just been in with Detective Bowman where people did various things to one another and in different combinations on tables and chairs. We wanted to have sex while watching the movie but it was so bad we realized we didn't need it and turned it off. I was tired and my mind was free associating in a million directions when I realized that there was nothing more to talk about but that Ms. Kuten didn't seem like she was anxious for me to leave her office. I'm sure she wouldn't have minded if I had gotten down on my knees and buried my head between her legs, but it never happened.

I worked until seven and took the train home. I bought a salad at a new gourmet market that opened recently on 15th Street. I sat at the small dining room table in the alcove near the kitchen, big enough for two people, and drank a bottle of beer and listened to the radio. They were playing some songs from the 1960s which I liked. Songs by English groups like Cream and Procol Harum and Traffic. I knew more about music that had been popular before I was born than the music that was popular now. It was dark out and the sky was purplish and a few airplanes flew low over the river on their way to Newark Airport. I thought if I could make my mind go blank for a few minutes that I would feel better and the static in my head would begin to fade. The person I was thinking about most was Linda Kuten. I had seen her later in the day and she had smiled at me as if we had something in common and I had been tempted to go back to her office just to see what would happen. What I wanted was for her to call me up and come over as quickly as possible. "I was in the neighborhood," she would say, as if she needed a reason.

The idea of me calling *her* up, on the other hand, was out of the question.

A half-hour later someone was knocking on the door, and when I opened it without asking who was there it turned out to be Jill. I hadn't seen her much in the last few weeks and in the dim hallway light I thought she looked tired. She always stayed up half the night reading and the circles under her eyes seemed even more pronounced. Her hair was tied back with a green ribbon and looked lighter than I remembered. Maybe she was tinting it as some women do when they grow older but Jill wasn't exactly old. She was wearing a blue t-shirt turned inside out and a short denim skirt, no jewelry except for a string of beads, and no make-up. She was carrying four or five paperbacks in one arm, hugging them close to her chest.

"I've been cleaning up and I found these books. I think they're yours."

She didn't say "how are you?" or "how you've been?" but she didn't seem particularly hostile either, just matter of fact. The words meant what they meant. Here are your books, do you want them? They were some Penguin classics that I would sometimes read before going to bed on those nights I stayed over in her apartment. Boccaccio's *Decameron,* Henry James' *Portrait of a Lady,* Balzac's *Père Goriot* and *Vilette* by Charlotte Bronte. As I took the books from her hands and looked at the titles the essence of each of them came back to me and I realized that these books would now become more meaningful by the fact that they were associated with this moment.

"Do you want to come in?" I asked.

She stepped tentatively over the threshold but stayed there, looking around at the kitchen and the entrance to the living room.

"I'm really busy right now Hark, but I just wanted to give you your books back and let you know that I'm moving out tomorrow."

I tried to pretend that it made no difference to me—whether she was there, whether she wasn't there, whether she had a boyfriend, whether we ever saw one another again.

"Where are you moving to?" I asked, as if I was genuinely interested in the problems of relocation. The next thing I knew, if I went down this path, I'd offer to help her pack her things.

"Well Sven has a new job up in Portland, Maine, so we're going to go there. I'm going to finish my dissertation and he's going to work."

"Sven?"

"This guy I've been seeing. I don't think you ever formally met but I'm sure you've seen him. We once passed each other on the street when I was with him. Don't you remember?"

"Well, that's great," I said, trying to make it sound like I meant it. Did I mean it? 'Sven' was like a child's word, a word that a child repeats until it loses its meaning. I had trouble associating Jill with someone named Sven.

"I have some other news too, just wanted to let you know. I'm three months pregnant."

It's true we hadn't talked much in the last year and there was no way she could know all the feelings I still harbored for her. When we were together we had talked frequently about having a baby and it was she who always said she wanted to wait until she finished her dissertation and had a teaching job. I'd made it clear from the start that I would be willing to have a child whenever she felt she was ready and if she didn't want children that was fine with me also. Truthfully, I was deeply ambivalent about my potential talent as a parent, and the idea of moving into an apartment or a house that would accommodate all of us—me, Jill, all the children and even a dog—made my head spin. My parents weren't people who I would ever want to emulate and I thought by doing the opposite of what they did I might actually make a success of it all, whatever that means. But to think that what I wanted was what she wanted was enough.

It gave me comfort that I could put her needs above my own. It made me think anything was possible.

I felt dizzy, for a moment, wanted to sit down or hold on to something. I felt like I had something lodged in my throat. Jill's matter-of-factness was one of the reasons I had fallen in love with her, it was so much the opposite of how I was. I was the impenetrable one, or so she had often told me, the person with secrets who never said what he was thinking.

"I'm going to have a baby and write my dissertation and live in the woods," she said. It occurred to me that this might be the last time we ever saw one another. I put the books down on a table in the foyer and stared at my feet.

"Aren't you going to wish me luck?" she asked.

"Luck is important," I said. And she put her hand on my arm.

"I try to have good memories of you, you know? Of us. I know I hurt your feelings but things like that happen every day. Things happen." And then: "Are you seeing anyone?"

"I'm thinking of going back to school myself," I said.

"That's a great idea. I always think you underestimate yourself—how much you know about everything. I sometimes hear you leave the apartment in the morning and I think about your job, the same job, he's going to the same job. And it seems like you can do better. And then at night—I hear you come home at night—eight or nine, or even later. And I wonder why you care so much about your job that you'd work until late at night. Why it's all so important."

"It's not that important," I said, wanting to tell her about the nights that I'd hear *her* come home, from wherever she was with this person named Sven, their laughter in the hallway, and how I used to press my ear to the wall that separated our two apartments, my kitchen wall, in an attempt to hear what they were saying. "It's just what I do."

"Tomorrow the movers are coming and then the next day we're flying to Norway to meet Sven's parents."

I had the odd thought that we could have sex one last time, that that was the real reason she had come to see me. Returning the books was just a pretense. But to think something might be true doesn't mean you can assume it's true, or that something might be more true, or less, or that your instincts are correct, or if you act one way and not another everything would be different, and if you don't act at all you miss out on everything. Better to have loved and lost and all that crap made some sense but I rejected it, I wanted to trample on the fucking words that were all in my head. It was like there was this wall inside me and on either side of it there was turbulence and static and there was a rift in the sky that was like a dividing line and I was on one side and Jill was on the other. And for a moment I was frightened. When she moved out of the apartment for good it meant I was alone, I was really alone.

I put out my hand and touched the side of her face and I realized that wasn't what she wanted at all. Her skin was icy and she moved her head away.

"I'll be in touch," she said. Touch. That's what I had tried to do and it didn't matter.

She backed out of the door into the hallway, but I couldn't look up. I knew she was looking at me but I felt lacking in kindness, the reservoir of kindness if it ever existed at all had dried up. I had the feeling that if I looked back she would interpret it as an agreement that no matter what happened between us we were going to wish each other well. There was a long life up ahead and who knows what might happen and we had fun together and now let's be decent, let's say goodbye like decent people, let's not hold any grudges. The problem with this way of thinking was that she had hurt me, she had left me, she had been sleeping with someone else at the time she had been sleeping with me, she had lied to me for how long I don't know, and the good question was why I didn't hate her, why I wasn't consumed with anger, that's what my friends wanted to know, why I could actually say, as I once told my friend Mark, my gay friend Mark who's had a complicated love life himself, who's been around the block a few times, how I could actually say to him that no matter what Jill did and how often she lied to me I was still in love with her, and that none of this mattered. She wanted me to look back at her so she didn't have to feel guilty but I have a feeling she was passed that stage, that the question of innocence or guilt was no longer relevant for her. She was caught up in her new life, there was Sven and the baby, and she didn't waste her time staring into space thinking about what might have happened if she had stayed with me. She didn't suffer because of me, or relive our past, or feel nostalgia for the nights watching movies and the sex, the porno movie about the office, all the shit that keeps circling around in my head all the time like a fucking ferris wheel in some small town amusement park that my parents took me to when I was a kid, the blur of lights and the vertigo when you reach the top and look down and look up and there's the moon and the belly of a blimp hovering in the sky. She didn't want to be back there in the dark, having sex in front of the movie. But I don't think she felt guilty about anything. My father had been married before he met my mother and now he was marrying someone else. And my mother seemed to have given up on ever living with anyone again. She was comfortable with her peripatetic life, with her solitude. People recovered from separation even though sometimes it feels like death. It means that the person you were so close to is no longer in your life, that this person might as well be dead. I'd been in mourning for a year now but the idea that Jill was leaving raised it all to some new level. There was no longer the possibility of fantasizing about some future where she would have a change of heart and come crawling back. I don't mean that she'd have to come crawling back. All she had to do was show some interest in getting back together and I would do the rest.

I was glad when she closed the door so I could ease myself down on the chair in the kitchen, at the table near the window, and light a cigarette. The table was empty except for some menus that had been slipped under the door. If she stayed a moment longer I'm not sure what might have happened. I felt like I was on the verge of losing control and that at a certain moment I would no longer be responsible for my actions. I felt like going into the hallway and pounding on her door. I didn't care if the neighbors called the police. I could take a kitchen knife with me and when Sven opened the door I could plunge it into his chest. This was the last time I would be able to play out this kind of scenario in my head. Tomorrow the apartment next door would be empty.

Slowly I began to drift away from myself, from the dead self with its self-inflicted wounds, and I tried to remember the person I was before I met Jill two years ago. We had been living next door to one another for over a year before we met. It was she who made the first move. We were standing outside the building—she was going out, I was coming in—when she invited me for a drink later in the evening. I remember that she was wearing a big floppy hat and that her upper arms were as thin as a child's. Her invitation took me by surprise, I must admit, and since I was already going out with someone else at the time, a woman from the office named Rita, I wondered whether going to Jill's apartment was a good idea. As it turned out, within an hour after I entered the apartment we were in bed together. It had felt like the natural thing to do and our bodies seemed to connect in a way that made sense. The next afternoon, at lunch, I broke the news to Rita. We were sitting in a French restaurant around the corner from our office when I told her that I had met someone else, that I had fallen in love with someone else, though that was hardly the truth even though I could see it happening, I could see into the future where love might be possible between me and Jill where with Rita it was mostly sex and a bit of love. She was certainly someone I respected and sometimes when we were both working late we would have sex in the supply room, amid the boxes of staples and file folders. "You can't do that," was what she said when I told her I was breaking up with her. She was holding a glass in her hand and I had the feeling she was going to smash it in my face. "I'm going to kill myself," she said. "I'm going to fucking decapitate myself. Just you watch."

There were other women in my life before Rita. I thought of their names: Ronnie, Yvette, Cassandra and Beverly. I thought of each of them separately and wondered what they were doing. I had heard that Cassandra was in rehab because she had overdosed on heroin but I don't think it was because of anything I had done. I wondered what Rita was up to and what she would say if I called her and asked her out for a drink. Casually, as if nothing had ever happened. I know for a fact that she didn't kill herself after I told her it was over and I have a feeling she's probably married and living in some place like Connecticut or Northern California. Once, when we were in bed together, she broached the subject of marriage, but I think she wanted to marry someone who had more money than I did. I certainly had nothing to lose by calling her up.

I sat at the window smoking and looking out at the building across the street. One of the windows was lit, and a tall young blonde woman was standing in front of a full length mirror. I had seen her before, on other nights when I returned home late from work. I liked sitting in the kitchen, reading the newspaper while waiting for water to boil for coffee. On some nights, like tonight, I just liked to smoke and look out at it all. I had seen the blonde woman before. Most of the time she was accompanied by a young man who was obviously her boyfriend. They would enter the bedroom together, often late at night, and I had the feeling they were both coming home from work, that possibly they both worked in the same office. Maybe they worked in different offices and met for late dinner when work was over. Sometimes, when I left for work in the morning, I would see them emerge from the entrance of the building across the street, holding hands, the woman with her blonde hair piled on top of her head or braided or just hanging loosely down her back, the young man with his fuzzy beard and dark-rimmed glasses. They looked like they had just stepped out of the pages of a fashion magazine, one of those glossy magazines that Rita used to read and which always smelled like perfume. Tonight the woman was alone, at least for the moment. She stared at herself critically in the mirror and lifted her hands to her hair and began to unfasten the ribbon that held it in place and when she lifted her arms I could see her breasts swell against the cotton material of her dress. She reached behind her, and with her back to me, began to unzip her dress, and then she stepped out of it slowly and turned to face me. For a moment I had the feeling she knew I was watching, and that she was taking off her clothing for my pleasure alone. But then, as if an invisible hand had turned off the switch, the window went dark.

G & A

She was convinced that a life of solitude was the only way to accomplish anything. That if she fell in love the feeling would eat her alive and she would never do anything with her life. That the need to be with another person all the time would devour her energies. That she would end up falling in love with someone who would discourage her from being a painter. That she would submit to another person's desire to shape her life because it would make that person happy. That's what her mother had done and her mother before that. She didn't want that kind of life with anyone yet she hated being alone. She spent years of unhappiness thinking that no one would ever love her.

He had asked her if she would let him take photographs of her. He gave her the address of his apartment. One of the reasons she had come to New York was to be with him, listen to him talk about the new artists: Picasso, Rodin, John Marin, Marsden Hartley. She wanted to be with someone who shared the same interests. Living in Columbus, South Carolina had its charms and she could imagine living there when she was older. But not now. She was only 28. She had heard that this man who asked to take her photograph was married and that his wife gave him money to finance his gallery and his photography magazine but that otherwise she had no interest in her husband's work, that they had nothing to talk about except their daughter who was sick, who had had a nervous breakdown and was locked away in a mental hospital.

That's what she knew about him. And that he liked her work. He had written her a letter praising her drawings. He had even offered to give her a show of her watercolors at his gallery.

She took off her clothes and posed naked in a chair in front of him. He adjusted her legs, slightly apart, she liked his hands on her skin. He said, turn your head sideways, and she did, she did what he said.

The fact that he was twenty-three years older didn't mean she was searching for a father. It's too simple to make this kind of interpretation. In the same way, critics discussed her first paintings as symbolic representations of a woman's sexual organ. According to them, a woman painting a flower is painting her cunt. That was the equation, but she wouldn't buy it. The critics refused to see her as an artist first, then a woman. The only way they could write about her paintings was by talking about them from a woman's point of view.

She closed her eyes and let him touch her. She was lying on the couch listening to the rain at the window. She felt his lips on her breasts. She cupped them in her hands to make it easier for him as he knelt beside her. Neither of them heard the door open or saw his wife standing a few yards away, her hands on her hips. It was like an aftershock, a tremor, the earth moving beneath their feet.

He had seen her out of the corner of his eye as she turned around to leave and then the movement of her hips as she banged into the coffee table so that an expensive vase fell to the floor and shattered and then she slammed the door. For a moment he felt guilty but then he remembered that this was exactly what he wanted to happen. They had been married for fifteen years and it had been a big mistake from start to finish. Now he was free.

No one could understand why Georgia was interested in this man who was so much older than she was. He was a bore, everyone thought so. What he liked to do was hold forth in his gallery to anyone who doubted the merit of the paintings and drawings and photographs on the walls. Someone would walk in and say "This isn't art" and Alfred would start making his speech and the person would walk away feeling like an idiot. That's what he did every day of his life. No wonder his daughter went crazy. The first time Georgia went to the gallery she stood in the corner, too shy to say anything. She was with her friends, Dorothy and Anita, who were much more glamorous, and Alfred didn't even notice her. What Alfred did was come on to the young women who entered the gallery. He would take them into the office adjoining the gallery. He would say, "I want to take your photograph." There was a bed in the office.

What do you think happened?

Georgia wasn't the first woman he fell in love with. There had been a woman named Katharine Rhodes whom he had seduced in the gallery. She had shown him her paintings and he had praised them though they weren't very good and she was flattered enough to make love to him in his office. But it had ended badly and she destroyed all her paintings and fled to Europe.

Georgia was teaching in Virginia. She had lost her virginity with Arthur MacMahon, an art student from New York. Arthur visited her in Virginia and they made love in the backseat of his car. It was she who shocked him by her willingness to have sex before they were married. She was almost twenty-eight. It was her idea—she reaching out to him. They made love at her insistence; he was frightened of getting her pregnant. They were outside, in the darkness, at the end of a deserted road. What sounded like a wild animal scratching at the window of the car. He was frightened of being committed to one person—he sensed she was a virgin—she had been alone too long. Solitude was necessary for her to get any work done but the absence of another person's body at night was driving her crazy. All her work was about the absence of sex. When Arthur returned to New York, he wrote Georgia letters promising to visit her again over Christmas, but he never did. It was just a matter of time she found out he had another girl friend as well.

Shortly afterwards, Georgia wrote to her friend Anita Pollitzer: "I want to love as hard as I can and I can't help myself."

It was during this time that Georgia did the charcoal drawings she sent to Anita in New York with strict instructions not to show them to anyone. And of course, Anita showed them to Steiglitz, who immediately wrote to Georgia, showering praise on them. He wrote almost every day to this person he didn't know but whose work he felt communicated something that no woman had ever expressed before.

Georgia dreaded going to get the mail. She was frightened of his letters.

She moved to New York briefly, staying at the home of Anita Pollitzer's uncle, in midtown.

It was during this time that Steiglitz decided to show Georgia's charcoal drawings in his gallery, but he did it without telling her.

Drawings by Virginia O'Keeffe. It was part of a group show. Georgia and two men. He had even forgotten her name. She stormed into the gallery—how could he show her work without telling her first?

He assumed she was a virgin and that she was expressing something she had yet to experience and that it was his job to discover her, to turn her into the first great American woman artist. Georgia was aware how much Steiglitz could help her career. She arrived at the gallery filled with anger—"How dare you show my work without telling me"—and left filled with gratitude and trust. As a way of seducing her, he convinced her that they were the same person. That the reason he liked her work so much was because he saw himself in the drawings. The same longing, the same frustration.

She returned to her teaching job in Virginia and he wrote her every day.

The only person she ever painted nude was Leah Harris. They were both living in San Antonio, where Georgia was teaching. Leah, who was born in Texas, taught canning and food preservation at a local college. It was 1917. Both of them were thirty years old.

Steiglitz, in New York, had a plan to get her to return to New York. He felt like he couldn't live without her. He dispatched Paul Strand, his surrogate son, to Texas. Steiglitz knew that Strand and O'Keeffe were in love with one another but Strand didn't know that O'Keeffe and Steiglitz had already become lovers. It was Strand's job— as Steiglitz's emissary—to convince O'Keeffe to return to New York.

Strand and O'Keeffe were the same age. They were like Steiglitz's children, in a way, and if they were smart they might have seized the moment and gone off together. It was inevitable that they would break free from his parental influence.

O'Keeffe couldn't understand why Strand didn't take the initiative. All he had to say was "come with me" and she would have followed him anywhere. Instead, he seemed to be a puppet without a mind of his own. He sent her poems from New York. He sent her a copy of Dostoyevsky's *The Idiot* for Christmas. He didn't know about Leah Harris.

Part of her wanted to be with Leah Harris. Part of her wanted to be with Paul. And there was always Steiglitz, looming in the background. Strand's letters to her made her weep. Until now, the only way she could express her emotions was through her art, but even that wouldn't work. It was Leah who broke the ice, so to speak, by confessing her love for her. Georgia went to live with her at her family farm in Waring, Texas. She wrote to Paul, telling him that she had changed. She was a different person. She wrote to him in bed, with Leah Harris lying beside her. "Don't come," she wanted to write to him, but she didn't have the nerve. She sensed that the only reason he was coming to see her was because Steiglitz had asked him to. Why didn't he have a mind of his own? Why couldn't he think for himself? She put out her hand and touched the arm of the woman lying beside her.

Strand arrived in San Antonio in May. He didn't get it at first. Who was this other woman?

He and Georgia would spend a few hours of every day together and then she would go off with Leah. He had to remember that the purpose of the trip was to convince Georgia to return to New York. Steiglitz, before leaving, had confessed his love for her.

There was this woman named Leah Harris. He wrote to Steiglitz about her. Strand and Leah spent a day together in San Antonio, wandering through the Alma gardens. Thinking about Georgia from a distance was different from actually engaging her on real terms. Her life wasn't easy. There was the question of money, how she would support herself if she came to New York. The last thing she wanted was to be dependent on anyone but that was all Steiglitz could offer and he was still married. Steiglitz and Strand had an image of her that was different from the real person. Strand wrote to his mentor that Leah was the only person who understood Georgia. She wasn't going to let Georgia go to New York without any reassurance that someone would take care of her as well as she did. She told this to Strand as if she was speaking for Georgia herself. As if Georgia was a child and didn't know how to express what she wanted. As if she—this other woman—knew best.

Strand wrote Steiglitz about Leah. He refused to admit that Georgia and Leah were lovers. He felt like he was falling in love with Leah as well.

She was lying in bed with Leah and Leah was asking her if she was sure that she wanted to go to New York and Georgia said, "Only if you come with me," and Leah said, "you know that's not going to happen."

"Not now it's not, but once I get there. Once I'm settled."

"And how are you going to get settled?'"

"Alfred will give me some money. He'll find me an apartment."

"So you'll be dependent on him, right?'"

"He'll show my paintings in his gallery. He'll sell my paintings. I'll have some money, my own money."

"The only thing you're selling is yourself—to him. He hates his wife, his daughter is crazy—why do you think he wants to support you? Without him he's in prison. He has nothing, no life."

"It'll just be for awhile," Georgia said. She lifted the

hem of Leah's nightgown and rested her head on her stomach. "If you want me to live here, I will. I'd rather paint here than in New York."

Her first night in New York Georgia stayed in the back room of the gallery at 291 Fifth Avenue. Steiglitz stayed with her until after midnight, and then returned to his wife in the apartment at 1111 Madison. Even though he returned to the apartment they didn't share the same bed. He had a bed in his office at home. Returning to the apartment was just a formality; his whole life was a formality, really, except for the time he spent in the gallery talking about painting.

Georgia didn't mind being alone, but not in New York, and not on her first night. She called Leah in Texas. "I shouldn't have left," she said, "I hate it here." She could hear the anger in the silence on the other end of the line. Leah was angry, she had reason to feel abandoned and angry. She said, "You want to have a career in New York? That's what you want? Have fun." Then she hung up.

She was using her power to get what she thought she wanted. But for a moment, as she lay awake in the dark studio, she felt like she was losing control. She heard a noise in the gallery that might have been a mouse or a person and she said, it was the first thing that came to mind, "Strand, is that you?'" Strand had left the city to enlist in the army. There was a war going on, a slow moving war in which stick figures pursued each other through swamps and patches of scrub, where the bodies of dead soldiers were unearthed in narrow trenches. Georgia claimed to be against the war—against all wars—but she felt that if she was a man she would enlist immediately, that fighting in a war was the experience of a lifetime. She had made fun of Strand—questioning his masculinity—and he had enlisted in the army to prove something to her. Now she was worried that he would turn up dead, that he would die among strangers. She regretted, now that he was gone, that they had never slept together.

She had given up on Leah Harris and Paul Strand and late at night, in the closet-like office of the dark gallery, that's who she wanted. Sometimes the choice that you don't make is the one you always regret. Steiglitz had assured her that he would take care of her—that's what he said to seduce her—but where was he now?

The worst thing to do is to make a decision and then wonder if it was the right one. She had given up on something—she had neglected her feelings for Leah—with the hope of becoming a successful painter. It was Steiglitz's promise—that he would show her work every year—that had swayed her in favor of returning to New York. But now that she was here all she could think about was what she had left behind.

The next morning, when she was still half-awake, craving a cup of coffee, Steiglitz arrived at the gallery with his camera. He undressed and got into bed with her but to his disappointment she didn't want to have sex. Instead of getting angry, he went down to a nearby restaurant and returned with containers of coffee and fresh rolls from an all night bakery. He leaned back against the wall, playing with his moustache, and watched as she hunched her shoulders over the cup, as the smoke from the hot container blew through her hair. He had almost never seen her hair loose before; most of the time she wore it tied back like a helmet. Her hair fell over her shoulders and breasts and she stretched out naked, unselfconscious, and reached for her blouse which was folded over the back of a chair. He watched her button the blouse, as if in slow motion, and sip her coffee. He watched her hands, the curve of her thigh. He reached for his camera. You could see the outline of her nipples beneath her blouse. She held her hands in front of her breasts as if she were offering them to him. He circled around the room. She lay back on the bed and stretched her legs and thought about Leah Harris. She thought about Leah's shoulders and all the mornings of the rest of her life.

She lay back on the bed and he started taking photographs of her. It had always been his dream to do a portrait of a person by taking many photographs at different angles and at different times of the day. He had wanted to make a portrait of his daughter Kitty but his wife didn't want him to follow her around all day with a camera. And certainly he wasn't going to take naked pictures of his daughter. He wasn't sure whether it was what Georgia wanted but she wasn't saying "no." She stretched out on the bed and spread her legs and he hovered over her with the camera.

Every night, at one or two in the morning, she would call Leah Harris. She would let the phone ring, knowing her friend was there and that she refused to answer. She had made a choice and now she had no one but this man with a camera.

Inner Circles

It's not easy to become part of the inner circle. By definition, an inner circle is closed to outsiders. There are always soldiers with rifles at the gates, metaphorically speaking. One way is to marry someone who is a member of the inner circle, though this is tricky, since at any moment the person you marry can fall out of love with you (or fall in love with someone else) and file for divorce. And then where will you be—back where you started, scrubbing pots, used car salesman, street vendor specializing in fake handbags. You can always turn the tables on your former wife by having an affair with the wife of some other member of the inner circle. In a sense, you must trade places with yourself, and swallow your pride, whatever's left of it. There are many people who are not part of the inner circle who couldn't care less.

Think of it like this: I was married to someone in the inner circle. I went to all the parties, teas, private concerts and lectures. At first, I was greeted with open arms, so to speak, like a novelty item. But when I fell from grace, I was banished from the inner circle forever. At least that's what it felt like. Then a little voice reminded me that I had a future, and it wasn't selling used cars, or collecting bottles for deposit. It was just a matter of time before I took up with Josephine, the widow of one of the former members. It was like being part of a circle inside a circle, if you hear what I'm saying. (If you can't hear, there's nothing I can do about it.) I had to bite down hard on my lower lip, but it was worth it to walk into a party with Josephine on my arm, and see my former wife and her new husband across the room. My former wife's new husband is a bad drunk, or so they say, and at every party he hides out in the bathroom, with his head in the toilet. My former wife favors low cut dresses, with hems ending a few inches above her knees. She has beautiful knees, I must admit, and it was hard not to feel a little sympathy for her as she sat by herself in a corner of the large ballroom, nursing a daiquiri. Everyone was having fun except her. The last thing I heard was that my former wife dumped her new husband—literally dumped him out of the back seat of her car onto the side of the road in the middle of nowhere. They were coming home from a party where he had thrown up on one of the guests.

At the next party, a few days later, my former wife was standing alone in a corner of a small living room, like a pariah. It was the saddest thing I had ever seen. No one would talk to her. Josephine could see what was about to happen. She took my arm and said: "If you as much as look at her, I'll have your head. I mean really: I'll decapitate you with my bare hands." When we came home that night, Josephine said: "I have a surprise for you." She opened the bedroom door and there was her younger cousin Samantha lying naked on top of the sheets. She was lying on her stomach. I could tell that a new phase in life was beginning, and I immediately felt a yen for eggs with sausages, my breakfast of choice for years before I ever aspired to becoming a part of the inner circle. I would go to the diner across the street, maybe two or three times a week, and Ernesto, the waiter, wouldn't even bring me a menu. I would drink more coffee than humanly possible and watch the people on their way to work—the young women in flimsy dresses especially who disappeared down the steps to the subway. It was embarrassing to have so much time at my disposal, but I wouldn't have it any other way. My first wife used to bring her maid to sleep with us sometimes, just for the variety of it all, so I wasn't really surprised when Samantha entered our bed. And sometimes it was just me and Samantha. When Josephine wasn't feeling well, she liked to sleep alone, in the bedroom downstairs. She was self-conscious about coughing and sneezing in the presence of another person. She was frightened of germs.

Samantha, to her credit, had no interest in being part of the inner circle. Once, when we were taking a shower together, she said: "What do you see in her?" She was referring to Josephine, of course. Samantha lived in the south of France and offered to take me there on a kind of permanent vacation, even though she knew how much it meant to me to be part of the inner circle. I could have stayed in the shower forever, with Samantha locked in my arms, and the water temperature changing from scalding hot to icy cold. It felt like the high point of something, and I could sense that Samantha felt the same way, as I dried her legs and shoulders. The secret of life is to try to make these moments last forever. Sometimes, when I'm on the rush-hour subway, going to and from my job at Citibank, a job which I had to pull strings to get, I remember what it felt like to stand under the shower, her blonde hair pasted to the sides of her face as she knelt in front of me, so long ago and far away. Everything else—every other memory—pales in comparison. I can look back on my days as part of the inner circle and try to laugh through my tears. And when I read articles in magazines about the initiation rites inflicted on candidates to sororities and fraternities—how a young woman, no more than five feet tall, was required to have sex with every member of the varsity football team, for instance—I remember the feeling of being an outsider amid the barons and counts and corporate CEOs who comprised the inner circle— how they stopped talking whenever I approached and literally spat their words at me whenever they deigned to include me in their conversations. Once, at a Christmas party, I was handed a glass of punch spiked with LSD, and everyone at the party burst out laughing as I stumbled around the room, bumping into tables and chairs, before finally passing out on the living room rug. They walked over me as if I wasn't there. One drunk woman even tripped as she tried to get around me and hit me with her purse. I just closed my eyes and imagined what it was like to be in heaven. At another party, I was forced to strip in time to some old disco record, while Josephine and all her friends stomped their boots on the tiles. Some of them even stuffed dollar bills down the front of my underpants.

Samantha still sends me a Christmas card from

Fontvieille, the small town where she lives in the south of France, not far from Arles, where Vincent Van Gogh painted some of his greatest works, but I never hear from Josephine. I did hear, recently, that my first wife died in a car accident. She was with her new husband, her third one, and both of them were drunk. My first wife was naked—at least that's what the police report said. My first thought, when I heard about this, of course, was to imagine her naked. We had gotten into bed together at least a few thousand times in the years that we were together and it amazed me how little I could remember. It was like all these nights had dissolved into one big blur. Her eyes, the highlights in her hair, the curve of her breasts, the two bodies—hers and mine—reflected in the mirror at the foot of the bed, moving together as if we were one body, the smell of her lilac-scented perfume, all the oils which she ordered from South Korea and which smelled of mangoes and coconuts. Whenever I eat a coconut, which isn't often, the smell comes back to me, and I remember my first wife sitting on the side of the bed rubbing the oil between her legs and thighs, night after night.

THE MERIT SYSTEM

He assumed he was doing her a favor by telling her what he was feeling. He assumed that honesty in any form was a virtue and that there was no point in keeping secrets from the person you lived with, pretending you felt one way when the opposite was true. It was only later, when he left the apartment and walked across town to his brother's apartment to spend the night, that he began feeling guilty about hurting her feelings. He realized that the only reason he had said what he did was to get back at her for something equally hideous she had said to him a few weeks before. He knew that he didn't want to go through life hurting people. What he had said to her, her reaction, the way he was feeling about it now, was familiar to him. He had played out this scenario years ago with other women. It never occurred to him that she might be relieved by what he had said, that she had sensed the depth of his enmity towards her for years (impossible to disguise when you live side by side), and that she was growing weary of living in the shadow of the illusion that they were going to spend the rest of their lives together.

No, on the contrary, she wasn't suffering at all. The minute he walked out the door she put on her suede jacket and went downstairs to the bar across the street to be with her friends. "I shouldn't have spoken to her like that," he said to himself, replaying everything he had ever done in his life to hurt anyone. It's possible that she was suffering over what he had said, but she wasn't the type who was going to wallow in her unhappiness. Didn't he know that about her? She wasn't going to sit home alone and brood. If she was going to drink, which she did almost every night whether she was suffering or not, she would do it among friends. It proved how little he knew about her after ten years of living together to think that she was lying in bed at that moment suffering because of what he had said. That his words really had that kind of effect.

He had spoken to her, he had told her what he was feeling, he had tried to be honest with her. There was no way what he was telling her couldn't be hurting her in some way. He assumed, after all their years together, that he had the power to hurt her. He didn't realize that in the course of their life together she had managed to insulate her real feelings for fear of getting hurt. The disguise she wore had become more comfortable, more fleece-like, than her own skin. After awhile she had forgotten what she had been trying to hide to begin with. It was only while he was telling her what he was feeling, that he had stopped loving her, that she remembered why she had armoured herself in the first place. The look on her face, which he interpreted as a sign of suffering, was really the shock of remembering that this was the moment she had been preparing for, like the meaning of a moat around a castle isn't clear until the castle is attacked. Her expression was also an acknowledgment of the fact that she had known for years that he no longer loved her, so it was no big deal for her to be hearing it now. His actions, over the last few years, had communicated his lack of love for her, so that hearing it all now was a redundancy, to say the least, like he was trying to underline something that was already written in boldfaced letters, large enough even a blind person could read them. It was like he was trying to rub it in, making it worse by talking about it, and it was all she could do to prevent herself from yawning. "I just want to be completely honest with you," he repeated, and she nodded at him quickly, as if she understood everything, as if she agreed with him, as if she admired him for his truth-telling, as if she was about to get down on her knees and beg him to stay, as if she cared.

After he left, she brushed her blonde hair over her shoulders, staring at herself in the full-length mirror on the inside door of her closet. She had a sullen expression on her face, even when she smiled. She put on the suede jacket, which she had recently stolen from A&S, and walked to the restaurant-bar across the street. The bar was called Leon's. It was always crowded. Her best friend Kathy worked there as a waitress. Other friends hung out there as well and she sat in a corner booth talking to them all, occasionally yawning because the conversation was dragging. She would wait till the bar closed and she was alone with her friend before she told her, almost as a joke, what Tom had said to her that night. She would present it almost as an afterthought, as if talking about it wasn't important. She would describe how solemn he had been about it all.

Her friend, the waitress, wore a tight black off-the-shoulder blouse and a short skirt. The owner of the bar, Leon, whom Nora had never met, had a reputation for sleeping with all the women he hired. Sleeping with Leon, at least once, was a condition of the job. He was in his late thirties, not particularly unattractive, and many of the women who applied for the job were desperate enough to go through the motions of having sex with him on the floor of his office if it meant that he would hire them. It didn't take long, really, the sex part, five, ten minutes. And if it meant so much to him, as it seemed to, then there was nothing wrong with it. Their own reputations weren't going to suffer because they'd slept with him to get the job. There was even something exciting about having sex on the carpeted rug in the office in the back of the bar. It didn't mean undressing, either. All you had to do was close your eyes and pretend it wasn't happening.

Kathy admitted that it was a form of prostitution to fuck someone in order to get something in return. It excited her while it was happening, but afterward she felt demeaned by it all. At least that's what she told her friend Nora who lived across the street from the bar. She told Nora that while it was happening she wanted to kill him, get a gun and point it to the side of his head and pull the trigger. Yet the odd thing, at least it seemed odd to Nora, was that a week or two after Kathy began working at the bar she began going out with Leon after the bar closed. They would go to restaurants or dancing or to hear music at an after-hours club near the Holland Tunnel that Leon knew about. There was a rumor among the other waitresses that Leon had fallen in love with Kathy, that he was planning to leave his family so he and Kathy could get a loft together, that he was paying her double what he was paying them, that he had offered to pay the entire rent of her apartment in exchange for sleeping with him.

Sometimes Leon and Kathy would go to her apartment after the bar closed, sniff heroin, and fall asleep. They fell asleep on the couch, with their clothing on, listening to a tape of Billie Holliday singing "God Bless the Child" or Messiaen's "Quartet for the End of Time." Then he would wake up, suddenly, in a daze, usually the light at the window was what got him up, and he would rush off to his wife and children. He would take a cab to his apartment on the Upper East Side where he lived with his family.

Nora had the feeling that her friend Kathy was falling in love with the owner of the bar. She was tempted to apply for a job there herself just to have the experience of turning him down when he propositioned her. She wondered whether she would have the strength. Kathy had told her that the day she applied for the job he had walked around from behind his desk and had stood behind her chair. He had placed his hands on her shoulders, lightly, talking all the time. He never stopped talking, massaging her back, he had a beautiful voice. He could seduce anyone with that voice. She could feel the tension easing from her neck and shoulders. Nora wondered how Kathy felt whenever a new waitress was hired. Did it make her jealous? The longest anyone ever worked at Leon's was six months so he was always hiring new women, new girls. Nora couldn't understand why none of the women who applied for work at the bar ever complained about Leon's behavior. But who could they complain to? He never came out and said "If you want the job, you have to sleep with me—now," but the message was implied. He wasn't forcing you to do something you didn't want to do. It was common knowledge that you had to have sex with him to get the job. You were free to walk out of his office at any time.

Nora wondered how many job applicants had turned down his offer. "I wanted to spit in his face," Kathy told her. At this point she had been working in the bar for about a month. But if she feels this way, Nora thought, then why did she sleep with him again? "He's not really a bad guy," Kathy told her friend, unaware of the contradiction. "You should meet him." She sat alone at the end of the bar counting receipts, waiting for Leon to emerge from his office. They returned to her apartment almost every night. She would put on a record by Dinah Washington that he liked a lot. Sometimes he complained of a headache and she brought him an aspirin and a glass of water. "He's different from all the other men I've known," she said to Nora. "Every night we're together is different. Sometimes we just take off our clothes and sit on the couch without touching. Some nights we shoot up and fall asleep on the couch. Other times...." It was true, Nora thought, she's in love with him, but she isn't suffering.

Tom dialed her cellphone number, lying in bed in his brother's apartment with the phone against his ear, counting the rings. Then he dialed the number in the apartment but she had disconnected both the phone and the answering machine as she sometimes did when they were making love. Her mother was sick, lived in another state, and she worried, when the phone rang late at night, that it was someone calling to tell her that her mother had died. A stranger's voice, a doctor or nurse she had never seen. Her mother was seventy-five years old and lived in a nursing home in a small town near the ocean where she had many friends. Whenever Nora spoke to her mother she felt guilty for not giving her more attention, for not visiting more frequently. Her mother was always careful never to say anything to make her daughter feel guilty. She assumed that Nora had better things to do than devote her life to nursing a sick old woman. There was no reason for her to do it. Nora's mother had lived a full life and wasn't frightened of dying. She hated the pain that accompanied the disease, the loss of concentration and mobility, but she could still take pleasure in looking out the window at the ocean or listening to music, especially opera.

Nora visited her mother in North Carolina every three months and talked to her on the phone every week. It was a pleasure to visit her since it meant that Nora could spend a few days near the ocean as well. It was almost a vacation. One night, after a particularly grueling day with her mother in the nursing home, she went for a walk on the beach and met two men. She made love to both of them, willingly, desiring to give pleasure, the sound of the waves crashing against the shore in her ears. It was a way of wiping out all thoughts of illness and death, of transcending the inevitability of dying, at least for the moment. Anonymous sex is often more exciting than sex with someone you know. Nora knew that she wasn't the only person who felt this way. She wished that the scene on the beach with the two young men would go on forever. She hadn't gone to the beach with the thought of meeting someone. It had been her idea to make love, to fuck right there on the beach, not theirs. They would never have dared try anything if she hadn't reassured them that she wasn't planning to call the police afterward and accuse them of raping her. That she wouldn't lose her nerve once it began.

The doctor in the nursing home had told her that her mother had an infection on the heel of her right foot that was possibly life-threatening. In order to prevent the poison from spreading they would have to amputate her mother's right leg. The doctor touched the place right below his own knee. "We'll have to cut if off here if we want to save her." Nora was an only child. Her father had died when she was fifteen (the day after she lost her virginity) and none of her mother's brothers and sisters were still alive. The decision whether the doctor should amputate her mother's leg was up to her. "If we don't amputate," the doctor said, looking out the window at the ocean, "she could die any time." Nora knew she would have to decide before she returned to the city. She called Tom, the man she'd been living with for the last ten years, but he didn't answer. Tom and her mother had never gotten along and he never accompanied her when she made her trips to North Carolina. She heard his voice on the machine and hung up without leaving a message.

Nora assumed that Tom slept with other women when she went to North Carolina. It was the only time they were really separate from one another. She couldn't believe he had remained faithful to her for the ten years they had been living together. Sometimes she asked him whether he ever felt like sleeping with someone else and he just shrugged. "Aren't you tired of me yet?" she would ask, turning it into a joke.

She stood on the boardwalk outside the motel near the ocean and called him on her cellphone, listening to the waves of static inside the receiver. Then she heard Tom's voice asking to leave a message and she said: "It's me, I'm still in North Carolina. I may have to stay longer than I planned." Maybe she would call him back later? She went down to the beach, it was after midnight, and met the two men. They were walking in her direction. There was no way they were going to pass one another on the beach without talking. She could see the outline of their bodies in the sand. She had to convince them that there was nothing to be nervous about. It wasn't the first time she had been with two men. One of the men seemed more willing to have sex than the other. They were both still in college. One of them entered her while the other looked on. One of them was strong, a weightlifter, maybe six and a half feet tall. Both of them had blonde, shaggy, shoulder-length hair, just like her. It was a clear night, filled with constellations, and the moon was almost full.

She assumed that Tom had gone to the bar across the street for some company. She didn't blame him for feeling lonely when she was visiting her mother. Kathy, the waitress, had told her that the last time Nora had gone to visit her mother, Tom had come to the bar every night trying to convince her to go back with him to the apartment after work. It was on a night when the owner of the bar was sick, or so he said, home with his wife, and Kathy was angry at him. Obviously, no matter what he said, he had no intention of ever leaving his wife. Also, Leon had just hired a new waitress named Samantha, and he was interested in her as well. For one thing, she was prettier and younger than Kathy, and seemed to be popular among the regular customers. So when Tom came into the bar that night when Nora was in North Carolina and Leon was at home with his wife she just shrugged her shoulders as if she were inwardly resigning herself to her own fate and leaned towards him so that her breasts were touching his arm and told him she would be happy to go with him to the apartment after she closed up. He waited on a stool at the end of the bar, nursing his drink. He helped her draw down the shutters over the windows of the bar. The apartment was a third floor walkup across the street. They sat on the futon in the living room, smoking, listening to music, nodding out a bit. Then Tom lifted her in his arms and carried her into the bedroom, to the bed which he and Nora had shared for ten years. They stayed in bed until three o'clock the next afternoon.

"Tom's a wonderful lover," Kathy told Nora when she returned from North Carolina. They were sitting together in a booth at the back of the bar. It was almost closing time and the owner, Leon, emerged from his office.

"I want you to meet someone," Kathy said. She kicked Nora's leg under the table. Leon slid into the booth and kissed Kathy on the neck. "Stop it," she said, playfully, but Leon didn't stop. He squeezed Kathy's breasts without looking at Nora. "Not here," Kathy said. "Later."

Nora walked across the street and climbed the steps to her apartment. She took off her clothes, slipped her nightgown over her head, drank a small tumbler of peach nectar and brushed the tartar from her gums. When she got into bed, Tom woke up briefly and she draped her arm around his waist, resting her chin against his naked shoulder. "I was dreaming about you," he said, without opening his eyes.

CRACK

He handed me his card as we stood in the hallway. We were waiting for the elevator, side by side, our shoulders touching, and he reached into his pocket for his wallet and fished out his card. It had his name on it, in gold letters, his address and phone number. If I ever needed help, he said, I shouldn't hesitate to call. I assumed he thought I needed help (if not now, then some day), though I didn't know how he could tell. I had been alert and restless all day but after the encounter with the stranger in the hallway I began looking forward to going home, getting into bed with a long novel, and falling asleep for twelve hours. The elevator was crowded; I stepped in and turned a full circle so I was facing the door. For a moment the smell of perfume, the physical contact with people I knew only by sight, the swift plunge from the fortieth to the twentieth floor, made me feel like I was going to faint. One woman, who I saw almost every day as I passed through the marble lobby, was pressing against me from behind, her hand on my thigh. But when I turned to say something she didn't even smile.

The phone rang that night and Irini answered it and said it was for me. The curtains were billowing at the open window and the radio was playing a song by Nat

King Cole, Irini's favorite singer. The song matched my mood (sullen, restless: why couldn't I sleep?), and the temperature outside had dropped ten degrees in the last hour. I was wearing the same pinstriped shirt I had worn that afternoon when I met the man in the hallway, the man with the card (which was in my jacket pocket), but I had removed my tie. I stared through the window, parting the curtains with one hand and lifting the phone to my ear. The woman who lived in the apartment above us was walking her dog at the edge of the curb. I tried to visualize the face of the man in the hallway but all I could remember was the band-aid on his chin where he had cut himself shaving.

"It's for me," I said to Irini when the phone rang again. She folded the newspaper she was reading and left the room. By now, there was another song on the radio and the voice on the phone said "Remember me? I gave you my card." I wanted to ask him how he got my number since it was he who had given me his, not the other way around. I don't have a card and even if I did I'm not one for giving my number away to strangers, even those who attract me. I knew that Irini was listening to the conversation at the door of the living room. Or beyond the door where I couldn't see her, but only a shadow. The voice on the phone apologized for calling once and hanging up. "A bad connection," he said, but I knew there was some other reason. I knew that when I got off the phone I would have to tell Irini who called and what had been said. It was our habit, after five years of marriage, to report back to one another about everything that happens when we're apart. And since we're apart most of the time there's always a lot to say.

She was standing in the hallway, in the vestibule near the mailboxes, when I returned home from work. I had loosened my tie on the subway ride home and I was carrying my jacket over my arm. It was a day in late spring; evening had slipped by without the usual drop in temperature. As I tried to brush by her, I had never seen her before, she put her hand on my arm and asked me if I would give her ten dollars. Not loan, give. Even when she asked me for the money, I noticed, she didn't look at me directly. Didn't make eye contact the way people do when they meet for the first time. When you want something from someone you look them in the eye (that's what I do). I knew I had a twenty in my wallet, a five and some ones. It was a warm evening in late spring and I had stayed at work longer than usual. I had no idea how long she was waiting in the lobby, or if she was waiting for me.

I asked the man on the phone where he got my number and he said "Bob" and I said "Bob who?" but it was just a technicality like running outside the baseline. I knew a lot of Bobs, from childhood on: Bobby Kennedy, Bobby McGee. I was glad that he had called but I didn't say that. Some music, the ideal form of communication (no words), filled my head, but I didn't say that either. I knew, if I said anything, Irini (who was listening) would ask: "What did you mean?" Later that night, lying in bed, she would question me about what he wanted and I would say: I don't even know him, I never saw him until this afternoon when I was leaving work. Then Irini would roll on top of me and let her nightgown slip over her shoulders. She has a closet filled with nightgowns, some of which she's never worn, at least not for me. This one was yellow, my favorite color, with doves embroidered on the sleeves.

That night, as I was going through the pockets of my jacket, I found the card which the stranger had given me. Irini was already in bed reading a volume of Proust. Before getting into bed she usually puts on lipstick: *mango, blushing tulip, panic pink.* Then she reads to me or we listen to music before going to sleep. She was lying in bed reading with the book balanced on her knees. Her knees (raised) made a tent of the sheets and blankets. Soon, I thought, we would no longer need the covers which had kept us warm that winter. We could sleep in the nude, with the window open, like we did last summer, and the summer before.

The woman in the hallway told me she could get me anything I wanted. "Anything?" (I felt sleepy). She held the bill I had given her in her hand, no longer desperate for whatever she needed that had inspired her to ask me for money. Now that she had the money she could get what she needed whenever she wanted. She had stringy brown shoulder-length hair and wore an old winter coat with wooden buttons. Possibly she didn't want to feel that she was taking from me without giving, without at least offering me something in return. The word "anything" hung in the air between us like a falling leaf buffeted by the wind.

The next day at work a woman named Sara asked me if I would join her for lunch. We sat at a table near a window in a French restaurant and she touched my knee. She put her hand on my upper thigh under the table and told me she knew I was married but.... "I can't help myself," she said. She was biting her lips and crying and I asked the waiter to bring her an aspirin but she shook her head and dabbed at her eyes, eyeliner running down her cheeks. People at nearby tables began poking one another and staring at me angrily as if I were the cause of her suffering. I looked through the window of the restaurant and noticed that the people on the street were wearing less clothing than the day before. The light on the street was golden and the buds were soaking up the sun.

I felt like I was part of everyone I knew. I felt I was divided into parts and that I wasn't a person who could say "I did this" and really mean that it was "me." The "me" seemed like someone else, or everyone else, and not only that: not only did I have to keep the faces of everyone I knew suspended in my mind at all times, but I also had to keep track of the lights of the city, the cars, and even the music floating out at me from an open window. I felt I was a composite of all these things; the absence of any one thing was the source of my sadness, my regret. If you asked about "me" I would say: look at the light on the side of this building. Look at this tree.

When I arrived home Irini said "He called again" and I thought of Sara. That night, lying in bed with Irini, I had to admit I was thinking about Sara, how she had wept in the restaurant. It was a hopeless feeling to make love to one person and think of another. The man with the card asked (when I told him about this): "Does it happen often?" The next day when I saw Sara at work I blushed but she averted her eyes (too painful). The man with the card said he had his office down the hall from mine and when I stepped inside he locked the door behind him and loosened his tie.

The advantage of friendship is that there's no jealousy involved. Plato said that, I think, in the *Phaedrus*, which I read in college. "To be curious about that which is not my concern, while I am still in ignorance of my own self, would be ridiculous" (Plato said). He said: "In the friendship of the lover there is no real kindness" (or not).

The man with the card said, we were in his office, "Why don't you make yourself comfortable?" I thought of the time my mother, who left me with a baby sitter when I was a child so she could go back to work, came home early one day, dropped her raccoon coat onto the living room rug, and announced: I'm quitting.

She was wearing the same coat and dress she had been wearing the week before. And this time, when I gave her the money and she said "anything," I followed. Across the street, down an alley, into the basement of a tenement. This is it, I said to myself, this is what I want, always want. She reached behind her and took my hand and led me into the darkness of rats scurrying and black plastic garbage bags and cans. It was the engine of the building down here, all the cables and meters. I couldn't imagine going any deeper but I wasn't sinking. My head was above water and I knew a few nouns and adjectives so that describing it to myself was still an endeavor I could aspire to at a later date. I heard voices (do rats speak?) and someone asked: "Who's that?" Someone was standing guard, in the darkness, like a sentry. And then the woman said, simply: "It's me, I brought a friend."

We were on our knees on the floor of the basement amid the garbage cans and rats. The vial of white powder had fallen from her hands and I lit a match but we couldn't find it. The woman and the men behind us were cursing and someone was laughing. It was probably odd for them to see a man with a jacket and tie crawling around on his knees. Until this happened I have to admit I didn't know it was what I needed. I saw Irini, just a flash, but she wasn't in bed reading. I could see her body floating out the window above the city. Irini, in her red nightgown, an adjective, a clause, her arms outstretched above the rooftops. It was all I could do to prevent myself from following her, but I knew that the experience of flying would be different for me. I knew if I stepped off the ledge I would plunge like a rocket to the pavement.

I put my hand through the broken window but I didn't feel anything. "It's like having an orgasm, isn't it?" the woman said, wiping away the blood. She had taken off her blouse but I didn't notice as she gave herself a sponge bath with the water from a basement tap. I no longer knew what "feeling" meant, only "intensity" seemed to convey the sensations I had previously described as "love" or "anger." The excitement was no longer prearranged but seemed to blur my sense of what was most familiar. It was like my first night in Paris, after taking the boat-train from London. Or Venice, getting lost in the maze of alleyways, canals and streets. So when I came to a new feeling I had to stop for a moment, like a tourist, and say: this is it.

I sat at my desk at work, in the large open area where everyone can spy on everyone else, and leafed through a book of photographs of Marilyn Monroe. I had a hard time focusing on words but I could still look at pictures and I kept going back to the one where she's running from the ocean in a white bathing suit holding an umbrella with red dots. "Obviously posed," I kept saying to myself, and then "larger than life." I was tempted (who knew who was watching me?) to press my lips to the different parts of her body when the phone rang and it was Sara to say she was feeling under the weather (her phrase) and wasn't coming in. There was a pause and she said "I'll be expecting you" and then "don't worry, you won't catch anything." Her assumption that I was planning to visit her caught me off guard and I started stuttering. "I'm b-b-backed up here," I said, which wasn't true. There's never enough work to do—I spend most of my time reading the newspaper—and she knew it.

The man who gave me the card locked the door of his office behind him. There was someone else in the room but he didn't introduce us. Instead, he addressed the stranger, a young man in a suit and tie. He said: "Ernie, I think our friend here needs a wake-up call. Don't you?" I was standing in the center of the room with my feet planted firmly on the carpet. Ernie walked out from behind the desk, stood in front of me, and punched me in the stomach. I fell to my knees and he hit me in the back of the neck and kicked me in the ribs as if I were a dog. "That's enough," the man with the card said. He knelt beside me and turned me over onto my back and slapped my face lightly with his fingers. I felt his hands on me, loosening the knot of my tie and unbuttoning my pants, and I felt like reaching out and pushing him away but I didn't have the strength. "I told you to call me," he said. "This is something to remember me by." He snapped his fingers. Ernie disappeared for a minute and returned with a glass of water. He propped my head beneath his arm and tilted the glass to my lips but the water spilled out of the corners of my mouth and down my chin. I tried to stand up but he kept pushing me back against the carpet. The office was empty except for a desk and a chair. There were no diplomas on the wall to indicate that he was a doctor or a broker. "Now you know what it feels like when you hurt someone," he said. "Like a punch in the stomach."

That evening, when I told Irini I was going out, she retaliated by saying that her ex-husband Sid was in town and they were meeting for a drink. In the past, I always expressed anger when she told me she was meeting Sid. He came to New York maybe twice a year and called her up every time. But this time it meant nothing to me. I genuinely hoped they had fun together. I thought of all my old lovers and how happy I would feel if they called me up. Then Irini said: "A woman named Sara called" and I stopped what I was doing. She said: "You're going to meet her, aren't you?" and ran into the kitchen in tears. I guess she assumed I was being unfaithful to her with the woman from my office and I realized that if she thinks that she doesn't know me at all. I had never lied to her once in the five years we were together. If I was going to see Sara I wouldn't try to hide it. "Believe me," I said, putting my hands on her shoulders, "I'm just going for a walk," but she wasn't listening.

This time I went directly across the street to the basement. I lit matches to see my way through the dark. "I knew you were coming," the woman said when she saw me. Some of the faces of the people there were already familiar to me but none of them said hello. There were two people having sex on a mattress in a corner with the woman on top. I took out my wallet and emptied it on the floor of the basement. "You must have robbed a bank," the woman said when she saw all the tens and twenties. "It's Cash McCall," one of the men in the background said, and everyone laughed. The woman scooped up the money and said "I'll be right back." I leaned back against a garbage can and lit a cigarette, trying to blend in.

My father was a dentist and encouraged me to follow in his profession but I dropped out of dental school in my first semester: it just wasn't for me. After that, I took some art courses, painting and sculpture, and for a few years I lived in a loft and attended parties and openings and even had a show, but nothing sold. I was going to have a second show but the gallery folded and I began doing office work, first as a temp, then as a full timer so I could get the benefits. For awhile I continued painting after

work and then I met Irini and we moved to the apartment
uptown and the past began to fade. All my old paintings
are still in storage somewhere. Occasionally I get an
invitation from an old friend who's having a show but
I never attend. The office work involves pieces of paper
(non-threatening) and voices on the phone. And then
there are my coworkers, Sara and the others, with whom
I try to get along, if only to make the job more interesting.
It's hard to spend forty hours a week with the same people
and not feel intimate in some way. I would have to be
blind not to realize that Sara was falling in love with me,
but I didn't want to admit it for fear I would do something
to hurt her. I became the personification of indifference:
who cares what you feel? She leaned over my desk and
I felt myself slipping down the side of a well. I felt like I
was lost in an endless sentence, a maze of words, where
my only escape was to reach out and touch her breasts:
what was being offered. We would go to lunch and she
would ask me about my past and I would tell her: "My
father was a dentist..." but I knew she wasn't listening.
I could feel the tip of her shoe against my leg and her
head would tilt to one side but I kept on talking if only
to appease the guilt, the mixture of guilt and longing. At
night, I would lie in bed and Irini would read to me from
the volume of Proust which she was finishing, and I felt
like I was sinking, clause after clause, into the maze of
words, where the only escape was to roll over on top of
her and lift her nightgown over her breasts, the pale blue
nightgown or the silk one, the one she had worn with her
ex-husband. I deluded myself into thinking that thoughts

were a form of action and that it was permissible to think about Sara while I was making love to Irini. I couldn't understand why Irini, with whom I had lived for five years, was incapable of reading my mind. It made me self-conscious, as if someone were looking over my shoulder as I turned the pages of a magazine with pictures of naked women in poses that invited you to enter their bodies. I could even pretend for a moment that these women weren't being abused, fucked-over, that most of them hated men. By day, during the week, I would literally push Sara away when she leaned over my desk, while at night I would pretend I was lifting her dress, right in the office, when everyone else had gone home. We would go to lunch together, maybe twice a week, at a small French restaurant near Eighth Avenue which we thought of as "our place." The same waiter led us to the same table and chatted with Sara in French. I let her pretend that I was available, that something was happening between us. I even let her hold my hand as we waited for the food to arrive. But most of all I never stopped talking.

The woman in the basement said I could spend the night there if I wanted or I could go with her to an abandoned building on the Lower East Side where she sometimes slept. I unlaced my shoes and sat on the edge of the mattress and I could sense that she was dozing off, that she was going to sleep in her clothing. I pulled at her hair and said "wake up" and she started cursing at me so I stopped. By now I was used to the sound of the rats and the hum of machines. At that moment I felt I could have sex with anyone, woman or man.

Everyone who lived in the basement had a name: Aloha, Conrad, Vitamin G, Washout, Bedtime Story. "You can call me Sylvia," the woman said, after we spent our first night together. She apologized for falling asleep when I was most awake and promised that she would make it up to me somehow. She leaned over and bit me on the side of my neck and told me that she had been living in the basement for almost a year. And before that? I asked. There was a child, a husband, a house in the suburbs. There was a station wagon with which she drove her son to school, trips to Europe every summer. As she told me her life story, she began licking a callous on the side of her thumb. She took my hand and placed it between her legs. I tried not to think what the man with the card had told me about what it felt like to experience pain, that it was worse than a punch in the stomach or a broken jaw. Is that what he said?

After a week in the basement I decided to return to my apartment, what I thought of as my "old apartment," and visit with Irini. I had lost my keys in the basement, the buzzer system wasn't working, so I waited in the vestibule until someone let me in. It was the woman who lived above us, walking her dog. I hadn't shaved in a week and I don't think she recognized me at first. Her dog was black with a white spot on the top of its head and began pawing the cuffs of my trousers, as if I had something he wanted. The woman, who was in her early forties, tugged at the leash and began climbing the stairs. Once, when I returned home from work, about a year ago, she had been sitting on the living room sofa next to Irini, who was showing her photographs from our album. She had stood up to leave almost immediately and lowered her eyes as she brushed by me. Her hair was almost down to her waist and as I followed her up the stairs I had to stop myself from touching it. At the third landing I paused to catch my breath but she continued on, without saying goodbye.

At first, when I knocked on the door of the apartment, no one answered. Then a man's voice said "Who is it?" and I shouted out my name. It was Sid, Irini's ex-husband. I could hear Irini's voice in the background: "Who is it?" All the furniture was gone and there was a stack of cartons against one wall and an open suitcase on the floor filled with Irini's clothing. "I don't think she wants to see you," Sid said. "She's moving out." Then Irini appeared and began pounding on my chest with her fists. "I think you better leave," Sid said. He took my arm and tried to steer me out the door but I pushed him away. "Five years," Irini shouted. "Five fucking years." I wanted to explain that I accepted the blame for what had gone wrong, that she shouldn't punish herself, that it had all been my fault. The apartment looked tiny with no furniture and

I couldn't imagine how we had ever lived there for so long without killing one another. The fact that we had survived five years together in such a close space was a kind of triumph. I wondered what she had done with all my possessions, all the things we had bought together and which, in a sense, were half mine. Out on the landing, Sid pressed a fifty dollar bill into my palm. "If you're going to kill yourself," he said, "do it in style."

Sylvia disappeared for a few hours every afternoon. She had a friend who worked in a hotel in midtown who let her use a room. The rest of the time we sat on the mattress in the basement listening to the radio or playing cards. If the weather was especially warm, we went to Tompkins Square Park and sat on a bench. My money had run out and we lived on the money Sylvia made at the hotel. As soon as she arrived at the hotel she called a woman named Dora and Dora told her the day's schedule and what each of the customers said they wanted. One afternoon, when Sylvia was at work, I dozed off on the mattress in the basement and when I woke up Aloha was kneeling over me. She was an Egyptian woman, with graying hair, who always wore a long striped ankle-length gown. "I wanted to surprise you," she said. "Sylvia won't mind." She unbuckled my pants, lifted her dress, and climbed on top of me. She leaned forward so that her mouth was against my ear and began humming a song that sounded like "Some Enchanted Evening," but more up tempo, in the old Bossa Nova style Irini and I danced to when we first met. Afterwards, she fell asleep in my arms, which is how Sylvia found us when she returned from the hotel. I sat up, quickly, as if one of the overhead pipes had exploded in my head, thinking Sylvia would be angry at me, but she just laughed, as if to say: We all need our privacy, don't we? Then she took off her clothing and joined us, with Aloha in the middle. I remember, hours later, leaning back against the basement wall smoking a cigarette, watching them make love, something I'd never seen before except in pornographic movies. *Two women.* My head began aching with the thought of all the time I'd wasted in my life, all the possibilities I'd backed away from, fearful of the risk, that I might go crazy if I acted one way and not another, deluding myself into thinking that happiness was a function of order, that security was like a tunnel where you never look back. Even when I was painting pictures I was never *inside* the painting (an experience which the painters I admired most had described) but thinking of the final result, wanting it to be over with so I could play the role of spectator (which I preferred), admiring my work from a distance as if someone else had done it. All my old paintings, locked away somewhere, resembled coffins, dead objects, and the last thing I wanted was to create something for others to admire, as if they were speaking a eulogy over my grave. What I wanted was to be like one of the stripes on Aloha's gown, not a line on a map between two points but something that was somehow bent out of shape and restored to life at the same time, so that the act of healing would go on as long as the body kept moving, but with no contours. I was sitting on the edge of the mattress, leaning back against the wall having these thoughts, when Sylvia looked up from between Aloha's legs and said, reaching out and taking my hand: "Don't be sad, honey, we haven't forgotten you," and we all laughed.

Sirocco

It's no use trying to pretend you're someone different. I've seen your type before. It's no accident that we're sitting across from one another on this train. We might as well say something. Hey, fuck your sister. No, not that. It's better to pretend that you like to do things in your spare time like go to museums and to the movies. Matisse. Did you see the recent Matisse show at MOMA? I belong to MOMA, you know, which means I get in free. Sort of, since I pay $150 a year, and that entitles me to free admission. Otherwise, it's $20 a pop. It feels like I'm getting something for nothing. I can go everyday and stay as long as I want. Once I was sitting in the garden at the museum and a girl sat down beside me and started talking to me and afterwards she gave me her phone number and then a few days later we went on a date to the movies and then later that night we went back to her apartment and had sex and then a few months later we got married at City Hall. And that's how things stand at the moment, five years later. Love—I'm not sure that's the word, but it's something, we get on well together, though I must admit I have a small crush on her younger sister Bethany. Last summer we went to visit her sister and her husband in California. They live in the country north of San Francisco, outside Point Reyes, right near the ocean. Beautiful, but I'd get bored in two seconds if I lived there. I keep my feelings for my sister-in-law to myself. I'm not crazy about her husband Blair either, but I don't let on. I ask him questions about his life and try to ignore the fact that he never asks me anything about mine. When I have sex with my wife I imagine making love to her sister Bethany. I know this is more than you want to know, but you asked me to say something that I never told anyone else, so here it is. I'm in love with my wife's sister. I sometimes think that the feeling is mutual, but who will ever know? I try to pretend the only reason she married Blair was because of his money. His father is CEO for some dumb corporation. A big time contributor to the Republican party. Bethany assures me that Blair isn't the conservative type, but I think she's kidding herself. The last time my wife and I visited them Bethany and I went for a walk on the beach. It was the first time we had ever been alone and I was tempted to tell her how I felt, how I had made a mistake by marrying her sister, Devon, that I was tired of living a life of disappointment, of living with one person when I loved someone else. I said nothing, of course, though in a restaurant overlooking the ocean she put her hand on my arm when she was saying something and I had to bite my lip to stop myself from spilling the beans. Then, before I knew it, Devon and I were on an airplane heading home, and the next thing I knew, not long after, Bethany was dead. She had jumped off a cliff into the ocean not far from where we were walking and disappeared into the waves. Devon and I flew back to California for the funeral. We rented a car in San Francisco and drove up the coast. Blair told Devon that Bethany left a suicide note and I like to think that the reason she killed herself was because she was in love with me. But I never saw the note, and Devon never told me what her sister had written. I felt like it was my fault—if I had told her how much I loved her when we were in the restaurant, when she put her hand on my arm, things would be different. I can still feel the pressure of her fingers on my bare skin. It's what I think about before I go to sleep. It occurred to be that I was doomed to spend the rest of my life sleeping beside someone who I didn't love and that I might as well jump off a cliff myself. "What are you thinking?" Devon asks, about ten times a day, and I want to tell her everything, but I don't. The only person I've told about my feelings for Bethany is my therapist Jill. Jill doesn't think it's a good idea for me to tell Devon, even though in almost every other circumstance she advocates telling the truth. Possibly, Jill suggests, I should wait until her sister's death sinks in before saying anything. Otherwise it's too much for any one person to deal with at one time. I imagine Bethany lying in bed next to Blair, thinking about me. I imagine her thinking about me when she's having sex with Blair. I remember the last time I saw her when she rolled up the cuffs of her jeans and ran into the surf. She turned to me and extended her arms as if she was going to lead me into the abyss but I backed away. I didn't want to get my feet wet. That's what I'm like, though you wouldn't know it from talking to me. I project something different. You wouldn't know, for instance, that I'm scared of my own shadow. But Devon knew, I'm sure, about my feelings for her sister. Maybe Bethany made some mention of it in her suicide letter. Maybe she wrote how much she was in love with me and couldn't stand it any longer and begged her sister's forgiveness. Maybe she didn't drown herself at all—the body's never been recovered—and one day I'll be walking down 8th Street in Manhattan, passed the old Studio School where my first wife Martine used to study landscape painting—and I'll see a person I barely recognize heading my way and realize, just as we're passing each other like fucking ships in the night, that it's Bethany McCarthy, my second wife's sister, the girl I love.

PICKUP ON TENTH STREET

I t was after midnight, a Wednesday, the bar was almost empty. Three women in their early thirties came in laughing and sat down at a booth. One of the women, Teresa, stood up almost immediately and announced to her friends that she was going to the bathroom, which was located behind a glass door and down a flight of stairs. On her way, she smiled at a man sitting alone at a table.

"Don't I know you?" she asked.

He shrugged, "Maybe," looking straight at her without recognition, taking her words literally and thinking, "no, I don't know you," and said, finally, "Can I buy you a drink?"

The woman leaned over his table and said, "I'll be right back." She walked down the hallway, the steps, opened the bathroom door, and stared at herself in the mirror. Took the brush from her pocketbook and lifted her hair from one shoulder and held it up to the light inspecting for split ends. One of the other women, one of her friends, Alison, came into the bathroom and stood directly behind her in the mirror. She put her hands on Teresa's breasts and buried her face in her hair. She tried to sneak a hand under her skirt but Teresa pushed her away.

She had already told Alison that she wasn't going to go home with her that night but Alison didn't want to hear about it and Teresa was frightened of inciting her anger. That's why she was letting her touch her breasts, now, in the bathroom, the straps of her bra sliding down her arms. She actually didn't mind fooling around outside, it excited her more than if they were back in her apartment, but she didn't say this to Alison. She kind of let it all glide for a few minutes, reciprocating by slipping her hand down the front of Alison's blouse and squeezing her nipple. She promised Alison that they would spend a night together next week.

"I can't wait," Alison said.

She went into one of the stalls and pulled down her pants without closing the door and Teresa, resisting the temptation to watch, took advantage of the moment of freedom to leave the bathroom and go upstairs.

The man at the table—blonde, moustache, his shirt unbuttoned midway down his chest—was waiting for her. He had already ordered her a drink.

"I took the liberty...." She waved her hand. It wasn't necessary for him to explain. She pulled the chair away from the table and crossed her legs, skirt pulled up, her knees touching his.

Christina and Alex came into the bar holding hands. Christina put a quarter into the jukebox and played

"Tonight, Tonight" by the Mellowkings but it didn't come on immediately. They sat at a booth in the corner, ordered two beers, and Christina told him how bored she had been earlier in the summer before he arrived. It had not been a very productive year, to say the least.

"One night," she said, "about a month ago, I was so restless I came here at about midnight and picked up this guy, a total stranger He lived right around the corner on Tenth Street. It wasn't a bad apartment, two bedrooms, a small living room, a kitchen and a full tile bath, and I could almost imagine living there with him, cooking his meals, but he said, 'Do you want to watch a movie,' and I said, 'That's not what I came here for,' and he said, 'But I'm not interested in women, I don't fuck women.' He said that many of his best friends were women. He said that when he first met a woman she assumed they would eventually become lovers, that that's what he wanted as well. They were shocked and disappointed when he told them he'd never been with a woman before. I was on the verge of falling asleep from the effort of trying to deny what he was telling me—the last thing I wanted was to be anyone's friend—when his roommate walked in and I asked them if they were lovers and they stared at their feet and the guy I met in the bar said 'Sometimes." And then I asked the roommate if he liked women and he said 'Yes' so I made it with him."

"What an asshole she is," Alison said. She emptied the last of her beer into a glass, swallowed it, made a face, and waved to the bartender to get his attention.

The bartender, who was watching television, saw the woman waving at him from the booth. He ignored her. There was no table service; even an idiot could see that. If she wanted a drink she'd have to get it herself.

Greta, who had met Alison and Teresa at a party the night before, hummed along to the song on the jukebox, "Devil or Angel," by The Clovers.

"You can have my beer," she said to Alison, tilting the bottle over the empty glass.

Greta's mother was German, but she had grown up in Fort Lauderdale, Florida. A year after her mother died, when she was twelve, she witnessed a murder from her bedroom window. She had identified the murderer to the police, a friend of her father's, but the lawyer for this man offered her father a large sum of money if he could convince her not to testify in court. A few months after her mother died her father introduced her to his new girlfriend. Apparently he'd been seeing this woman even when Greta's mother was alive. Her name was Molly Stone, and she had two sons, Harry and Darryl. Molly slept over at Greta's house almost every night. One evening her father called Greta into the living room—Molly Stone and her sons were there—and tried to persuade her to go to the police and tell them she had been mistaken about the murder. That the man she had seen kill the woman with the ice pick in the driveway of their apartment building was not Amos Akindo, as she had previously thought. He told her that he himself would call the police and tell them his daughter had made a mistake. She didn't have to do anything. He tried to persuade her by saying that he had been playing pool with Amos the night of the murder. Greta knew in her heart he was lying to save his friend and that he depended on her to lie as well; she knew nothing, at the time, about the money which Amos's lawyer had offered. She felt no particular loyalty towards her father, only a kind of fear of what he might do if she didn't go along with his plan. She hated him mostly for being unfaithful to the memory of her mother. It was Darryl who eventually told Greta that her father and Molly had been going out together for over a year before Greta's mother had died.

"I wish I was a stronger person," she confessed to Alison. "I wish I hadn't listened to him."

Greta's father used the money which Amos Akindo's lawyer gave him to take his family north, put a down payment on a house in a suburb of Boston, and purchased a share of the Oldsmobile dealership where he now worked. By this time her father and Molly Stone were married. Greta told Alison that she occasionally dreamed about the man with the ice pick (Amos Akindo) and the young woman whom he had met earlier that night in a bar, seventeen years old, her short white party dress covered with blood. Greta had many friends in Fort Lauderdale and one boy, especially, with whom she thought she was in love, and the last thing she wanted to do was move to a strange city, the last thing she wanted was a life that involved Molly Stone and her two slovenly sons. She didn't like the way the two young men looked up from their magazines when she entered a room; she couldn't sit in the same room with them without feeling they were undressing her in their minds.

One night, a month after they moved to the house in Boston, a month after they began living under the same roof in the three bedroom house where Molly and her father shared one bedroom and the two brothers shared another and Greta was given the smallest room, a maid's room really, no bigger than a large closet, the older brother Harry returned home drunk late one night and tried to get into bed with her, lifting her nightgown under the blanket and then climbing on top of her. She managed to push him aside, clawing his cheek with her fingernails (drawing blood), and escape down a ladder that was leaning against the side of the house. She told Alison how the next day, when she complained to her father about what Harry Stone had done, he laughed in her face.

Teresa said, "I told you I knew you," and Victor said, "It's possible. I didn't believe you at first."

She said: "You thought it was a line."

"I've used it myself," Victor said, "but not recently."

After five minutes of talk, they discovered they were the same age, born only five days apart, and they had attended the same college in upstate New York. Neither had graduated, though Teresa had lasted a year longer. She told him that she had lived for five years, the length of her marriage, in Santa Fe, New Mexico. He knew the street that she lived on and the bar named Claude's where she worked as a waitress. After her marriage ended, she said, she moved back east. Victor asked her about the courses she had taken in college: possibly they had been in the same class? He mentioned the name of a professor in the psychology department but she shook her head.

He told her that he lived a few blocks away, just below Houston Street, but that he didn't like his apartment, he was thinking of moving to Brooklyn to a bigger place, that he had two cats, that he'd been married once, as well, and though it had ended five years ago he was still getting over it in the sense that he assumed now that all relationships were doomed, that nothing ever lasts, and that it was pointless to get overly involved with anyone with the hope it might go on forever. It was the "forever" part that created the pressure on most people who lived together. He knew he was dominating the conversation but he had the sense that she was interested, that she was relating to what he was saying. As he talked, he was aware of her knee pressing against his thigh.

Teresa knew that Alison was probably angry with her for leaving her alone with Greta. As a way of retaliating, they—Alison and Greta—would probably go home together. In Teresa's mind this turn of events wasn't the worst thing that could happen. Alison had assured her over the phone that Greta didn't even like women, that she was lonely and wanted friends. Alison had stopped sleeping with men and couldn't understand why Teresa still bothered. She had been contemplating asking Teresa whether she wanted to move in with her. It was stupid for each of them to pay $800 a month for their tiny apartments. The only reason to sleep with a man, as far as

Alison was concerned, was to make babies. If that was the reason, she wouldn't mind if Teresa slept with someone (a man), but that was the only reason. She had a fantasy of being in the delivery room while Teresa was giving birth, of holding her hand, of breathing with her while she was in labor. The fact that men were even necessary to conceive a child was, from Alison's point of view, a crime against nature.

"Did you know Renee Jacobson?" Teresa asked.

"Of course," Victor said. "She was Tom Poole's girlfriend."

She would mention a name and he would nod his head as a sign of recognition. She had a hard time adjusting to life in college, to being away from her parents. Among her friends, she was the only one who was still a virgin. She didn't know how to drive a car or cook and she had never laundered her own clothing. She remembered spending her Saturday nights lying in bed in her dormitory room composing letters to her parents and to her sister Marie. People were laughing in the hallways and outside in the quadrangle she could hear firecrackers and the sound of a radio playing "You Send Me" by Sam Cooke. In subsequent years, whenever she heard the song "You Send Me" she remembered that moment, how lonely she felt, how separate from everyone else.

Renee would come in at two in the morning after a date with Tom Poole. Sometimes Renee would ask Teresa whether she could spend the night elsewhere so that she and Tom could sleep together in the room. They had nowhere else to go. Renee arranged for her to sleep in a room down the hall; the girls who lived there were going away for the weekend. Once, during the week, Teresa woke up in the middle of the night to the sound of Renee and Tom fucking in the bed across the room. "They think I'm asleep," she said to herself, "or maybe they just don't care."

Edgar always came to the bar after fighting with his wife. He sat on a stool, in the corner near the door, ordered a beer, drank it straight from the bottle, and then another, all the time replaying the argument, everything he might have said if he hadn't walked out. If I don't care about what she does when she's not with me, he said to himself, then I won't feel this way, right? It wasn't simply a rationalization but a plan, a way of being that actually made some sense. If I only think about what I do, at all times, and not concern myself with what she's thinking or doing, or who she might be with—something I'll never know anyway—then I'll never have to feel this way again. He felt like he needed a tourniquet or a giant band-aid to stop the pain.

He recognized that in his previous marriage the same thing had happened: he had driven his first wife away with his insecurity, his jealousy, his suspicion. But when his second wife accused him of being "crazy" (her word) for questioning what she did, he assumed (in the depth of his distrust for her) that saying this was the ultimate lie. I'm lying to you and if you don't believe me, you're the one who's crazy. He tried to deny that she was the type of person who would purposely try to hurt him. If she's lying and I know she's lying then it's my fault as well. He would accuse her of lying and she would accuse him of being crazy. She acted angry and resentful whenever he accused her of lying. Worst of all, Edgar knew that if he were unfaithful to her, he would say the same things.

When they first met, she already had a boyfriend, and he had waited, patiently, until she made her choice: him or me. He knew that she was sleeping with both of them, that she was capable of such a thing, but he managed—since they weren't living together yet—to hold that thought in abeyance, to keep his jealousy under control, to assume that what was happening was a prelude to the rest of their life together. (He refused to believe that she would some day repeat the same scenario with someone else.) He never once gave her an ultimatum—him or me, *now*—but let her play it through, the drama she loved so much, until finally she let her first boyfriend off the hook, told him the news, and showed up at Edgar's apartment one night, teary-eyed, suitcase in hand. They had been together for four years.

All his thoughts about their life together had nothing and everything to do with the pain in his heart. There was no way of thinking through a feeling so that it would eventually go away. Thinking never solved anything, yet it was all he had.

She had arrived home late, as she did every Wednesday night after class (the class ended at eight, she had returned at eleven-thirty), and he had asked her what she had done and she told him, as usual, that the teacher had kept them past the time the class normally ended, that she had to talk to the teacher after class about a paper she was writing, that she had gone out with a friend—a woman friend, she even mentioned a name—for something to eat, that the train was delayed and she had to wait for forty minutes at the 68th Street station, that she fell asleep on the train and missed her stop. All these excuses added up to how many hours? In her school notebook she had written a phone number and he had called it up one night and a man's voice on the answering machine said, "This is George, I'm not at home now, please leave a message." So there was the issue of this person George and who he might be. And sometimes the phone rang when he was at home and the person at the other end hung up. Once, a man asked to speak to his wife, who wasn't home, and when Edgar asked if he could take a message, the man said, "No, not necessary," and hung up. The asshole refused to even give his name, Edgar thought. So there was the lateness after class and the feeling that every time he left the house she left too, after him, that she was waiting for him to leave so she could go out to see—whoever!

Once, with his first wife, Yvonne, in an attempt to either appease or confirm his suspiciousness, he had decided to spy on her. He stood across the street from the office building where she worked. He watched her leave, holding the arm of a man he'd never seen before. He followed them for a few blocks until they reached the building where he lived (or so Edgar assumed), a high-rise with a doorman. She was with him for an hour. He watched her walk across the lobby, carrying her coat.

"Enough time for a quick fuck," he muttered bitterly to himself, wanting to kill someone. As soon as the doorman saw her coming, he rushed out into the street, blew his whistle and flagged down a taxi. She was already home when he returned (Edgar had taken the subway) and when he asked her what she had done after work she said that she went to visit her mother. "Where were *you?*" she asked, diverting the suspicion. A typical ploy. He lit a cigarette, opened a beer, and told her everything he had seen. She hung her head momentarily, anticipating punishment, a slap, the rush of footsteps which meant he was leaving. But he didn't say anything which was the worst punishment of all since she knew he was waiting for her to confess; she was cornered, she had no choice. After an endless unendurable silence, during which he finished his beer and lit another cigarette, she told him that she had been sleeping with her coworker for the last six months, but that she wasn't in love with him. "What's his name?" Edgar was tempted to ask, but what difference did it make? In a flash, he remembered all the nights when she returned home late and presented him with her repertoire of excuses. He had believed her, he had wanted to believe her, he had denied that she was lying to preserve their life together. If nothing else, now that everything was out in the open, he had the vague satisfaction of knowing his instincts had been correct.

Of course his new wife Lydia knew what had happened with Yvonne, knew that she had been unfaithful to him, Edgar had told her everything. And now, when he expressed his jealousy, which took the form of anger, saying the worst things that came into his head, she would turn to him and say: "I'm not Yvonne, don't confuse us. When you shout at me you're really shouting at her."

Edgar knew this was at least partially accurate but also sensed that to say this was part of a complicated subterfuge that involved transferring the burden of guilt from her to him. What it always came down to was that he was the crazy one. "Why don't you follow me like you did with her?" Lydia would say. He knew that he would feel the same way about any woman, that he was attracted to women who had the potential to deceive him, but that it was also possible for Lydia—or whoever—to give him a sense of reassurance so that he didn't have to experience the torments of jealousy, especially if there was no reason. He wasn't sure, exactly, what she could do to make it clear to him that she wasn't lying, but he wanted her to do something.

And meanwhile, there was always this bar, where he could slow down, take a break, watch his thoughts come and go, one thought bleeding into another, as if he were observing himself from a distance, this is me feeling these things. The last thing he wanted was to go through life repeating what he had done before. The last thing he wanted was to feel like a victim, a person whose nervous system was dependent on what someone else did.

And the only way out, it always came down to the same thing, was to live his own life irrespective of anyone else. Even the person you married, this person you called your wife or husband, was a separate being. It was a dumb illusion on his part to think you could be connected so intensely to anyone else, yet it was what he wanted, not the illusion but the luminous thread of longing that extended to infinity. The impossibility of it all, with anyone, ever, was the source of his strange sadness.

"I want another beer," Christina said.

Alex was due at the airport at seven the next morning. That's when his plane back to California was scheduled to leave. He assumed, since it was already almost one, that he would stay awake all night. It was pointless to insist on going to sleep and then wake up exhausted, as exhausted as he might be if he never slept at all. His plan was to take a seconal and sleep on the plane, close his eyes in New York (while the plane was still on the ground) and wake up five hours later as it was circling above San Francisco Bay.

He had come to New York three weeks before to see a publisher who was interested in a book of his stories and to visit with his father who was recovering from open heart surgery. Before leaving California, his wife Arlette had called her friend Christina to ask whether she had room in her apartment for Alex to stay. Christina and Arlette had known each other since high school. During this long distance phone conversation between Arlette and Christina, Alex hovered in the background, not certain whether he was really happy with the arrangement. In his imagination, he had seen himself in a hotel room on the Upper East Side, looking out over the city, drink in hand. It was his reward for selling the book, but Arlette thought differently. Look at all the money he'd save if he stayed with Christina. Be practical for once in your life.

The last thing Alex imagined was that he and Christina would become lovers. For the first week, he slept on an air mattress on her living room floor. There was only one bedroom in the apartment, only one proper bed. Every afternoon Alex went uptown by subway to the hospital where his father was recovering from his operation. Alex's stepmother usually visited in the evening, after work, and Alex wanted to avoid seeing her. As soon as he arrived in New York, he called up all his old friends. He had dinner at their homes or met them in restaurants or for drinks, but after five years there was no way he could re-enter their lives in any real way. Most nights he spent alone in Christina's apartment, watching the news on TV or one of her many tapes, until she returned home from her film classes at New York University. One night a week she worked for an escort service; she accompanied men, mostly elderly or middle-aged, to cocktail parties, or to the opera. She was writing a screenplay about a young woman, much like herself, who worked for an escort service, and what happened when one of the men fell in love with her. Christina told Alex that after an hour or two the man she was with tended to forget that she had been hired to go out with him and began to think she was willingly providing her services because she enjoyed his company. Sometimes, if she liked the guy, she would give him a blow job in the back of the cab on the way to his hotel. It was rare for one of these men not to assume that she would eventually go to bed with him.

Often, before falling asleep, Alex and Christina watched a movie together on Christina's bed. They saw *The Manchurian Candidate, 400 Blows, Suddenly Last Summer.* One night they both fell asleep in front of the TV fully dressed and woke up in each other's arms. They removed their clothing in slow motion and made love like zombies in the dawn light, with Christina on top. Since then they slept together every night, easing into one another's arms as the characters in the movie they were watching faded into oblivion. Christina had never lived with anyone who was always there when she came home. There was no need to tell one another how they spent their respective days, no need to talk. She undressed in front of the full-length mirror on the door of her closet while Alex watched her from the bed. She knelt alongside him, taking his cock in her mouth. She buried her face in the pillow and spread her legs. "Slap my ass," she ordered, as Alex hovered over her. It was something that Arlette had never permitted him to do.

"If you want," Christina said, as they were sitting in the bar, "I'll call up Arlette and tell her what happened. I'll tell her we fell in love and want to live together forever."

"In My Diary" by the Moonglows was playing on the jukebox. As Alex approached the bar to get more beer, he noticed a couple in the back, in the space between tables, dancing to the music. He saw the woman's golden hair as she tilted her head to be kissed. He noticed the two women, surrounded by empty beer bottles and ashtrays, sitting at a booth holding hands. One of the women was crying while the other was attempting to comfort her.

He noticed a man with a beard, perched on a stool near the door, drinking beer from a thin-necked bottle that seemed as long as the arm that was holding it. When the bartender came by to take his order, Alex pointed to the bottle which the man was caressing and said: "I'll take one of those."

THE RIGHTFUL HEIR

For the moment, the throne is empty. The rightful heir has decided to stay in bed this morning with one of his girlfriends. Myra rolled over in bed and watched the rightful heir as he slept. She lit a cigarette and blew perfect smoke rings up to the ceiling which was covered with paintings of angels and harps and clouds. She wondered if she was cut out for this life—girlfriend of the heir—and what it would mean once he took his place on the throne. A nonstop round of parties—in which she, as the first girlfriend, was required to strip naked and dance in a circle while the other men in the court whistled and shouted at her. And perhaps she would be required to sleep with the other men in the court, while her husband looked on, if that was his pleasure. In her short life she had known men like him before. Perhaps it is simpler to be a citizen than the heir to anything. Perhaps it is safer to be a decoy than the real thing. The rightful heir has only one life to give to his country, or so they say, but the citizen can live forever in the comfort of his or her bed. As a private citizen, far from the glare of the klieg lights and the TV cameras, you do not have to attend parties, strip naked in time to the beat of the tom toms, or have sex with strangers, both men and women, and in some case very young men and women, at your husband's behest. All you have to do is take the trolley line into the center of town and check into a hotel under a false name. Then you can go about your business with no one watching over your shoulder. You can stare at the rooftops of the city through a telescope which the rightful heir gave you for your fifteenth birthday and see all the couples sunbathing in the nude. You can see their private parts, covered with sweat and lotion, and remember how the rightful heir used to wake you in the middle of the night or at the crack of dawn after a night spent drinking with his lackeys, how he pried open your body with his fingers when you were half-asleep. Now you can stay in bed all day or lie naked on top of the sheets and no one will bother you. Only the maid, a young girl like yourself, will disturb your solitude, same time every day. Her name, you learn, is Natalie, and she was born in a town on the banks of a nearby lake. "Natalie, will you bring me some water," you say, as a pretense to draw her closer to your bed, so that you can smell the lavender cologne on the side of her neck and her mint-flavored mouthwash as she smiles. It's just a matter of time before she arrives at the door of your room in the middle of night. "I thought you might want some company," she says, kicking off her loafers and lifting her skirt to exhibit her flowery underwear. The days that turned into weeks that you spent with the rightful heir, the weeks that turned into months, seem to vanish into the near distance, as Natalie, who thinks only of your pleasure, massages your pointy shoulders with coconut oil from the island of Kuwaii, and slips her tongue between your knees without asking. Sometimes you wonder what the rightful heir is doing at the very moment that Natalie falls asleep in your arms, but all you can see is the body of an anonymous woman leaning over him in his king-sized bed while "The Four Seasons" by Vivaldi plays in the background. And for the rest of your life, every time you enter a room, with Natalie on your arm, and "The Four Seasons" is playing, all eyes on you as you descend the staircase in your see-through muumuu, whether it be a restaurant or a private party, you will remember your moment in the sun as the girlfriend of the rightful heir, and recall his bad breath and broken fingernails, his rough beard against your skin, the way he farted in his sleep, the smell of piss everywhere.

SPECIAL FRIEND

It's important to let the grass grow a little while longer. It's not necessary to cut the grass, let it grow for a few more days. You can wait until it's up to your waist, then you can cut it. You can wade into the water until it's waist-high—then you can dive in. Even on the coldest days, I take a swim in the ocean. I swim out to where the horizon meets the sky, and then I swim back to shore. A strange woman awaits me on the shore, holding a towel, just like my mother did when I was a child. "Let me dry you off," my mother said. I would change from my wet suit to a dry suit in the men's bathhouse. Some girls were peeking through the windows of the men's bathhouse, watching the men undress. It was strange to be standing around in the bathhouse with a lot of naked men. My father was there, and some of his friends. The girls were at the window, staring at the naked men. I had seen my mother naked, and maybe my sister, and that's it.

I like to hold my head underwater and count. Sometimes I stay under for more than a minute. I like to swim past the ropes to the diving board with my father watching me from the shore. My mother sits on a blanket with her friends. She doesn't swim. One night a week we have dinner at a restaurant, The Knotty Pine. It's still there. A few years ago my wife and I visited this town from my distant past. We went to the restaurant, where I used to go with my parents, but the food was horrible. First we had a drink at the bar. Then we sat down. It was a special occasion—going to this restaurant with my parents. It's the end of summer and the water is too cold to swim. All we can do is sit in our bathing suits on the shore. My father plays hearts with his friends on a blanket. It's important to let the grass grow—but now it's time to cut it. I can feel it in my bones—time to let it all go. The beach, the shoreline, the horizon, the diving board, the bathhouse with the girls peeking through the window at the naked men. And the restaurant where we used to go on warm nights, after a day at the beach, walking single file along the side of the road.

Maybe once a week we went to this restaurant. I always ordered the same thing—Southern Fried Chicken. It seemed to be something an older person might eat. I wanted to be older than I was. We went to the beach every day. I stood in the cold water. Then I swam past the ropes to the diving board. You could see the trees and the houses on the opposite shore. Then it was time to swim back with your head underwater until you reached the ropes. Your mother was waiting on the shore with a towel. You went to the bathhouse to change into a dry suit and there were the girls, peeking through the window. You knew their names: Joyce, Margaret, Ellen-Sue. Their parents were friends of my parents. It was odd that no one complained. The men just walked into the bathhouse and began taking off their clothes. The girls hid under the window. My thighs were chafed. At night I put talcum powder on my thighs. I thought of the girls at the window and of people back home in the city, the girls in my classroom. Sometimes, in the evening, we went to the movies. There was one movie theater in town. One night we watched *The War of the Worlds* and the sister of one of my friends started screaming and ran down the aisle of the theater. It's time to let it all fade away. The town, the movie theater, the girls at the bathhouse window watching the men take off their clothes. What were they thinking? I turned my back to them. I could hear them whispering. I was alone in the bathhouse and they were watching me undress.

There was a rumor that some of the parents went swimming at night. In the nude, of course. But not my parents. I wondered what it would be like to peek through the window of the woman's bathhouse, but I never did. Instead, we were on the beach, and I was swimming past the ropes to the diving board with the trees in the distance and a motor boat chugging through the waves. The sound of the motor boat, the wind through the trees. The sound of the crickets as we walked home from The Knotty Pine, the snakes slithering through the grass. The body of a dead chipmunk. The moss on the side of a stone.

I imagined all the bodies of all the adults on the beach swimming in the nude late at night. Getting out of the water naked in front of everyone and no one minded if one husband saw another man's wife or some woman saw another woman's husband. I wondered what happened afterward when they came out of the water into the moonlight on the sand. I imagined the girls in my class back home and some of my teachers when they turned their backs to the class and a woman on TV who swirled her skirt when she was dancing and you could see the tops of her thighs. It was what I thought about when I was lying in bed.

The tops of the trees were moving in the wind. There were people sitting in beach chairs on the docks outside their houses. A motorboat, a rowboat, a canoe. Some people fall asleep on the blanket in the afternoon. There were two couples fucking on the beach at night. The friends of my parents. I wondered what I would do with the woman on TV in the short skirt. It all came back to me, as if in a dream. You could see the reflections of the trees and the houses in the water. My suit was wet. "You can change in the bathhouse," my mother said. The girls were on their knees at the back window. I took off my bathing suit in the bathhouse and turned around. I could hear them laughing.

We went there every summer. And then we stopped. Things were the same and different. I was different, but I can remember everything. I can remember the couples fucking on the beach. The husband with someone else's wife, the wife with someone else's husband. I can hear one of the women crying out in the night. There was a full moon and you could see the bodies covered with sand. They were the parents of my friends. I knew them all well. It was easy to imagine running out of the water onto the sand, like in the movie *From Here to Eternity*, but in this case everyone is naked. In *From Here to Eternity*, Deborah Kerr and Burt Lancaster run out of the water and lie down on the sand. They're wearing bathing suits. Half-naked bodies rolling around, one on top of the other, as if they were fucking. I lay awake in bed thinking of someone I had seen for a few moments. We had stopped for gas—me, my parents and my sister—and she was sitting in a convertible at the gas station. She was wearing a straw hat, and a white dress. Her arms were bare. I could see her blonde hair under the hat. It wasn't hard to imagine what it would be like putting your hands under her dress in the car if you were driving. It was possible to drive with one hand and put the other hand between her legs. That's what I thought about when I was lying in bed—and what else? Everyone I saw on the street, every teacher who stood in front of a class, every girl in the class, the mothers of all my friends.

You knock on the door and there she is. Paul's mother, Dorothy. But he isn't home. "Do you want to wait for him?" Dorothy says. Paul is your best friend and once, when you were visiting him, you saw his mother undressing . The door of her bedroom was half-open but she didn't see you. Or possibly she left it open on purpose? You saw the reddish hair between her legs and the tips of her breasts. It seemed possible to reach out and put your hand down the front of her blouse. That she would let you do anything.

Once I went to the movies on Saturday afternoon with a girl in my class named Bettina. Everyone sitting around us was locked in a passionate embrace. I wanted to watch the movie. It was starring Cornel Wilde. Bettina was looking at me as if she was waiting for something to happen. I thought I should take her hand and put it down the front of my pants, but I didn't. I put my arm around her shoulders and she inched towards me. The top buttons of her blouse were open and I placed my hand on the skin below her neck. I could see the tips of her breasts pointing outwards. Her breasts were larger than most of the girls in my class. Cornel Wilde was riding a camel across the desert. The sand seemed hot and there was no water for miles.

She leaned towards me in the movie theater and we kissed with our mouths closed. Everyone around us was doing the same thing. It didn't take long to forget where I was. She took my hand and placed it down the front of her blouse. I didn't move. She was wearing a bra, of course. I was touching the tops of her breasts and we were pressing our lips together. It would be awhile before I learned how to kiss in any other way. Or what you were supposed to do, even now, touching her breasts, if you were supposed to go further, whether she wanted you to or not. It was up to you to take the initiative but you didn't want her to push you away. You wanted to do whatever you wanted. That's what it was about, in bed, before going to sleep. It was as far as either of you wanted to go, especially in the crowded movie theater. Maybe some other time, when you were in her house after school, and her parents were at work. Then it would be different. I had to admit that I wanted to go further. I touched her nipple for a second and felt her breath in my ear as if I had done what she wanted. I didn't know anything. The movie wasn't very good. There was no incentive to stop what we were doing. All around, people we didn't know were kissing and touching one another. I could only imagine what anyone else was doing. It's something I'll never know. Later we walked home, holding hands in the evening light. She lived in a private house on Mulliner Avenue, two blocks from where I lived. Her parents were often gone during the day but I didn't have the nerve to visit her in her house. Every week, for a long time, we met outside the theater on Saturday afternoon, and every time, in the dark theater, she let me put my hand down the front of her blouse.

We no longer went to the lake for the summer. The kids were older and wanted to do other things. I wonder what happened to the people on the beach and whether the couples stayed together. It wasn't like they exchanged partners in secret. They took off their clothing and ran into the water. Afterward, you could see them having sex on the sand. There were some people there who I didn't know. Ellen Sue's mother was lying on the beach and some men were standing over her. I didn't know how long I could continue watching or thinking about what had happened. I wanted to say, "Nothing happened," but it isn't true. Something had happened. She was lying on the beach and there were two men leaning over her. Then a third man joined them. She was on her knees. This is what I wanted to happen. This is what happened. I was lying in bed. My sister and I shared a room. I was twelve. She was fourteen. My parents slept in the living room. My sister was asleep. I was thinking of the woman on the beach, surrounded by three men. They were the parents of my friends. The woman was crying, but one of the men put his hand over her mouth. All the windows in all the houses across the lake were dark. It was the middle of night.

The scenarios were endless. I played them over in my head. The woman in the gas station, the teacher who turned her back to the class. The smell of the teacher's hair as she leaned over your desk. Her name was Miss Patrick. All the boys were in love with her. The girls too. Everyone wanted to be her special friend. Sometimes it's important to have a special friend. Someone no one knows about but you.

One evening Bettina and I walked home from the movies and she asked me if I wanted to come in. Her parents weren't home. I hesitated for a moment, not knowing what it meant. "You don't have to," she said, looking like I'd done something to hurt her feelings. Part of me was content just to kiss in the movie theater. I didn't know what else was expected of me, or what I wanted to do. She locked the door behind her and we went to her room. I felt envious of her for having her own room, for living in a big house, while I shared a room with my sister and my parents didn't even have a room of their own. But here we are. "My parents won't be home till late," she said, sitting down on the side of her bed.

It was what I imagined, lying in bed at night, what I would do if we were ever alone, and here we are. But it was different to imagine something. The reality of it all was too strange. I wasn't ready for it, in a way, though it was what I thought I wanted. Sometimes there's pleasure in thinking about things. Sometimes there's no reason to venture outside. It's all happening in your head and no one knows anything.

She unbuttoned her blouse and lay back on the bed. I thought that the next step was removing her bra. I fumbled around in the dark but couldn't do it. Instead, I pushed the straps of her bra down her arms. Then I touched the tip of her breast with my tongue. That was something I had never done before. Everything was new. Everything was happening for the first time. We were kissing and I was touching her breasts and pushing her skirt up over her knees. I thought she was going to stop me but she didn't.

Money Under
The Table

You can say I was holding out my hand to one of them. There were two of them with me in the room, one in a silk dress that resembled a short slip, the other in cutoffs and a Chinese blouse. It had been my suggestion to go to her room before I was too drunk to walk. The mother of one of them was somewhere behind the door. I could hear her rustling around outside and I knew it was just a matter of time before she would enter without knocking and turn on the light. The one with the slip was lying alongside me, playing with the buttons on my shirt, while the other was sitting on the edge of the bed. Except for my shoes, I was still fully dressed.

It was a novelty to be in an apartment on Park Avenue, the largesse of one room expanding into another. Closets as big as the rooms I lived in with my mother and sister in the Bronx. There were paintings on every wall, clusters of small ones or one large one, all of them in ornate frames, as well as vases with fresh flowers, a whole table of potted plants. In one painting, above a mantelpiece with another row of vases, a young blonde man on horseback was rescuing a woman wearing a white cape from the arms of a gray-haired man brandishing a whip. The woman was clinging to the man's waist, pressing her breasts against his back, her cape flying behind her like a wing. There was a spotted dog running alongside the horse, nipping at its heels.

In another painting, a teenage girl wearing horn-rimmed glasses and a long Victorian dress with a high collar was sitting at a dining room table surrounded by plates of rotting fruit. A rat hovered on the edge of the table, waiting for the girl to turn her head so it could take a bite out of a rotten pear. The fruit and the plates made shadows on the white tablecloth. The girl wasn't shocked by the world of the painting in which she was the only human inhabitant. She stared straight ahead, her eyes bulging behind her thick lenses, but she obviously knew the rat was there. Her gaze was filled with the acceptance of a world where a rat had as much place at the dining room table as a person. Just because she wasn't going to eat the fruit didn't mean it had to go to waste.

I imagined secret hallways, tile bathrooms with gold faucets and monogrammed towels, guest rooms, a room for the *au pair* girl or the maid, storage rooms and rooms where people had died. My soul flew out of the top of my head as soon as I passed over the threshold; I felt like lighting a cigarette and stamping it out on the Persian rug. There was a lifetime of sadness hidden in the folds of the drapery that sealed off the apartment from the life in the street. I was grateful to my friends for inviting me into their world but redundancy of possessions made me feel crazy. The rooms resembled tombs or caves, places to hide. It was possible for members of a family to live in an apartment like this for years and never see one another.

I assumed that the woman who opened the door for me was the "cook" or the "maid." She didn't look as if she had lost her sense of pride or was embarrassed by her color. Why should she? Her license to be here was her willingness to serve others. She studied me carefully, my face and clothing, to see whether I worthy of the company of her employer's daughter. The door closed on my fingers and I bit my lips to fight back the pain. For a moment I wondered if I'd come to the right place. (It was the right place, but it wasn't "me" who was there.) The maid told me to wait; when she disappeared I unbuttoned my coat. It didn't sound like a party. (When Linda called, earlier in the week, she had said, "I'm having a party Friday night—why don't you come over?") In fact, I wouldn't be surprised if Linda's mother, or a surrogate mother, suddenly appeared to inform me that her daughter was sick. It wasn't the first time I'd traveled on the subway to Manhattan only to be disappointed by a last minute change of plans. No doubt the girl, Linda, or anyone, if this was the case, was standing behind a door at the far end of the apartment, hand over mouth to muffle laughter. Getting me to travel all the way to Manhattan from the Bronx was a way of testing her power, the equivalent of tossing a dog a bone at the end of a string and then withdrawing it until it was out of reach. Only a few weeks ago, in the pouring rain, I traveled for an hour on the subway to a new high-rise on the Upper East Side overlooking Central Park only to be greeted at the door by the mother of the girl I was going to see.

"Amber's not home at the moment," the woman said, "but I know she'll be happy to hear you stopped by."

Only the night before on the phone Amber had made me promise to arrive any time after eight o'clock. Her parents were going to the theater; we could be alone for a few hours. I was amazed how little effort her mother put into lying in a convincing way. The least she could do, I thought, was offer me a cup of hot chocolate before sending me home in the rain, but as an accessory to an act of cruelty such gestures weren't permitted. She aimed her gaze at a point directly above my head and spoke without moving as if her jaw was wired in place. It was the same remote tone she used when she talked to one of her servants. What difference did it make to her whether I believed her or not?

It wasn't unusual to make love to someone over the weekend and ignore the person when you passed her in the hallway at school a few days later. I saw Linda coming and looked the other way. Once I had gone out of my way to meet her in front of her locker or on the slope of the ball field behind the school. Now I left the school early, before her last class ended, going out the back entrance and cutting across the parking lot to avoid meeting her. When I arrived home there was a note in my mailbox—"I miss you"—with her initial. Later that night my friend Harris called and asked me for details about my weekend and I told him everything, not realizing how jealous he could be, though I knew he was no longer a virgin and had numerous girlfriends of his own. I hadn't planned to mention Linda's name but he kept asking questions — "What's she like in bed?" — goading me on until I said something worth repeating. In this way, what people said about you determined your reputation, your popularity or lack of it. No one I knew went to church or believed in a religion that discouraged you from touching another person's body, though there were some who were less curious than others, who were too engrossed in their dutifulness towards schoolwork and getting into college to pay much attention, while still others — a few of us, anyway — were frightened of falling in love and getting hurt. I was in the latter category, though my curiosity was stronger than fear, and getting hurt (being rejected or spurned, I realized, once I'd experienced it a few times) was something I'd learn to survive. Someone older than I once told me that if I wanted to be a writer I had to experience everything, the whole spectrum of emotions that went along with being in love, but I never sought out pain that wasn't worth it in the end.

The two girls came out of nowhere and told me they were hungry. I only knew one of them, the one who had called me about the party. Apparently the other was her out-of-town cousin. That's how she introduced her. "We're hungry," they said, in unison, as if it were somehow in my power to provide food for them on the spot. I assumed if they were hungry they could always ask the maid or the cook to prepare something. I could hear a voice from another room in the apartment that was probably Linda's mother talking on the phone. The cousin was the one wearing the short silk dress. We were standing in the foyer, surrounded by more paintings and flowers. Linda's cousin brushed her wiry hair away from her face and showed me the stud in her ear. She had gone to MacDougal Street to get her ears pierced that afternoon. The jeweler had tried to put his hand between her legs and now she was frightened that her ear was infected. Both of them complained about how much they hated school. The one from out of town, who was taller than I was, said she had a crush on one of her teachers, her biology teacher, and that it was just a matter of time before they went to bed together. It was a common practice, in her town, for the teachers and students to sleep together. The teachers often called their students into their offices after class for "special conferences" and locked the doors. No one seemed to mind, the students least of all, though no doubt some of their parents would have complained if they knew.

We were sitting on the sofa in the living room smoking when the doorbell rang and Linda's mother appeared.

"It's her boyfriend," Linda said.

Her cousin, Devereaux, who had been yawning ever since I arrived, suddenly looked interested. "Is he cute?"

In fact, he was in his early seventies, and walked with a cane like a retired Russian count. Linda's mother led him across the threshold into the apartment, holding his arm and taking small steps to match his, but she didn't bring him into the living room to introduce him to her daughter or her friends.

"What do you think they do together?" Devereaux

asked.

She slouched against the cushions at the end of the sofa, swinging her legs in my direction. I noticed that she was wearing a gold chain around one of her ankles and when I asked her about it she said that her boyfriend had given it to her. Apparently her boyfriend was much older than she was — "He's twenty-two" — and had just been expelled from the Naval Academy at Annapolis for cheating. "He didn't want to go into the Navy anyway," she said. Now he was back in the small town where she lived, hanging out on the town commons while he pondered his future. She had actually known him when she was much younger, when she was eight and he was fifteen and he used to deliver groceries to her house from the local supermarket. She remembered that she was often alone in the house when she was eight years old, especially between the hours of three-thirty and five-thirty, and that it was then that he usually came by with the groceries. Her mother often gave the people in the supermarket a list before she went to work since she had no time to go shopping herself and he would deliver the groceries in a shopping cart and carry the bags into the kitchen. Much later, when they had become lovers, she reminded him of their first encounters but he scratched his head and claimed he didn't remember anything.

"I delivered so many groceries to so many people, why would I remember you?"

She would stand at the window waiting to see him coming down the street wheeling the cart filled with groceries. Then she would race to the door and stand there with a dollar bill in her hand (her mother had instructed her to give him the dollar after he finished the job) as he carried the bags into the kitchen. She had been tempted to offer to touch his penis (they could go down to the basement to do it) just to see what it looked like but she didn't have the nerve. Now she was thinking of dropping out of high school so they could travel around the country together. He had been offered a job in Chicago and had asked her to come along.

"You and your boyfriend can live here," Linda said. "I'm sure my mother wouldn't mind."

I was sitting on the sofa. Linda was kneeling at my feet with her arm on my knee. Devereaux was lying lengthwise across the couch with her feet on my lap. Linda and I had slept together earlier in the year but had ignored one another at school as if we were sorry it had ever happened. I had thought she was angry at me for never calling her and was surprised when she invited me to her party. I was going to ask whether anyone else was coming over but I didn't want to give the impression that I was bored with their company. On the contrary, I was flattered that I was the only guest. I lit a cigarette with a gold lighter and put my hand on Devereaux's leg. Her skin was white and smooth and she didn't push my hand away. It was then that I looked up and saw the painting of the young blonde man on horseback and the woman in the cape. The gray-haired man was standing with a whip in his hand. His arm was raised but it was a meaningless gesture. The woman, who was possibly his daughter, had already made her escape.

I always enjoyed traveling from the apartment in the Bronx where I shared a room with my older sister to the apartments of classmates who lived in Manhattan. Central Park West and Park Avenue were my favorite streets. If I had a choice, I guess I would have preferred a room with windows overlooking the park; if the apartment was high up, a view of the East River or the Hudson. I came from a world where anything that wasn't purely functional was considered a luxury, and where there was no value attached to an object that was beautiful for its own sake. I passed through the marble lobby of Linda's building as through a hall of mirrors, the potted trees and imitation Louis XIV chairs upholstered in burgundy, and smiled at the doorman when he asked "What apartment?" and called me "Sir." No doubt one of the girls had answered the intercom and assured the doorman that it was appropriate for me to come upstairs. But he eyed me suspiciously nonetheless, just in case the police questioned him later about a rape or burglary. I wanted to assure him that I wasn't going to tie anyone up or ransack anyone's apartment, but it wasn't something I could put into words.

The doorman, who was in his mid-twenties, looked at me curiously as I headed towards the elevators. I sympathized with him as best I could. How could he feel anything but envy? I knew what it felt like to go to a party and meet someone I was attracted to who was obviously with someone else. I remember, at one party, going to the bedroom where I had put my coat and where two people I knew were fucking on the bed. They had swept all the coats onto the floor and were making love with the lights on. I don't think they knew I was in the room and if they did they wouldn't care. They wouldn't stop what they were doing because I had come in looking for my coat. It was probably on the floor, under the pile of other coats. The woman might even ask me to join them. She was on top of the man, her back facing me, as I entered the room. I remember how empty my own life felt at that moment, seeing the couple on the bed while I was about to go home alone, and how much I envied them, as no doubt the doorman envied me (wasn't he sick of his life, as well?) as I walked through the lobby.

I could imagine Linda teasing him (in the same way I had seen her flirting with her teachers at school), playing with the tassels on the shoulders of his uniform or leaning forward so he could see down the front of her blouse. "Let me try on your cap," she said, snatching it from the top of his head before he had a chance to stop her. She preened in front of the mirror, tilting her head from side to side.

"I won't give it back to you," she said, holding the cap behind her, "until you kiss me."

Sometimes she flitted through the lobby without even glancing at him. Other times she arrived at the building in a taxi and he helped her carry her packages to her apartment. On other occasions she engaged him in long intimate conversations. "My period started today," she said to him as if she were reporting the evening news. She would talk, until her face was red and perspiring, about how much she hated her mother, how she wanted to kill her. As a joke, she offered him a thousand dollars to murder her mother. When he told her he had more important things to do than talk to her about her problems, she acted insulted and ignored him for days. She had lived her entire life among servants, maids, nannies, doormen, *au pair* girls and private tutors. She had bathed in their subservience. It was the privilege of people with money, or so she assumed, to treat the people who worked for them as they pleased.

It was almost midnight when I suggested we go to her room. We were drinking beer and listening to a record of Frank Sinatra singing "The House I Live In." I didn't drink much and after two or three beers I began nodding out. Linda said she had once met Frank Sinatra at a party. She was about to tell us the story when Devereaux swung her legs over the side of the couch and stood up.

"Well, let's go inside," she said, smoothing her dress over her thighs.

She had obviously heard the story of how Frank Sinatra had attended a party at Linda's mother's house (it was Linda's mother's birthday and she had given herself a party) and how Linda—who was only five years old at the time—had sat on his knees while he sang "The House I Live In." (I guess there are some things you never forget.) Devereaux hated Frank Sinatra but knew better than to voice her opinion. There was a rumor that Linda was Frank Sinatra's daughter, but no one knew for sure. I followed them from the living room down a hallway into Linda's bedroom. It was the same room where we had made love earlier in the year. All the beer and the music was making me feel drowsy (it seemed like yesterday that

I had been there) and I stretched out on Linda's king-sized bed and closed my eyes. I don't know how much time passed, probably only a minute or two, when I heard the sound of someone outside the door of the room. It was Linda's mother.

Devereaux was lying next to me on her side studying the lines in my hand. Linda was sitting at the end of the bed. I was thinking that I would reach out and pull her backwards in our direction when I heard the sound at the door, a kind of rustling. We were all in bed together, we were all fully dressed. Linda's mother opened the door of the bedroom and turned on the light. She gasped when she saw us and crossed her arms over her breasts. She had short silver hair, a wide face with a long pointy nose, and a blunt disapproving expression, like the warden in a woman's prison. We were the inmates and she had come to check on what we were doing.

"Can't we have *any* privacy?" Linda said.

She spoke in an accent that reminded me of a movie actress playing the role of a spoiled southern belle, the daughter of a plantation owner, but I couldn't remember the name of the actress or the movie. Her mother made a noise in the back of her throat that sounded like a key turning in the lock of a prison cell or the rotted latch of an old trunk. It was the sound of moral superiority and hypocrisy, of growing old in the absence of desire and pleasure. She stood there for about thirty seconds like a dog lost in the rain, breathing heavily. Finally, she closed the door behind her but didn't turn out the overhead light.

The two girls couldn't contain themselves. They

laughed loud enough so that Linda's mother, retreating down the hallway, could hear. "What would Frank think?" Linda asked. It was a private joke. She rolled around on the floor, pounding her fists into the carpet. Then she crossed the room to the mirror above her vanity and unfastened her blouse

I had never been in bed with two women before. I had the feeling that they were both more experienced than I was (I'd been a non-virgin for two years and I could still name all the people I had slept with). They helped me undress, each of them tugging at the legs of my pants. Then Devereaux pulled me on top of her and we made love while Linda watched. She was thin and bony, flat-chested, with hips like a boy. Occasionally I reached out and touched Linda's breasts or put my hand between her legs so she didn't feel left out. The overhead light was still on and I could see every pore in the skin of the neck of the girl moving beneath me.

"You can come inside me if you want," Devereaux said. "I don't care."

And later: "I want your baby. I want to have a baby. Make me pregnant."

The first time Linda and I had sex it had lasted only a few minutes. We were both half-drunk and didn't even bother taking off our clothes. I knew that being "good in bed" was defined (at least from the man's point of view) by staying power and frequency. The best lovers were those who could do it four or five times in a single night. I wondered if I had the reputation, as a consequence of coming quickly when I was with Linda and then leaving immediately afterwards, of being an indifferent lover, someone who cared only for his own pleasure. I wondered whether Linda had told her friends about me. Truthfully, I had no real idea about how to give another person pleasure. I assumed that when a woman cried out it meant she was having an orgasm. I didn't know how to differentiate cries of pleasure that led up to having an orgasm from the cries that accompanied the orgasm itself. I never made any noise when I made love, not even when I came. I think I was too conscious of what I was doing (at being "good") to really enjoy it.

"Harder," Devereaux kept saying, and Linda, leaning over me like an animal trainer, repeated what she said just in case I didn't hear.

"Don't come yet," Linda instructed me. "I'm too sore to make love."

"You're sore from fucking the doorman," Devereaux said. "I heard you."

She turned her head to one side, not looking at me, and stared at her cousin defiantly.

"Shut up," Linda said. She toppled backwards as if struck by a blow.

I continued to push against her but I was just going through the motions. I felt like slapping Devereaux across the face just to see what she would say. I pretended that I was making love to Colleen McGrath, my English teacher, to keep myself interested: she was leaning over her desk in the deserted classroom and I was lifting her dress from behind. I decided that I didn't care about my reputation as a lover. Linda could tell her friends anything she wanted. I began moving rapidly. Devereaux wrapped her legs around my back and lifted her ass off the sheet.

"Have you ever made a baby before?" she hissed in my ear. "This is your first one, I bet. Do you want a boy or a girl?"

I was lying on top of her, still inside, my face buried in her neck. For a moment I didn't remember her name.

"I feel like a dog," Linda said. "A sheepdog."

Someone was hammering against the bedroom door.

"Who is it?" Devereaux and Linda shouted in unison.

"Telephone for Devereaux. Long distance." It was a woman's voice, not Linda's mother, but the maid who had let me in.

"Get off me," Devereaux said, but I didn't move. "Linda, tell him to get off."

I was tempted to hold her down until she begged me to let her get up, until she started crying, until she began whining like a dog in a cage. She punched my arm and bit my shoulder but I grabbed her by the hair and pulled her away.

"I think she wants you to get up," Linda said.

As soon as Devereaux left the room, Linda rolled towards me. She put a pack of Old Golds, a silver lighter, and a glass ashtray on the sheet between us. She looked genuinely happy to have me all for herself. The first thing she did was apologize for what happened last year, for not calling me back after we slept together. I told her I was sorry as well for never responding to her note. She looked at me as if I was crazy (what note?) and I wondered if I was confusing her with someone else. I could visualize the note, the words "I Miss You" followed by the initial "L." I assumed that Linda had written it but I could have been wrong.

It was raining out and I told her that maybe I should begin thinking about going home and she suggested I spend the night. Her mother wouldn't like it but I could always sneak out before dawn. I asked her if she was really having an affair with the doorman.

"You'll tell everyone at school," she said.

"I won't," I promised, trying to reassure her, but I knew she had the right to feel concerned.

"You'll talk to Harris—he's your best friend, isn't he?— and he'll tell everyone."

She paused to crush her cigarette in the ashtray and light another.

"I'm so sick of all the kids at school. Some of them are such babies, especially the guys. I wanted to see what it was like with someone older. Lenny is twenty-six. He just comes up here, stays an hour. Sometimes we don't even take off our clothes." She blushed. "I love his uniform. I have to admit that's part of it. He even carries a gun in a holster strapped to his shoulder. Sometimes we stand at the window and point it at the people on the street. My mother's been traveling recently and I'm alone here most of the time except for Juanita the maid and she won't tell anyone. Not about Lenny. She likes Lenny and knows that he'll lose his job if my mother finds out he's been here."

She propped a pillow under her head and stretched out on her back, blowing smoke rings at the ceiling.

"Devereaux's really beautiful, isn't she? Every guy I

introduce her to falls in love with her. I was so jealous of her when we were growing up."

Her hair was mostly brown with red highlights and fell in long waves over her forehead and shoulders. It was Linda's hair that had attracted me when I first saw her in the hallway at school. My friend Harris had pointed her out to me. When we were freshmen she sat in front of me in French so I had a whole year to study her hair. Even then, she was absent at least once a week and failed most of the tests. She always smiled at me when she stood up after class but I was too shy to talk to her.

"I'm going to nap for a few minutes. You have to promise that you're not going to leave."

Then a minute later: "I was in love with you last year. Did you know that? At least I thought I was. I had a crush on you even when I used to sit in front of you in French. I used to wear special clothing but you never even looked at me. I followed you around school. The only reason I took that class was because you were in it."

She was asleep now. It felt odd to be lying next to a naked woman and feel no particular excitement or pleasure. Only two years ago I spent half my waking hours studying the pictures of naked women in magazines like *Playboy* and *Adam* and reading the sexy passages of novels like *The Amboy Dukes, A Stone for Danny Fisher, Battle Cry* and *The Hoods* until I knew them by heart. I reached out and put my hand on her thigh and she murmured contentedly but didn't wake up. There was a rumor around school that she had an eating problem, that she went on binges where she ate nothing but chocolate for days and that's why her skin was so bad. Her face was white and puffy and was covered with tiny black dots. She was wearing too much make up: purple eye shadow and pink lipstick. I was beginning to feel like I didn't know Linda at all. I never realized how much she liked me when we were in French together and regretted that I missed my chance to go to bed with her then. Even when we finally did sleep together last year she had been more serious about me than I ever imagined. We had met at a party and she had asked me back to her apartment for a beer and we had ended up in bed. That was it. I guess I hurt her feelings by never calling back and by avoiding her at school. It was impossible, I realized, to know precisely what anyone was feeling at a particular moment. I didn't have enough experience to trust my instincts. It was rare for someone like Linda, who had no trouble finding boyfriends, to confess that she once had a crush on me, and I wished I could reciprocate by telling her that I had loved her too. But all I remember feeling when we had sex together was indifference. As soon as it ended I wanted to pull up my pants and leave.

I thought I heard voices in some other part of the apartment but I couldn't tell if it was Devereaux or Linda's mother and her boyfriend. I rolled over to the edge of the bed and walked naked to the window. Looking straight down, through the rain, I could see the doorman run out into the middle of Park Avenue to flag down a taxi. He didn't have a raincoat or an umbrella, only the cap that came with the uniform. I wondered if he and Linda had sex in the bed where she was sleeping now or whether they went down to the basement where there was a mattress behind the boiler. It was my turn to feel envy. As doorman of a large building he had his pick of women to sleep with. He knew everyone's schedule, when a husband might be out of town, when it was convenient to suddenly appear at the door of someone's apartment. He had access to the intercoms of all the apartments in the building and could call up at any time to see if Linda was at home. If she was interested in seeing him. "My mother's gone for the day, why don't you stop by?" Or: "I'm expecting a package. Why don't you bring it up?" No one minded if he was gone from his post for fifteen or twenty minutes, or even longer. He was always doing errands for the older people in the building. He had been working as the doorman of this particular building for five years. Before that, he had worked as an elevator operator in an office building on Wall Street. Everyone called him by his first name. "How's it going today, Lenny?" they said. At Christmas the tenants of the building pressed twenty dollar bills into his palm. He kept photographs in his wallet of his wife and daughters, to show off if anyone asked, as well as a picture of his ninety-year old grandmother who lived in Lithuania. It was common knowledge among the tenants in Linda's building that he was trying to save money so he could buy a house in New Jersey, in a town like Hackensack or East Orange. He told everyone in the building about the problem his grandmother was having getting a visa. He told them about the house in New Jersey. He showed them pictures. There was a rumor that his wife was pregnant again. Even Linda gave him a ten or a twenty dollar bill when he visited. She showed him the drawer where her mother kept her money. There was a gold bracelet on top of the bureau in Linda's mother's dressing room and he slipped it into his pocket before he left the apartment. Once he stole a twenty from Linda's wallet when she was asleep.

It was two in the morning. I had told my mother that I was planning to stay out later than usual. It was my habit to call her before midnight so she wouldn't worry that I had been mugged. I knew she was lying in bed at that moment waiting for me to call. The last thing I wanted to do was put on my clothes and go looking for the telephone. I didn't want to get into the subway, which ran irregularly if at all this late at night, and return to my apartment in the Bronx. ("A ten minute walk from the Bronx Zoo," I said, when people asked me where I lived.) The last time I went home on the subway this late a tall black man in a tan trench coat asked me if I wanted to "mess around." I wasn't sure what he meant and I didn't ask. I had enough money to take a taxi but the idea of waking up in the bedroom in the Bronx with my sister sleeping in the bed across the room didn't appeal to me as much as waking up between Linda and Devereaux.

In a corner of the room there was a floor to ceiling bookcase containing magazines, stuffed animals, a radio and a portable record player. There was an entire shelf devoted to records. The first record I noticed was a boxed set of *Tristan und Isolde*. I remembered that after we made love a year ago Linda had asked me what kind of music I liked and I said "opera," though I only liked one opera, and when she asked me my favorite I said *Tristan und Isolde*. I wondered if she had bought the opera on my recommendation, in an attempt to impress me so that when we saw each other again we'd have something to talk about. I thumbed through the other records on her shelf but *Tristan und Isolde* was the only opera. Her taste in music, as far as I could tell from her record collection, tended towards show music like *Oklahoma, The King & I* and *West Side Story*, and albums by popular singers like Frank Sinatra, Eddie Fisher and Nat King Cole.

I remember telling my friend Harris that I had spent the night with Linda.

"She'll sleep with anyone," he had said, emphatically, as if I'd cheapened myself by going to bed with her.

I was tempted to ask whether he had ever slept with her or if he had wanted to sleep with her and she had rejected him but by then he was telling me about his new girlfriend Margot. I held the receiver away from my ear and thought guiltily of how I had purposely avoided Linda at school. We had met at her locker in the basement every day leading up to the night we spent together. We had talked on the phone in the evening. She had asked me questions about her English homework—we were both reading *Sons and Lovers*—and I had tried to help her, but she had little confidence in her ability to learn anything. She had failed half her subjects the year before and was on probation. That day, in the mail, I had received a note with the words "I miss you" followed by her initial. After making love (in this room, in this bed) she had started crying. It wasn't the first time I had been with a girl who had burst into tears immediately after having sex. I asked Linda what was wrong and she said that she liked me a lot, more than she ever liked anyone, but she knew I didn't care for her at all. "I hate myself," she said. I put my arm around her shoulders to comfort her. "I like you a lot too," I told her, willing to say anything if she would only stop crying. "I really do."

As soon as she quieted down, I went to the bathroom and threw up. I washed my face in the sink with its gold faucets and inspected the medicine cabinet. The only prescription medicine was a jar of skin cream with Linda's name on it. Before leaving the apartment, I returned to her bedroom. She was lying on her stomach, as I'd left her, with her skirt hiked above her waist. I found a blanket which had fallen to the floor and covered her naked legs. She spread her legs slightly and lifted her head from the pillow and moaned.

"I'm going now, Linda," I said, but she didn't respond.

My mother had a subscription to the Metropolitan Opera for her and my father but my father was sick so my mother asked if I wanted to go. I was twelve years old.

"It's in German," my mother said. "Sprechen Sie Deutsch?"

On the train downtown she told me what she knew about the story.

"It takes place on a ship," she said. "At least that's where it begins. Later they go to a castle. Tristan is bringing Isolde to marry his Uncle Marke. It's a complicated story.

Apparently Tristan murdered Isolde's former boyfriend. Isolde was planning to revenge her boyfriend's death by killing Tristan but they fell in love instead. Tristan was sick and she nursed him back to life. They just looked at each other and fell in love. I guess neither of them had ever seen anyone as beautiful as the other. Anyway, Tristan feels guilty about murdering her boyfriend. He won't admit to himself that he's in love with her so he offers her to his Uncle Marke. Isolde isn't happy with this arrangement. She loses her boyfriend, she falls in love with her boyfriend's murderer. Now she's being forced into a marriage with a person she never met. The last thing she wants to do is get married to Tristan's uncle. She complains to her maid Brangaene that she wants to kill herself. Brangaene has two magic potions, a death potion and a love potion. Just before the ship arrives at King Marke's castle, Tristan goes to Isolde's cabin. She's been insisting all the time that he come to see her but he's been trying to avoid her the whole trip. So he's there and the first thing he does is give her his sword. He hands it to her and orders her to kill him to revenge the murder of her boyfriend Morold. Instead she points to the cup with the magic potion and tells him to drink. She assumes it's the death potion. He drinks without hesitating and then she grabs the cup and drinks the rest. All this is taking place as King Marke and his entourage are gathering on the shore to meet the ship. All the sailors on the boat are going crazy. Both Tristan and Isolde assume they're about to die. In the last minutes before they're going to die they feel free to admit their love for one another. But they're not going to die. Brangaene poured the love potion into, the cup instead. They can't believe that they're still alive.

I thought she had finished, but that was only the end of Act One. It took almost an hour to get from our neighborhood in the Bronx to the area south of 34th Street where the Met was located. I rarely went anywhere alone with either of my parents. I had reached the stage where I defined independence as doing things on my own or with my friends. I hoped that I didn't meet anyone I knew on the train or at the opera. My mother told me that I couldn't go unless I wore a jacket and a tie and I was tempted to tell her she could rip the ticket into tiny pieces for all I cared. She buttoned my shirt until it pinched the skin on my neck. She flattened the tie under the collar and held the wide and narrow ends in front of her. We were the same height now but I could remember when I came up to her waist and then her breasts. The tie had a pattern of playing cards against a gold field. It took her three tries before she tied it in a way that satisfied her.

"Maybe if you wore ties more often," she said, "you'd learn how to do this yourself."

The seats were in the second balcony, a few rows back, near the center. My mother kept exclaiming how perfect the seats were, and how expensive. She told me that when she was younger she and her friends would sit in the last row of the top balcony where it was impossible to see anything but where you could still hear perfectly. My mother kept looking around to see what other people were wearing. We were a few minutes early and I sat back on my red cushioned seat and studied the program.

"A lot of people hate Wagner," my mother said. "He was Hitler's favorite composer."

The two seats to my right were empty. They were still empty as the lights began to dim and the conductor took his place on the podium, turned and bowed to the audience. There was a small lamp on the podium so he could follow the score. The orchestra had been warming up for some time, but after the applause for the conductor died down there was total silence. Behind me I heard the sound of human voices: apparently the usher was arguing with some latecomers. "It's started," he was saying. "You can't go in." There was a commotion in the aisle. Then a man and a woman made their way down the steps to the row where I was sitting. A man behind me remarked how inconsiderate some people were. The lights were fading but I caught a glimpse of the woman. She was wearing a conservative gray and black striped dress, black stockings and high heels. The man who was with her was much older and had a white goatee. Both of them were carrying their coats over their arms. As the woman sat down she brushed my hand with her elbow, we were both vying for the arm rest between our seats, and pressed her face close to mine, close enough so I could smell her lilac perfume, and whispered: "I'm sorry." She settled back in her seat, with her coat on her lap, just as the overture began.

I tried to concentrate on what was happening on the stage but I couldn't resist glancing at the woman about once a minute. (On the train ride downtown, my mother told me that my father often fell asleep before the first act was over.) The stage was still very dark. There was the vague outline of a ship painted on the far wall. Sailors were lying around near the mast in the center of the deck. It was an old-fashioned wooden ship with a wide curve in the middle. The sailors were apparently just waking up or had been awake most of the night. There was a man standing alone, looking out to sea. I assumed that was Tristan. Another man with long curly hair was lying at his feet like a huge dog. There was another area of the stage that resembled a tent at the far end of the ship with a ladder leading from the tent to the deck below. This was Isolde's tent, or so it seemed. She was lying on a couch, her face buried in the cushions. Her maid was looking wistfully over the side of the ship. The wall of the stage was painted two shades of blue to distinguish the sky from the water. It was either dawn or late evening. The woman next to me stared directly in front of her, but once when I glanced over she tilted her head towards me and smiled. She was sitting closer to me than she was to the man with the goatee who might have been her father or uncle or an older brother. I shifted towards her in my seat (it was just a matter of inches, of fractions of inches), so that eventually I was sitting closer to her than I was to my mother.

I realized that it wasn't necessary to know the story. What was important was to get caught up in the immensity of it all. The characters in the opera were speaking to each other, but instead of talking they were singing. There was often nothing particularly dramatic about what they were saying. The singing made it seem more dramatic than it was, only because the voices sounded so beautiful set to music. I began to listen more closely, despite myself, in an attempt to understand what made opera so interesting to so many people Also, I wanted to impress the woman sitting next to me with my devotion to the music. I even forgot about her for a few minutes; then I felt the toe of her shoe brushing my leg. I looked over and she was staring at the stage through a pair of opera glasses. Without saying a word, she offered them to me, as if she assumed (because of my proximity) I had as much right to use them as she. I think she was in her early twenties but she might have been a few years younger. Isolde and Brangaene were on stage. Isolde was wearing a long white dress which trailed behind her when she moved. Her hair was loose but not very long. She wore a complicated series of necklaces, gold and amber and lapis, which dangled almost to her waist. Her dress was very tight, especially around the breasts, and I wondered how she could breathe. She looked older than Tristan. More like his mother than a potential lover. She had a wild concentrated look in her eyes as if her mind was a tunnel with no light at the end and she gestured with both her hands as if she were gathering the words from the sky and then offering them back to the air itself in return for nothing. "They're talking about the potion," the woman next to me said. She put her hand on my arm. I felt like the drama had moved from the stage up into the balcony and that it was just a matter of time before everyone in the audience had their binoculars trained on us. Didn't she know that I was only twelve years old? Some people told me I looked older—fourteen or fifteen—but to my mind, when I stared at myself in the mirror, I looked like a child.

The man sitting on the other side of the woman was breathing heavily, occasionally taking a handkerchief from his jacket pocket and spitting into it, careful not to make any noise that might disturb the people behind us. "Here," I whispered, returning the opera glasses. The man behind me cleared his throat: we were disturbing his concentration. Once, on the bus ride home from school, I reached out and put my hand on the leg of a girl who was standing in the aisle near my seat, but she didn't tell me to take my hand away or cry out that she was being molested. I had seen her every day on the trip home and I had been trying to get the nerve to touch her. I tried to catch a glimpse of her face when I put my hand on her leg but her head was turned away. The bus was crowded. I was sitting down, she was standing next to me in the aisle. It occurred to me that I should offer her my seat but instead I reached out and put my hand on her leg. First I just grazed the skin with my fingers. She was wearing a gray skirt, knee-length, and carried her school books against her chest. Once my mother told me that a girl in the neighborhood, someone I knew, had been raped on the way home from school. My idea of rape had nothing to do with sex. It simply meant that someone had taken away her clothing and she was forced to walk home alone. I had an image of a naked girl wandering the winter streets. As Tristan and Isolde were vowing their undying love for one another (they had just sipped from the cup with the magic potion), I was sitting in the dark wondering if I should put my hand on the woman's leg.

At the end of Act One everyone stood up and applauded. The singers came out from behind the curtains and took their bows. The man with the goatee whispered something to the woman. With the lights on she looked older, maybe in her mid or late thirties. The man patted the breast pocket of his jacket to indicate that he wanted to smoke. It was a gesture my father made every night after dinner. My mother didn't like him to smoke in the kitchen so after dinner he left the table and sat in the living room with a cigarette and a cup of coffee and the newspaper. But first he patted his shirt pocket where he kept his cigarettes as the man with the goatee had done. The woman nodded her head in response to what he had whispered. They started towards the aisle, leaving their coats on their seats. My mother, whom I'd almost forgotten about, asked me if I wanted to get up and stretch.

I assume she was proud of me because I hadn't fallen asleep. The opera had started at seven and it was already eight-thirty and there were two more acts to go; it wasn't even half over. All about us people were talking, humming the music, comparing notes on previous performances which they had seen in Vienna or Milan. We were standing in the lobby and most of the people were smoking. Some of them talked in heavy accents. Some of them were talking about subjects that had nothing to do with the opera. I saw the woman talking with the man with the goatee. She was leaning against him as if she was having difficulty keeping her balance. She was drinking something out of a long-stemmed wineglass and holding the man's arm as he puffed cigarette smoke towards the ceiling. The heels of her shoes were pointed and very thin and maybe that was why she had trouble standing on her own. My mother always complained that she had difficulty walking when she wore new shoes. She said she hated to wear high heels but that they made her legs look more shapely. The woman who was sitting next to me was as tall as the man with the goatee. Her black hair fell like a dark cloud around her shoulders and along the sides of her face. We were standing a few yards away but I couldn't hear what they were saying. There were other women in black dresses with bare shoulders who were clinging to the arms of men in black pinstriped suits. My mother asked what I thought of the opera and I said that I wished it was in English so I could understand all the words but that otherwise I liked it quite a bit, especially the voices of the singers, especially Tristan. "He looks like a movie star," my mother said, "doesn't he?" There was the sound of a bell ringing in the distance and my mother said that was a signal to return to our seats. The people began putting out their cigarettes in the standing ashtrays but the man with the goatee and his tall girlfriend didn't move.

We made contact again during the second and third acts but not as often as before. There was almost no action in Act II except at the end. Most of the time Tristan and Isolde were standing on the stage singing to one another. I put my elbow on the arm rest and she leaned her arm next to mine. She turned her body in my direction and crossed her legs. I felt the toe of her shoe rubbing against my leg.

It occurred to me that possibly such contact was normal. We were sitting so close together it was impossible not to touch one another, if only accidentally. I had the feeling, as Act II stretched on into a kind of infinity of unrequited longing and despair, that if I put my hand under her dress she wouldn't mind. (My friend Harris had a theory that if you didn't act aggressively when you were with a woman, she assumed that you didn't like her.) At one point she tilted her head towards me and I thought she was going to rest her head on my shoulder. I was beginning to feel drowsy and I had to fight from dozing off. Occasionally the audience burst into spontaneous applause and I stared at the stage to see what I had missed but nothing was happening. All my attention was centered on the woman sitting beside me. I had the feeling that she would lose interest in me if I fell asleep. I had the fantasy of meeting her again, when I was older, how we would talk about the night we first met at the opera. "I kept wanting you to touch me," she said. "I thought I was going crazy." Her long dress, her black stockings, her high heel shoes ("stiletto" heels, as they were called), her black opal earrings, the sweep of her black hair as she shifted towards me in the dark. My mind began to wander. Someone on the stage was shouting and the voices of the singers had become louder and shriller, almost hysterical. It was a Friday night, at least I could sleep late the next morning. I had planned to go to the local movie theater, the RKO Pelham on White Plains Road, with my friend Harris. We often went on Saturday afternoon when the theater was crowded with people from the neighborhood, mostly kids our age or older. In every row there was a couple necking, oblivious to the movie or the people around them. Once I saw my sister, who was three years older than I, sitting in the back row of the balcony with a young black man. They were necking and the man had his hand down the front of my sister's blouse. Later, I saw my sister outside the theater. She was holding hands with the black man and told me if I ever told my parents what I had seen she would decapitate me, that was the word she used. I knew that it was just a matter of time before Harris and I went to the movies with the intention of picking up girls. (I envied the aggressiveness of the young man in front of me, only a few years older than I, who without thinking twice rested his hand on the front of the blouse of the girl sitting beside him.) Now Harris and I divided our time staring at the heads of the couples necking and the Biblical epic on the screen. Harris, even more than I, was preoccupied with the girls in our class at school. He had magazines with photographs of naked women hidden beneath the copies of *Sports Illustrated* under his bed. The theater smelled of hair tonic, eau de cologne, disinfectant. A halo of cigarette smoke (smoking was permitted in the balcony) blossomed in the air above the orchestra, slowly descending in an ever-expanding cloud above the embracing couples. Ushers patrolling the aisles directed their flashlights in the faces of anyone who was smoking or (sadistically) in the faces of the couples who were making out. There was a candy store next to the theater that had been closed by the police for selling pornographic comic books. That's where Harris and I were going to meet at 2 P.M. I tried to imagine telling him about the woman at the opera but I knew he would never believe me.

My mother opened her pocketbook and took out a wad of tissues and pressed them to the side of her face. It was the third act and everyone was dying. Tristan was lying on a small sofa in the center of the stage. His servant, Kurvenal, had just killed Melot, Tristan's false friend. The woman next to me leaned towards the stage, holding her face in her hands, as if it were too painful to look. It was obvious, even to me, that Tristan was dying, that they were all going to die. But Isolde was still singing and the music was rolling over the sound of her voice like an immense wave and I knew that we had been sitting in the darkness for hours waiting for this moment. It was only at the very end that the words and music suddenly came together. It was almost as if Wanger had been teasing us up to this point, holding back, developing a theme and then cutting it short. Now the melody seemed to last forever, withdrawing into itself until it reached the boundaries of infinity. All the waves in the ocean were pouring over Isolde's outstretched arms. She was melting into the meaning of the words, clinging to each syllable. She was giving new meaning to the words with the sound of her voice. "Soon I'll be with you," she was singing, addressing Tristan's soul. They had planned to die together at the end of Act I but had sipped from the love potion instead. The music was like a ladder to heaven which they were climbing, step by step. Then the woman sitting beside me and my mother and the man with the goatee were on their feet. Everyone was applauding, tossing hats and flowers onto the stage. People were shouting and stamping their feet like young children. The woman next to me was crying too, wiping her eyes with a handkerchief which she had borrowed from her friend. The man with the goatee was standing on his seat shouting "Bravo!" The singers who played the roles of Tristan and Isolde were taking their final bows in the center of the stage. The singer who played Tristan gathered some of the flowers that had been thrown from the balcony and presented them to the singer who played Isolde. The woman next to me tilted her head in my direction, biting her lips as if she wanted to say something. I leaned towards her, the sleeve of my jacket touching her arm. It was pointless to say "Goodbye" when we had never really met. I felt like saying "I want to see you again" but I didn't have the nerve. I felt like embracing her, in the spirit of the moment, as Tristan and Isolde had embraced at the end of Act One. I had an image of her floating in the air above the orchestra. Self-contained, like an angel with blue hair. In another image, I saw her sitting on the side of an unmade bed in a hotel room. "It's unusual to find someone your age," she was saying, "who loves opera as much as you do." Her dress was pulled up to her waist and she was peeling her black stockings from her long legs.

I wondered if my mother was crying because of the opera or because she was thinking of my father, all the nights they had taken the subway downtown together to see a play on Broadway or a concert at Carnegie Hall. Maybe she realized that they would never go to these places again. They had met twenty years before at a singles weekend in a hotel in the Poconos. At the time, they were both in their mid-thirties, and each of them had been married once before. My father was working as a letter carrier for the post office. Later, at my mother's insistence, he went back to school, and when he graduated with a degree in engineering he found a job as a city housing inspector. His job was to meet with landlords and housing contractors and check that they were maintaining proper standards in the buildings which they owned or were renovating. Often, contractors and landlords used the cheapest materials for their buildings. After a few years the pipes eroded and the wooden floors rotted away and tenants ended up suffering because the landlords tried to raise the rent so they could pay the cost of maintaining a building that was barely liveable.

He would inspect buildings with people living in them where previous violations had been cited. Sometimes, when the violations were serious and the landlords and contractors didn't want to spend the money, they offered my father a bribe if he promised not to report them. They would hand him an envelope containing a hundred dollar bill, sometimes more than one. Maybe it was as simple as repairing a staircase or plastering a leaky ceiling. The landlords tried to get away with doing as little as possible. There were enough contractors who committed violations who didn't offer bribes to avoid suspicion when he accepted the bribes of the contractors who did. You could never be too careful. Some of the contractors gave him money every month. They would leave the money in a locker in Grand Central Station for which my father had the key. Every month he went to the locker and took out a white envelope filled with cash.

He spent his days driving around in a city-owned car, a Buick. Once I went with him on his rounds and he introduced me to some of the landlords and contractors. They had sagging jaws and stomachs, just like my father, and their skin was mottled from too much drinking. They called me "Albie's boy" and said I looked just like my old man, though I knew this wasn't true and that they were just saying it to please my father. I saw the white envelope pass from the pocket of one of the landlords to the breast pocket of my father's jacket. I saw the walls of corroded tenements, I climbed the urine-soaked staircases. While my father conferred with a man in a yellow hat, I stood in the rain and watched a tractor excavate some old stones. "It's not a bad job," he said, as we drove back to the Bronx. I sensed that he wanted some kind of confirmation that what he was doing was worthwhile, that I understood why he took the money, that it wasn't a crime, but I didn't give it. Every minute or so he patted the breast pocket of his jacket. *That* was his confirmation. I was just along for the ride.

My father kept all the money in our apartment. If he put any of it in the bank he would have to report it to the government and he didn't want anyone to ask him questions about where it came from. His bank account was regularly audited by the city to discourage him from taking bribes. The only people who knew he had this money were the members of our immediate family. The only way I knew about it was because I overheard my mother and father talking. Apparently, all her sisters and brothers wanted to borrow the money from him for one business venture or another and he refused to lend them a penny. Once, in the back of my father's closet, when Harris and I were playing, I found a shoe box containing a stack of hundred dollar bills. I made Harris promise never to tell anyone about the money but I always worried that he would tell his parents and his parents would inform the police and that my father would lose his job and end up in jail.

We lived in a three and a half room apartment in the Bronx, a ten minute walk from the zoo. My sister and I shared a room. My father and mother slept in a bed in the living room. With all the money my father hid away, we could have moved at any time. But he was frightened that the housing commission would question where the money came from if he ever bought a house in the country or a new car. He had friends who had been investigated for withdrawing too much money at one time from their bank accounts. Any sudden transaction aroused the suspicions of the investigators. If he bought anything that cost a lot of money, they would question him immediately. How could he afford a house in the country on his salary?

I asked my sister how much money she thought we had and she said that we probably had a hundred thousand at least. She was mad at my parents for never buying anything. What she wanted most of all was an apartment with a room of her own. She was sick of sharing a room with her brother. Who could blame her? When she was younger I used to watch her get dressed when she thought I was asleep. Now she put on a bathrobe, collected her clothing, and dressed in the bathroom. She wanted to live in an apartment where she could invite her friends over without feeling embarrassed. She had lost her virginity a few months before, or so I learned from reading her diary. She thought it was wrong for my father to take bribes. What difference did it make since we lived like paupers anyway?

My mother asked me what I wanted for Christmas. I surprised her by requesting a recording of *Tristan und Isolde*. She didn't realize that the opera had made such a big impression on me. She had canceled her subscription to the Met because my father wasn't well enough to accompany her and she assumed that my sister and I weren't interested. My feelings about the opera were inseparable from my thoughts about the woman who had been sitting beside me. I masturbated daily, imagining her in different settings and in different poses. We were in a hotel room and she was lifting her dress over her head or we were in the last row of the balcony at the local movie theater and I put my hand down the front of her blouse. Listening to the opera was a way of reviving her image, of reliving the moment. I wanted my life to be like the explosion at the end of the opera when Tristan died and Isolde extended her arms toward heaven as the world crashed around her. The music accompanying her final song was what I imagined heaven was like, a continuous orgasm, building up and then exploding but never really subsiding. My sister was particularly impressed with me for requesting a record of an opera for Christmas and told all her friends that her brother was interested in classical music. She had one friend who played the piano and studied voice. When my sister told Jennifer that I liked *Tristan und Isolde* she clapped her hands (or so my sister informed me) and said that it was her favorite opera too.

My father's stomach problems grew worse. The word "cancer" was never mentioned but what else could it be? I guess they thought I was too young to deal with the truth. Twice a week he went to the hospital for treatment. Often, when I said "Good night" or "Good morning" to him he stared at me from the bed in the living room as if I were a total stranger. The only person he enjoyed talking to was my sister Liddy. She sat on the side of his bed and read the newspaper aloud to him and told him about the courses she was taking in school and what her favorite teachers were like. Sometimes she sang him one of his favorite songs, "I'm Walking Behind You," which Eddie Fisher had popularized a few years before, or "Hey There," in a voice that sounded like a scratchy record. She had perfected the technique of talking without demanding a response. She took it for granted that what she talked about was interesting to him, that it was more important to say anything than sit in morbid silence staring into space. When he didn't feel like talking he would communicate to her by writing notes. The fact that he preferred my sister's company over ours was obvious to my mother and I but neither of us minded. It was one less burden off my shoulders was the way I saw it. The only thing I could think of talking about with my father was sports. He liked to watch the Friday night boxing matches and I would join him in the living room, prop his pillows behind his back and adjust the antenna so the picture was clear. But I don't think he cared whether I was in the room with him or not.

He was on extended leave of absence from his job. It occurred to me that if he quit his job he would be able to spend all his money and no one would question where it came from. Sometimes all he could eat for days was chicken broth which he drank through a straw. There was always a pot of broth warming on the stove. He had lost thirty pounds in the last year and I had to admit that he looked more handsome now that he was thinner. He had weighed over two hundred and twenty pounds before he became sick. I guess he assumed that the one thing he could spend his secret money on was food. He liked Chinese and Italian food, especially, but he hated going to restaurants. He would call up the restaurants in the neighborhood and they would deliver the food. The exception was a dairy restaurant on 2nd Avenue in Manhattan called Ratner's where he liked to go on Sundays. When he was well, we would all take the subway downtown to Orchard Street on Sunday afternoons to go shopping and afterwards we would eat at Ratner's. There were two Ratner's, one on 2nd Avenue and one on Delancey Street. My father preferred the restaurant on 2nd Avenue. He knew the waiters there and always over-tipped. On the subway uptown my mother scolded him for giving the waiters so much money. "The last of the big time spenders," she would say, though it was anything but true. I remember there were big baskets of bread and rolls on the table and my father ate practically half of them before the actual meal arrived. He would order mushroom barley soup and potato pancakes or cheese blintzes with sour cream. For dessert he had a bowl of fruit, nuts and raisins.

One afternoon I met my sister and her friends on the street and she introduced me to Jennifer, the girl who loved opera. She was a tall, awkward-looking girl with high cheekbones and a mass of unruly knotted reddish-brown hair which looked like it hadn't been washed in weeks. Not the type of girl I was attracted to, or who normally entered my fantasy life. She was wearing an oversized car coat with a hood so there was no way of knowing what her body was like. As far as Harris and I were concerned, and even though we knew that a girl's "personality" was important, the size of a girl's breasts was all that really mattered. Unlike my sister and her other friends, Jennifer wore neither make up or jewelry, none that was visible anyway.

"I've heard a lot about you," she said, and I averted my eyes, trying not to blush, while my sister and her friends laughed.

"They're a perfect match," one of them said.

A few days later, a Saturday when my parents were at the hospital and Liddy was at the movies with one of her boyfriends and I was lying on my bed reading *79 Park Avenue* by Harold Robbins which I had found in the back of my sister's bookcase, the phone rang and a woman's voice asked to speak to my sister.

"It's Jennifer," she said. "Remember me? We met on the street."

When I told her that Liddy wasn't home she paused for a moment as if she was saying a prayer for the dead and then asked if she could stop by anyway. She wanted to hear my recording of *Tristan und Isolde,* if I had the time to play it for her.

"I was really calling to see you," she said. "Are you alone?"

She was over in fifteen minutes. I helped her off with her coat and hung it in the closet while she sat on a chair in the small foyer and unfastened the snaps on her boots. It was snowing out but she wasn't wearing a hat and the tips of her hair glistened with melting crystals. She was wearing a black turtleneck and a red and black striped skirt with a big safety pin holding it together, black tights, and a necklace of small bones. I guess I was supposed to ask her where she bought the necklace but I didn't want to be obvious, to be like everyone else. If my interest in opera set me apart from others then I had to act different in every way, or pretend to. All I wanted to do, from the moment she entered the apartment, was put my arms around her and bury my head between her breasts. I led her to the bedroom which I shared with my sister and she told me I should put on the last act of the opera. She stood very close to me, studying the record jacket, as I brushed the dust from the needle. My hands were trembling. Her hair, straighter and cleaner than it had been when I first saw her, hung over the sides of her face and alighted on her shoulders like wings.

I had to admit, as we stood there listening to the music, that I was thinking of the woman who sat next to me in the opera house. Whenever I looked at Jennifer I saw the woman's face. It was the moment when the lights in the opera house came on at the end of Act III and her eyes were swollen with tears. Yet she was smiling at me as a way of acknowledging what had passed between us in the dark. Nothing much had happened; but the fact that anything had happened was a kind of miracle.

I thought of my parents. The last thing I wanted was for them to return home suddenly and find me with my sister's friend. They'd been gone a few hours already and there was some talk that my father would have to stay over night at the hospital so the doctors could do some tests. I had asked my mother when she was going to come home. She had hung her head and muttered, "I don't know," which of course she didn't. It was out of her control. These days she rarely gave me a specific answer to anything. If he wasn't going to stay then they would come home together. But possibly they would wait until the snow let up. They might be forced to stay at the hospital if the storm became much worse. The night before I went into the kitchen at 2 A.M. for a glass of water and saw my mother sitting at the table with her head in her hands. My parents never discussed my father's illness with me but I was beginning to get the impression that they had given up hope.

Jennifer sat down on the side of my bed and beckoned me to join her. She told me that her parents were separated and that her father lived on MacDougal Street while her mother still lived in the Bronx and that she spent her weekends with her father but that this weekend he was out of town, he was a jazz pianist and sometimes he went on the road for a week or two with his band. So it was just by luck that she was in the Bronx today and she thought of calling my sister Liddy but realized that she really wanted to see me (it was her turn to blush). "If Liddy answered the phone," she said, "I was going to hang up." She said that her parents had taken her to see *Tristan und Isolde* when she was ten and that it had made a lasting impression on her. She began voice training lessons at the neighborhood music school and wondered if she'd ever be good enough to sing at the Met. She tried to learn some popular songs by listening to the radio and to her father's records, but when she fantasized she was always in the center of the stage of a huge opera house in Italy or France, engulfed by waves of applause and adoration. She said that the reason her parents split up was because her father didn't make enough money as a musician and her mother wanted him to quit playing music and get what she called "a real job." She said she preferred going downtown on weekends and being with her father, she wished she could live with him all the time, that her mother had a boyfriend who stayed over twice a week while she was there (and probably on weekends as well). He was a foreman for the sanitation department and left the apartment at about four in the morning to go to work. He had massive hands and a thick moustache and ate enormous platefuls of beef and chicken. He was always knocking on the bathroom door when she was taking a shower and asking if he could come in and pee. There was no lock on the bathroom door and she was frightened he was going to come in and rape her when he was drunk. Her mother kept saying that no one wanted to be a sanitation worker but the people who did the dirty work in life made the most money. Her mother wanted a lot of money, though she wasn't always this way. At one point in their life together she had encouraged Jennifer's father to pursue his career as a musician. They went to concerts and nightclubs and parties almost every night. It was when they moved to the Bronx, a few years after Jennifer was born, that things began to change. Maybe if they had stayed in Manhattan their lives would have been different. Now Jennifer's father had to ride the subway an hour each way to go to work, when he had work, playing in nightclubs in midtown or the Village. Sometimes he wouldn't return home till four or five in the morning. They didn't have enough money to hire a baby-sitter so Jennifer's mother could go with him, like in the old days. Her mother had wanted to be a painter but she had no confidence in herself. She felt about painting the way Jennifer herself felt about singing, that she was good up to a point. She couldn't decide whether she wanted to devote her whole life to singing any more than her mother could or couldn't decide whether to devote her energies to being a painter. It was after Jennifer was born and they moved to the Bronx that her mother began losing interest in both music and painting. She became obsessed with clothing, with her body, she went on a diet and lost so much weight all her old clothing no longer fit. And of course there wasn't enough money to buy a new wardrobe. She had an old sewing machine and began making clothing for herself. That's how she spent her days when her daughter was in nursery school and her husband slept. That's what she did when her husband was out all night at his job. They no longer slept together so she assumed he had girlfriends as well but after awhile she ceased to care. She had a dream of becoming a clothing designer or at least opening her own store. She began making clothing—dresses and skirts—and selling them to her friends. Eventually, as her reputation in the neighborhood grew, people she didn't know began calling her up and giving her work. But she could never save enough money to open her own business. There were weeks when Jennifer's father was out of work and all they had to support them was the money she earned making clothes. She tried to encourage her husband to find a job with a regular income so she could save some money but he refused to give up playing music. If he worked during the day he couldn't play music at night. He couldn't go out of town if he was asked. Jennifer's mother wanted money so she could move out of the Bronx and open her own store. Her dream was to live in the suburbs, Westchester or Nyack. The sanitation worker boyfriend was a ticket out of the Bronx.

"I used to hear my parents fighting all the time," Jennifer said. "It was like being in hell. Our apartment wasn't large and I think my father hit my mother a few times, they would throw plates at one another and frying pans until the neighbors complained. I knew my father was hitting her when my mother shrieked loudest—there was always a point in their fight when this happened. It was like her voice stopped sounding human, more like an animal when it's been stepped on. Once one of the neighbors called the police. I tried to cover my head with my pillow but it didn't help. Usually, after all the noise subsided, my father would look in on me and sit down on the side of my bed and wipe the sweat from my forehead. I was always recovering from a fever of some kind. I had fantasies of killing myself, which I could never tell anyone, about strangling myself with the telephone cord, taking fifty aspirins, slitting my wrists. I actually saw a movie with my friends where a woman kills herself in the bathtub by slitting her wrists with a razor and the water turns red. I wanted to do something that would wake my parents up but the only thing I could think of doing"— she lowered her voice, as if someone was listening—"was committing suicide."

There was death in the air, in her words, and in the opera where Tristan was dying. The difference between art and life was that you could start the opera from the beginning. You could turn back to page one, when the characters in the book were still alive. But when people die all that remains are memories, as meaningless as ashes in an urn. I tried to speed up the tape of my life and imagine what it was like to be fatherless. It occurred to me that I had been living with my father's absence for a long time, and that dying was just another version of not being there. Most of the time I tried not to think about dying. When I did, usually late at night lying in bed, I would rush to the bathroom and stare at myself in the mirror. The idea of not being was frightening to me. The cold porcelain against my skin as I leaned over the sink reassured me that I was alive at that moment. I made a vow to live my life as if any moment might be my last. To sleep no more than two or three hours a night, since sleeping was like being dead. I was shocked at the idea of suicide. For a moment, as she uttered the words "committing suicide," my desire for Jennifer vanished. The last thing I wanted was the idea of dying to intrude on my thoughts. Jennifer was like a character in a movie who had stepped off the screen into my arms. I wanted to fall in love with her in the moment of our being together but her words got in the way.

We stood at the window watching the snow blanket the parkway below. The cars were moving very slowly in the half-blizzard and I knew it would be a long time before my parents would ever return home. There would certainly be no point for my father to travel in this weather. Maybe my mother would come home later in a cab if the blizzard stopped.

"It's so beautiful, isn't it?" Jennifer said.

I didn't know whether she was talking about the opera or the snow.

"It's unusual for someone as young as you are"—the words stung for a moment— "to appreciate beautiful music."

I wanted to admit to her that I wasn't listening to the music, that whenever I played the opera I thought of the woman who had been sitting beside me in the opera house. By now I couldn't even remember her face. The man with the goatee was a stranger who had hired her to accompany him to the opera. She went with him to the opera once a week. On other nights she accompanied other men to dinner parties or the ballet. Sometimes she returned with them to their hotel rooms or apartments. They always paid her in advance. She was only nineteen years old but she looked older, mid-twenties at least. The man with the goatee liked her to take off her clothes and sit in a chair facing the bed until he fell asleep. Then she would join him in bed and fall asleep beside him. He never touched her.

Jennifer reached out and drew a heart in the frost on the windowpane.

"A cold heart," she said, and we turned to face one another.

"Don't you want to kiss me?" She was a few inches taller than I was and I had to raise my head so our lips could meet. Her mouth was open but as our faces collided she pulled away.

"Don't bite," she reprimanded me, in a way that reminded me of my mother. "Didn't anyone ever teach you how to kiss?"

She extended her tongue and touched the corners of my mouth, my lips, darted her tongue between my teeth. I tried to follow her movements as if we were dancing. For a moment just the tips of our tongues were touching. She took my tongue between her teeth. But it didn't hurt. She closed her eyes and darted her tongue in and out of my mouth. "This is called tongue-fucking," she said. She reached for my hand and as we stood at the window with the snow falling she guided it under her skirt. We came up for air but she continued kissing the side of my face, my neck. Then our mouths connected again and she grabbed my arm to keep from falling. Her breasts, I noticed, were larger than my sister's. She unbuttoned my shirt, kneeling slightly, so she could kiss my shoulders and chest. I remembered all the couples I had seen in the movie theater on Saturday afternoons, how it seemed like they could go on kissing one another for hours without stopping. The only time I ever kissed anyone before was during kissing games at parties, spin the bottle or post office. I'd never done it with my mouth open.

"Wait a minute."

She pulled away from me and took my hand and led me towards the bed which suddenly seemed too narrow for both of our bodies. Her skirt with the immense silver safety pin settled over her thighs.

"Did your sister tell you anything about me?" she asked.

"She said you liked opera. That's all. That your favorite opera was *Tristan*."

"What do you think she'd do if she knew I came to visit you? I'm three years older than you, at least. What would anyone think? If I put on a lot of make up I can pass for twenty. Most of my friends are older than I am. I wish Liddy liked me more but I understand why she doesn't. For a while we were both going out with the same guy and one time, at a party, he made love to both of us. First he took Liddy into one of the bedrooms, then me. Afterwards he took me home and left your sister at the party. Ever since then I have the feeling she hates me."

I was frightened that it was going to end here, that the words were going to take over. I was suddenly aware of the faces on the wall above my bed, a collage of magazine photographs of baseball players and movie stars. I saw them through Jennifer's eyes as if they were the remnants of an earlier life. The room I had lived in since I was a child was no longer familiar to me. The opera was still playing but I didn't recognize who was singing.

"Do you have a boyfriend now?" I asked, trying not to sound like a fool.

"I've been with lots of guys," she said. "The first time was with one of my father's friends. My father would kill him if he ever found out."

I was sure that at any moment she was going to get up and leave. She would make some excuse, a forgotten appointment, she could say anything. She would struggle into her boots, button her coat, kiss me on the cheek and leave. There was no way I could hold her here if she didn't want to stay. I couldn't understand why she wanted to stay, given my lack of experience.

She knelt on the floor at the foot of my bed and began fumbling with my belt. She unlaced my shoes and lowered my pants over my knees.

"You're a virgin, aren't you," she said. It wasn't a question but simply a statement for which she knew the answer. "Most of the guys I know go to a prostitute for the first time." She touched my cock with the tip of her tongue. It was something the woman from the opera house did in my fantasy. I put my hands on the top of her head, my heart beating too fast to speak. I was worried that I was going to come in her mouth.

"There are a lot of girls who charge money to do this," she said. "But I'm going to do it for free."

After a few minutes she stood up, unfastened her skirt, and took off her tights.

"It must be strange to share a room with your sister," she said, glancing at the wall of photographs as if she was seeing them for the first time.

Her hands were cold. I thought of the woman at the opera, how she had leaned against me in the dark, the sleeve of my jacket brushing against the sleeve of her dress. Jennifer stretched out on my bed like a cat and pulled me down on top of her. The bones of her necklace scratched against my chest. She spread her legs, reached between our bodies and put my cock inside her. I knew I was supposed to move but I wasn't sure how. I couldn't understand how the weight of my body, pressed flat against her, wasn't causing her pain.

I thought of the shoe box filled with money in the depths of the closet. My sister said she knew where our parents kept the rest of the money, but she wouldn't tell me. I thought of Harris and what he would say when I told him I was no longer a virgin, of the singer who played Isolde lifting her arms towards heaven, of the woman in high heels sitting beside me at the opera, of my mother weeping at the kitchen table, of my father drinking soup through a straw. I saw my sister Liddy running into the bathroom to get dressed so I wouldn't see her naked. When we were children it never bothered her whether I saw her naked or not, but now she had to close a door between us whenever she wanted to get dressed. All the images of everyone I knew faded away and there was only Jennifer's eyes staring up at me.

The great melody that encompassed Isolde's final song pulsed in the air around us. Jennifer twisted her head from side to side as I moved inside her, laughing and crying at the same time. My pants were tangled around my ankles but I didn't want to stop to take them off. She had pulled up her turtleneck so that her breasts pressed against my bare chest.

"It's so beautiful," she repeated. The music, the snow, our bodies—I assume she meant everything. I felt a kind of desultory happiness, like I was floating on the surface of a lake covered with weeds. The music was subsiding, growing fainter, but Isolde's voice echoed in the distance as if she was calling my name.

I slipped out, breathing heavily, and rolled onto my side on the narrow bed.

Jennifer, still on her back, touched the wetness between her legs, put her fingers in her mouth and sucked them dry.

"All your stuff is coming out of me," she said, pulling up her tights.

No Vacancy

All you have to do is open the door and step outside. It's strange that you have a choice, whether to do this or not, and that necessity rarely beckons you anywhere but your own room. Flirtation with some inner being, who changes continuously, as the day lengthens, is often enough to keep you occupied, as much as the breeze coming through the open window ruffles your hair and sends the lace curtains into a small frenzy. You can flail about at will, or occupy yourself with old photographs, or let your thoughts mingle with the words in a book, something Melville wrote on a bad day, perhaps. You can imagine Melville, in middle-age, sitting at a desk in the Customs House in Lower Manhattan, not far from where you live, and where there's a street named Gansevoort, leading down to the river, and you can only consider the consequences of not doing what you want at any given moment. Still, something tempts you to put your hand on the doorknob, and open it, walk down five flights of stairs, or take an elevator into the street. You like to sing to yourself as you walk, to deflect the bombardment of faces with the words of a song, as simple as "Dancing In the Dark," or "I Left My Heart in San Francisco," but you keep moving, even when the light is red and a car seems to be approaching rapidly across the intersection. Gravity is no small achievement, or so they say, what holds you and everyone else to the sidewalk under your feet, and all the senses have a purpose, as well, and sometimes two or three senses are in play at the same time, for instance touching and smelling often go hand in hand. Perhaps you will meet someone you know, or haven't seen in awhile. You can pick that person out of a crowd, you can recognize her anywhere, she hasn't changed much, and nor have you, or so she says, as she leans forward for a kiss, first one cheek, then the other. Anything can happen when you walk outside, you can be innocently thinking one thing one moment and then suddenly two worlds collide, your world and someone else's, or you can trip on the sidewalk or someone on a bycycle can run you over. Some stores, I notice, have closed—"Thanks to all customers," a sign on the window reads, "it was a pleasure to serve the community for thirty years." And you are part of the community, though rarely seen. Young children don't rush up to you as if you were their uncle. And you don't own a dog, so complete strangers don't feel compelled to ask you questions relating to pedigrees and breeding. The man selling sausages doesn't wave to you as you walk by. You don't genuflect, or kneel down, when you pass a church, and there are many of them, religious institutions of different denominations, and you never cease to wonder that religion is a living reality for millions of people you don't know. Billions perhaps—not everyone, but a lot. It's your lot to simply be who you are. Cordoned off. Surrounded by bodies of water. Only reachable by boat. Not available. No one home. Do not disturb. All of the above.

Outside Boston

"You look just like your father."

A man reaches out and pats the top of my head; the gesture accompanies the words, a disembodied hand parting the curtains of air. The words are spoken to please my father, of course, who stands alongside me, a firm hand on my shoulder to emphasize possession, but I don't know what it feels like to feel proud—is this it? I don't feel I've done anything to deserve the compliment.

Sometimes, if my father isn't standing nearby, the stranger presses a folded five dollar bill into my palm.

"You look just like your old man," he says, closing my fingers over the bill.

Then he shakes his head in disbelief and turns away. The assumption is that I'm going to tell my father the identity of the person who gave me the money, that I'm going to put in a good word for him. It's like I'm the middle person in some secret adult game where strange barrel-chested men with square jaws and receding hairlines give me money in order to get something from my father. The only problem is I have a hard time remembering names. "Tell your dad Jim Somebody says hello," and I forget the name immediately. I forget when I want to forget, and even if I could remember the name I would never dream of telling my father. I unfold the bill to check the denomination and then add it to the roll in my shirt pocket. It's my money now, the less anyone knows the better.

It's the last memory of my father, but the most insistent one. The anonymous stranger mouthing the words: "You look just like...." and then wandering away. The ritual of slipping me the money as if it was something I deserved. My father drapes his arm around my shoulder and looks proudly into my face as if he can't believe I'm his son, that after he's gone strangers will approach me and say: "I remember your father...."

The scene of this memory, this glimpse of the past, is a roadside bar called Eugene's outside Boston, or the house my father rented after he and my mother split up, or a larger party at someone else's house, where different people, both women and men, all say the same thing, every sentence begins "You look..." and then they present me with money, especially if they're drunk. My work is done. I've played the role of my father's son, I've watched my father play the role of the proud parent, his hand on my head as if he were a ventriloquist working the strings, mouthing my response (but I never say anything) without ever moving his lips. I feel like I'm at the mercy of what other people choose to say, that if I go up to my room or leave the bar unnoticed and stand in the driveway watching the lights on the highway, my father will be angry at me, and nothing's worth that. Someone will approach him and he'll say "I want you to meet my son" and I won't be there when he needs me. Even now, fifteen years after he died, I can stare into his photograph and compare it to my own face in the mirror, or to a photo of myself taken at the same time, and there's nothing, not the slightest hint of resemblance.

"Maybe," I once told Angela, a woman I lived with for a year after graduating from college, "maybe they were just saying it to be polite. But if that's the reason it wasn't me they were talking about. I could have been anyone. The whole point was to kiss my father's ass by playing on my vanity. They'd say anything to me whether I looked like him or not."

It'll go on forever, this memory, outlasting all the silences, another myth of childhood, last glimpse of dad blowing smoke into my face as I look up into the eyes of a man with pink jowls and a handkerchief folded neatly in lapel pocket, some strange oily substance coating his fat pink lips, this friend of my father, this colleague whom I was supposed to call uncle, Al or Fred.

"Shake on it partner," the guy said. "Did anyone tell you you look like your dad?"

The spitting image: that's the expression they used. It was the last time I saw my father though I wasn't aware of it then. He was being honored for something in a nightclub in Boston and had to make a speech. But beforehand, everyone mingled around drinking and shaking his hand, and shaking my hand. So I remember his face that night as a blur of smoke and I remember the women in short dresses and long hair entering the sphere of his conversation as he sat on the edge of a barstool, a drink in his hand, a cigarette, while some people dropped out of the immediate circle and others stood in the background waiting to be introduced, while still others just shook his hand, said "Congratulations," and moved on. And I was there beside him, he had a hand on my shoulder at all times, while the other hand never stopped moving, lifting the cigarette or the glass to his lips, as he talked and smoked and drank simultaneously: was anyone listening? Two men stood behind him at all times like bodyguards who did nothing but nod their heads in encouragement and laugh in the right places. He was talking about nothing. Every few words he said "fuck" and then apologized, squeezing my shoulder. All of the men, and even some of the women, as if he had given them permission, used the same word to punctuate their various responses. Even the women with their permed hair and their perfume that smelled like lilacs used the word "fuck" as a hinge at the end of their sentences. Possibly they would use this same word later in the night in another context, as in "do you want to fuck?," initiating the idea that anything was possible. Yet it was the first time I ever heard a woman speak this way. The woman who perched on the barstool near my father smiled at me lovingly with the hope (the same hope as the men who offered me money) that I might play favorites and put in a good word with my father. As if it were up to me to choose a new mate for him, a new sleeping companion. One woman with silver lipstick even kissed me on the mouth. I watched my father's hand disappear beneath her skirt as she threw back her head and exhaled the words "Fuck him!" to describe a mutual friend, her boyfriend or husband whom she would leave in a minute to be with my father.

After awhile, he was so drunk I don't think he realized I was there. Someone drove us home, eventually, my father in the front seat, dozing off, me in the back between two women, the windows wide open so no one would get sick. I was aware of their thighs and legs pressing against me and I held my hands in my lap for fear that I might reach out and touch them, put my hands between their legs (I was a step away from believing they wouldn't stop me if I did), and when the car stopped suddenly feel their breasts push against my shoulders, and one of them said "Fuck" again, because that's what we were doing, in a way, and no one cared. I was happy that when we arrived at my father's house my mother wouldn't be there, that they lived separately, since I knew how angry she would be if she saw him drunk, unable to walk. I knew that my mother, who hated being alone for even one minute of the day, had left my father because he wouldn't stop drinking, because he went out every night, because he slept with other women and because he did all these things openly, as if he purposely wanted to hurt her. It was logical that they should separate. At least now I didn't have to lie in bed listening to them fight at three in the morning.

But before we went home he made a quick speech to his constituents. He pontificated drunkenly into a microphone about labor unions and strikes and the relationships between management and workers and the laws, the "fucking laws," that allowed management to hire replacements when the workers went on strike.

I can't imagine that anyone was listening. I stood in the corner, trying to make myself invisible, frightened that he would call me up to the platform with him (as if the fact that I existed somehow validated his principles), drape his arm around my shoulder, as he sometimes did, and introduce me once again to all his cronies. The last thing I wanted was for anyone to mistake me for him.

"He got drunk again, I bet," my mother said. Those were her first words when I called her the next morning. Followed by a sigh. My parents lived all of ten blocks away from each other. Two weekends a month and special occasions like this one I slept over at my father's.

"I bet he brought someone home with him," she said.

Before calling her, I looked into my father's bedroom, which was empty of furniture except for a king-sized bed, and he was alone, lying on his bloated stomach in a white undershirt, one arm hanging over the side. I knew the women who had accompanied us on the ride home, either one of whom would have been willing to spend the night with my father whether he was drunk or sober, had stayed in the car while the driver carried him into the house and dumped him onto the bed. That was really the last time I saw him. When my mother came to pick me up, though I insisted I could walk home alone, was the last time. My mother never came inside when she picked me up. She was certain, if she ever crossed the threshold, that a strange woman in a short red nightgown would appear, my father's latest "piece of fluff," and question her right to be there. Before I left I went into his room, said "Goodbye Dad," but he didn't hear. Then I put on my jacket and closed the door behind me.

The Acting Lesson

The movie opens with a shot of a middle-aged man in steel-rimmed glasses emerging from the back of a taxi in midtown Manhattan. As the credits roll, he enters an office building, nods hello to the security guard in the lobby, and takes his place in front of the express elevator: first stop twentieth floor. The camera adjusts to the lines of his face as they merge with the intricate shadings of marble and chrome. There are other people in the elevator, strangers who work on different floors and who know one another by sight, and the camera observes them as well: alert to the silence, the boredom, the resignation, the inevitable bitterness that surfaces when you work at a job you hate. As he steps out of the elevator, the camera pans to the end of a long corridor where a young woman is staring transfixed at the name on the door of an office. It's not clear whether she emerged from a staircase or from another elevator. There's a close-up of her face, how she lowers her eyes when she sees the man walking towards her. There's a shot of her blue high heel open-toe shoes, the way the light from the window behind her frames her hair like a golden tiara. With every step forward the distance between them decreases: we see the woman from the man's point of view as a vague outline which slowly evolves like a Polaroid into a whole person with recognizable features. There's a quick shot as the woman lifts her hand to brush a strand of blonde hair from in front of her eyes, a nervous gesture, or stares down at the black and white tiled floors of the corridor. There's a shot of the man's face as he undresses her in his mind. Though in some situations mouthing "hello" or "good morning" to a stranger is an appropriate response, the woman doesn't want to send a message that might be interpreted as a sign of interest. As they draw closer, it becomes increasingly difficult for the man to avert his eyes, while the woman edges closer to the wall of the corridor, bumping against it like a blind person. "If he touches me," she thinks, playing out the worst possible scenario, "I'll scream."

Equidistant from the points at which you and the woman first begin approaching one another, there's an office with a doctor's name stenciled on the door. It's your name, and the woman is your first appointment of the day. In a minute you'll see her naked body under a white open-backed gown on a table, her platinum blonde hair hanging over the edge. You'll hammer at her knee to check her reflexes but she won't even flinch. You'll pretend that your thoughts are organized into fleeting units of desire which you can instruct the way a sign on a road signals a car forward, or simply to yield. The dialogue in your head (between you and yourself, between her and you) consists of words of anticipation, reassurance and pleasure. You keep her at a distance, tempting fate, as she turns on her side, adjusting the gown over her shoulders and breasts. The brain might burst under the weight of a million sentence fragments, the actual words you attribute to the parts of her body or your emotions, but you don't say anything for fear she'll slam the door and leave, or sue you for taking advantage of her in the privacy of your office. In a space behind a curtain, in a corner where no one can see her, she lifts her dress over her head in a comedy of errors which spells out the ambivalence of desire. What was once an abstract idea of a body under a short, sleeveless pastel dress, is arranged in front of you on a table, an *object d'art* for your pleasure alone. As you press the end of the stethoscope against her bare skin you can hear the sound of her heels (as you heard them a few moments before) on the tiles of the corridor, echoing to you out of the recent past, the gray and blue light from the windows at either end framing her waist-lengh blonde hair like an aura, an angelic halo. But the person who turned away in fear when she saw you coming isn't the same person whose body you're scrutinizing now. "How long have you been feeling this way?" you ask, in your most professional manner, and without hesitating she responds: "All my life, doctor. All my life."

The actor's day begins the moment he awakens. It's possible to say that he's never not acting, never unaware that he's playing a role. He pretends that he's at a table in a restaurant and that he's addressing a waiter who hovers over him and points out the day's specials on the menu.

The scene in the play for which he's auditioning involves talking to a waiter in a crowded restaurant. He acts out the scene, improvising his own gestures, remembering what it feels like to eat alone, all the times he's dined alone in the evening after working in an office all day. He pretends to drink from an invisible cup of coffee which the waiter has just brought him. He bends his fingers into the ear of the handle and lifts the cup to his lips. Then he replaces it on the saucer, careful not to spill. It's his job, as an actor, to convince the audience that he's drinking from a real cup of coffee. He runs his tongue over his chapped lips to convey a sense of pleasure at the taste of the coffee. A woman he knew as a child, a friend of his mother's, appears at the door of the restaurant, her stringy brown hair hanging straight down over the frayed collars of her fur-lined coat. He pretends not to notice her (he wishes he had brought a book with him so he could bury his head) but she recognizes him at once. He stands up to meet her embrace (a kiss on either cheek) and watches as she drapes her coat over the back of a chair. She doesn't ask permission to sit at the table nor inquire whether he's expecting anyone to join him. The actor rehearses the scene, alone in his apartment. He tries to communicate to the imaginary audience a sense of annoyance at the woman for distracting him, but she's too self-involved to notice. (The audience sees everything; the woman sees only herself.) It's just a matter of time before she's confiding her most intimate secrets: that she's been married for five years ("to a doctor") but that she's unable to have his children. "Any" children is more accurate but by saying "his" she puts part of the blame on her husband, inaccurately implying that she might be able to have children with someone else. She's the type of person who confides her secrets to anyone, who talks without listening, a rush of sentence fragments with no boundaries. The actor, playing the role of a young man, shakes his head as if to deny what she says is true. He's secretly worried that he looks too old for the part, that no one will believe this woman is twice his age. He attempts to convey to the woman that he understands the extent of her unhappiness but there's nothing in his own experience to compare with her inability to have a child. There's no way he can imagine what it feels like to be her.

The actor sits at a table in the center of the stage, pretending to drink from a cup of coffee. He wants to give the members of the acting class the impression that the coffee is too hot to drink. There are twenty students in the class, not counting the teacher, who is also the director of the play, and who stands behind the students in the back row of the small theater. The actor tilts the imaginary cup to his lips and winces as he swallows the hot coffee. Then he returns the cup to the saucer without spilling it. He uses both hands, focusing all his attention on the empty space between his fingers. A second actor, playing the role of the waiter, approaches the table and offers him a menu. The actor listens attentively as the waiter recites the day's specials: braised duck in red wine sauce with mashed potatoes, grilled salmon, a Black Angus steak in sauce Béarnaise. Then he opens the menu, which is the size of a large magazine, and begins studying the lists of appetizers and desserts. He pushes the imaginary cup and saucer to one side to make room for the menu. In a few minutes the waiter will return, but the actor isn't ready to order.

Where does the coffee go when it passes between the lips? He feels the warmth of the liquid through the handle of the cup. It's his job, as an actor, to express the sensation he's feeling in his fingers as he lifts the cup to his lips. If the cup is full, won't he need more than one finger to lift it? The last thing he wants is to spill coffee on his shirt. He tries to take into account the smell of the coffee (smell and taste are different pleasures) and he does this by closing his eyes in a kind of ecstasy as he takes the first sip. In this gesture, the pleasure of taste and smell are combined. He puts one hand under the imaginary cup to prevent it from spilling. It's at this point that the waiter approaches the table with a large cardboard menu. But first he introduces himself: "My name is Alex," he says. "I'm your waiter."

The woman patient says: "I like it when you touch me." The doctor, either absentmindedly or purposefully, has neglected to put on his latex gloves when he examines her. She's lying on a table in his office, her white gown untied, her legs raised slightly, her long platinum blonde hair hanging like a waterfall over the edge. A still life of a waterfall. Her eyes are closed. The doctor places his hand over her heart and for a moment her whole body grows tense, then relaxes, as he massages her shoulders, then tense again, as he touches her breasts. More than once, when she was younger, a teacher in school tried to molest her. "You have a beautiful body," the doctor is tempted to say. He pushes her hair away from her ears and massages her neck with both hands. It's then that the woman tells him how much she likes it when he touches her. He translates her words into an invitation, then rejects it. For emphasis, she relaxes her legs on the end of the table, parting them slightly so that the gown slips away.

He can hear the sound of her heels as she approaches him from the end of the corridor. (Already, even before he sees her close up, he can imagine her naked body on the table in his office.) She's wearing a dress with a short skirt and stockings, a heavy gold belt, a velvet jacket with wide collars. The corridor is lined with doors, heavy fake wooden doors, leading to the offices of doctors and dentists and lawyers. When he first sees her, he has no way of knowing that she's coming to visit him. It's five minutes to nine, a Thursday morning, she's his first appointment of the day. Apparently, she just stepped off the elevator a few minutes before him and is reading the names on all the doors of the offices. At least that's what she's pretending to do when he sees her walking towards him from the other end. It's no accident, then, that they meet in front of the office with his name. "Are you here to see Dr. Inrati?" she asks. "I am Dr. Inrati," he says. His hands tremble as he turns the knob.

One wall of the office is covered with framed diplomas from universities and medical associations. You can buy them anywhere: who can tell whether they're authentic or fake? On another wall a cluster of photographs, typical of many doctor's offices, black and white photos of Venice, the roofs of Florence. A couple (doctor and wife?) step into a gondola. The same couple at a table in an outdoor cafe. The woman enters the office without seeing any of it. She sees everything but translates it all into a single impression: no details, no identification of objects, no names, just a sense of the way everything fits. Is this place threatening or not? Ever since the accident, or so she refers to it in her head, voice one talking to voice two, she assesses every situation as threatening, possibly threatening, or safe. All her actions are determined by this gauge which is active twenty-four hours. Sometimes the messages she gives herself contradict her voices: sometimes, when the gauge reads "threatening," she doesn't flinch or turn away. There's often a pleasure in the possibility of experiencing something potentially dangerous or frightening. You lose a sense of where one thought starts and another begins. You wake at noon and don't know the name of the person sleeping beside you. Fear is seductive if it talks to you sweet. What's shocking to the woman as she enters the doctor's office is the emptiness of it all. No fear, but something unnameable, worse than fear, ghostlike, the pretense of living. She had felt it on the first visit, this twinge, her third or seventh sense warning her that emptiness (the absence of feeling) is worse than fear. Or could be. Those diplomas in their cheap silver frames, those photographs in homage to some ridiculous moment of illusory happiness, all communicate one thing: the person who works in this room doesn't know what it means to be alive. One way of dealing with fear is to be aware of the possibility: to court it, let it swallow you whole, while staying outside yourself. The only way to survive is to cheat a little, seeing yourself from a distance, from the sky, until you no longer know your own body. "You can go in now, Ms. Hendrix," the receptionist says, pointing towards the hallway leading to his office. She stands behind the partition and strips, ties the gown behind her back. This is her second visit, she knows the ritual. "And how do you feel today?" the doctor asks as he enters the office, clipboard in hand. Empty, like you, she feels tempted to say. She's lying on the table, her long bleached blonde hair hanging over the edge, staring up at the ceiling, aware of every movement, the pen slipping from his hand and striking the metal bridge of the clipboard, the way he clears his throat to fill the silence, the strip of plaster dangling from the ceiling (not only isn't he alive, but this person going through the motions isn't even aware of his surroundings, can't even see), the music *easy listening* from another office. "Any better today?" he says, the machine says, forgetting that he already asked, unnerved by her beauty, the way her body fills the whole table, the largesse of her presence.

It's been so long since he felt anything about anyone he doesn't even recognize what's happening to him. Two phrases, *reflecting emptiness* and *being alive,* contest one another in the air, in his head. All he knows is that he wants to cross the room, remove the photographs from their hooks on the wall, and smash them to the floor. His hands tremble as he massages her neck and he backs away, takes off his glasses and wipes them on the sleeve of his jacket. The woman lowers the gown to her waist and raises her body on one elbow. "Is there anything wrong?"

It's late afternoon, not quite dinner hour, and there are more waiters than customers in the restaurant. All the waiters are dressed alike: loose black pants, red cummerbunds, white shirts (no ties). When the woman enters, they surround her like suitors at a party vying for her attention, but she doesn't even see them. Her gaze is fixed on the young man sitting in the corner, the young out-of-work actor (the actor playing the role of actor), who has barely enough money to buy himself a decent meal. The waiter named Alex who brought the actor his coffee and took his order assumed he was dining alone. The woman scrapes the chair back, drapes her coat, flattens ankle-length woolen skirt over thighs. If there were a full-length mirror nearby she would inspect herself carefully before sitting down. But the only mirror is in the eyes of the young actor eating his imaginary dinner. The woman, the doctor's wife, played by another actress also hoping for a role in the play, another member of the acting class, settles into the chair, leans her elbows on the table. "And what have you been doing all this time?" she asks the actor. Only the night before, actor and actress rehearsed this scene together, pretending that the kitchen table in the actor's apartment was the table in the restaurant. After several hours, the actress, in her mid-thirties, the mother of a teenage son, suggested that they go to bed together. She assumed that their range of emotions as actor and actress would be enhanced if they got to know each other more intimately. People who get up on a stage night after night have to do something to keep their performances from going stale. Besides, it was too late to take the subway home and the woman didn't want to spend the money on a taxi. She took the actor's hand and placed it down the front of her blouse, but he pushed her away. It was then that he confessed to her that he wasn't interested in sleeping with women.

An orchestral version of "Greensleeves" was playing over a hidden speaker in a corner of the doctor's office. The woman lay on her stomach on the table while the doctor massaged her shoulders and back. Instead of saying "How do you feel today?" he had merely smiled at her when she stepped from behind the screen in her white gown. This was her third visit, but she felt like she had known the touch of his hands for years. She had knotted her hair into a braid so it wouldn't get in the way. "I like your hair loose," the doctor said. "It makes you look younger." She reminded herself to wear it down for her next visit. She told him how all the boys in high school used to make fun of her because of the size of her breasts. She felt the weight of her breasts against the white napkin that covered the length of the table. An oval of morning sunlight expands across the wall, reflecting the glass in which the doctor's diplomas are encased. He was tempted to tell her about his wife, how they were trying to have a child, how she had begun taking drugs to make her more fertile but without any success. After the visit, the woman stands very close to him as she buttons her blouse. There's no reason, at least in her mind, to feel self-conscious about dressing or undressing in his presence. She sits on the edge of the table, legs crossed, brushing her hair, while the doctor writes meaningless numbers on her chart, pretending she isn't there.

Sometimes, to amuse him, she would enter her bedroom in a white gown similar to the one she wore in his office. They would pretend he was "the doctor" and she was "the patient" (since by now she considered herself "cured" of whatever had been wrong with her), only instead of the hard table in his office she was lying on her stomach across her bed, and he was leaning over her, massaging her neck and shoulders ("How are you feeling today?"), while with his free hand he would unzip his pants and hover between her legs. By then, he had told her more than once how his marriage was falling apart over the issue of having a baby, that when he was home he felt he was playing the role of "dutiful husband," that when he made love to his wife he pretended he was making love to her. As he drove home from her apartment after midnight he rehearsed what he would tell his wife if she asked him where he had been. That they could no longer live together, that it was insane to continue this endless role-playing, that he had fallen in love with someone else, that his new lover (his former patient) was pregnant with his child. His wife never questioned why he was coming home so late, night after night. She assumed he was sleeping with someone else (this wasn't the first time he had been unfaithful to her) but it was beneath her dignity to act jealous, to play the role of the jealous wife. She sat in bed reading until she heard his key in the front door; then she turned out the bedside lamp and pretended to be asleep.

The doctor's wife told the out-of-work actor what had happened to her the last time she was in this restaurant, maybe ten years before. They were lifting imaginary forks and spoons to their mouths, going through the motions of carving and chewing (in the actual play, of course, there would be real food on real plates), gesticulating with their hands and faces to simulate the pleasures of eating. "It was before I was married," the doctor's wife said. "I would often eat out alone. The restaurant was more crowded than it is tonight. I was sitting at a table in a corner"—she gestured with her fork—"when four men came in with ski masks over their faces and guns in their hands. Almost every table in the restaurant was taken. People were eating, laughing, talking. Music was playing in the background, recorded music, the kind they play in elevators. The four gunmen ordered all the men to empty their pockets into a black garbage sack. One of the gunmen herded the waiters and the cook into the kitchen. The men in the restaurant were forced to undress, while another one of the gunmen went around and gathered all the jewelry from the women. One of the men refused and the gunman who seemed to be the leader shot him in the side of the head. There was one young woman who seemed paralyzed by what was happening; she sat at a table crying and refused to give up her ring. The head gunman tied her hands behind her back with wire, taped her mouth, pulled up her dress and raped her on the floor of the restaurant in full sight of everyone else. I gave them everything they wanted, of course. When the rape was going on there wasn't a sound except for the young woman's muffled cries; and then the cry of pleasure as the gunman with the ski mask collapsed on top of her. The three other gunmen looked envious of their leader. For a moment it seemed that each of them was going to take his turn with the young woman on the floor. There was a pool of blood surrounding the body of the man they had shot and I guess they figured they had wasted enough time torturing us. They backed out of the restaurant with their guns raised, carrying the sack of money and jewelry, and disappeared into the night. The police arrived, in due time, and questioned everyone who was there. The man who had been shot was dead; I don't know what happened to the young woman. I had to go down to the police station and answer questions for hours." Her food was getting cold as she told the story. The young actor, his fork raised, stared at her in disbelief. "You mean it all happened here? In this restaurant?" "Right here," the woman said, pointing to a spot on the carpet. "That's where he raped her."

"More than once," the woman says, "when I was younger, a teacher tried to molest me." They're lying across her bed, both fully dressed, a bottle of cognac and two wineglasses on a tray between them. The doctor is too exhausted to pay attention to yet another chapter of her life story; in his fantasy, he had imagined arriving in her apartment, making love on the living room floor, and leaving. For weeks now she's been trying to convince him to spend the night with her. It's been years since she slept with anyone, since she woke up in the morning with another body lying beside her. The doctor is thinking about his wife, what her life will be like after they separate. He feels like taping the woman's mouth, shackling her wrists, and forcing her to do whatever he wants. But when he actually suggests having sex in this manner, simulating the rape scene which took place when she was nineteen, she shakes her head sadly. "You're missing the point," she says. The doctor has the impression that they'll never get beyond this moment, never move forward into a present tense free from the shadows of the past. His wife, the rape scene, the way the teachers used to go out of their way to touch her arms and shoulders and breasts, casually, as if they were just being affectionate, as if they weren't aware of what they were doing; all associations related to the stigmas of the past will linger forever. All these wounds feel like they were inflicted yesterday. He tries to convey to the audience his frustration without losing their sympathy, but the point of view has changed from the doctor to his former patient. He reaches out and touches her shoulders and begins to unbutton her blouse as she talks but she pushes his hand away. "I won't fuck you again," she says, loud and clear, "until you leave your wife."

The waiting room of the doctor's office is filled with young women. Some of them are reading magazines, others stare into space. None of them are happy, the woman thinks, not certain whether she's projecting her own feelings or whether what her instinct tells her is true. Since she met the doctor, she no longer thinks of her life as "happy" or "miserable." There's no longer a fixed boundary between one emotion or another. The receptionist calls out her name, "Ms. Hendrix," and the doctor's assistant leads the patient behind the screen. "You can undress here," she says, "the doctor will be with you in a minute." The patient lifts her dress over her head, reaches behind her back to unfasten her bra. She remembers the way her first boyfriend, when she was in high school, used to fumble at the catch of her bra while she pretended she wasn't aware of his difficulties. Finally he gave up (she felt like laughing in his face), lowered the straps of her bra over her arms, and buried his face between her breasts. She stares at the gown hanging from a hook on the wall and decides not to wear it. By the time the doctor enters the office, clipboard in hand, the young woman is lying naked with her knees raised on the silver table.

Lying in bed waiting for him to appear, each night a little later and with a different excuse, the doctor's wife reviewed their life together as a series of glyphs which translated into a small gallery of memories with no continuity and no emotion. The person she had married six years ago in a ceremony in a church was more alive in memory than the absent lover, but even that spark was going out. The fire was out, there were only dead embers, wet kindling, who cared if he came back or not? She wanted to tell the young man whom she had met earlier that evening in the restaurant how her husband slept with other women (as if no one had ever been unfaithful before) but she was frightened that he would hate her for breaking down in public, that her tears would embarrass him, that he wouldn't know how to react. Even telling him that she wasn't able to have babies had been a mistake. She had to admit that meeting him had distracted her in a positive way from her problems with her husband. One day, she told herself, when he returned home late, she wouldn't be there. She laughed out loud as she imagined him standing over the empty bed. She pictured herself with her own lover; the young actor she had met that day, his tiny one room walkup, the loft bed, the alcove which served as a kitchen. She had to remind herself that she was only thirty-five, still young enough to change her life, that it wasn't unusual for women her age to have lovers who were ten years younger. Most days she lacked the strength to lift her head from the pillow. Most days she didn't even bother getting dressed. Before leaving the restaurant, she and the young actor exchanged phone numbers and he told her she could call him any time. The idea that he might be waiting for her phone call right at that moment, though it was two in the morning, was enough to get her out of bed and search through the pockets of her coat for the old matchbook on which she had written his number. She could see him lying in bed, wide awake, fully dressed, smoking, listening with anticipation to the sound of the phone. "Answer it, you bastard," the woman said. But as soon as she heard his voice—it seemed to be coming from a thousand miles away, lost in space—she hung up.

I used to meet people in parks or bars, the young woman told the doctor, and take them home with me. The only men who interested me were men I'd never met before and would never see again. I haunted deserted playgrounds late at night and if I saw a young man on a bench I would make eye contact and approach him. The only men who interested me were men I didn't know. Sometimes I would meet someone at a party and make love in a deserted bedroom with the lights off so I couldn't see his face. Once, in a taxi late at night with the driver, a Palestinian who had the word "Allah" tattooed in a heart on his arm. We made eye contact in the rearview mirror,

I unbuttoned my blouse. The only men I was attracted to were strangers, men with no names. I would arrive at parties in a short skirt with no underwear and sit in a corner until someone approached me. I liked to have sex with two or three men at one time. Some of this is true, some of these are my fantasies. If they wanted, I let them tie my hands behind my back with a nylon stocking or a scarf and tape my mouth so I couldn't cry out. Afterwards, I would lie on my stomach while they got dressed, not moving until I heard the door slam behind them. That was my dream, anyway, but it never worked out. The first time, with you, in the office, I can't tell you how much I wanted you to touch me. I didn't want to get dressed. I felt it the first time I saw you, in the corridor, coming towards me. Whether we made love or not, I knew I'd come back for more.

I was only nineteen. We were going to be married that fall. My fiancé had given me an engagement ring and we went out to a restaurant with members of his family to celebrate. We were just finishing our dinners, my fiancé was drinking coffee, I was sipping Chivas Regal, when four men with ski masks pulled tight over their faces entered the restaurant. Each of them was carrying a gun. My fiancé, his father and brother were forced to undress, along with the other men in the restaurant. They were led into a room in the back, the freezer, while one of the men went from table to table gathering the jewelry from the women. I refused to give him my ring. He pulled me by the hair and dragged me to a space between tables in the center of the restaurant. He tied my hands behind my back and taped my mouth. I have to confess that I wasn't a virgin. My fiancé and I had been sleeping together for over a year and I'd had other boyfriends before that. Don't ask me how many. The man with the gun rolled me over onto my stomach and forced me to spread my legs. I don't know how long it lasted; maybe five or six minutes. They had already shot one of the men in the restaurant and I was frightened they would kill me as well if I refused. At some point I stopped struggling; I felt like I was going to faint. I kept going to the verge of blacking out and then snapping back. There was a voice in my head reminding me that it wasn't a dream, no nightmare, but really happening. I can still feel his hands in my hair, the smell of his breath on the back of my neck. When it was over he pulled off my ring and put it in his pocket. He stood up, buttoned his pants, and kicked me with the toe of his boot. I could hear his friends laughing in the background. 'It's my turn now,' one of them said, but he never did anything. I kept lying on the floor of the restaurant waiting for one of the other men to climb on top of me. Of course, the wedding was called off. I refused to even see my fiancé. He would call me every day for months afterwards but I refused to speak with anyone, especially him. I dropped out of college and hid myself in my bedroom in my parents' house. There was my photograph in the newspaper, the girl who was raped in the restaurant. Some days I didn't even get out of bed. I would come downstairs to eat and watch television with my family but my father always ended up carrying me upstairs. The police questioned me over and over again, but they never found the men. They assumed because I was raped by one of them that I knew something no one else did. Apparently one of the customers in the restaurant was a state senator so the story received more publicity than it might have otherwise. One of the detectives who was assigned to the case kept calling me long after the publicity had stopped. I realized that he wasn't just calling me because of what happened in the restaurant but that he was falling in love with me. He would call the house to assure my family that the case hadn't been forgotten, that he was still working on it. But after awhile I told my parents to say I wasn't home, that I was busy, that I had moved away. Part of me, I know, didn't want him to find the man who had raped me. I wanted the event to recede, as doctors assured me it would; I wanted to get on with my life. I even knew that I could deny it had ever happened if I wanted to. I was good at denying, good at lying to myself, good at pretense. Just when I thought I was almost cured I started falling down at unexpected moments, paralyzed, gasping for air. It was as if my body was trying to remind me that it was stronger than any attempt I was making to pretend that nothing was bothering me and the only way I could get beyond the experience was by accepting it as something that could have happened to anyone. I lingered over the moments in the restaurant like frozen stills from a grade-B movie. I wanted to think so hard about what had happened that I'd bury it forever under the weight of my obsession. I even returned to the restaurant and sat at the same table where I was sitting the night it happened. I went there more than once. I would go alone, hoping a stranger would join me. I'd stare at all the single men standing at the bar and dare them with my eyes. I was like the shell-shocked veteran of some meaningless war who has to relive her combat experiences in order to integrate them into her present reality. Most of all, I remember the way he kicked me when I was lying on the floor. I can still feel the toe of his boot against my ribs. As if I were a bag of trash. Trash! And that's what I've felt like ever since.

The play consists of four main characters: a doctor, his wife, the patient who becomes his lover, and an out-of-work actor who is also an old friend of the doctor's wife. There are other characters as well: the four gunmen who raid the restaurant, all the customers in the restaurant (including the young woman's future husband and father-in-law), the waiter, the doctor's receptionist. In the first scene we see two people walking towards one another down an empty corridor lined with doctors' offices. It takes about five seconds for the two strangers to meet, center stage, at the door of the office with the doctor's name on it. Their hands reach out simultaneously for the doorknob but the doctor gets there first. He smiles at the woman who removes her hand and holds it behind her back as if she's frightened that touching the doctor's hand will contaminate her. Subsequent scenes include the doctor's waiting room, his office, and the restaurant where the actor and the doctor's wife meet accidentally.

The doctor's wife (Clarissa) tells the young unemployed actor (Bob) that ten years ago, more than that, four men with guns entered the restaurant and murdered one of the customers and raped a young woman. How the male customers were forced to strip naked and were herded into the freezer and how the women were forced to turn over all their jewelry. Unlike Greek drama, the murder and the rape take place on stage, in full view of the other customers in the restaurant and the audience. There's another character I've forgotten about: the detective who falls in love with the woman who was raped. Neither the playwright nor the director are sure how old the detective should be. The director insists that all the actors and actresses are chosen from his acting class. The playwright wants a well known actor and actress to play the parts of the doctor and his lover. For a week, playwright and director don't speak to one another. There's a rumor that the play will be canceled or that the playwright is going to find another director. All the students in the class are aware that this power struggle is going on. Each of them takes a turn on stage playing the roles of the doctor, the patient, the doctor's wife, or the young actor in the restaurant. Everyone has a different theory how the rape scene should be treated. One student, a male, feels that the young woman and the rapist should really do it, really fuck, really make love, every performance. Others think it should happen off-stage or behind a screen while still others think that the actors could simulate the rape like they do in the movies. One of the students, a young actress named Natalie, confesses to the class that she was raped when she was nineteen, in circumstances similar to those in the play. The last thing she wants is to relive this experience night after night. Yet the fact that she knows what it feels like is also a point in her favor.

The director lies in bed and imagines a possible movie version of the play. The credits roll over a shot of the doctor entering the office building where he works, riding the elevator, stepping out and seeing the woman at the end of a long corridor. There's a close-up of the woman's face, how she lowers her eyes when she sees the man walking towards her. There's a shot of her blue high heel shoes, the way the light from the window behind her frames her hair like a golden tiara. The director turns over on his side and touches the face of the woman named Natalie who's sleeping beside him, the actress who's going to play the role of the young woman. "You're not giving me the part because I'm sleeping with you?" she had asked him earlier, knowing the answer in advance, but wondering whether he had the nerve to tell her the truth. There's no reason why she would dream of sleeping with him if he wasn't the director of the play. She had been abused enough by men in her short life. She knew how to lie back and spread her legs and endure it, close her eyes, until it was over. There was no question in the director's mind that she was perfect for the role. He reminded her, as he did all the actors and actresses in the class, about Stanislavski's theory of "emotion memory," how you relive your emotions about an event in the past in order to communicate a similar emotion to the audience. So that it was up to Natalie, when she was being raped on stage, to remember how she felt when she had really been raped, no matter how painful the memory. The more she remembered, the better her performance would be. The director forces her to explore every detail, every nuance of feeling surrounding the event. "He wants me to tell him that I enjoyed it," she says to herself. "But it isn't true."

Pedagogy of the Oppressed

His name was Hector. Whenever I called his name, "Hector," and asked him to answer a question, he didn't respond. Finally I checked the official list of students and discovered that his name was Hernando, not Hector. But the next day, when I called him by what I assumed was his proper name, "Hernando," he still refused to answer. Most of the semester he sat in the back of the room reading the newspaper or drawing pictures in his notebook. Occasionally, I would say "Hernando, pay attention," but he would always ignore me.

There was a fly buzzing in a corner of the classroom, alighting occasionally on the edge of my desk or on the bare arm of one of the students. It was one of the hottest days in recent memory and everyone was sweating in the airless room as I tried to define the tables of history in terms of class relations and individual achievement. But after awhile I gave up, wrote a sentence on the blackboard, and asked the students to put it into their own words.

"You mean paraphrase?" a voice called out from the back of the room.

It was the first time Hector or Hernando had spoken in weeks.

"That's what I mean," I said.

"That's what I thought you meant," he said.

While the rest of the class dutifully took out writing implements and ripped note paper from spiral bound books, Hector or Hernando continued to read the newspaper. The fly had landed on the desk of the young woman sitting closest to me, but she didn't seem to notice it. (As she lifted her arms, to pin her hair back from her face, it flew away.) The young woman's name was Alicia, but she always reminded me to call her Alice, though I preferred Alicia. As the weather became warmer, she wore less and less clothing to class, and the presence of her half-naked body made it difficult for me to concentrate on what I was supposedly teaching. As the students began writing, I pretended to read; in reality, I was memorizing the angles of Alicia's body as she fidgeted in her seat.

Then a girl named Roxanne raised her hand and said that she didn't understand the words I had written on the blackboard. She didn't understand, for instance, what was wrong with capitalism, why my questions always implied that I thought there was something wrong with the world in which we all lived. As far as she was concerned, coming to this country from an island in the Caribbean was the greatest thing that had ever happened to her. If I was so keen on living in a classless society then I should get my ass out of this country.

"You should go to Cuba or somewhere," she said.

She slammed her notebooks together into a colorful

shoulder bag and left the room.

Hector or Hernando said: "Can I leave too?"

A Japanese guy named Tayama said he was finished, could he leave, and I said are you sure you're finished, you've only been writing for ten minutes. He said he was sure, he agreed with me about capitalism, he believed an armed uprising was inevitable, that all rich people were assholes.

"You mean we can leave after we're finished?" Hernando or Hector shouted.

"I never said that," I said.

"But that guy just left."

Alicia yawned, crossed her legs, and I noticed that the paper on which I thought she was writing her response was empty. I also noticed for the first time that she had a tattoo on her left breast. She was wearing a low-cut blouse and I could see the stem of a rose as she tilted forward in her seat. I could see the stem but I couldn't see the rose.

Hector or Hernando said: "My name is neither Hector or Hernando. If you call me by my right name, I'll pay attention."

I closed my book and stared at the sky. A helicopter was floating against a back drop of gray clouds. All the light had vanished from the sky, even though it was still early in the day. The heat had sucked out all the light. The helicopter was moving very slowly and the trees outside the window were still.

My job as teacher or guide suddenly seemed without purpose, as if I were just going through the motions like a warden in a correctional facility, keeping order, deriving sustenance from peripheral observation, extending myself outwards until I became the rose flowering at the tip of Alicia's breast, succumbing as much to the pull of gravity (which drew everything downwards) as to the enclosed space which I occupied with these strangers whose purpose in life was to be loved and to give love in return, but who had taken a detour (much like myself) only to discover (like a wake-up call from the beyond) that dignity has as much substance as the paper-thin wings of the fly against my skin, or the beads on a thread.

DUBROVNIK

As it turns out, I'm not happy with the view, which looks straight down into the parking lot below, not to mention the smell of the dumpster every time I open the window (I like to sleep with the window open, no matter how cold), so I ask the man at the front desk, Ralph, so the name tag on the front of his shirt informs me, whether there are any other rooms available. It seems to take an interminable period of time, during which Ralph combs the spread sheets in front of him, and then consults his computer, just to make sure he doesn't give me a room that someone else has reserved.

"Yes, there is," he says, "I'll have Bertha make your bed immediately."

Bertha, it turns out, is a small pouty redheaded lady from Eastern Europe—tiny waist, pointy features, thirty-five at the oldest. I always like thin women, my wife was anemic and had to take massive doses of iron pills every four hours, so I make a point of keeping my distance. I don't want her to get the wrong idea, or maybe I do? People tend to misinterpret the body language of people they don't know, not to mention actual conversations in which people say things they don't really mean, in a tone of voice that conveys the opposite of what they mean, so sometimes it's best to keep one's mouth shut in the presence of strangers. But as a person traveling on my own, it was just such a random encounter, like the one I was having with Bertha, that I imagined before boarding the plane. I had the fantasy that at every step along the way a stranger would rub her body against me. Anything could happen, for instance, flying over the Atlantic, in the middle of the night, but the girl sitting beside me was young enough to be my granddaughter, and fell asleep almost immediately. I once had sex on an airplane with a Romanian woman named Gina, an all night flight from New York to Seoul, but that's a different story. I lean back against the window of my new room, which faces the front of the hotel, whistling an aria from "La Traviata," while Bertha folds back the sheets.

"Can barely speak English," she says, when—feeling desperate, middle-aged, and alone—I try to engage her in conversation.

Happily, it's a room where smoking is allowed, so I open the window, twenty stories above the Rue Magdalene, and stare at the window of the building across the narrow street, where a woman and a man are standing, leaning forward out the window, almost dangerously so, the man behind the woman, his hands on her bare breasts. Her shoulders are bare as well, and it looks, for the moment, as their bodies rock back and forth, that they're having sex out in the open, in broad daylight, for everyone to see, though at twenty stories above the street it's unlikely that anyone is watching them but me. The woman has short curly black hair and the man is wearing a wide-brimmed hat, not quite as big as a sombrero, but almost, and he has the biggest moustache I've ever seen, curling at both ends. His eyes are closed and the woman is making small sounds, like a hungry terrier nipping at your heels, and the man is grunting each time he moves forward as if it was all too much work and he'd rather be anywhere else, though that couldn't possibly be true.

It's just a matter of time before I turn away from them—it's boring, beyond belief, to watch other people having sex, though I'm sure some people disagree—and stare at the room, as if it was a kind of prison where I would spend the rest of my days, the painting of a beach on the wall above my king-sized bed, a sailboat on the horizon, a young blonde girl with a pensive look sitting alone beside a rock that juts out into the bay, all of it enclosed in an ugly metal frame, and I wondered if I had made a mistake by boarding a plane and coming to a city where I didn't know a single person, though I've met a few, Ralph, at the main desk, and Bertha, with her wild red hair, among them. And no doubt I'll meet others, if that's what I want. People seem to like me, I make a good first impression, especially on women, though I have a number of men friends, as well, people I've known for years. I find it easier to be with women, as lovers, and especially as friends. I've only had one sexual encounter in my life with a man. I've never fantasized about having sex with a man. Men are impossible to love—you can't talk about love with a man, not as a friend. With women everything is clear. There's either one thing or another. It has to do with love, sometimes, and sex, most often. And then there's a third thing, which is impossible to figure out. With men, it's hit or miss. You never know whether the person (man) is interested in what you're saying, or even listening. It's hard to communicate who you are to another person and it's even harder if you're on the other end, listening to what someone else thinks is important. We all have to think that what we do is important, closing our eyes to the reality that no one really cares.

I was like that for awhile. "Who cares?" I responded, as an answer to almost any question. Then I changed directions, turned my life around, so to speak. I met someone, we fell in love, and then I met someone else. And it was the "someone else" who made the difference. I thought I was in love with the first person, but with the second person it really happened. I could actually compare one with the other and see how, in one case, I'd been kidding myself, and in the second case, something real was occurring, something I'd read about in books, something other people had told me about, something I never thought would happen to me. It was no fun saying goodbye to the first person, who I thought I was in love with, and who said she was in love with me, as well, and who I had known, in this way, for over six months. I couldn't, of course, tell her how I'd felt one thing for her, and something else for someone else, and how it was possible to measure the difference, as if on a scale, from one to ten. And I never thought my life with the second person would ever end, but here I am, in this strange city, on a bed with a woman named Bertha, my head in a vise between her legs, her red hair going up in flames.

MIDNIGHT SUN

Lauren passed a special statewide test when she was thirteen that allowed her to enter high school early. Most of the other students in her grade were two or three years older. As a consequence, and in an attempt to fit in, Lauren tried to look older—she wore make-up (lipstick, eye shadow) that she stole from Duane Reade and tried to wear tight clothing. At five foot eight, she only weighed about a hundred pounds. A photographer friend of her uncle suggested she audition at a modeling agency and the next thing she knew her face was on the cover of Vogue. That was her fantasy anyway. The people at the modeling agency thought she was too thin. They didn't want to project a look that other young women would attempt to imitate. They didn't want young women to starve themselves in order to look like Lauren. She looked unhealthy, in their eyes, and they had already been accused, more than once, of using anorexic women in their ads. Women who never ate.

Mike Divak was the first to spread rumors about her. He was a boy in her class who asked her out on a date. There isn't much to do in a small town if you don't have a car but there's a local movie theater and that's where they went. They both lived near the center of town so getting there, and back, wasn't a problem. Mike Divak walked her home and they kissed on the front porch. In Divak's version of what happened, Lauren let him do anything he wanted. It's not a good idea to discuss your sex life in intimate detail but Mike Divak told everything to anyone who wanted to listen and no one questioned whether it was really true. He told one person who told someone else and within twenty-four hours everyone knew that he had sex with Lauren. By nightfall, all the boys at school were calling to see if she would go out with them. They figured that if she was going to "put out" to Mike Divak, not the most handsome or most athletic and certainly not the brightest bulb among them, she would certainly bestow her favors on them. Lauren could have a date with a different guy every night, if she wanted. Wasn't that what everyone wanted? She was only thirteen. Her guidance counselor, a born-again type, said that her life's journey was just beginning. He put his hand on her leg. He had also heard the rumors. Lauren lived alone with her mother, Dorothea. Her father had been badly injured in a car crash. He was still in a rehab hospital but it was doubtful that he would ever walk again. Once a month she and her mother visited him. His brain had been injured in the crash as well and he gestured wildly with his hands to explain what he could no longer express in words.

Dorothea had already begun dating other men. Lauren could hear them—her mother, her mother's boyfriend—behind the bedroom wall. She could hear her mother's cries and the way the bed slammed against the wall. Didn't they know she was lying awake, just a few inches away? That she could hear everything? It never seemed to occur to them. Once, in the middle of the night, one of her mother's boyfriends tried to get into bed with her, but she managed to fend him off. Sometimes when she came home from school one of the boyfriends was sitting on the couch watching television while her mother was at work. Sometimes, if she was bored, she would join the boyfriend in front of the TV, and they would share a joint, and she would let him touch her breasts, if that's what he wanted to do, but most of the time she walked by him without even saying hello and closed the door of her room. She'd had enough touching for one lifetime, it seemed, and she had to admit that she was attracted to a girl named Agatha, two grades ahead, whom she saw in the hallway at school, between classes. Sometimes she followed Agatha from one classroom to another. Often, she was surrounded by young men in the upper grades. Lauren decided the way to get Agatha's attention was by getting the attention of some of these young men. Soon she had the reputation of someone who would go "all the way," the days of "putting out" were far behind, and soon the young men who were trying to seduce Agatha began showing her some attention, and Agatha herself began to wonder about this young spindly person named Lauren, and why everyone seemed to be falling in love with her, she looked so bird-like, a stork wading in a tide pool, while Agatha herself was more peacock-like, her extravagant clothing and hairdos, her voluptuousness, the rings on her fingers and the silver bracelets which orbited her wrists. She seemed to be in the center of the universe, or a universe of her own, self-contained, preoccupied, yet aware—vaguely—that there were others around her, lesser beings who existed simply to provide her with pleasure, often two or three at a time. There was rumor of a movie—Agatha having sex with two men— not students, older men, but no one had seen it, though some of the young men at school, who would lie about anything, described it in detail—a figment of their own fantasy world. Lauren was the anti-Agatha—accessible to everyone—and it was only a matter of time before they were seen making out in a booth in the back of Lloyd's Sweetshop on the Main Street of Greensboro. There was even a rumor that Lloyd had appeared in the video with Agatha.

Lloyd was over fifty, a former linebacker with a semipro football team, who never stopped eating. He weighed more than three hundred pounds, but he'd lost the will to keep in shape, and the three hundred pounds was mostly fat, while in his playing days it was mostly muscle. It was hard to imagine having sex with him without being smothered under his weight. Crushed, really. A pounding. Especially if you were a tall thin person like Lauren. How could you survive?

One afternoon Lauren returned from school and there was Lloyd sitting on the living room couch where all her mother's former boyfriends had sat and now Lauren realized that the person she heard in the bedroom with her mother the night before was this hunk of flesh whom she saw every other afternoon behind the counter of his sweetshop. If you wanted a job at Lloyd's you had to— it was unthinkable, but that's what people said. You had to—I can't say it—I can visualize Lloyd and I can't imagine how anyone could have sex with him. It made me think differently about my mother, to say the least, who was not a big person herself. All I wanted, in those days, was to bury my head between Agatha's legs, and stay there—I would have stayed in that position forever. I began going over to her house after school every afternoon. Once, she said, let's play a game, and she blindfolded me and tied me to the bed, with my legs spread. Then boys from school, who must have been waiting in the next room, climbed on top of me, one at a time. They paid Agatha for doing this—but I don't know how much. My reward was her. And as soon as I got home from Agatha's I had sex with my mother's boyfriend if he was around. It didn't matter anymore—whether I did it, or didn't—whether it was Lloyd or anyone else, and to be honest with you, I don't think my mother even cared. She returned home from work, had a few drinks, and fell asleep on the couch. That's how I'd find her, the TV going, a low hum of voices, all the lights burning brightly, and no one in sight.

Sadness on Ludlow Street

It doesn't matter where she went. There were probably stories about her, all the unmentionable things, which I was meant to write. I knew I would write them in the future, that writing about her would be part of my future, but I didn't know it would happen so soon. It's only when something's over that you can dream of writing about it. That you can't dream at all, even with your eyes closed, pretending to be asleep so that when a stranger enters the room and gets into bed with you you can roll over into her arms, just like you did with the person who's gone.

People aren't interchangeable. At least that's what we want to think. When I met Jennifer she didn't even own a skirt. Just some t-shirts and baggy pants and a sweatshirt two sizes too big. We went shopping together, at my insistence, on Lower Broadway, but being in clothing stores was confusing to her and made me feel claustrophobic, like I felt when I went shopping with my mother when I was a kid. Now I was the parent leading the child by the hand into a circle of hell where I didn't want to be. I didn't like the idea that I cared about the way she looked more than she did. She was comfortable not caring, it was part of the style that conformed to the way she felt, and I was confusing her by taking her hand like a parent and forcing her to change, to grow up, so to speak, into an icon of vanity. She cared about some sixties version of what a political activist looked like and that meant not giving a shit about the way she looked, even though it was the late nineties and part of the politics of the present moment involves an engagement in a relationship with yourself. Your sense of who you are is a form of politics. The image she emulated had faded into a caricature of a place in time that had as much relevance to the present moment as a song by Grace Slick. I had to lead her in the direction of the skirts and dresses which were usually in the back. A saleswoman in a black slip and perfect shoulders slid towards us and I waved her off. I had to choose a skirt for her and point to the dressing room but Jennifer always tried it on without even showing me. Finally I said, "this is it, just get this one." And she said: "I don't think it's going to fit." We left the store empty-handed and for a long time didn't say anything. It was up to me to buy her clothing for her birthday or Xmas. Otherwise she would wear the same thing every day. She would never have even changed except for the times she wanted to please me, which was a mistake, since the whole point was that I wanted her to please herself. She knew that I wanted to see her wear something other than t-shirt and jeans. It was also my mistake to impose what I wanted on her, some image I imagined that she was supposed to conform to, like a page out of a fashion magazine that would stimulate me into thinking she was someone else when we got into bed. I didn't want to accept her except in a diminished way without realizing that the only person I was diminishing was myself. If you don't love the person as she is get out of it. There are reasons for everything.

Things were not that simple for me then. It's already part of my past. My past, these days, let me say, is not high on my list. It's just there, like a train wreck, with a lot of cars piled up, and people screaming. The sound of ambulances in the distance and medics with stretchers. I want to blot out whole years as if they were part of a war, a skirmish on some different continent. Like in war movies, when the men on boats arrive and are ambushed by the enemy soldiers hiding with machine guns behind the bluff. But if you want to know what I was fighting about I can't answer, not truthfully, and it's not as if it still matters enough to go into detail about what I was feeling. Eventually, she went somewhere else, packed up and left, and that was that. We were together for a few years and then she was gone.

The first time she came to my house, with her cigarettes, which she rolled at the dining room table, and the first time we slept together, actually, when she walked in the door and I pushed her down on the bed. That goes back awhile but I can remember what she was wearing. She was hiding her beauty behind something, enclosed under a dome, the upper story of a dollhouse, and I wanted to get at it, saw a glimpse of what she might be like, some image I had of her, and wanted more. Her blondness was too blonde, her skin too pale. Her forehead had lines in it. She was worried about something but she wouldn't say what and it was only later I found out that it wasn't me she had fallen in love with but a person in her past who I resembled and who she had been in love with once before. The whole point was that I would reject her the way he had done. The pain was part of the fantasy. It wasn't important to be adored.

We went shopping for bad food but before we ate it we had sex with our clothing on. It was what we both wanted. I was the adult and she was the child, only a few years older than my oldest daughter. It was still possible, in the early days, to come and go as we pleased. I began to lie to her about what I was doing when we were apart. I was older but could merge with a part of myself that had stopped growing a long time ago, a half-brother hidden in the indentations beneath my skin. We dropped the food on a table and fell into bed. Sometimes we cooked food and had sex watching television. We had rituals that had to do with going into the world and working and returning home and making food. One of us would buy the food and one of us would cook it. We watched cop shows and ate in front of the TV and argued, mostly, about music.

It felt like if I touched her skin she would bruise. There were rashes on her skin. Stitches on her breast. "Let me touch them," I said. The problem was that I'd lived with someone else in this apartment and now she was here among the ghosts and echoes. I knew that if I were her I'd feel the same way. "Let's move," she said. "I want to move." But I didn't listen. I didn't want to lose the past

I'd had with this other person. I didn't want to liquidate what had happened before, even though it was I who had been hurt. The person whom I'd been living with in this apartment had left me but I didn't want to let the memory of it all go. Whenever I left my mark on her, I had the feeling we were the same person, holding on to the pain, reducing it to a headline on a scrap of newspaper that was floating across the pavement. Some detritus out of the past that seemed to hover over the present moment. Make it last, we both said, even if it causes us pain.

If you let go of your fantasies you'll die, I know that much. Whenever we fucked I assumed she was thinking of someone else. I always knew when she was about to come. She was concentrating on the image of someone else in her head. We had arguments about everything but it all amounted to nothing. There was a period where we had sex as soon as she walked in the door. Where we stayed in bed all afternoon, letting the phone ring, letting the messages add up. Jennifer said, "You can do whatever you want with me." I knew that meant I could hurt her, in ways I didn't even know about, and she would stay.

The last thing I imagined was that she would end up hurting me. She found out I was sleeping with others; that was the first prong in the sentence, like a German translation, where the verb follows the pronoun or comes at the end, a feeling of self-doubt when you know something's over but it's not. In this case, I let it happen and watched her suffer, saw her withdraw for a moment out of a sense of pride, and then return, as if, on her hands and knees, it was she who was begging me for forgiveness for betraying her. I wanted her there but I had a sense of commitment to myself that made it impossible not to betray her. The commitment to myself involved a commitment to others as well. I made excuses to myself, as if I had no other choice. I could see the pain in her eyes and I thought to myself: this is what she wanted. It was an unwritten contract, that she would stay with me no matter what happened.

You could say that I hurt her during the first two years that we were together, but there was an illusion of happiness and I was really there, inside the pleasure and the possibility that it might end, but living in the moment. Then we broke up, but only for a few weeks. During that time she called me every day. There was a possibility that my old girlfriend and I might get together again, the woman who had left and who was now pregnant with someone else's baby, someone she didn't love. The possibility of playing the role of father was part of it even though I already had two children who were older. It seemed like I wanted a person who acted younger than her age, who needed something I could give, as a father might, but in exchange for sex.

To say that I was "confused" or that I created a problem for myself was an understatement. It was my problem really. We broke up, and then I suggested we get back together. Not with pressure, but because I assumed it was something she wanted to do. She had made a scene when we broke up and then she had called me every day so I assumed it would please her. The new plan. I was committed, I wouldn't sleep with anyone else, I would always tell the truth. She hedged, but only for a moment. She still wanted something from me that had nothing to do with her feelings but with her identity, that it meant something to other people. I forgot how slowly she moved in her head. But it was really a way of letting her get back at me. Why not? I made myself vulnerable so she could even the score. We would live together and she would lie to me about everything as a way of getting back. As a final act of compensation, I fell in love with her so that she could hurt me if she wanted. I'd made a mistake, it was all a mistake, but I was trying to make things better. I felt guilty for hurting her in the past. It was my old-world self taking over, the guilt I'd inherited from my ancestral tribe. She was upset with herself for not breaking up with me when she found out about my past crimes so as a kind of delayed response she was enacting revenge when there was no reason to get back at me in the present. We were adding up the score. I wanted the ledger to add up—both sides. It had less to do with love, except for a moment or two, than with greed. How much can you endure? What is your capacity to deflect pain? How much unhappiness can you absorb without going crazy?

Sweet Sixteen

They were driving south on Route 13 through Maryland and Virginia when a blonde shirtless young man appeared with his thumb in the air on the side of the road. Elizabeth guided the car onto a strip of gravel fifty yards ahead of where he was standing, rested her arms on the steering wheel, and stared at his figure in the rearview mirror. As the man ran towards the car, dragging his duffel bag on the ground behind him, Maureen turned to her friend, adjusted her skirt over her knees, and said: "I trust your instincts, but he looks like a killer." The hitchhiker opened the back door, threw his duffel bag onto the seat, and climbed in.

"Thanks for stopping," he said, in a way that made it sound like he was doing them a favor by accepting the ride. "How far you going?"

As Elizabeth eased the car into the flow of traffic, the hitchhiker leaned forward, looking over the front seat at the bodies of the two women, trying not to be obvious but wanting them to know what he was doing. He carried with him the smell of pine cones or maple syrup, something musky, like he'd been rolling around naked on the ground.

Elizabeth told him that they were heading for the

North Carolina coast, the area known as The Outer Banks, a town called Nag's Head where her parents owned a house. They were going to spend a week in a house near the ocean.

For a few minutes they drove in silence, like characters in a pornographic movie, the two young women in short dresses up front, the bare-chested young man in the back looking out the window. What he saw when he looked were farms, some of them deserted, cornfields and vegetable stands, an occasional billboard warning of the evils of television—how it corrupted the morals of young people and would eventually lead to the end of the world. Then Maureen turned around and asked him where he was from. It was the usual question that a driver or passenger asks a hitchhiker but she couldn't think of what else to say.

"Canada," he said, mentioning the name of a city or province where neither Elizabeth nor Maureen had ever been.

Elizabeth, who had driven this route before, told them about a 25-mile long bridge spanning Chesapeake Bay and Maureen took out her old-fashioned Minolta and said she wanted to take some photographs when they crossed. Elizabeth didn't know how long it would be before they reached the bridge but she hoped it would still be light out. The hitchhiker, who hadn't told them his name or how far he was traveling, asked to see the camera and Maureen handed it back to him.

"I used to have one of these," he said.

He focused on the back of Maureen's head and when

she turned in his direction he snapped her picture.

"Hey," she said, "don't do that." She tried to sound annoyed, but she was smiling. "I look horrible."

From time to time, during the drive, Elizabeth and Maureen stared at one another covertly, or so they thought, trying to communicate their feelings and impressions of the hitchhiker without using words. Already they could imagine the dingy motel room where the three of them would spend the night: the glow of the TV, the spray of the shower on their backs, the smell of the sheets as they spread their legs.

They stopped for late lunch at a roadside diner called The Paradise Grill and Elizabeth and Maureen were surprised that the hitchhiker, whose name was Eddie (at least that's what he told them), had enough money to pay for himself. Before entering the restaurant, he fished in his bag for a clean work shirt which he buttoned up in the restaurant parking lot and tucked into his pants. They sat in a booth covered with blotchy chartreuse upholstery which stuck to their thighs, the two women facing him, and during the meal (omelets, cheeseburgers, French fries, milkshakes) Elizabeth felt the pressure of his foot against her ankle. Then his knee touched her knee, pressing against it firmly, and she didn't move away, but parted her legs slightly and pressed back, smiling at him. Over coffee he began to open up, telling them about the one time in his life he'd been in New York and how he got lost on the subway and ended up in Brooklyn.

"So you're from Brooklyn?" he said, shaking his head, as if he couldn't believe people actually lived in such a place. "To me it's just a place to get lost in, not to see."

Elizabeth said that the next time he came to New York she'd give him a tour of the city. He slouched in his seat, the leg of his jeans scratching the inside of her thigh, and told them that his parents had died in an auto accident when he was ten, and that's when he moved from Florida (where he was born, where he was heading) to Canada (where he was coming from) to live with relatives. As he talked, bumming one cigarette after another from Elizabeth's pack of Kool Lights, Maureen thought: I don't believe a word, it's all a big mistake. She could sense something was going on between the hitchhiker and her friend (the way he lit her cigarette, the way he addressed his words mainly to her), and she was jealous.

It was raining when they left the restaurant and Eddie offered to drive. They had stayed in the restaurant longer than they had planned and would never reach the bridge before dark. The car was a brand new Chrysler Le Baron which Elizabeth had rented in New York with her American Express card. It was silver, with gray trim, her favorite colors. Elizabeth sat up front and Maureen moved to the backseat. She fell asleep and Eddie took Elizabeth's hand and held it between them on the front seat as he steered with the other. Every few minutes she lit a cigarette with the dashboard lighter, one for herself, one for him. Maureen was still asleep, her head resting against Eddie's duffel bag. The rain had stopped, but the sky was one immense cloud, and some of the drivers passing in the opposite direction had already turned on their brights. There was a station on the radio playing songs from the fifties and sixties, music by groups of black women with names like the Shirelles and the Chiffons and the Ronettes, music that had been popular before Elizabeth, Maureen and Eddie were born.

Elizabeth asked him what movies he liked and he said he didn't like movies much, he liked sports if he liked anything, and so she said "What sports" and he said "Volleyball" though he'd never played it and Elizabeth said that she'd been the captain of the volleyball team when she was in high school and he said "You don't seem tall enough" and she said "I was the tallest person on my team." As if to prove a point, she pulled the hem of her short dress above her thighs and shifted her legs in his direction. He reached out and put his hand on her knee and looked at her for a moment, taking his eyes off the road just as a truck passed in the opposite direction with its brights shining in Eddie's face, blinding him slightly and forcing him to grab the steering wheel with both hands and turn it to the right to prevent a head-on collision. Elizabeth laughed, pulled her dress down, and straightened her legs so that her knees hit against the dashboard. When he offered his hand again she made a circle in his palm with her finger.

Elizabeth and Maureen had met when they were sophomores in high school and now they were going to be seniors in college and they were still friends. They had gone to different colleges but had stayed in touch. Elizabeth remembered at the end of their junior year in high school when Maureen called her up late one night to tell her she was no longer a virgin. She remembered enduring a lengthy description of what it had been like to have sex with her boyfriend Alex, how she had been drunk but not drunk enough not to know what they were doing. Maureen insisted that she had enjoyed it, that she was in love with Alex, that they were going to apply to the same college and live together in an apartment off-campus, none of which ever happened. Elizabeth remembered the night Maureen called her up from college to tell her she was pregnant, that she was going to have the baby even though she didn't know the identity of the father, and then calling her back the next night to say she was going to get an abortion. The towns where they were going to college, in upstate New York, were only fifty miles apart. Elizabeth picked up Maureen on the steps of her dormitory and drove her to the abortion clinic and waited in a lounge filled with comfortable threadbare sofas and armchairs and a brown mahogany coffee table with piles of magazines: *Vogue, The New Yorker*. There was only one other person in the lounge, a woman in her mid-thirties with prematurely white hair who was wearing a ring in the shape of a snake that curled the length of her middle finger. Elizabeth, unable to concentrate on her German lesson (she had an exam the next day) asked if she could see it. The woman, who was wearing sunglasses and turning the pages of a magazine with glossy reproductions of Renaissance paintings, looked up and smiled. "It's just some cheap ring I bought on the street," she said, crossing her legs. "You can have it if you like."

Eddie told her that his father had been in the army and that they had lived (he, his parents, and two sisters) on various army bases in the southwestern part of the United States until he was ten and the accident happened. He said the word "accident" and swallowed and then didn't say anything, forcing Elizabeth to ask: "What accident?" which is what he had intended her to do, giving him time to make up the story as he went along. Apparently his parents were driving home from a party with another couple and they were hit by a truck. Everyone died, including the truck driver. After that he was sent to live with his mother's brother in the city he had mentioned earlier, Port Elgin, on the coast of Lake Huron. Elizabeth moved closer to him, not knowing how much she believed of his story, not caring.

They were still a hundred miles from the house in Nag's Head when the cat leapt in front of the car. Eddie pressed down hard on the brakes and Maureen fell forward out of sleep and hit her forehead on the back of the seat. Each of them had heard a thud, the contact of the fender or tire with the body of an animal, but neither of them suggested they stop to see if the animal was alive. It could have been a raccoon or a skunk, but it had looked to both Eddie and Elizabeth like a big cat with bright eyes, more like a leopard or a cougar. Elizabeth wished she could be alone with Maureen, if only for a moment, so she could tell her everything she was feeling.

"I'm sorry I stopped so suddenly," Eddie apologized. "Are you O.K.?"

The motel was called Whispering Pines. It consisted of a dozen connected units, one story high, with a slanted tile roof, modest red brick in an L-shape around a tiny swimming pool. There was a grove of exhausted weather-beaten pinetrees behind the motel. A beach chair had fallen over onto the grass alongside the pool and some purple and yellow leaves floated on the water's surface. Maureen went into the office and paid for a room with her Visa card. As soon as they were alone in the car (it was the first time they had ever been alone), Eddie put his hand between Elizabeth's legs, biting down gently on her lower lip as his finger moved inside her. In the office of the motel a woman in pin curlers ("dead batteries" as they were called when Maureen and Elizabeth were in high school) asked how many people were going to sleep in the room and without hesitating Maureen said: "Two, me and my friend." Maureen asked the manager of the motel if there was any place nearby where she could buy some food. It was almost nine o'clock and everyone was hungry again. The manager told her that there was a strip of restaurants about a mile down the road: Bob's Big Boy, Hardees, KFC, Burger King, MacDonalds, Pizza Hut, Taco Bell. One after the other, maybe a drive-in bank or an auto supply store in between. Maureen didn't bother getting back into the car but pointed to Eddie to follow her to their room. He stopped the car outside the door which Maureen had opened and helped Elizabeth unpack the trunk, what they'd need for the night. Maureen offered to drive down the road to buy some food and bring it back to the room.

"You don't mind?" Elizabeth asked. "Shouldn't we all go?"

Maureen winked at her.

"Don't worry about me," she said. "Think about yourself for a change."

She went to the bathroom and locked the door behind her. She peeled the wrapper off a miniature bar of Ivory soap and washed her hands. Rubbed skin moisturizer over her face, put on lipstick, blush and mascara, changed from her white dress into jeans and a tank top. When she emerged from the bathroom fifteen minutes later, Eddie was sitting on the floor in front of the TV watching the Olympic Games, looking bored. Elizabeth was lying on the bed behind him. She was leaning back against the wall, skirt tucked between knees, brushing her hair.

Maureen drove past the strip of fast food restaurants. About a mile further down the road she saw a sign, Little Anthony's, and turned into the parking lot. She could hear a woman laughing out of control from a car parked nearby and music from behind the door of the bar, not live music, but a jukebox turned on full blast. The people in the bar were laughing and dancing. It was Saturday night. Most of the women in the bar were in their late twenties and wore long frilly cowgirl dresses or tight jeans with crocheted blouses. Many of them were divorced from their husbands and lived alone with their children and worked during the week while their children were in school. Some of them had dyed their hair to make them look younger. The men wore cowboy hats or baseball caps and didn't seem to pay much attention to the way they looked. Some of them had beards, some of them needed a shave, others were obviously more interested in drinking than dancing or picking up women. There was a group of men sitting at a table at the far end of the bar playing cards. There were women of all ages, though none as young as Maureen, carrying pitchers of beer and bowls of chips on trays and laughing with the customers who stood on the dance floor when the music came on.

Maureen found a place at the bar and ordered a Jack Daniels with ice. At the sound of her voice, obviously she wasn't from around here, the man to her right turned a full circle and tipped his hat. He asked her where she was from and she said New York City and he told her that he had been in New York a year ago to visit his sister who lived in Brooklyn. Saying you were from New York always inspired some kind of response. The top three buttons of his denim shirt were open. He was wearing a wide leather belt with a gold buckle and his face twitched slightly. When he caught her noticing his tic he said: "I do that when I'm nervous." He had a tattoo of a rose on his left wrist. His hair was thinning. He wore a ring that looked like a wedding band and when Maureen asked him if he was married he said his wife was dead. He smiled when he said it and Maureen felt like laughing in his face. She sipped her drink and he ordered another beer, calling the bartender by his first name. As she stared into the drink, Maureen saw the faces of her friend Elizabeth and the young man named Eddie whom they had picked up hitchhiking. She saw Elizabeth's black hair spread out on the pillow. She saw their bodies, surrounded by a silver glow, moving rhythmically on the unmade bed. Then a person who was a friend or acquaintance of the man at the bar came up from behind him and slapped him on the shoulder and said, "Why don't you introduce me to your friend," motioning to Maureen, but the first man, whose name was Rex, said: "I would, but I don't know her name," and Maureen smiled as his face jumped again and said "I'm Maureen," and the second man offered his hand and said, "I'm Davis, nice to meet you."

Maureen guessed that both these men were twice her age, forty or more, though she also knew that people who drank a lot usually looked older than they were. A Randy Travis song was playing on the jukebox and the man named Davis asked Maureen if she wanted to dance. She put down her glass on the bar, it was almost empty, anyway, and glanced back at Rex, whose face was going crazy. She rested her head on Davis's shoulder and could feel his breath against her cheek. It was a familiar smell, beer and smoke, but she didn't want to kiss him, not yet. He placed his hand on the small of her back and guided her in a slow circle around the dance floor, gyrating slowly with his hips to see if she would respond. Maureen pressed him closer, her hands on his ass. Then the first man, Rex, came up to them, pushing his way through the crowd of dancers,, holding a beer bottle by the neck, and tapped Davis on the shoulder. "My turn, friend," he said, though it was obvious he wasn't feeling very friendly. Davis looked at Rex with disgust and then at Maureen and said, "I'll be back, sweetheart, that's a promise," as if she cared one way or the other about either of them. A minute later the dance ended and a fast song came on and Rex, who had stepped on her toes twice, said: "I don't dance fast." He took her arm and tried to steer her back to the bar, but she slipped free and stood on the edge of the dance floor watching a black man and a younger white girl with blonde hair down to her waist. The black man was the only nonwhite person in the bar as far as Maureen could tell. He lifted the young girl in his arms and swung her around while the people on the sidelines stomped their feet and applauded. Then the man named Davis came up behind her and circled her waist with his arm. "It's my turn," he said to Maureen, kissing her on the side of the neck. "I'll show that nervous fucker how to dance."

Après Le Bain

"I wish I was marrying you instead of her," Richard said. He was sitting at the kitchen table in Deva's apartment drinking coffee from a porcelain cup she had brought back from Cancun. There was an empty vase, a glass ashtray, a container of skin milk, a box of Strike Anywhere, and a bowl of sugar on the wooden table.

Deva leaned back against the stove smoking a cigarette. She crossed her arms over her breasts and studied the back of Richard's head as he sipped his coffee.

"You can still come over for lunch," she said in response to his remark about getting married.

Richard worked as a clerk in a hardware store down the street from Deva's apartment and had been visiting her during his lunch hour, twice a week, for the last year and a half. He'd call at about ten, while she was still half-asleep, and ask if it was a good day for him to come over for lunch. "Lunch" meant going to bed together, it was the word they used to equate desire with hunger, and Deva couldn't remember ever saying no. It was a perfect arrangement, except that she had fallen in love with him, something she had promised herself she wouldn't do, and Richard had met someone else, a Swedish woman named

Britta who worked as an assistant producer for *Good Morning America*, an early morning television program which Deva had never seen. One of the reasons he was marrying Britta was because she promised to support him so he could quit his hated job at the hardware store where he'd been working for three years. The convenience of the arrangement between Richard and Deva had something to do with the proximity of Richard's job to her apartment, but neither of them knew how much. When he told her he was quitting his job on Friday and getting married on Saturday she was tempted to ask—*When will we see each other?*—but didn't. She could hear the desperation in her voice even before she opened her mouth.

Richard squinted morosely into the depths of the coffee cup. There was no handle on the cup and the heat of the coffee was burning his fingers. He remembered the day Deva told him about her trip to Cancun, how envious he had felt. "I've never been anywhere," he said, though this was only partially true. He'd spent a month in Alaska when his father was in the hospital, an afternoon in Tijuana, a weekend with a girlfriend whose parents owned a house in Key West. He was born in a suburb of Boston and had lived there with his mother and stepfather until he was seventeen. Then he went to college in upstate New York but it was too cold so he transferred to a college in Jacksonville, Florida but never graduated (his stepfather once called him a "faggot" because he liked to read poetry). He and Britta were flying to Los Angeles after the wedding (she had to interview the wife of a soap opera star who had died in a boating accident) and then to Hawaii for a week. Richard wanted to stay longer, especially since her parents were paying for it all, but Britta was worried about losing her job.

He had assumed that this would be their last lunch hour together, that when he told Deva he was planning to get married she would end their relationship. Certainly, no one could blame her for not wanting to share him with someone else. Not only was he quitting his job but he was moving out of his studio apartment on Ludlow Street into Britta's co-op in the West 90s. It was a much larger apartment, with a terrace and a team of doormen patrolling the lobby, and he could have his own room, with a view of Central Park. If he and Deva wanted to see one another again it meant he would have to make a special trip downtown. It also meant that they were free of the parameters of the lunch hour ("is it a good time?") which had previously defined their relationship. When she said that he could still come over whenever he liked, even though he was getting married, he turned in his chair and spilled the coffee down the front of his shirt. "Are you kidding?" he asked. Incredulous, childlike. Deva crossed the room with a paper towel and wiped the front of his shirt so it wouldn't stain. As she bent over him, Richard untied the belt of her robe and pressed the side of his face against her stomach. "I don't joke about things like this," Deva said. Britta, Richard was thinking, often left for work at six in the morning, and didn't return home until seven or eight o'clock at night. Enough time to take the subway downtown to visit Deva whenever he wanted. If Britta called him at home he could always say he had gone for a walk in the park.

They were getting married on Saturday, in a town north of the city where Britta's parents owned a restaurant on a hill overlooking the Hudson. Both Britta and Deva were thirty years old. Richard was a year younger, but looked older than both of them. His hair was prematurely gray and he was beginning to put on weight. Since he met Britta, who didn't like to cook after working all day, who had grown up in a household where food and restaurant business was all anyone talked about, he had been eating out almost every night. "Too much restaurant food," he said, as he sucked in his stomach in front of Deva's mirror. The first time he visited Deva she had even prepared a real lunch for him, thinking that lunch meant eating food, and that he would be hungry after working all morning. But five minutes after he arrived they were rolling around on the kitchen floor. "Let's go into the bedroom," she had said, her willingness to comply registering as an aftershock to her own needs, "it'll be more comfortable." (After he left, and without realizing what she was doing, she sat at the kitchen table and devoured a bowl of avocado salad and a plate of prosciutto and melon, the food she had prepared for both of them and which neither had touched.) Sometimes they had sex leaning against the kitchen table or sitting half-dressed in one of the kitchen chairs. He arrived at five minutes after twelve, out of breath from running up the three flights of stairs (anticipating the pleasure was part of the excitement), and she greeted him at the door in a nightgown or a robe or a slip. It was only the first half-hour that they could concentrate on sex; after that, she could tell he was thinking about having to leave. Sometimes they made love twice, quickly up against the stove or table, and then a bit more leisurely in her bed, ending with just enough time for him to pull up his pants, run down the stairs, and get back to his job.

In the days before he met Britta he had been concerned about alienating his boss at the hardware store. He hated the job, hated the wisecracks of his boss and his coworkers ("There must have been a special on pussy today") when he came in late, as if they could smell it on him or see Deva's reflection in his eyes, or read his mind. When Britta offered to support him, at least for a year while he worked on his stories, he realized that practical considerations, when it came to marriage, was as good a reason as being in love. In his past relationships, he had been the person who had fallen in love first, who had opened himself to the possibility of being hurt. And he had been hurt. Most of his previous girlfriends had deserted him for other lovers. He had the bad habit of falling in love with everyone he slept with. He couldn't imagine sleeping with someone and never seeing the person again. His girlfriends were often shocked at his willingness to commit himself to a relationship where the only thing in common was an interest in sex. All they had wanted was someone to sleep with for a single night — and here he was practically suggesting that they live together. His willingness to express his feelings, whether they were genuine or not, scared them away.

Britta didn't know how Richard spent his lunch hours. She had to wake at five to be in the TV studio before the show began. Her job, interviewing and researching pseudo-celebrities to determine whether they were suitable to appear on the show, was "all consuming," as Richard sometimes described it to Deva, and she was too distracted to keep track of how her future husband spent his days. Sometimes she didn't return home until eight at night. Working in television involved endless meetings, conference calls, lunches, dinners. She had been attracted to Richard because he didn't seem like the type who would pressure her to choose between their life together and her job. He didn't need her attention, nonstop, the way other men did. Most of her previous boyfriends expected her to act like their mothers. Richard made it clear that he had no interest in sabotaging her career. Neither of them wanted children, not yet, anyway, if ever. She was anxious for him to quit his job at the hardware store. She offered to support him while he worked on his novel. She had read copies of the stories and poems he had written before they met and had decided, though she hardly qualified as a judge, that he had some talent. More than that, maybe. Her plan was to encourage him to write stories that were accessible to a lot of people. She fantasized about being married to a best-selling novelist. She wanted her husband to be someone who she could introduce to her friends at the TV station. Someone with stature. Maybe she could even help him get a job writing for a soap opera? She imagined herself as Richard's muse, the person to whom he would dedicate his books. "For Britta, without whom nothing is possible," was her favorite imaginary dedication. Many of her friends from ABC were coming to the wedding and if any of them asked Richard what he did she prayed he would tell them he was a writer.

Britta had given him a set of keys to her apartment so he could go there after work. Either they'd meet back in her apartment or she'd call him at the store during the day. She always tried to call him at least once a day under the pretense of asking where he wanted to meet her for dinner. Richard preferred Indian food but Britta didn't like to travel downtown after work. She didn't want to go to Chinatown either. She insisted there were Chinese restaurants on the Upper West Side that were as good as the restaurants in Chinatown, but Richard knew this wasn't true. All the best Japanese restaurants were downtown as well. He eventually acquiesced; wherever you want to eat is fine with me. He felt like they had already been married twenty years and had exhausted every possible topic of conversation except what to eat for dinner and where to go. Some nights when they met at the restaurant of choice she would surprise him by ordering only an appetizer or a small salad. Apparently she'd already eaten something at the station—"I was starving, I couldn't wait"—and wasn't hungry. Richard preferred eating alone to eating with someone who was just drinking but he swallowed his food with alacrity and told her how good it was and brushed the crumbs from the corner of his mouth and offered her a taste and refilled her wineglass from the carafe he had ordered and poured a bit more for himself. He ate and drank continuously to avoid going crazy.

The apartment on Ludlow Street was one medium-sized room with a loft bed. There was a separate bathroom with a shower, a small kitchen alcove, high ceilings. The desk where he worked was an old door propped on gray filing cabinets. What he longed for most in life was a desk with drawers, maybe an old secretariat with numerous tiny compartments where he could file all his papers. He and Britta would walk passed an antique furniture store and Richard wold point out a desk he liked and she would say, "Let me buy it for you." She once visited him in his apartment and couldn't get over his old laptop. For Christmas, she thought to herself, that's what I'll get him.

A desk, a chair, a new computer—what else did he need? He was subletting the apartment on Ludlow Street to a friend of his brother's, leaving all the furniture behind, even the radio, TV and DVD player. The only things he was taking up to Britta's was his computer, his books and papers, a trunk filled with clothing. He had been in the apartment for seven years but he wouldn't miss any of it.

Some new people, a couple, had moved upstairs about a year before and they liked to play music late at night, jazz mostly, so loud he could feel the ceiling vibrate. He could hear bedsprings creaking as they had sex at five in the morning. He could hear them fighting, what sounded like plates smashing against the kitchen wall. The next day Richard invariably saw them in the street with their arms around each other as if nothing had happened. The man had a blonde ponytail and a beard and never acknowledged that Richard was his neighbor no matter how frequently they passed in the hallway. His companion, a small dark-haired woman with bright eyes and a mole under her lower lip, was more outgoing. Once they met at the mailboxes and she asked Richard if all the noise bothered him. She looked at him wide-eyed, apologetic, and Richard interpreted her gaze as a cry for help. At least that's what he wanted to believe. He tried to catch a glimpse of her neck under her sweater to see if she had any visible bruises. He wanted to think she was asking him to help her escape her lover, but he couldn't be sure.

The anxiety attacks occurred without warning. Sometimes there was a specific reason: Britta would call Richard at the store or at his apartment and he wasn't there. She would hear his voice on the answering machine and feel like the slightest breeze could blow her away. Often, she would hang up without leaving a message. As far as she knew, he was dead, or with another lover. It was the uncertainty of it all that made her heart quiver; she raced to the bathroom to be alone with her imaginary fears. She wanted to throw up, but couldn't. She knelt in front of the toilet bowl until the pain in her chest subsided. She had lied enough to others in her own life to know how easy it was to deceive someone. She had no evidence that Richard was lying to her but she knew if she looked hard enough for a sign of betrayal she would find it somewhere. The man at the store, Richard's boss, hung up on her when she began questioning him.

She had the feeling that Richard was pretending not to be there in order to torture her. She never knew for certain whether the person she talked to would tell Richard she called. There was no certainty he would get the message and call back. When she finally spoke to him, later, she would ask, in the calmest of voices, where he had been when she called, and he would say, deadpan: "I was on a break" or "I went for a walk." There was no way she could keep track of what he was doing every second of the day. He wasn't a dog, after all, with a leash and a collar, but maybe that's what she needed. She had a dog once, but it was killed in an accident. It had run into the street and was hit by a truck.

"Why don't you take the whole day off?" Deva said.

He had told his boss at the hardware store that he was quitting on Friday. There was no reason why he couldn't call him today and tell him he was never coming back. They would deduct some money from his last paycheck, but what did it matter? He went into Deva's bedroom, carrying the cup from Cancun, and dialed the number of the store. Deva followed him, draping her robe over the back of a chair. She sat down beside him on the bed and put her hand down the front of his pants. He wondered what Britta would think when she called him at work and his boss or one of his coworkers told her he had quit. Maybe she would change her mind and cancel the wedding?

HOLY CITY

She had been teaching for twenty years and in all that time she had only slept with one student, a young woman named Arlette. It was during the time in her life that she referred to as "the worst time" when talking with friends. Between marriages, she was living alone in an apartment in Brooklyn, a ramshackle neighborhood near the Gowanus Canal. The smell of the water from the canal pervaded her small railroad apartment, combining with the smells of her two cats. "It was my most reclusive period," she once told me, apropos of nothing. It was the apartment where Arlette came to see her after school.

Carla taught French in a private high school in Brooklyn Heights. Her first novel, published when she was fifty, is dedicated "to A." By the time the book came out she and Arlette were no longer in touch. There was a rumor that Arlette was married and living in Detroit. After the book was published, Carla was tempted to send a copy to Arlette, with the secret hope that it would inspire her to visit her again, like in the old days. Carla herself had remarried and was living with her husband on the Upper West Side of Manhattan. I had never met her husband who was in his early sixties and worked as an executive in a bank near Wall Street. If Arlette ever came to town she and Carla could always meet for an afternoon in a hotel. That's what she would say when we went out drinking together.

The novel was about an older teacher who falls in love with a student. It was more than a thinly disguised recounting of her relationship with Arlette. She had written it in a moment of deep despair, not long after she married Seth, her new husband, in an attempt to recapture that moment in her life when everything seemed bathed in starlight, when she could name all the planets and the stars and the constellations, when it seemed like all the stars, moons and planets were perfectly aligned, that for the first time in her life she was getting what she really wanted. It wasn't easy to stand in front of a classroom, day after day, and deny your attraction to the bodies of the young women and men staring up at you. They gave you the impression, approaching your desk after class or visiting you unexpectedly in your office, that they would do anything you wanted—all you had to do was ask. In the book, Carla changed Arlette's name to Simone. She was no longer teaching so she wasn't frightened of people's responses to a book about a teacher who seduces a student. She wasn't frightened that anyone would think she was writing from her own experience.

What Carla implies in her book was that the student had seduced her. It was the young girl, only fifteen, her hair tied back in a French braid, who invited herself over to her teacher's apartment after school, who asked for a glass of Merlot and drank it down in one long gulp and then asked for another, who lay on her bed with her pleated skirt bunched up around her waist, who sucked on Carla's fingers, each one, and then placed Carla's hand between her legs.

"At any moment," Carla said, "I could have told her to go home." She paused to look at herself in the mirror behind the bar where we had gone for a drink to celebrate the publication of her book. "But I didn't."

It was hard for me not to feel empathetic with her. Hard not to identify. It's no accident that Carla and I are friends. There was a time, soon after we first met, where it seemed we might become lovers as well. It's hard to become lovers with a person with whom you've been friends a long time. Both of us knew that if we became lovers it might end badly and we would stop being friends. Neither of us wanted to take the risk of losing what we had. We depended on one another—for something, possibly, that no one else in our lives could give.

I had been teaching in a small college in Brooklyn for about ten years when it happened. The class in twentieth century European literature ended at 8:40 at night and Laura—that wasn't her name—came to my office afterwards. There was no one in the building except for the janitorial staff and a few security guards. We weren't supposed to smoke but I opened the window of my office and we lit up. She came to my office ostensibly to go over one of her papers. She wanted to improve her writing, how could I help her? How could I not? We sat side by side in my office while I pointed out her grammatical mistakes. Sometimes she lost control of her sentences, inserted commas instead of periods, forgot to create paragraphs. I told her that she was writing too fast, that she should try to be more methodical about her work. It went on like that for awhile, with her coming to my office after class. We sat very close together and occasionally she put her hand on my arm to get my attention, to interrupt me. I had the tendency to just go on, as if I were still lecturing in front of the classroom.

It wasn't long before we began sending e-mails to one another. Again, it was she who initiated the correspondence. There was a misunderstanding about one of the writing assignments, at least that was the pretext. I had told the class to write a paper applying the quote from Plato, "The unexamined life is not worth living," to the works of European literature we had read that semester: *The Death of Ivan Ilych* by Tolstoy, *Metamorphosis* by Kafka, *Death in Venice* by Thomas Mann, "The Dead" by James Joyce and "To Room Nineteen" by Doris Lessing. I had planned to include Camus' *The Stranger* but we had run out of time. The question involved the word "unexamined" — she wasn't sure what that meant.

My wife had gone to the Berkshires to visit her brother for the weekend so for the moment, as I read Laura's e-mail, I had the illusion I was free. It was a taste of what it would be like, I realized, if my marriage ever ended. As in the case of Carla and Arlette, it was Laura who invited me over to her apartment. I know that this is no excuse, that no one will believe me if I say that nothing would have happened if she hadn't called me and invited me over, but I'm saying it anyway. It was my job to shift gears no matter what the student wanted. There has to be something wrong with a student to invite her teacher to her house.

She lived in the depths of Brooklyn, some neighborhood where I'd never been. As soon as she invited me over I realized that it was what I had wanted all along and I wasn't afraid of anything. It occurred to me for a moment that I was misreading the situation and that she just wanted me to come to her apartment so I could help her with one of her papers. But hadn't we already kissed in the office after class? She had stretched out on my desk and let me touch her breasts. I'm the older, mature person and I should probably have backed away. I often had fantasies about sleeping with one of my students but I never propositioned anyone. As soon as she invited me over I knew I would go. I would go even if my wife was in town. Lie to her, say anything. I knew that I was risking a lot: my job, my marriage. No one would believe me if I said that she had invited me over, that there was no coercion on my part, but who would care?

Her name was Laura. Of course, that's not her real name. She had been in one of my classes and then she dropped out and instead of failing her I gave her an incomplete. She came back a semester later and began making up the work she had missed. This involved coming to my office, not only at night but in the middle of the day when other students and teachers were around. She would come to my office in between classes. One of my colleagues—someone I confided in, who I thought was my friend—told me I was taking a big chance, that if anyone found out I'd be fired on the spot, but at the moment it seemed worth the risk. The time I spent with

Laura, in my office and the few times we met in her apartment, gave my life meaning.

"All I care about is this," Laura once said, in my office, pressing my hand between her legs. She didn't seem to care about what might happen if we were caught. She didn't seem to realize that my job might be in jeopardy. I had the feeling she was telling all her friends that she was having sex with her former teacher. I began thinking that the students I passed in the hallway were laughing at me behind my back. Pointing a finger in my direction when they thought I wasn't looking.

Even so, my relationship with Laura ended after a few months. She left the city for the summer and met someone else, someone closer to her own age, and in the fall she dropped out of school again. For awhile, after she dropped out, we continued to talk on the phone, maybe once every two weeks. Then I left town and that was that. The idea that we might never see one another made me sad for awhile and more than one night I spent lying awake remembering her body. I was thirty years older than she was but she never once referred to our age difference when we were together. If she didn't care about it why should I?

I began to fantasize about what might happen if I was living alone. It's typical of people who are married for many years to forget what being alone is really about. How hard it is, especially after you've lived with someone a long time. If I lived alone Laura could visit me any time. (What I forgot, of course, was that if I was available Laura wouldn't be interested; marriage created the context where desire could take place. Once I was free that desire would no longer exist.) My wife and I had been married fifteen years and we had sex maybe twice a month. The absence of sex didn't seem important to our relationship. Something else was more important but I couldn't really define what that was. We had many interests in common and we never argued about petty things. I imagined renting a one-bedroom apartment, hopefully with a garden, in one of the neighborhoods on the outskirts of Brooklyn, or possibly even in Queens, where I didn't know anyone, and that after some time had passed Laura could move in with me. I knew that as long as I stayed married nothing would ever change. I was fifty years old and if anything was ever going to change it had to be now. I lay awake, my wife sleeping beside me, and reviewed the contours of Laura's body, the way she sat on my lap in my office with her shirt unbuttoned, the way she unfastened my belt. Once, in her apartment, she asked me to hit her on the back with my belt, and when I refused to do it she got angry. Not long afterwards she went away.

Carla told me that she and Arlette used to lie in bed in the afternoon, with the windows closed so you couldn't smell the dead bodies in the Gowanus Canal, and that Arlette would tell her stories about all her lovers, most of them classmates who Carla also knew, but some older men as well, fathers of her friends. She had lost her virginity when she was twelve with her older sister's boyfriend who had come to her parents' apartment thinking her sister was home. At least that's what he said. Later, when they were in bed together, he confessed that he knew her sister

Samantha wasn't going to be home, that he had come to see her, Arlette, but that he was too shy to make the first move. It was only when they were in bed together that he felt he could be honest with her.

It was after they had sex for the first time that Arlette realized her older sister and her boyfriend Tony had never made love before, even though they'd been going out together for almost a year. She realized, when she first let him in and they sat together on the living room sofa, that Tony had really come to the apartment to see Arlette, that was the truth, but now that they were together he was frightened to touch her.

It was Arlette who said: "I had a dream about you the other night," and when Tony said, "What happened in the dream?" Arlette started laughing. One of them had to say something to break the ice. It was Arlette who took Tony's hand and led him down the hallway to her bedroom at the end of the apartment. She was twelve but looked older when she wore make-up and she had been experimenting with her sister's eye shadow when the doorbell rang and there was Tony, too nervous to say what he wanted. For a moment Arlette had the feeling that Tony wasn't even going to enter the apartment. "Is Samantha home?" he asked, and when it was obvious she wasn't home (he knew she wouldn't be home), he started walking away.

"You can wait for her if you like," Arlette said.

She had been aware of Tony's interest in her for awhile. Whenever he came to the apartment to pick up Samantha he stared longingly in her direction. Arlette was aware that men on the street were watching her as she walked by. She could sense Tony's gaze following her whenever she left the room. Whenever she took the subway she was aware that men were staring. What she wanted most was to have sex with someone she didn't know. To meet someone on the subway and go home with that person. A room with a mattress on the floor, lights out, the tip of a cigarette glowing in the dark—two strangers.

"You're the first woman I've ever slept with," she told Carla.

The sun was going down over Brooklyn, it was almost winter, and she had to be home for dinner. Usually, Carla called a car service to take Arlette home to the apartment in Brooklyn Heights where she lived with her parents. Her older sister, Samantha, was away at college. Apparently Samantha never forgave Arlette for sleeping with Tony. She had found out about it by reading Arlette's journal. They had never been very close before this happened so it didn't seem like a major loss. Nothing to lose when there was nothing there to begin with. Arlette hadn't told anyone, except for her closest friend Kristin, that she was sleeping with Carla.

It was Arlette who had made the first move. There was a book in French that she wanted to borrow from her teacher. That was the excuse. Arlette waited outside the school and they drove to Carla's apartment, with the smell of the murky water. There was a rumor that there were dead bodies at the bottom of the canal. That Mafioso hit men dropped the bodies of their victims in the canal. Dumped them there in the middle of the night. The water had a green film covering the surface that reflected nothing.

She was lying on Carla's bed, drinking wine, listening to a record of Edith Piaf. It was during a time when Carla thought she would never sleep with anyone again, man or woman. She was between marriages, but still recovering from the hurt of the marriage that had ended. She never dreamed that she would fall in love with one of her students. And a girl, no less. She had fooled around with girls in college, but nothing serious. She had married a few months after graduating college and it had lasted twenty-five years. She had a child, a girl, older than Arlette, who was studying art history at Brown. Presently, she was in Italy for her junior year. She was in Florence, living with an Italian family. Maybe it was because her daughter Melissa was so far away that she craved the company of the younger girl. That's what Carla talks about in her novel, the reasons she didn't tell the girl to leave. That she was lonely for her daughter. It was raining out and they were listening to the music and drinking wine when Arlette reached for her hand and took each of Carla's fingers into her mouth one at a time. You could see the Gowanus Canal from her fourth story window, the lights of the boats in the distant harbor, the housing projects in Red Hook. From the roof of her building you could see The Statue of Liberty. The younger woman reached out and touched the older woman's hair, tugged at it gently. It was early autumn and they spent the winter together in bed, the older woman and the younger girl, two or three afternoons a week. It wasn't the end of the world, but it was something.

NONE OF THE ABOVE

It was the summer of 2005. She was living in a small town in Western Massachusetts with her parents, Otto and Georgia. People would call her up and ask her to baby-sit. She had a boyfriend named Leon whom she had known since she was a kid. One night he picked her up from a baby-sitting job in his white Volvo station wagon, a late 90's model, with his friend Mark. Mark was a transfer student from a high school in Los Angeles and had lost his virginity when he was twelve with a friend of his mother. His front tooth was chipped and he had excema on his cheeks and hands. There was a rumor that he also slept with men.

Alicia had been looking forward to spending the night with Leon. What was Mark doing there? She bit her lip and didn't say anything. She didn't want to make Leon angry—he had a bad temper, even as a child, breaking his toys when he didn't get his way and thrashing out blindly at whoever was around him. And as a boyfriend, he was erratic, moody, rarely affectionate, and often showed up late to their dates. Sometimes they just drove around for hours, listening to the radio, not saying anything. He never even came inside the house anymore to chat with Otto and Georgia, not that they cared. He drove up to her house, honked the horn, and she came out. Her parents didn't let her go out much at night during the school week so sometimes—when Leon's mother wasn't home—she went over to his place after school. They listened to CDs, mostly bands from the 60's like The Doors, and had sex in his bedroom.

She had seen Mark around school but they had never talked. Leon called her on her cellphone at the house where she was baby-sitting and they made plans to meet later that night. But he neglected to tell her he was bringing his friend.

"Call me when they get home," he said, "and I'll come and get you."

He picked her up after midnight outside the house of the Wysacks, Regina and Michael. The Wysacks lived on Rutland Road with their three year old daughter Fiona. They were part of a Polish community, an extended family of cousins, who had settled in the town over the last decade. Alicia's father was a mix of French and German and didn't have kind words for the Poles, but Georgia, whose family originated in Canada and then settled in Minneapolis, liked them for their blondness, their pale meaty features. "They all look like butchers," Alicia once heard her say.

The Wysacks drank a lot. There was a bar in the living room stocked with bottles of vodka, bourbon, rum. They would go to parties at the houses of their cousins and come home drunk. Alicia was amazed they didn't crash their car into a tree or swerve off the road into a gully. She had the feeling that they didn't get along. Michael Wysack was at least ten years older than his wife. He had no neck, a receding hairline, and a double chin. He had played center for his high school football team in Pittsburgh and had suffered more than one concussion as well as a leg injury which derailed his career in his senior year. He walked with a limp and was addicted to Oxycodeine to kill the pain. He heard voices in his head shouting out signals and he could still hear the buzz of the crowd in his ears. His eyes were different colors—one hazel, one blue.

Regina had married him to escape an abusive father. She had had sex with her father and her uncle for two years, age fifteen to seventeen, but Michael didn't know this. She had been tempted to tell him when they first met and then she realized he would kill them if he knew. He would end up with a life sentence and her chance for normalcy (whatever that meant) would be gone. Of course she might meet someone new when he was in jail, but who would want to marry her once the story of her life became public knowledge? She had married Michael Wysack with the promise that they leave Pittsburgh—that's where her father and his brother Alvin lived. She was very blonde and skinny and wore short skirts and halters in the hope that someone might find her attractive. Her chin was pointy and she didn't know what to do with her hair so she let it hang down her back or occasionally tied it in a ponytail. When she stared at herself in the mirror with her hair hanging loose she pretended she was a cheerleader in high school—that's what she'd been doing when Michael saw her for the first time. He was coming back to his old alma mater and there she was on the sidelines kicking her long legs into the air and shouting the name of the school. Michael was just recovering from an operation on his left leg. The first time they had sex she told him to just lie there and she would do everything. She was interested in what it might feel like to have sex with someone other than her father or uncle. Michael had been all-state as a high school football player and there were always recruiters in the stands to check him out. Her neighbors were impressed when Regina told them they were getting married. She went around talking to herself in her head. "Fuck you," she would say, addressing her father and her Uncle Alvin. It was all she could think about when she was having sex with her crippled husband.

Alicia could imagine Regina and Michael fighting and breaking things. Once they came home and it was obvious that Regina was crying about something. She ran upstairs, clutching the front of her dress, without even saying hello. And once Michael ("call me Mike") offered to drive her home. Regina had gone upstairs again and Alicia could smell the alcohol on his clothing from across the room. As if someone had spilled a drink down the front of his shirt. Part of her was tempted to say yes, you can drive me home, just to see what might happen. Yet another part of her knew it was a bad idea. The last thing she wanted was to be alone with Michael Wysack in his car. He was too big and too strong and she wouldn't be able to defend herself if he tried anything.

Years later, when she was living in New York, she would remember all of them. She would lie in bed and the faces of everyone in the town would flash through her memory. Not just the other students but all her teachers, Mr. Allen, the school principal, who was having an affair with the school librarian, Constance Liu, and all the couples whose children she tended while they were out getting drunk and flirting with each other's spouses. It excited her, especially, to think of the night Leon picked her up and she had sex with the two boys in the backseat of Leon's car.

She remembered that it was raining on the roof of the car and how the flashes of lightning over the treeline illuminated the dashboard and how afterwards she got out of the car, pulled up her skirt, and peed in the grass while the boys watched. Leon lit a joint and passed it to Mark. Then the boys got out of the car and stood in the rain. Leon unzipped his pants and Alicia knelt in front of him while Mark looked on and Leon peed on her face. Then Mark took his turn and she opened her mouth as the stream of urine passed from his body to hers and the rain poured down on all of them.

Her parents were out when she got home that night. They didn't seem to care if she stayed out late. It wasn't like the city where you might be raped walking home from the subway. It was less dangerous in the country. There was an occasional break in, a drug bust, domestic violence, but no homicides. When she first started going out, her mother asked her to call if she was going to come home "after midnight." But whenever Alicia called one of her parents on their cellphones, no one answered. She left a message: "I'll be home by one, don't worry."

She couldn't escape the feeling that her parents didn't care about what she did. It was something she had felt since she was a child. She couldn't explain it, really, but there was something stagnate in the air of all the houses she lived in with her parents, first in Boston, a one-bedroom apartment in the South End, and then in North Adams, Mass., where Otto drove a taxi, and now here in Hartsdale, where her parents finally settled when she was seven. Leon had been one of her first friends in town. Georgia would drive her over to Leon's house and dump her on the lawn. Leon's mother sat on an old rusty beach chair at the edge of her tiny swimming pool, wearing a bikini, smoking a cigarette and drinking a glass of orange juice laced with vodka, though who would ever know, and waved as Georgia drove away. The next week Leon's mother would drop him off at her house, and they would play together in the basement, mostly board games, Monopoly and Clue.

Years later, she remembered the smell of the rain and the ache in her lower back as first Leon, then Mark, climbed on top of her in the car. Mark was the bigger of the two and her head banged against the door handle as he pushed against her. Happily, he came quickly. "Oh shit," he said, "I'm coming," and pressed even harder. He was unaware that he was causing her discomfort, or knew and didn't care, and Alicia had the feeling he was embarrassed for coming so quickly. She knew that it was a matter of pride, something the boys could brag about. How long could you fuck without coming and then how many times you could have sex in one night. The boys talked about these things incessantly among themselves. They lied to one another. Twenty minutes, a half hour. We did it three times. But the girls talked as well. Her girlfriend Joan told her that the senior class president, Avril Johanneson, had trouble getting an erection, and that she ended up giving him a hand job instead. Leon went first while Mark stayed in the front seat. He pushed her skirt up around her waist and pulled her underpants down over her legs. He had long stringy black hair and the skin on his face was prickly where he forgot to shave. His lips were very close to her ear and when he came he bit the side of her neck. It made her want to scream. It seemed like he was inside her for about thirty seconds before he started coming but that the actual orgasm lasted about five minutes. The only time she'd had an orgasm was when she masturbated before going to sleep and so she had some idea what Leon was experiencing. The way it all built up out of nowhere. When it was over, when she had fucked both of them, the car smelled like smoke, stale cigarette butts and weed in the ashtray, and beer, empty beer cans on the floor of the front seat. The residue of everything was in that car. And now it smelled like sex. Licorice sex.

She wondered what they would tell their friends. How they would brag about what they had done and how word would get around that Alicia Germaine had let them pee on her. It was just a matter of time before everyone at the school found out. Being with two guys at once made a good story. But the fact that the other thing had happened was something else. And it was the other thing that interested her the most, that excited her when she thought about it afterwards. She could see them laughing with their friends at a table in a corner of the school cafeteria. She assumed, though it wasn't necessarily true, that they were laughing about her.

The night in the rain marked the end of her relationship with Leon, but a few weeks later Mark asked her if she wanted to go somewhere and "fool around." She made up an excuse—she couldn't imagine having sex with him again—but as he turned away she saw the rash on the side of his face and for a moment she wanted to reach out and touch it. As if she had the power to heal someone, to clear the scars from his skin with a touch of her fingertips. If he hadn't told anyone what had happened in the rain he'd certainly do it now. Both Leon and Mark had used condoms but she wanted something different, an experience that was out of the ordinary, or what she thought of as "ordinary," not to get pregnant like everyone else and have a baby when she was sixteen or go to Boston and get an abortion. Weren't there any other options? She wanted to do something no one else had done, to amaze everyone in the "have done" column, as if anyone cared. If someone asked how far did you go you could say "all the way," but there was more than that, there had to be. "All the way" was just the first stop on the map.

Maybe there wasn't anything else. It was a deadening thought. She had already done enough. It was graduation day. Most of her friends were going to college in Boston but she had opted for New York. There were all the parents of all the graduates sitting out in the sun. She was getting the prize for languages. She had studied Italian, German, Spanish and French. She could speak French fluently, and read the others. She knew enough vocabulary to get by if she ever visited any of the countries where these languages were spoken. She even knew some Latin. She had asked her parents for a summer in Europe as a graduation present, or even two weeks. They claimed they didn't have enough money, that they had taken out a loan to help pay for her college. Also, the idea of their only child traveling alone though Europe, which is what Alicia wanted to do, frightened them. There were stories about young women who had disappeared—kidnapped and sold as a sex slave to the highest bidder. There were terrorists in every country and as an American you were a marked person.

She felt an ache in her heart for something that hadn't happened. She was only eighteen but she felt like she had lived a long time. It made her wonder whether she had been someone else in another life and that some part of this other person's life had carried over into her. It was like someone had injected a serum under her skin for a disease that she didn't know she had. She would wake up in the middle of the night covered with sweat and then, unable to fall back to sleep, sit in a chair at the window of the apartment she shared in New York, smoke a cigarette and listen to the sounds of night, the occasional high-pitched siren playing in the distance, growing louder before fading away. Her roommate, Alexandra, was sleeping over at her boyfriend's. She had met Alexandra through an ad on the internet. They both attended New York University. Alexandra was a year ahead and was majoring in psychology. Alicia was still studying languages but was also majoring in nineteenth century French literature.

It was because of Fred Lustig that she was studying literature at all. He had called the other night and she was debating whether she should see him again. She hadn't seen him since the night of the train crash two years ago. One of the reasons she couldn't sleep was because she couldn't decide what to do about Fred. It was hard to escape all the memories connected with her life in Hartsville, but there was Fred, a person from that life, e-mailing her every day whether she responded or not. He was teaching in a private school in Brooklyn and lived in an apartment near Prospect Park. And he wanted to see her.

After the scene with Mark and Leon in the back of the car she began to think something was wrong with her (maybe I need a therapist?) She made an appointment with the school guidance counselor, Bethany LaMar, but realized that she couldn't tell her what had happened that night in the rain. She wanted to tell somebody what it felt like to kneel on the ground while the two boys peed on her face. She wanted someone to assure her that there was nothing wrong with what she had done. She wanted Bethany LaMar to tell her that she liked doing things like that too, that she did it with her boyfriend all the time, not because he wanted to but because she did. She wanted Bethany LaMar, with her painted fingernails and her necklace of turquoise stones that hung down the front of her blouse like a snake, to tell her there was more than one way of having sex. Bethany brushed her red hair out of her eyes and crossed her legs. Alicia stared at the flower patterns in her black stockings and wondered why some people were more beautiful than others. She knew that the words she wanted to say were locked inside her in some place that resembled a prison cell, dark and airless. How could she tell anyone that the night in the rain with Leon and Mark was the only time she felt really alive?

She decided not to date anyone and concentrate on her school work. She wanted to do well so she would be accepted by a good college. She wanted to get out of town, to a place where she didn't have a reputation as a person who would do anything, where people didn't call her up and ask her if she would suck their dicks. They were just drunk teenage boys who didn't know better.

Once her mother answered the phone, which was in the kitchen, and it was one of those boys. "It's her mother," the boy shouted gleefully to his friends in the background. And then he asked Georgia Germaine: "Want me to suck your pussy?" Her mother notified the school principal, Mr. Allen, and told him what the boy had said and Alicia was summoned into his office and admitted that she had received similar calls over the last few months. How many calls, they wanted to know, but there had been too many to keep track. Do they really think I keep a record of every call? She told them she had been too embarrassed to tell anyone and they looked surprised. And no, she had no idea who might be making the calls, which was true. She doubted that it was Mark or

Leon, more likely one of the innumerable kids in school whom they had told about the night in the rain. "She'll fuck anyone."

Her decision not to have sex lasted almost a year, but everything changed when she met Fred Lustig. First she fell in love, or so she convinced herself, and that's what made it possible for her to change her mind. She had made a contract not to have sex but the person she made the contract with was herself and that meant she could break the contract whenever she wanted with no hidden fees.

Fred Lustig was in his early thirties and lived in a two-story brick house on the outskirts of town. The house had been on the market for awhile but no one wanted to buy it so the owner consented to rent it for the year. Fred lived alone which targeted him as an object of gossip: is he gay? Why did he move here? What does he do at night? There was nothing to do at night except go to one of two bars, Splash, on the main street of town, and Smiley's, about a mile down the road. No one had ever seen Fred in either of these two places—at least, there was no rumor that he went to these places looking for company, male or female.

Alicia was positive that he wasn't gay though she could understand why he might try to hide it if he was. There were plenty of people in town who had a problem about people who were different from them. Different color, race, sexual preference: the phobias spread outwards, overlapping, like ripples in a polluted lake. No one knew when a storm would erupt out of nowhere and batter the sandbags protecting the shoreline. A man living alone in a house in the country could be anyone. Maybe he was simply an eligible bachelor who had taken the job in the country to escape his former life. An "eligible bachelor," stupid expression, implied that he might be available if there were any single women who were interested, or even women who were married but anxious to escape their lives. Isn't everyone? Maybe that's what Fred was doing in town, making an escape. From his former wife? No one knew for certain. Even Georgia, Alicia's mother, brought it up over dinner.

"What's the new English teacher like?"

There was something devilish about Fred Lustig, like he knew something about you that even you didn't know. He might tell you, but only if you did what he wanted. And what was that? His hair was very black and he wore it shoulder-length so that it flowed over the collars of his plaid sports jacket. He had two jackets and a purple blazer and he alternated wearing them but he never wore a tie and sometimes he neglected to button his shirt all the way and she could see the top of his hair curling on his chest. He was barrel-chested and dark-complexioned and had a wide forehead with one long wrinkle—just a thin line, like a paper-cut—which disappeared when he smiled. But mostly he didn't smile—he stood in front of the classroom, leaning back against his desk, or stood at the blackboard with his back to the class. He was not a large person and Alicia had a hard time imagining what his body was like under his clothing. She couldn't understand, or didn't want to, why people had so little to occupy their attention that all they could do was think about other people's business. She felt protective of Fred, who she studied every day from her seat in the third row. She wondered if he knew that people were talking about him and whether he cared. No one had a clue what he did when he left school. Some people said he drove to Boston on weekends. That's where his lover lived, they said, implying that his lover was a man. Everyone was anxious to think he was gay so they could show how tolerant they were by pretending they didn't care or become indignant and self-righteous at the thought that some faggot had come here to corrupt their kids. And he was Jewish as well. There were a handful of Jewish families in town, the Grossberg's, the Coen's (formerly the Cohen's), the Lubin's (Alicia had baby-sat for Agnes Lubin), maybe a few more. You can often identify a person's religion or ethnicity by their name. Lustig sounded like a Jewish name. There was also talk that people saw him in town on weekends. They saw him drive by in his Hyundai, but he never seemed to drive too far. He bought his supplies in the stores on the main street of town rather than driving to the mall a few miles away. The main street was dying and the stores that hadn't gone under appreciated his business.

"You're the new teacher," they would say.

And after he left: "Do you think he's gay? He doesn't sound gay to me."

American literature with Mr. Lustig, second period, right after Spanish. She wanted to do something to get his attention. She wore a short skirt and thought she caught him glancing in her direction. Staring at her legs and then trying to pretend he wasn't. If he didn't look at her maybe that meant he was gay after all. He didn't seem to pay more attention to the boys in the class. He seemed present and absent in the class at the same time, as if he'd left part of himself in the city before moving to the boondocks. And maybe she was only imagining that he was staring at her legs. Why would he be interested in me, anyway? She could stay after class and ask him some dumb question. She could wear a low-cut blouse and lean over his desk and ask him about the essay by Emerson they were reading. "Self-Reliance," for god's sake. A hundred people think one way and you think another. Trust yourself. Isn't that what we should do? Even if people hate us? Mr. Lustig, I don't understand. She tried to act like she was interested. Whenever he asked a question she raised her hand. Sometimes she was the only student in the class who responded. She crossed and uncrossed her legs, but he didn't notice. Leon was in the class and he turned around and smiled at her as if he knew what she was thinking.

She assumed that Fred Lustig spent most of his time reading. There wasn't much else to do. She couldn't imagine him sitting at a bar, flirting with one of the married women who was stepping out for the night. There weren't many single women or men in the area, and he could have his pick, if that's what he wanted. People who lived in small towns were always craving some excitement. Look at all the movies about what happens when a mysterious stranger comes to town. All the women come out of the woodwork to compete for his attention.

It occurred to Alicia that Fred might be a writer as well. Ms. Beckman, her junior year English teacher, had told her that most English teachers ("including myself") were frustrated writers. She googled Fred Lustig and of course there was a list of his publications. Stories and poems had appeared in numerous small magazines, but there were no books, as far as she could tell. So it turns out he was a struggling writer who had taken a job as a high school English teacher in a small Massachusetts town. He had answered an ad, he had been interviewed, that was that. The school board was unanimous. Of course he had teaching experience in New York as well, but our students—according to the members of the school board who had interviewed him—are different. Watch out! They all laughed and congratulated him: you're hired. His previous address was in New York, a place where Alicia had been only once, when she was ten. And somewhere she read that he was born in San Francisco, another place where she had never been, and graduated from Macalester College in Minnesota. She sat in the class as he paced back and forth in front of the room, scribbling on the blackboard, posing questions that not many students (since who could be interested in this shit?) could answer, and tried to imagine what he might be like in bed, the weight of his body as he lowered himself on top of her. She tried to imagine what his face would look like when he came, all twisted and crazy. She wanted to get to know him better, no matter what. The fact that he was twice her age—that he could be arrested for seducing a minor—only made it more interesting.

Her visit to New York City had lasted only a few days. They had stayed in Brooklyn with a cousin of her mother's, and all that Alicia remembered was taking a boat ride around Manhattan and seeing the Statue of Liberty in the distance. And the World Trade Towers, they were still there, looming over the tip of the island. It seemed as if all the rays of the sun were directed towards the windows of these buildings. After September 11, which happened one morning when she was at school, she remembered the boat ride around Manhattan and later that night she and her mother sat around the dining room table looking at the photos they had taken on that trip. There was the one with Alicia and the towers and the clouds in the background. Yet part of her couldn't remember being there at all and she had a hard time summoning up any sadness about the fact that she would never see the buildings again in person and all the people who had jumped out of the windows and died. She had more empathy with the characters in the books she read. If a person in a book was walking down a street in a particular city, she could feel what that person felt, even if she had never been there. She had never been anywhere. It wasn't necessary to do something or go somewhere to imagine what it was like and sometimes imagining the thing was more interesting than actually doing it. She had the ability to enter into other people, like a parasite, to invade their beings, or so she thought. She lay awake at night thinking about Fred Lustig. They were in the shower at his house, the spray of water on her back. She was kneeling in front of him with his penis in her mouth.

She sat at the kitchen window in her apartment in New York. It was two in the morning but impossible to sleep. Alexandra and her boyfriend Raymond were sleeping in the other room. Fred had called again and she had finally consented to see him. They made plans to meet at a bar in the East Village. She didn't want it to go on for too long. She could drink a beer and leave. He had resigned from his teaching job the day after the train wreck. Of course everyone knew they had been together, in the backseat of his car, when the train went off the tracks. It was the summer after she graduated from high school, a few weeks before she moved to New York. Everyone in town knew they were having an affair. It's hard to keep a secret in a small town. All it takes is one person for everyone to know. The woman who lived in the house next to Fred's, Laura Matlack, saw Alicia ride up on her bicycle. Laura was curious about Fred Lustig. She was in her mid-forties and lived with her seven year old son, Spike. And Fred, ten years younger, was one of the few unattached men in town. It was hard to meet any single men around here. Most of the men were married. About once a week she went to Smiley's, one of the local bars, just to see who was around. Just to get out of the house. She was having an affair with Michael Wysack. They had met one night at the bar and she had taken him home. He complained incessantly about his bad knee, which he had injured playing football. He complained about his wife, the scrawny blonde lady with no breasts. Laura had once seen her in the bar as well, sitting alone at a table, as far back into the shadows as possible, staring furtively at everyone who walked by. Michael liked to lie there while she massaged his back and shoulders. She thought of him as "the cripple." Once, when she was massaging his back and singing "You are the sunshine of my life" in his ear, he fell asleep. It was pathetic. Sometimes he came to her house and he was too drunk to have sex. It was hard for her to say no to him when he called her up and said he was just driving by and wondered if she wanted a visitor. And two minutes later he was there.

She sat on the porch at night in the darkness with a glass of Merlot and a hand-rolled cigarette and Alicia rode up on her bicycle. She parked it under a tree in Fred's front yard and entered the house without knocking. Laura tilted back into the shadows, took the smoke into her lungs until it burned, and listened hard to the voices in the house. The light in the bedroom on the second floor went on. Then a minute later it went out again. And someone lit a candle, she saw it flickering on the ceiling, she could hear the muffled voices coming from far away but maybe she was just hearing the voices in her head, or the wind blowing through the mangled branches of the old elm tree between the two houses. And music, the thud of a bass guitar lurking like the heartbeat of an animal trapped in the bushes. A raccoon waiting for the lights to go out so it could rummage through the garbage. The bedroom window was open at the bottom, just an inch. It was Fred's bedroom, no doubt, and they were inside, on the bed. Sometimes they played something classical, an orchestra warming up. Fred was trying to interest Alicia in classical music. Rachmaninoff's Second Concerto was her favorite and he put it on whenever she came to the house. He even gave her a CD so she could listen to it when she was alone. It put her into a kind of trance state and once she even undressed in time to the music while he lay back on the bed and watched. The music with its air of melancholy, its unexpected crescendos, swirled around them as she unbuttoned her blouse and stepped out of her skirt.

Sometimes she came over and five minutes later they walked out the front door and drove off together. Laura Matlick was tempted to get into her car and follow them, just to see where they ended up. She didn't recognize the girl on the bike but she did tell her closest friend, Betsy Malone, that Fred Lustig, the new high school English teacher whom everyone was talking about, was having an affair with one of his students. A girl, of course, why would anyone think he was gay? She was certain that she saw them kissing against the curtains in the upstairs bedroom. It was a kiss that seemed to go on forever. And weren't they holding hands as they left the house? Betsy thought that Laura should notify Mr. Allen, the principal, but Laura was frightened of the consequences, whatever they might be. She worried that someone would find out she was having an affair with Michael Wysack. She assumed that someone in town must know about it, someone besides Betsy Malone, whom she told everything.

The train wreck happened on the tenth of August, one of the hottest nights of the year. In two weeks Alicia was scheduled to move to New York. She was going to live in the dorms at New York University. She had been accepted by Smith in Northampton and the University of Massachusetts in Amherst, but she was intent on moving to New York. She wanted to get as far away as possible—from the town, from her parents, from Fred Lustig, from Leon and all the other students who taunted her when she entered the cafeteria and spread rumors about her and made anonymous obscene phone calls to her house. This was only her second trip to New York. She remembered, from the first time, people panhandling on the subway. A woman pushing a baby in a stroller through the subway cars asking people for money. And people sleeping on the street, their heads propped on old garbage bags. A man with blood on his face and broken teeth staggered towards them in broad daylight. Alicia's parents were already cautioning her about walking the streets by herself, especially at night. And Fred Lustig didn't want to talk about it at all. They'd been meeting for six months and she was tired of living a secret life, tired of Fred's demands to see her more frequently, especially now that she was leaving town, tired of his jealousy whenever he thought she showed the slightest interest in someone else, accusing her of wanting to fuck her old boyfriend Leon just because he had seen them talking in the hallway between classes. Everywhere there were stories about bishops and priests and coaches who molested young children. Of course this wasn't the same. Alicia didn't feel coerced into sleeping with him—if anything, she had seduced him, or so she thought. Many girls in the town had sex when they were twelve or thirteen.

She knew other girls who traveled to Boston to see rock concerts and then went back to the hotel where the band was staying and fucked everyone including the roadies and then came back to school and bragged about it. She had gone to his office and perched on the edge of his desk with her legs dangling in his face. She had taken his hand and put it between his legs.

Fred knew that he would be fired if anyone found out. He didn't know that his neighbor, Laura Matlock, was spying on him from her porch, or that Betsy Malone, the town librarian, was spreading rumors behind his back. For Alicia, who lay in bed at night fantasizing about her life in New York, her relationship with Fred was fading into the background, into the near distance, like a dead animal in the rear view mirror. She needed to get away from Hartsville, from her parents, from her classmates who spent all their time watching porn on their computers and talking on their cellphones, and who never read books, and now she wanted to escape from Fred as well, something he refused to accept. Hard to believe that she ever had a crush on him. It was another life lesson, something to learn from. His bad breath on the side of her neck as he lowered his body on top of her. The days when she used to linger in the classroom after all the other students were gone—those days were over. If it was up to her, she would end their relationship right now, and if he didn't like it she would threaten to tell someone. She didn't want it to come to that, she felt sorry for him, if anything, so she continued going over to his house, at least once a week. This time they decided to take a drive. Laura Matlock watched them from her porch. Alicia preferred having sex in his car to staying in his bedroom. It reminded her of the night with Leon and Mark. He pulled the car off the dirt road into a grove of trees, not far from the railroad tracks. They had been here before. It was easier not to resist, to let him do what he wanted. She took off her clothing and they climbed into the backseat.

Fred's rough beard scraped the side of her face. She was pinned down beneath him and he was moving too quickly, as if he wanted to get it all over with. It was a clear summer night, a three-quarters full moon in the distance over the treeline. She thought of Leon and wondered if she would ever see him again after she left town. He was attending the local community college, but only because his mother insisted. If it was up to him he would get a job in the supermarket—the butcher's apprentice, perhaps. The last time she saw him in the hallway at school he looked like he was putting on weight. His head seemed twice the size. She remembered when they were ten years old, in the basement of his house, when he showed her his penis for the first time. She encircled it with her small fingers as she watched it grow larger in the palm of her hand. Mark was long gone, probably back to L.A. Maybe their paths would cross again some day. Stranger things have happened. Alicia had a yearning to go to California, but not to Los Angeles. She wanted to go north, to the forest of redwoods in Sequoia National Park, and then up the coast, to Big Sur. She'd seen pictures of Big Sur, people lying naked on a balcony with the ocean right below. She wanted to wake up with the sound of the ocean in her ears. She wanted to walk by the ocean every morning, sipping from a mug of coffee. It was good to know that she had almost her whole life up ahead and that anything was possible. There were oceans near New York City as well. She could always take the subway to Coney Island. It was different of course. In her imagination she wanted the wildness of it all. She imagined herself on a beach, running naked into the surf. There was no way you could go swimming near Big Sur. The water was too rough and would pull you under.

They were parked in a small valley, near an incline leading up to the tracks. And they could hear the train coming, as if the ground beneath the car was moving. The last time they were here the train had passed by as well. They had spread a blanket on the ground. No one looking out the window of the train could see them having sex on a blanket a few yards away, especially at night when all you could see, when you looked out the window, was your jaundiced reflection in the dim light above your seat. The train sounded like it was going at top speed when suddenly, as it rounded the curve and came into view, not far from Fred's car, the engine made a long hissing sound, someone must have pulled the emergency brake, and the pressure of the sudden stop blew the train off the tracks. All Alicia had to do was close her eyes and it came back to her as if she was seeing a movie and acting in it at the same time. Fred pulled away from her and she felt the pasty warm fluid running down the insides of her thighs as the screams of the passengers filled the night air and the trees nearby began to bend under the weight of metal as if they were being yanked by their roots from the ground. The earth itself seemed to be opening up in the abyss created by the crash. The car that had gone off the tracks pulled the rest of the train with it.

It was the loudest sound she'd ever heard. Almost as if she and Fred were aboard the train, but nothing could be comparable to that. Except the oddness of the circumstance, being naked, with this stranger on top of her, and how the sound wrenched them apart until all that remained was the aftermath—the actual moments after the crash, when there was only the wind carrying the cries of hundreds of voices through the night. She moved her legs out from under him, found her clothing in the front seat, opened the door, pulled on her pants and blouse, and staggered towards the wreck.

"No," he said. "We have to go. They'll find out about us."

What was he thinking?

That's what she remembered—the sound of his voice at that moment. Everything else that had happened between them faded in comparison. He just wanted to drive away from it all. She ran down the incline towards the fire and the people staggering around, some of them half-naked, just like she was.

She lost track of him completely. But what was she doing there in the middle of the night? She had to tell someone about Fred Lustig—her parents, Mr. Allen. It was no longer important. She hung her head and wept. Her mother put her arms around her shoulders, but she didn't want anyone to touch her. She didn't want their comfort. Her father held back—fucking German, she thought later. Child of Nazis. She wouldn't forgive him, ever, for the way he treated her that night. Refused to talk to him. Called home and hung up whenever he answered. Her mother begged her to make amends, but something had snapped.

People died in that train wreck. It was on the evening news, but her name was never mentioned. She had been the first one there, before anyone else, but her parents or Mr. Allen kept it out of the newspapers. Fred had driven away. People lost their legs. There were dead bodies everywhere. A child—she was only a child—naked—no more than ten. Writhing on the grass—calling for her mother in a language that Alicia could understand. She could speak it fluently. *Ma mère,* the girl was saying. Alicia knelt next to her and put her ear to her lips. The girl's teeth were chattering and blood trickled from the corner of her mouth. And there were other people, she was surrounded by them, their arms outstretched as if they were walking in their sleep. People were dying around her. It was like a battlefield, Dresden after the bombs fell. How long would it take before the ambulances started arriving? Before the helicopters arrived to take the wounded to the nearest hospitals? It felt like hours had gone by since she was in the backseat of Fred's car and the moment when the first ambulance arrived. She could hear the sirens from a long way off as she held the girl's hand. A light rain was falling over it all but small fires were burning everywhere. The girl on the grass was pale and beautiful but her face was covered with soot and her red hair was singed at the ends and she died in Alicia's arms, she could feel the life fade out of her like a dead bird. She once had a rabbit named Jasper who died in her hands, but this was different. She took off her blouse and covered the front of the girl's body. That's how they found Alicia, naked to the waist. She had a bruise on her left breast from something Fred had done. She had to explain herself to her parents, to Mr. Allen. Her father slapped her—that was the end of it all.

They took her to the hospital. They—the ambulance drivers—thought she had been on the train. What else was she doing there? It was hard to explain. She had blood on her hands and face—it was the girl on the grass who had died. Her parents came to the hospital and took her home. The silence in the car was overwhelming and when she got into bed she could hear them fighting in the living room. Her father was not a pleasant person to be around when he was drinking. Nothing like this had ever happened before to this town. Once a girl had drowned in a nearby lake. Nothing—hundreds of people dead or wounded. The helicopters and ambulances shuttling people back and forth to the emergency rooms. Newspaper reporters camping out on everyone's front lawn. It was Georgia who called Mr. Allen and some time later the next day Alicia was sitting in his office at school with her parents. She had never looked closely at the school principal before and now she realized he was frightened of something terrible happening on his watch—frightened of making a mistake he would regret his whole life. It wasn't his fault that she had an affair with Fred Lustig (though someone might question why he had hired him in the first place), and it wasn't his fault that the train had crashed. Alicia's father hit her when she told them all about Fred and even Mr. Allen couldn't believe it. That this man had hit his own daughter and that she and Fred had been sleeping together literally under his nose. He had the feeling that everyone at the school knew about this except him, which wasn't exactly true. Alicia stared at her feet and hands, thinking—in two weeks I'll be gone.

Her name was Catharine La Page. Alicia read about it in the newspaper. They had a list of everyone who had died in the wreck. She was twelve years old, on her way to Montreal.

She could smell the burnt flesh, she could taste the soot-filled air. It was two years later but it would never go away. She walked across town to meet Fred, through the streets crowded with people on their way home from work, everyone muttering into their cellphones or gathering in outdoor cafes. A feeling of sadness and freedom in the air. It was hard to tell who was happy and who wasn't, who was wearing a clown's mask, who was returning home to a person they loved or hated, or alone, who was returning home alone. She could smell the smoke in the air and could hear the cries of the wounded and dying and that's who she was—if it was only that simple. Once a week she sat in a therapist's office and went over it all one more time.

Fred had left town immediately—she never saw him again after that night. She never answered his e-mails or cell phone messages. He wouldn't dare call her at at home. Her father had already threatened to kill him. He left messages at the NYU dorm—somehow he'd discovered where she was living. Once she thought she saw him leaning against a lamppost across the street from her dorm, smoking a cigarette like a character in a 50's movie, but when she looked again he was gone. Somehow he had found another teaching job in Brooklyn. Obviously, no one had checked his references, or he had neglected to include the year in Hartsdale on his resume. He lived in Brooklyn, not far from the Gowanus Canal. Alicia changed her e-mail address but he found her out.

She wanted to say, when she saw him at the table at the bar: "That night—with you in the car—was the last time I had sex with anyone." But she didn't want to send the wrong message. He'll think I'm saving myself for him.

It had been two years, almost to the day, since the night of the train wreck. He looked smaller than she remembered, sitting behind a table in the garden behind the bar. There were circles under his eyes and he had lost some weight. He'd been a track star in college, or so he had bragged to her, lying in bed in his room. He took her hand and put it on his stomach. Flat, you see, nothing but muscle. He looked like—a dried fruit—was that the right analogy? But he was only in his mid-thirties, if even that. Some fifteen-year-old girls, looking for attention, would find him attractive. No doubt he was a different person when he stood in front of a classroom. Here, nervous, on the defensive, he could barely look at her. She remembered how he tried not to stare at her when she was sitting in front of him in class. She uncrossed her legs and arched her back so that her breasts pointed straight out, daring him to look. It seemed a lifetime had passed since she bicycled to his house in the evenings. She remembered the way his beard felt against the inside of her thighs when they were having sex in his upstairs bedroom. You're hurting me, she wanted to say. Why didn't he shave before she came over?

He stood up when he saw her enter the garden and held out his arms as if he expected her to embrace him. Didn't she feel anything after all this time? She realized, from the first moment she saw him, that meeting him was a mistake.

He was drinking a beer, clutching the bottle tightly in one hand. All the tables around them were full—it was happy hour—and an old song by The Who was coming in over the speakers. Music for old men played by people who were once young. It was the kind of music Fred liked—what they listened to in his bedroom. There was always music playing in the background as he undressed her. It gave him pleasure to unbutton her blouse in slow motion. Sometimes he lay back on the bed and watched her undress in time to the music. He wasn't aware that people in town knew he was sleeping with a student, that eventually one of his neighbors would tell the principal. There was a mirror propped at one end of his bed so they could watch themselves having sex. I should have known better, she thought, shaking her head, but I didn't. So far her life was just a series of regrets. When she was alone, when she was studying, when she was reading—that's when she felt different. Her mind began to expand to include every fact, every detail, every person—real and imaginary—who had ever existed. Her personal problems seemed small in comparison. All the slums in all the cities where people lived five to a room, with nothing to eat but a bowl of rice a day, if they were lucky. At least she didn't have to worry about where she was going to get her next meal.

Her mind had a life of its own. One thought led to another. She looked into the eyes of every person in every store she entered. She said good night to the security guard at school, locked in his little cubicle for ten hours a day. She wanted to know what other people thought about, how they were content living their lives, watching all the minutes and the hours slip away. It was the mindlessness of it all that upset her. And who am I, she wondered, to spend all my life worrying over the books that someone else had written. A note-taker, if nothing else, a person who spent most of her time in her head. That's where it all made sense to her, the interrelation between books, between events, how one thing led to another. She could understand how a book written in 1750, for instance, might link up with a book written two centuries later, why people died from The Black Plague in 1350 and why people died of consumption in 1820, why some people took xanax when they were too frightened to get out of bed in the morning, when people first started using condoms and what methods of birth control they used before, how so many people who were sympathetic to Communism were blindsided and disillusioned when

Stalin came to power, (it was one thing to say one was anti-Communist and another thing to say one was anti-Stalinist), and all the animals that died in the Iraq war, the stray dogs, much less the thousands of people, and then the drones suddenly appeared, dropping bombs on civilian populations, before disappearing into the night. It went on forever, all the events of history, all the people who were alive at the same time you were, who leapt from the hundredth floor of the World Trade Center, who seemed to be suspended in air forever before they crashed to the pavement, the photograph of the young girl running naked down the road in Vietnam, the body of the girl who died in the train wreck, who was going to meet her father in Montreal. She didn't want to regret everything that ever happened, but she had to admit that being with Fred Lustig had been her biggest mistake. Nothing to do but cut your losses and move on.

The waitress, a tall young woman with long bony arms in a white t-shirt and ankle-length skirt, and a small black mole in the corner of her mouth, approached their table and asked her if she wanted something to drink but she shook her head, finding it difficult to even say the word "no." If she ordered a drink it meant she was going to stay.

"You can get me another," Fred said, and Alicia watched his eyes wander over the waitress's body as she turned her back.

"You wanted to see me," she said, "so here I am."

"Why have you been avoiding me? I always thought we had something to talk about—something in common."

"I'm studying French literature now."

"I mean other things as well."

"You mean sex? That was a long time ago. I was too young to know better."

"There was nothing wrong with what we did."

"We never talked," she said. "It was just about sex." And then: "Why did you run away from the crash?"

"To protect us—to protect you. I wish you had come with me."

"There were people dying out there. All you could think of—"

"I knew what would happen if they found out. They would fire me in a minute. I could go to jail. I thought if we just drove off nothing would happen."

"I was leaving town anyway, remember? And they would have found out about us no matter what. Half the town probably knew. It would have ended, either way. I was already thinking of the future, that I had made a mistake by sleeping with you."

"And now—who are you sleeping with?"

"I'm at school, I'm a student. And who I'm sleeping with isn't your business."

"I'll wait for you," Fred said, looking into his beer. "It meant a lot to me, what happened between us. You might think it was all about sex but it was more than that. I was risking everything. Soon—some day—you'll be old enough to understand."

"If you ever come to my dorm I'll call the police. I'll get you fired from your job. You'll never be able to teach anywhere again. This is it—this is the last time we're going to see one another. If we pass on the street just pretend you don't know me."

"You'll figure it all out some day," he said.

"And you, who are *you* fucking? One of your little students, no doubt."

She felt like yelling at him but she was aware that they were in a public place—at a table surrounded by groups of young people who were laughing and embracing one another. She envied them, but only for a moment. She knew she was different, that there was no way she could act as if nothing mattered, as if she didn't have a care in the world. Maybe she had been that person once, bicycling through the evening light on her way to see Fred, but it was too long ago to remember.

"It doesn't matter," Fred said, apropos nothing, like an actor in a soap opera. Like someone had written a script for him and he was reciting it from memory.

"Remember," he went on, "we were going to travel together. We were going to Paris together. We had it all planned."

And then he said: "I'm writing a novel—it's about you—what happened to us. I want you to read it."

She looked at him and remembered the smell on the inside of his car after they had sex. The feeling of anticipation she felt during the day when she knew she was going to meet him that night. They only had a short time to spend together. She had to lie to her parents— every time she went over to his house at night she had to make up some lie about where she was going or where she had been. That's what she did on her way home, bicycling in the dark. They had to make every moment count, up in his room, where he played music for her, Rachmaninoff, a piano quartet by Brahms, or in the back seat of his car. She remembered wanting something when she was with him and then the feeling of disappointment when she returned home. It was one thing to have a fantasy about someone and then there was the reality of actually being with that person. She thought he would open a door to something she didn't know anything about but all she learned from him was what to avoid the next time around.

But there was no next time. The young men in her classes at NYU asked her out and she turned them down. They called her and she said no, she was busy, she had to study. She was only nineteen. She didn't want to repeat the mistakes she had made before. There was Leon— that had gone on for awhile—and then there was Fred. That was it. She met women in her classes and in the dorms and she went to cafes with them at night. Some of them propositioned her but she turned them down as well, though part of her was curious. It was like opening a book by an author she had never read. What it was like to be with a woman—she would learn about that soon enough. But not yet, she thought, there was too much to do. She could see men staring at her as they passed on the street. Or in the subway. Everyone was looking at everyone else. Once someone tried to talk to her on the subway and she was tempted by the anonymity of it all. "Does this stop at Sheepshead Bay?" he had asked. She didn't know the answer to his question, but she liked the name, Sheepshead Bay, she would go with him anywhere. It was near the ocean, and she'd never been there, not even to Coney Island. She didn't want to go alone. Here in the subway was her chance. He was very tall and spoke with a Russian accent but at the last minute she backed away, she retreated to the opposite end of the subway car. And he didn't come after her, but just turned away. No doubt he was cursing her in his mind, the same way that Fred was cursing her but for different reasons. Cursing himself for being so pathetic.

The blinders. She had an image in her mind of a horse with blinders. That's what he was like. One of those horses that was trained to lead a carriage through Central Park. You wear the blinders so that nothing can distract or frighten you and somehow you kept going forward, oblivious to everything. If something distracted you there was the driver with a whip in his hand to get you back on track. While some couple made out in the back seat. Or fucked. It was what you did on prom night, or after graduation: you took a carriage around Central Park and fucked in the backseat. The girl lifted her prom dress and the man unbuckled his pants. That's what they were doing. That's what everyone was doing. That's what Alicia and Fred had been doing the night of the train crash. Then she ran half-naked into the night into this bad dream which never stopped happening. And that's what Fred was like—he couldn't remove the blinders. She realized that he himself didn't believe they were ever going to get back together again, it was just words, he would say anything, he didn't care. It was just some game that involved trying to convince someone else to do what you wanted, but it didn't really matter whether they did it or not. Nothing mattered. That's what she had learned from reading all those books. She sat up all night reading. She took speed pills to make her concentrate better. She went to the library where recently someone in one of her classes had committed suicide by jumping from the top level of the stacks to the floor of the lobby. There was too much pressure going to school, too much emphasis on getting good grades, too much money, too many loans to pay back, too many relationships that went south, too many temptations. It had been worse during her freshman year when she lived in the dorm but things were easier since she had her own apartment. A room in an apartment. But having a kitchen nearby was important. It meant all she had to do was go downstairs once a day on the weekends and buy food. The rest of the time she could sequester herself at her desk, among her dictionaries and papers. Once a week she spoke to her mother who told her all the latest gossip. All the news of small town life. I have some bad news, her mother said. Regina Wysack committed suicide. Do you remember her?

She had taken sleeping pills and then she had filled up the bathtub and slashed her wrists. She wasn't taking any chances. She knew that her husband was having an affair with Laura Matlack. But Laura was only one in a long line of girlfriends. It had been going on for years. He would sleep with anything that moved, or so people said. But her real pain had started when she was younger, when her father used to come into her room, and then, when her father was on one of his interminable trips to the West Coast, his brother Alvin, Uncle Alvin, would come into her bed in the middle of the night and clamp his hand over her mouth so she could taste the oil (he was a car mechanic) on his fingertips and she knew it was hopeless to fight back. She hated herself for the pleasure she was feeling. It was some kind of pleasure that overwhelmed everything else and she didn't want it to stop. There was a dull pain, and then there was the intoxication, as if she was drunk and had forgotten where she was or what she was doing. It was the same way she felt—eventually— after her second or third beer, after her first joint, and it didn't matter whose body she was touching. She never told anyone, she was only in high school, she would go to parties and someone would pass her a bottle from someone's parents' liquor cabinet, and she would drink as much as she could, she drank it straight, no ice, no tonic. Her father had died by then and Uncle Alvin had moved to another town. Once, when all this was happening, she thought she was pregnant, but it was a false alarm. She sometimes drove to the garage where Alvin worked just so she could see him from a distance. She wanted to get back at him for what he had done, but she wasn't sure how, or who she could tell, what she could do to make a difference.

Alicia's mother described the funeral, how everyone in town had turned out, even Laura Matlock. It was just a matter of time before Laura Matlock and her son Spike would move in with Michael Wysack and his daughter. She wold sell her house. Life would go on, but in a different way, as if the world had shifted a few inches in one direction and then shifted back into a different place entirely. Something can be different and the same at the same time and if this was true of anything it was true of people's lives. "The more things change," people liked to say, "the more they stay the same," whatever that means. People looked at Laura oddly on the street—at least for awhile—and no doubt they talked about her and Michael Wysack over dinner or in bars or in bed. They whispered about her behind her back and wondered what he saw in her—she was more like someone's mother than anyone's potential lover, and maybe that's what Michael Wysack needed, though who would know? Laura Matlock certainly didn't think of herself as the motherly type. Soon enough, even the small-minded people who were her neighbors forgot about it all. They accepted the idea—that Michael and Laura were a couple. They forgot about Regina, who no one liked very much anyway. Everyone had turned out at her funeral, even her uncle Alvin, but no one in town knew what had happened when she was younger—how they had come to her room, when she was fifteen, and taken turns in the middle of night. How, after a point, she lay awake waiting for them. Soon enough Laura and Michael and their children would move to another town, some place where no one knew their names or anything about their pasts and eventually, as time went by, and Michael Wysack's knees ceased to function, even after numerous operations, she would wheel him down the street and into and out of stores, and all the storeowners would nod at them graciously and everyone would wave at them when they said goodbye.

It was done. That part of life was over. All she had to

do was stand up and walk away. Fred was still sitting at the table in the garden, and the tall short-haired waitress with tattoos running up and down her bare arms was taking a beer and a glass from her tray and placing it in front of him. Alicia walked past the crowd at the bar. The television above the bar was on and there was a close up of Barak Obama's face making a speech, and someone at the bar asked her if he could buy her a drink, why was she leaving since she had just arrived, he had seen her come in and now she was leaving, and she felt like thrashing out at him, at whoever, it didn't matter who was saying what, but she kept on moving until she was beyond the sound of the music from the jukebox and Obama's voice, all the voices and sounds mingling together like one big wave crashing in her ears, out into the street which felt safe in comparison. She looked around to make sure Fred hadn't followed her, or anyone else. It was still light out as she crossed Second Avenue, walked up St. Marks Place, engulfed by the crowd of panhandlers and tourists. She had lived in the city for two years and she was used to the smell of garbage on every street corner and men pissing out in the open against the side of a building, the pasty look of human skin under neon, the billboard signs of half-naked people towering over the intersections, the smell of Macdonald's mingling with the garbage and the piss, all of it the same, and all the obese people staggering around barely breathing, the take-out bicycle drivers who lived six to a room in a rotting tenement in Chinatown, the kids with Mohawks and kilts sitting against a wall like mirages from another place and time drinking wine from a paper bag—all of it had become familiar to her, part of a world that she couldn't imagine ever leaving.

She was sitting at the kitchen window, smoking a cigarette, five flights above the street, waiting for rain—she could hear thunder in the distance across the purple sky—when someone knocked on the front door. It was Raymond, Alexandra's boyfriend, his shirt soaked, looking serious and unhappy. Can I come in? Apparently he was supposed to meet Alexandra in a coffee shop on the corner but she called at the last minute and said she was going to be late without saying why and that he should wait for her in the apartment if Alicia was home. He talked at top speed as if reading the words off a teleprompter. If not he could wait outside the building, she wouldn't be that late. Or if he wanted to go home—this is what she told me— that's what he should do—she actually said that—we can always see each other tomorrow. Raymond's long black hair was plastered to his forehead, one wet strand hanging over his right eye. He was wearing a salmon-colored shirt buttoned halfway up his chest. He was very thin, but graceful, like a ballet dancer, someone who was starving himself so he could move fluidly across a stage, someone who drank too much coffee and hardly ate anything. Raymond always looked discontent about something but this was a different kind of sadness—desperate, afraid, ready to explode. His bloodshot eyes were half-closed, as if he was squinting into a blizzard, and filled with rage.

Most of the time he came home with Alexandra, from wherever they had been, and went straight to her bedroom. But a few times Alicia emerged from her room when they were watching television and joined them for a beer. ("Ray," Alexandra said, "get Alicia a beer.") Alexandra always acted relieved when she joined them. She acted like she was frightened of being alone with her boyfriend and wanted someone else around in case anything happened. Or—more likely—she was just bored to be with him. It took a lot of work to keep Alexandra happy. Raymond was a graduate student at Columbia, also studying psychology, at least they had something in common, and according to Alexandra he was jealous of everyone in her life—her teachers, fellow students, boyfriends out of her past, girlfriends in the present, people who stared at her legs on the street or on the subway, imaginary lovers. And Alexandra, in her perverse way, fed into his obsessiveness, canceling appointments at the last minute, arriving late, not answering his phone calls or e-mails for days on end.

Jealousy, Alicia thought. It's like an epidemic.

"Who's she sleeping with?"

They were sitting opposite one another in the living room waiting for Alexandra to come home.

"I know when someone's lying—she says she's going to be an hour late—it's not as complicated as people think—you can be in bed with someone one minute and the next minute with someone else and no one knows but yourself—you're different, you never go to bed with anyone—that's what Alexandra says about you—I can't spend more than two nights alone—not since I was fifteen, can you believe it, I can't stand waking up alone—I can't sleep if I'm alone— sometimes I wait downstairs when I know she's not home just to see if she comes home alone or if she comes home at all—you have to tell me if she ever brings anyone else back to the apartment—I know she has a lot of friends and I'm uptown most of the day and she doesn't have a clue how I spend my time or who I talk to and if I was fucking someone else she wouldn't know—she doesn't care—just tell me to shut up if you want to go to sleep—it must be boring as shit to hear all this stuff—more than you want to know about anyone— about me—"

He started crying. She sat down next to him on the couch and put her arm around his shoulders. He was shivering and couldn't stop talking. She could smell the rain on his skin, could see the tufts of dark hair on his chest under his shirt. He was like a wolf or a wild dog who had come in from the cold.

She had had very few lovers compared to other women she knew. Sometimes she went to a coffee shop after French literature class with some of the other woman students and they would talk about their old lovers and sometimes even their present lovers in intimate detail and Alicia wanted to tell them about the night with Leon and Mark in the back of Leon's Volvo, but she couldn't. She couldn't tell them about Fred and the train crash either. She would smile enigmatically when it was her turn to speak. It was hard to link the words that would create the sentences that would describe what had happened. Who were her lovers: Leon, Mark (just that one time in the back of the car) and Fred. That was it. Alexandra offered to introduce her to her single male friends—friend's of

Raymond, among others. But Alicia enjoyed being free of the encumbrance of any relationship—of anybody at all—and she didn't want to give it up, the freedom to do whatever she wanted when she wanted and not feel dependent on another person even if it meant missing out on the feeling of anticipation that she remembered as she bicycled to Fred's house in the evening with the light streaming down onto the road through the tops of the trees. She liked to walk around the city late at night after studying for hours and stare at everyone and at the windows of the stores and know if she wanted to she could meet someone. The temptation of a one-night-stand was always in the air—but there was time for all that. She didn't want to be filled with regret and sadness, the way she felt when she thought about Fred.

"You know," Raymond said, wiping his eyes with his shirtsleeve, "I've always been attracted to you."

She tried to move away from him but he grabbed her hand.

"I mean I always wondered about you—Alexandra said you didn't have any boyfriends and I thought—that's amazing. I wonder what her life has been like. Everyone has this stupid past they're hiding—that they can't escape."

It wasn't something she had thought about beforehand—to have sex with Raymond on the couch. Alexandra would be home any minute. It's just a kiss, the beginning of something, and then he put his hand between her legs. She was wearing cutoff jeans. She parted her legs for a second and then pushed him away. Still, it was a struggle to stop, and he was breathing heavily. Obviously, he was losing his mind. One minute he was crying about Alexandra and the next minute he was trying to have sex with her roommate. In a way it made sense. If Alexandra was really sleeping with someone else this would be a way of getting back at her. She wasn't sure why she had tried to comfort him when he burst into tears. She would have done it for anyone. And here she was, pushing him away, but not wanting to.

And then she was there, in front of them, her clothing soaked through. Alicia had gone to the kitchen to get more beer.

"What have you two been up to?"

It was a way of deflecting the conversation from whatever she had been doing. She looked suspiciously at Raymond as if she guessed that just a few minutes before he had been fooling around with her roommate on the couch.

"Where were you?" It took him awhile, but finally he said something.

"First I was in the library, you know I have this paper to write for Doctor Phelps and then I have to give this presentation and while I was there, I was just about to leave and meet you, I saw Toni Fredricks from New Orleans and her new boyfriend Alonzo so we went—they insisted I go—to get a beer with them and catch up on everything, and I kept thinking I knew this guy Alonzo from somewhere, that we had met before, but we couldn't figure out where—he doesn't go to NYU and according to Toni they just met a month ago—he was born in El

Salvador, apparently, but he moved here with his family when he was ten—so that's where I was, that's where I've been, I'm sorry you had to wait but as I said there was nothing written in stone about meeting tonight—we were together last night if you don't remember and we can be together tomorrow night so there was no necessity about meeting each other tonight far as I can see, if it happened it happened and it if didn't happen it didn't—doesn't that make sense? And I can tell you're mad at me for saying that we were going to meet and then not even calling and coming late but here we are now—isn't it great, isn't this what you want? I'm here, I saw my friends, there's no rule that says I can't see my friends when I want to, even if it means we spend less time together, right?"

And when Alicia returned with a beer for Raymond and one for herself:

"So you like my boyfriend? He has a hairy chest, did you see?"

"He knocked on the door. I opened it."

"Did he tell you about me—how he thinks I'm cheating on him?"

"He's right here," handing the beer to Raymond, "why don't you ask him?"

"I'm asking both of you—were you having fun without me? Because I can tell you both—I was having a great time with Toni and Alonzo."

"Maybe I'll go to my room now," Alicia said.

"Wait—this is the first time you've come out of your room in months—and now you're going to disappear again? Raymond, you know, I never see this person—we live in the same apartment, right?—but she's always in her room, she's up all night, I can hear the music coming from her room at three in the morning, and then she sleeps till about noon and then goes to the library—and that's it, Raymond, that's what her life is like, imagine what it would be like if you were her boyfriend, Raymond, you like to go to parties, don't you, and to clubs, we've gone to some of the most boring clubs in the city, you and me, Raymond, so I'm just warning you, if you have any ideas about making a play for my roommate don't say I didn't warn you, and now—if you don't mind—I'd like to go to bed, and I'd like you—Raymond—since you're here, since you bothered to wait around for me though I wouldn't have blamed you if you had gone home, if you had called me and told me you were going to be late I wouldn't have waited around for a minute—I want you to come to bed with me too, if you're not wiped out from being with my roommate doing whatever you were were doing before I came in—"

"We weren't doing anything," Alicia said. She looked from Alexandra to Raymond, who was staring guiltily at the floor, his fingers knotted together as if he was waiting for the foreman of the jury to pronounce his fate, and then back to Alexandra.

"Have fun," she said, and left the room, ducking beneath the Tibetan flags that were hanging over the entrance to the living room, and closed the door of her own room behind her. It was still her own room, unless Alexandra decided to kick her out. They had nothing in writing about how long she could or couldn't stay in the apartment. Alicia had agreed to pay her six hundred dollars a month for rent and utilities. She had never asked Alexandra to see the lease to find out whether they were splitting the rent equally or whether she was paying more than her share, whether Alexandra was profiting from the arrangement as many people do, often doubling the rent to subletters who don't have a clue. Every month Alicia handed over the money in cash, and that was that. They had been living together almost a year and it was true, what Alexandra said was true, they hardly saw each other. Alicia had the feeling that Alexandra regretted choosing her as a roommate. She had interviewed several people for the room and Alicia had seemed like the best match in the moment. At least she was the best of everyone she had interviewed, and possibly if she had interviewed more people she might have found someone more suitable. Alexandra liked roommates who brought home their boyfriends. Randa, the roommate before Alicia, had numerous boyfriends, mostly one night stands, and one night, everyone drunk, they decided to swap—Randa went to bed with Scott, Alexandra's boyfriend at the time, and Alexandra with the guy who Randa brought home, and whose name she couldn't remember. It wasn't a fair trade, really, since he was too drunk to do much except climb on top of her like a dead weight and then roll over and fall asleep. While Scott was no doubt taking advantage of the moment. Randa had put on an old Motown record, Marvin Gaye's greatest hits, and had extended her hand to Scott, while Alexandra and Fernando, that was the name of the boy she brought home, were sitting side by side in silence on the couch, and within a minute Randa had put her hand down the front of Scott's pants while Alexandra was leading Fernando, who could barely walk straight, into the bedroom.

Alicia lay on her bed smoking, listening to music through headphones. She wanted to recapture the equanimity she had felt before she went to see Fred. It had slipped away during the few minutes they had been together in the bar and the walk home through the crowded streets and then just as she felt like she was settling into some place in her mind that she recognized there was Raymond at the door in need of someone and there they were on the couch together just as Alexandra imagined with his hand between her legs and the smell of rain in his hair. And there was Alexandra like a witch standing over them, lying through the side of her mouth about where she had been, trying to hide the fact that a half hour before she was in someone else's bed and that everything Raymond thought about her was true. And Alicia knew that it was time to move on. I'll look for another apartment, she thought. What she wanted most was to live alone but she couldn't afford it.

It was three in the morning when she went to the bathroom which was located on the other side of the apartment, closer to Alexandra's room, and she was sitting on the toilet with her shorts around her ankles when there was a knock on the bathroom door.

"It's me, Raymond," a voice said. "I have to pee."

Alicia lifted her head from between her knees and stared straight ahead. It was like a dream, and she could hear the rain falling on the hood of the Volvo, and the gravel scraping her knees as she knelt on the side of the road. She remembered trying to fix the straps of her dress as she stumbled up the steps of her house like a drunk person. It was like she had been dreaming all along and finally it was time to rub the sleep from her eyes and wake up.

"O.K.," she said, "you can come in."

And then he was there, in front of her, Raymond Octavo, her roommate's boyfriend. She pulled down his underpants, took his penis in her hand and opened her mouth wide. It was just as she had imagined it down through the years—only better.

She Was Working

She was working in an office on the top floor of a high rise in midtown Manhattan. It was just a suite of rooms with rented furniture behind a door at the end of a hallway. It was an open space where two other women worked at separate desks. You could see the World Trade Towers from the window. On clear mornings the sunlight cast a thin veneer over the Hudson like an astringent. On foggy mornings the Towers and the Verazzano Bridge were invisible.

The man who owned the business worked in a separate office adjoining the space where the women sat behind their computer terminals. His name was embossed on the door to his office. The letters of his name were the color of charcoal and glowed slightly like a night light when the office was empty. A friend who knew the sister of the boss had recommended her for the job. She had said, at the initial interview, "I have a friend who knows your sister." It didn't matter whether she had any experience. It wasn't the type of job that required special skills.

During the interview, the boss never stared at her once. Not the way a man stares at a woman when he thinks she doesn't notice. Or he stared at her covertly, through the corners of his eyes, in a learned manner that masked his secret pleasure. It was a matter of pride for a man to pretend he didn't care about the way a woman looked and this man obviously wanted to defy the odds by acting indifferent while in reality he was simply being indifferent to his own needs. Lorraine needed a job and didn't care whether he stared at her or not. She had once slept with someone in order to get something but she wasn't sure she would do it again. It was something she thought she would prefer not doing, though the one time she did it had been no less interesting than making love to someone you thought you liked and being disappointed afterwards. Charles, the boss, looked out the window when he talked to her. He looked at his hands.

One of the other women in the office was having an affair with the boss. Her name was Clarice. She was the best-looking of the three of them, or so Lorraine thought. Black curly hair and a ring on every finger. The look of a gypsy who lived near the Black Sea. Charles was married, in his mid-forties, and for all anyone knew the only time that Charles and Clarice made love was on the floor of his office. In a sense that was her job—to be on call whenever Charles wanted her. Lorraine and the third woman, Deidre, always winked at each other when Charles called Clarice into his office. She was often in the locked office for over an hour and she always emerged with a fake smile creasing her face as if making love to the boss gave her the right to feel superior. Supercilious, that was the word. As if making love to her boss was going to get her somewhere in life. A step up the ladder to nowhere anyone wanted to be. She assumed that Lorraine and Deidre were jealous—

that they would do anything to be in her place.

Lorraine had been hired without having to sleep with the boss. The company business involved distributing CDs produced by small independent record labels. There were hundreds of labels, new ones everyday. It didn't cost an enormous amount of money to produce a CD. There were orders coming in all the time. Announcements, catalogs. It was up to the company to coordinate the publicity surrounding the records. There were stacks of free CDs in the corner. Promo copies. There was music going on in the office all the time. It sounded like Philip Glass but it wasn't.

She had met Philip Glass at a party. Her boyfriend Steven was a jazz pianist. He had been trained as a classical pianist but he preferred to play jazz. He was often hired to do studio work—that's how he made most of his money. The rest of the time he played in nightclubs and bars. Once he had a job playing in a restaurant where no one listened. He played while people ate and some of them applauded politely when he finished but mostly he played to the accompaniment of coy laughter. Possibly the man at one of the tables near the stage had said something to the woman he was trying to seduce and she had begun laughing uncontrollably, oblivious of the music, of the other people at the tables around her, some of whom had come to hear the music, not just eat and drink. Steve sometimes thought he might be better off if he had a job unrelated to music so he could earn more money but he sabotaged the possibility by dressing sloppily at job interviews. No doubt it was his way of preventing something he didn't really want to do from happening. He didn't want to do anything but play music, even if it meant being poor, a throwback to a time when being poor was a badge of integrity. His practical side was just a vestige of something his parents had drilled into him when he was a kid. Make money, buy a car, a house on a hill on the outskirts of anywhere people didn't go. He could hear his mother's voice. That was all there was to it.

His goal was to lead his own jazz group and feel free to play whatever music he liked. A trio: piano, bass, drums. That was enough. Like Ahmed Jamal or Bill Evans. Those were his favorite jazz pianists. The group would be called the Steve Saxon trio. The word "Saxon" was more than a name, it was like jazz itself. It was like sex and jazz intertwined.

He didn't want to play what everyone else played. He didn't want to play like Ahmed Jamal or Bill Evans. There was a sound in his head that he couldn't identify when he listened to other people play the piano. It was just a glimpse of something that he could only touch by translating it into music. Very occasionally, when he was playing, he caught a glimpse of this inner feeling that he identified as himself. Then the music rolled out as if the veins in his fingertips were giving off sparks.

Lorraine was alone in her office when the young man arrived carrying a package of CDs. He was simply a delivery boy or bicycle messenger who had been hired to deliver product. As soon as he walked through the door and they made eye contact she began undressing him in her mind. It was hard to sit in an office all day and not think about sex. Some days the only man she encountered at work was her boss. Lorraine guessed the delivery boy's age as eighteen or twenty but looks were deceptive. People often told her she looked twenty when she was really a few months shy of her thirtieth birthday. For years she had wanted to look older than she was and now she was on the cusp of feeling older than she was. Some nights she would lie awake berating herself for wasting an entire decade taking odd jobs when she could have continued in school or focused on a career. She had friends she had known in college who were making salaries in the six figures.

When she complained about this to Steve he looked at her in disgust. "Fuck them," he said. He couldn't believe that she assessed her life by comparing herself to others. He felt disappointed, a bitter taste, as if he was swallowing his own sweat. He had assumed that Lorraine's passion for painting was equal to his for music and that they could pursue their interests with equal intensity. They had been together for two years and she spent little time doing anything except going to her office job and going out at night. She had a small room in her apartment that she used as a studio but whenever Steve came over the door was locked and whenever Steve asked to see her work she shook her head. "I'm not ready yet," she said, but he didn't believe her.

The problem with working in a small office was that she never saw anyone but Charles, Deidre and Clarice. Most of the people who did business with the company communicated by telephone or by e-mail. There was very little human contact in an office so small and in a way she was jealous when the boss called Clarice into his office and they fucked on the rug, if that's what they were in fact doing. If nothing else this little episode interrupted the boredom of a day filling orders from a catalog and talking on the phone to fledgling record producers who were desperate for a crumb of attention. Clarice's mid-afternoon dalliance with Charles stirred Lorraine out of her drowsiness but all she could think of doing was touching herself. She would call up Steve and say something obscene to him. She would suggest that instead of going to the movies as they had planned—that's all they did: go to see jazz and go to the movies—they stay at home. She would even prepare dinner for him if that was an enticement. She knew that Steve couldn't cook and that he appreciated the warmth that was implicit in the act of preparing food for someone else. Most of the time he ate in bad restaurants at odd hours before or after his jobs and his complexion was often sour. He had a cold sore in the corner of his mouth that wouldn't go away. He told her he would be over at about seven. The assumption was that they would make love before dinner. And then afterwards too. It would be the kind of date they used to go on in the weeks after they first met. Now, invariably, the only time they had sex was when they were about to go to sleep. As if they had been together for decades and had exhausted all possibilities. As if they were turning into their parents.

Lorraine knew most of the regular delivery boys by name. She had never seen this one before. He handed her the package. It was a small square package sealed with transparent scotch tape. The words: "Att: Charles Haas" were written in ink on the side.

"It's our latest stuff," the delivery boy said. "Our best, too."

"What label?" Lorraine asked.

"Albany. The Albany label. I'm from Albany."

"It's your label?"

"I'm the vice-president," he said.

He fished in his back pocket for his wallet and took out his card. It said: "Jeff Springer, Vice-President, Albany Records," followed by the phone number and the fax number and the e-mail number and the address. There was a logo of the state capital printed in red ink on the card.

Lorraine turned in her chair from in front of her computer so that she was facing him and she watched him stare at her breasts for a moment, the flicker of his eyes over her body as she bent towards him. Instead of being insulted, she was grateful for the attention.

"Jeff Springer from Albany," she said. "I thought you were the delivery boy."

Jeff laughed and swept his hair from his forehead. He was swarthy and self-assured. Whether she thought he was the delivery boy or the vice-president didn't matter much to him.

"I'm not a boy anymore," he said. "I bet I'm older than you are."

He stared around the office. She turned to look at what he was seeing. There were three desks with computers.

Clarice, who had worked in the office longest, had the desk facing the window. Above Deidre's desk there was a poster of the Eiffel Tower and a print of a Picasso painting. An abstract portrait of one of his mistresses. Deidre had a dream of moving to Paris with her boyfriend. The only reason she worked was so she could save money towards her goal. "I can do it, can't I?" she would ask Lorraine and Clarice whenever she felt insecure. Some mornings she came into the office and didn't say hello to anyone and Lorraine and Clarice knew she had had a fight with her boyfriend the night before. Somehow the goal of going to Paris was intertwined with her boyfriend, one thing was dependent on the other. The poster of the Eiffel Tower was the only decoration in the office except for some plants on the windowsill and a photograph of Clarice's parents above her desk. It was Lorraine's job to water the plants. Her desk faced the door. She was like the receptionist, in a way. The person who greeted the delivery boys and the vice presidents and the UPS workers.

"How long have you been working here?'"

"Two years," Lorraine said.

Jeff shook his head. "I couldn't do it. I'd go crazy."

"I know what you mean. You're the only person I've seen all morning."

"I want a job where I meet new people. That's what it's all about for me. I tried to be a musician but I wasn't any good. So I decided I could be in the music business but from a different angle. It's not like I couldn't do music and ended up doing something I hate just for the money. There isn't that much money doing this but at least it's something I like to do."

Lorraine said, "You're lucky. Before I took this job I wanted to be a painter, but now I'm not sure."

"What kind of painting?"

"Abstract stuff. Maybe that was the problem. I was trying to make the old stuff seem new and it just turned out to be old."

"Who's your favorite painter?"

"Georgia O'Keeffe," Lorraine said. She looked at her watch. Deidre and Clarice wouldn't be back for a half hour. They could make love quickly, up against the desk, before anyone returned. All she had to do was reach out for him and it would happen.

"She isn't that abstract," Jeff said. "Listen." He paused, staring at her breasts again. "I know someone who might get you a better job. I mean he's not someone I know well, really, but he can get you more interesting work than this."

"What kind of work?"

"Maybe modeling," Jeff said.

"I'm too old to model," Lorraine said. "Anyway, I'm too big."

"O'Keeffe's flowers are very sexy."

"That's what everyone thought when she did them. They thought she was painting cunts. They assumed because she was a woman she didn't know what she was painting."

"Listen," Jeff said. "I have to run. Here's the card of my friend. I would call him if I were you. You can't work here forever." He shook his head as if to imply, what a waste.

As soon as he left Lorraine went to the bathroom. She

was too excited to wait until she saw Steve. She rubbed herself until she came—it took about two minutes, the shortest time ever. She was thinking of Jeff Springer, going down on him in the deserted office and then leaning over the desk so that he could fuck her from behind. Sometimes, with Steve, it took her fifteen or twenty minutes to come, and sometimes she gave up, couldn't go over the edge. It was like crossing the desert with no water, only a distant mirage that disappeared whenever you thought it was a few feet away. Metaphors relating to sex were meaningless though, since the reality itself was so intense. On nights when she couldn't come she felt she should apologize to him for all his hard work, even though he said he enjoyed giving her pleasure. Her gratitude translated into a desire to do to him whatever he wanted as a way of reciprocating.

Deidre and Clarice came back from lunch. And then Charlie came back from a business meeting and called Clarice into his office. Deidre and Lorraine stared at each other and smiled.

On the way home from work Lorraine bought a special pasta to cook for Steve. She would make the pesto sauce that he liked. She stopped in a liquor store on the corner of 72nd Street and nodded to the man behind the cash register who was the owner of the store and who recognized her since she had been coming in about once a week for the last three years. It was his job to recognize his customers but sometimes she had the feeling he was coming on to her a little. She bought a bottle of chablis after practically falling asleep trying to choose, not wanting to ask the man behind the counter to recommend something because she really didn't know what she wanted and because the last time she had asked him he had followed her up and down the aisles like a ferret until she chose something that met his approval. Being in his store gave him permission to encroach on her circle of space. There was a cameo enclosing a winged angel on the label of a bottle that drew her attention, an angel hovering over a half-naked woman asleep in a garden. It was an old pre-Rhapelite painting, in blues and yellows. Steve was particular about wine and usually brought his own on the nights that he came for dinner. Even if the wine she bought was no good by his standards, he would never tell her. That was what was neat about Steve, or one thing. And there couldn't be too much wine, not tonight. Lorraine wanted a cigarette but didn't buy a pack, hoping that Steve would bring some and she could bum off him.

She tried not to think of Jeff Springer but she thought she saw him as she came out of the subway. He was crossing 72nd Street and Broadway, heading east, carrying a package under his arm, but she knew that if she ran up to him and called his name he would turn into someone else, a total stranger, another mirage in the metaphorical desert. Someone once told her that the way to meet people is to approach a stranger and pretend you know them and then apologize for the mistake. It's a good way of opening a conversation, an excuse for showing that you're interested. And if the other person didn't pick up on it that was his problem, his loss.

She had put the card which Jeff had given her in the

zippered compartment of her purse and while waiting for Steve, who always showed up late, even to his jobs, she dialed the number and a woman answered before it rang twice.

"Is Mister Carney there?'" she asked.

"Who shall I say is calling?"

"He doesn't know me, but Jeff Springer gave me his number."

"Jeff Springer?" she said. "Just a second."

A minute later a voice barked into the phone: "Carney here. What can I do for you?"

"Jeff Springer," she repeated. "He gave me your number. I'm looking for a job."

"Wow," he said. "Jeff Springer, huh? That's who told you to call?'"

She said it again. "Jeff Springer."

"And what's your name?" he said.

She almost told him her real name.

"Amber," she said.

He laughed. "That's as good a name as any, isn't it?'"

"It's my name."

"Well, I'm glad you like it, Amber, because I like it too."

She didn't know how to respond to this. She was frightened that Steve would arrive when she was on the phone. She had given him a set of keys so he could let himself into the apartment whenever he wanted.

"We're on a very tight schedule," the man named Carney said. She thought he might be bald and shapeless but she wasn't sure.

"A schedule for what?"

It was not the right question. "You mean that asshole Jeff didn't tell you?'"

"It's a movie," she said. She had guessed that much; she had guessed right.

"It's a fuck movie," he said. "I make porno movies. Have you ever fucked in front of a camera before? Do you think you can do it?'"

"I've never done it before" she said, breathing hard. "But I want to learn."

VICKI

We had reached the point of no return, and there was no going back. There was no going forward either. In fact, we could only move a few inches in any given direction, before we came up against a wall in our heads. This movement, back and forth, forward and back, was all in our heads. In reality, we could move in any direction we wanted. We could walk for a few miles without stopping, if that's what we wanted to do, in the heat of day and without a hat to protect us from the sun, so that when we finally stopped to rest our bodies were covered with sweat, as if our clothing had been left in the rain over night by mistake, and the wet clothing called attention to the shape of our legs and breasts. In fact—taking a long walk—that's what I'm going to do today. I'm going to put on my Hightops and head uptown, aimlessly, stopping whenever I want. I like walking around without any specific destination, turning left or right, walking west to the Hudson for a short stroll on the Highline, usually deserted on weekday afternoons, or east to a cafe on Avenue C where I can sit in a garden in the back, drink a double espresso and smoke. I like to watch all the bodies, the shapes, the bare skin, the nipples sharply defined. I like to stare at people and make eye contact with them. Some of them stare back, some of them blush, some of them pretend they don't see me. But some actually smile, invitingly, as if they're thinking the same thing as me. There must be a hotel around here where we can spend a few hours. I just live around the corner, why don't you come up for a drink? Sometimes this is what happens—all your fantasies come true—but not often. There's no way of knowing what's going to happen when you leave your house.

Even at home, though, it's hard to predict what will happen from moment to moment, the phone might ring or someone you haven't seen in forty years will send you an e-mail. Vicki, it was great to hear from you—I'm talking about my old high school girlfriend who wrote me yesterday from her home in Ann Arbor, Michigan. That was nice. We used to go to her house after school, maybe two or three afternoons a week, and then on weekends we would go to the movies. We would hold hands in the movies. At her house we would make out and she would let me put my hand down the front of her blouse, but that's all. I would fumble with the buttons on her blouse, wishing she would help me, and then slip the straps of her bra along her arms. That was it. I tried to go further but she made it clear that's all she wanted to do.

Then I went home and when my mother asked why I was late I told her I had joined a club after school, which in fact was true. It was the folk singing club. There was one guy, Johnny Blank, who played the guitar, and then we all sang along. "This Land Is Your Land," for instance. "Kumbaya." "Michael Row the Boat Ashore." We sang the same songs every week. I have a horrible singing voice and all I could do was stand in the background and mumble the words. It was no fun, to be honest with you, especially compared to going home with Vicki in the afternoon, and I only went to folk singing club twice before I began seeing Vicki. I was a junior and she was a senior and after she graduated we stopped seeing each other. But a few years later, when I was living by myself in an apartment on the Lower East Side, she called me up out of the blue and came over and we spent the night together. By then, of course, we were no longer virgins. That was the last time I saw her—we woke up the next morning, I made coffee, she got dressed, and then she left. I was involved with someone else at the time and there it was, my cards on the table. She—Vicki—even asked me about my new girlfriend. For a moment, I thought she looked disappointed. Like if I didn't have a girlfriend we could start seeing each other again. I can't imagine what she looks like now, she's almost seventy. I don't even have a photograph and no doubt, if we passed on the street, we wouldn't recognize each other. It doesn't matter. Her real name was Vera, but she changed her name to Vicki. And her sister's name was Billie, but she changed it from Paula. It was nineteen fifty-nine and we were both in high school—the Bronx High School of Science. I think we met on the bus going home. We took the same bus. I was waiting on line at the bus stop on the Grand Concourse and she started talking to me. I was too shy to start talking with anyone, so I never did. I would wait for the other person to make the first move. And that's what Vicki did. And then one day I just stayed on the bus and took her home and we sat on the couch in the living room and I began to open the buttons on her blouse. But when I tried to put my hand between her legs, she pushed me away. She made it clear (for some reason) that she wasn't ready—that this was enough. "I'm a prude," she said, though she seemed like the opposite of that, most of the time. It was she who started talking to me and invited me back to her house. There was pleasure in all of this. It was my whole life. And writing. I'd begun writing seriously, so this is what I did. School, writing, Vicki. And of course when I wasn't with Vicki I was thinking about her and we talked on the phone every night as well. It was a long time ago. Maybe once a year I take the subway up to the old neighborhood. I even walk down the street where she lived, but I can't remember which house. Mickle Avenue. Shit, there's the bus stop where I used to wait. My fingers touching her breasts. We would meet after school and then take the bus home together. Up the Grand Concourse and then change at Fordham Road. It took about an hour and then we were there. The hour on the bus gave us time to talk. Then, when we were at her house, we sat on the couch and made out. It was the same thing every time. We had reached our limit. This was as far as we were going to go, and that's it. I didn't care that much. I liked being with her, no matter what. And then my mother said—when I walked through the door: Why are you so late? I told her I'd joined a club, the folk singing club, and she smiled, because she knew I was lying.

None of this is true—I mean most of it's true, but the part that isn't true is the e-mail from Vicki. I don't have a clue where she lives. She never e-mailed me. I haven't seen her since the morning she left my apartment. We spent the night together—that was true. Somehow she found my phone number. She called me up and came over. It was easy to sit at my tiny little kitchen table and drink coffee and then get into bed. We were different people—I don't know what we'd say to each other now. It doesn't matter. Once a year I go back to the neighborhood where she lived. I walk down the street. This must be the house. Two or three times a week we went back to her place. In all the time we went out together I never met her parents. I did meet her sister one night when I took Vicki home from a date. Her name was Billie. I was smoking then—Kents. I would leave her house late at night and light a cigarette. I would stand at the intersection of Gunhill Road and Eastchester Road and wait for the bus. Sometimes I took a cab. Once, in the middle of a blizzard, I took a taxi. It was a miracle that a taxi came by in the middle of the night. I was only fifteen. This part is the true part. The wishful thinking is getting in touch. What difference does it make? Two or three afternoons a week we went back to her parents' house. There was a Catholic school around the corner and Vicki, who was Jewish, made fun of the Catholic girls and their funny uniforms. The school is still there. I sit on a bench in a small park near the intersection. I go back to my old neighborhood. I stare at the windows from the street. Somehow we lived there for seventeen years. My parents slept in the living room. My sister and I shared a room. Vicki is probably almost seventy now. Not quite. I wish I had a photograph of her, but I don't. But I can hear her voice.

I can hear her say "We shouldn't" as I try to put my hand between her legs. I can hear her say "How stupid they are!" as we pass the parochial school girls outside the church, which is also a school, right around the corner from where she lives. I can hear her say "I've been wanting to talk to you," as she approaches me for the first time. I'm waiting for the bus on the Grand Concourse. School is over for the day.

To Have
Or Have Not

When the war ended people came out of their houses and stood on the street corner and stared at the sky, looking for a sign, like the light of a meteor or a shooting star. Strangers kissed, it was the middle of summer, ninety degrees most days with intense humidity, and some of them took off their clothes. Caressing was permitted. Even the subway was crowded, during rush hour and at other times, with half-naked people, if you can picture it, and the people who were sitting down caressed the bodies of the people who were standing, if you can imagine that, an endless orgy from station to station.

The president made a speech from the garden outside the White House. He was wearing his usual outfit, except for a tie, and he looked tired, but happy, having been part of the negotiation that led to the end of the war, and all the rumors that he was having an affair with a woman named Astrid, a Brit whom he'd met on one of his frequent trips to London, no longer dominated the headlines, because it no longer mattered, and there was also the rumor that his wife was having an affair with a low level assistant to one of the members of her husband's cabinet, the assistant to the Secretary of the Treasury, Bob D'Angelo. There was a rumor that the president's wife also had a girlfriend named Tobey Caseras who accompanied her on her trips abroad under the title *personal assistant,* which wasn't far from the truth. Someone reported seeing the president's wife making out with Tobey Caseras on a park bench when, for an hour or two, they managed to elude the secret service agents, two men and a woman, who were assigned to the president's wife 24/7, in eight hour shifts. In other words, every eight hours a team of three secret service agents were never not aware of what the president's wife was doing and where she was. If she was in a hotel room with her boyfriend, Bob D'Angelo's assistant, one of them was outside the door, one of them was in the lobby, and one of them was in the street. No doubt one of the agents, under cover of daylight, leaked the rumor to a reporter from the Washington Post that the president's wife was sleeping with Bob's assistant, Dale, but the president himself couldn't care less.

The fucking war had gone on for a decade, so there was reason for celebration, except for the families who had lost a son, a daughter, a brother, a father, a sister, a mother, an aunt, an uncle, or a best friend, not to mention a niece, a nephew, a stepson or stepdaughter, a distant cousin. Just because the war was happening in a distant country didn't mean you didn't have to think about it, especially if you didn't have a relative or friend who was fighting. But it was actually possible to go for hours or days at a time without thinking much about the fact that people—many of them in their early twenties—were dying in the desert ten thousand miles away, especially if you didn't read the newspapers or watch the news on TV or on the internet. The number of people who died was in the hundreds of thousands, if you counted everyone, since there were many different countries involved, and the casualties add up over time, but it's impossible to estimate the dead and the wounded, not to mention the stray dogs who were killed in the crossfire. Some say a few thousand while others say a hundred thousand, and no one will ever know for sure.

Some people are not happy that the war is over. They don't rush into the streets and rip off their clothing, like so many others, the delicate flowers among us who think that war is hell. It's hard to say if there are more people who are happy that the war is over than there are people who want it to continue, who have an investment in the continuance of an event in which so many people have died. Undertakers, perhaps, or heads of corporations that provide weapons to the soldiers who go to war. "Coffin-makers, not coffee-drinkers." That might be a slogan for the people who wish the war would go on. There are some people who think it's good for the economy to be at war, for whatever reason. Certainly, if you are related to a person making weapons, or if you are such a person yourself, a factory owner, for instance, making parts for bombs, or simple ammunition, old-fashioned bullets, or bulletproof vests, your opinion about the war might be different from a person whose standard of living is not dependent on the war. If it wasn't me, these people think, someone else would be doing it. And now both your children can attend private schools and later, if they do well, they can attend the most expensive colleges. The tuition keeps going up. The war goes on and people enlist in the army with the idea that when the war ends they can go to college for next to nothing. And now that the war is over this is a real option. Even if you've lost an arm or a leg in the war you can still go to school. You can always find someone to wheel you across campus.

There are stories about how people returning home, men and women, people who were deployed for years in a foreign country, have a hard time adjusting to civilian life, and that some of them kill themselves, or the people around them. Some of the wives and husbands of the people returning from the war claim they no longer recognize the person they had married. There was the case of the wife who confessed to her husband that she had been seeing another man when he was at war. Months stretch into years, who can blame her? There was a rumor that he strangled his unfaithful wife in her sleep, but who knows for sure. There are other stories about soldiers who return from the war and who wake at night screaming out the names of the women whom they met in the war zone, and with whom they fathered at least one child, sometimes more. It's hard, on both sides, to go without love for so long. Most of the wives of the soldiers confess to having partners on the side. Often these women wrote to their husbands telling them that the marriage was over. It's hard, if you're a soldier, to get the news that your marriage has ended. And why? Your wife has fallen in love with someone else. It's hard to imagine your high school sweetheart in bed with another person.

It's hard enough to love someone during normal circumstances, much less during a war which involves long periods of deprivation and absence. And sometimes the soldiers fall in love with one another, out of desperation, men fall in love with other men, women soldiers fall in love with other women, and sometimes the men and women fall in love, though there are many more men soldiers than women, and often the women complain that the men are harassing them or touching them in a way that isn't appropriate, and it's not unusual for a woman soldier to report that one of the male soldiers tried to get into her bed late at night. Often the women are blamed for enticing the men into bed, for saying something that the male soldier interprets as an invitation to sleep with her. The woman is so exhausted she doesn't wake up until the man is already on top of her and both of them are naked. Often the male soldier is exonerated, if the woman soldier chooses to press charges, and at any rate there's no way to prove anything, it's her word against his, there were no witnesses or no witnesses who are willing to testify on the woman's behalf. There are always witnesses, but people are afraid to take sides for fear that someone will retaliate, that the family of the male soldier who tried to get into bed with the woman soldier will retaliate against the family of the woman soldier, and that this war within a war will go on ad infinitum.

Sometimes men go to brothels and fall in love with the prostitutes, many of whom are underage, sometimes as young as fourteen or fifteen. The younger girls are hidden away in the basements of the brothels. Only the very rich can afford to have sex with the very young girls. There's something addictive about going to the brothels and the soldiers can't help themselves. Sometimes they sneak out late at night. They bribe the guards so that no one reports them. Sometimes all they want to do is weep in the arms of the prostitutes and talk about all their friends who were killed. Sometimes they make promises to the prostitutes. When I leave, they might say, I'll take you with me, even though the soldier is married with young children. It feels like it all happened to a different person in a different world. You can't imagine going home to a house in the suburbs. You can't imagine sleeping with the same person every night for the rest of your life. It doesn't matter if you've lost an arm or a leg, you can still have sex with as many people as you like. There are some people who are excited by the idea of having sex with a person who lost an arm or a leg or an eye. Some women have sex with men who are missing a limb out of sympathy for the disabled person who risked his life for his so-called country. You want to reward the person by having sex— that's one way of doing it. Just lie back and relax, you say, let me do it. You can put on some music, a disco record by Donna Sommers, and undress in front of the disabled soldier.

The war is over and you can relax now. You can do whatever you want. You can go to the movies in the middle of the afternoon. This is the best time for meeting people. Many people go to the movies in the afternoon and have sex with the people sitting next to them. Many people go to the movie theaters just to meet people in this way. Once I went to a drive-in with my girlfriend and we had sex in the back seat, but that's another story. Soldiers returning home are mostly bored, even those who are married with young children. They wander the streets until they find a movie theater and wait for someone to sit down next to them. It's not uncommon for people to have sex in movie theaters in the middle of the afternoon. My girlfriend and I went to the drive-in, we had sex in the back seat. Another story, another time. Here, the war is over, people are coming home, some of them are handicapped, it doesn't matter. There are people who prefer life in the barracks to life in the suburbs, if you know what I mean. It's hard to live a so-called normal life after you've been in the desert for too long and all you can see is a body of water in the distance, but it's only a mirage, and all you want is a beer, thank you, a cold bottle of beer.

It's not clear whether you want to have sex with anybody—not the day you come back. Your wife complains that she doesn't recognize you anymore. War changes people. All you have to do is go to the movie theater in the afternoon. It doesn't matter what's playing. Once I went to a drive-in with my girlfriend. Her name was Angela and she came from Elmira, a small city in upstate New York, if you catch my drift. We went with another couple. They were in the front seat and we were in the back. The car smelled like sweat, beer, and licorice, and of course sex, whatever that smells like, the lilac-scented perfume that Angela was wearing, and in all the cars around us people were fucking, while on the big screen Humphrey Bogart was lighting a cigarette for a radiant Lauren Bacall, and Hoagy Carmichael was playing the piano in a bar in Martinique.

Story of the Kidnapping

"Joseph," Madeline said to the bartender, "this is my friend Scott. He's my new roommate."

"Scottie," Joseph said. He wiped his hand on a towel and extended it across the bar. "Good to meet you."

A flat-faced middle-aged man with a crewcut was sitting on a stool at the curve of the bar near the door drinking a beer from a thin-necked bottle. He held the bottle tight in one hand, a non-filtered cigarette in the other. All the barstools on either side of him were empty, as if he had a disease. Two young Asian women with short black hair and leather pants were playing pool in the back, lost in a private world, circling the table like lemurs. The people at the tables along the wall were engrossed in what sounded like a heated discussion about politics A few of them looked up as Scott and Madeline entered the bar.

"They haven't found her," Joseph said. "I wish that something would happen so the cops would leave."

He worked as he talked, polishing glasses with a rag

tied to his apron. A waitress came by and gave him an order. She nodded to Madeline though they didn't know each other's names.

Joseph put a drink in front of Madeline.

"What'll it be?'" addressing Scott.

"What's that?"

"Dewar's with ice," Madeline said.

"I'll take the same."

"The mother is really having a hard time. I mean, who wouldn't? She's slaved all her life for that kid. She was a waitress in this soul food restaurant in Harlem for awhile. She was in here one day and told me her life story. How this guy came into the restaurant every day for a week and offered to set her up in a hotel in midtown. She could make four times as much as she did as a waitress and she needed the money because she had a daughter to support and no future. That's what makes this whole scene with Lenora so sick. What's the point of kidnaping someone if the family doesn't have any money? I hear that they're asking for ten thousand—that's what the voice says on the phone. In return they'll give back the kid. Not a million but ten thousand. That's what Lenora Delray is worth.

"I mean," he says, "how much money can you make being a call girl? I've known Delores Delray for years. She was in here maybe four, five times a week. She would come in late afternoons, usually. Sometimes at night before closing. She hated not knowing what her daughter was up to during the day—when she was at the hotel— but she had no choice."

"And the father?"

"They're looking for him," Joseph said. "He seems to have disappeared. Last known address somewhere in Texas. Hadn't seen Lenora in years. Not even a Christmas card."

"How do you know all this?" Madeline asked.

"I'm a bartender. People tell me things. I don't even have to ask. Even the cops come in here for information."

"I can see the father kidnapping his daughter," Scott said, "but I don't think he'd ask for money. There's no reason to. Money isn't the issue."

"I knew someone who was kidnapped," Madeline said.

The people at the table along the wall wanted another pitcher of beer. The waitress drummed her fingers on the bar while Joseph worked.

"Dummy" by Portishead was on the jukebox. One of Scott's ex-girlfriend's favorite songs.

"I never told you this story." She sipped from her glass, rotating her glance from Scott to Joseph to see whether they were interested. "Before I came back to New York I knew this girl who was kidnapped. She wasn't my best friend but I went to school with her from kindergarten through fifth grade and when she was kidnapped she was maybe eight or nine. She was the daughter of the richest family in town. It wasn't a very big town, maybe two thousand people, and everyone knew everyone else's business. There were generations of families living in that town which few people ever left. Most people worked there all their lives. Anyway, the kidnappers sent the family a note and asked for a million in ransom. This family had more than enough to spare. Do you think they paid it?"

She didn't wait for either Scott or Joseph to answer.

"You better believe it. The family left the money in a suitcase outside an abandoned trailer at the end of a deserted road. A member of the family, the kidnapped girl's older brother, dropped the suitcase with a million in cash in front of the trailer. The instructions to the family were to sit by the phone. For some reason the family thought they had no choice except to do what the kidnappers said. They didn't even notify the police. They sat by the phone like zombies for two fucking days and nothing happened. It was only then that they called the cops, who were incredulous, totally pissed off. What can we do now? If you had told us before we could have traced the call. A week passed. You can imagine the anger that must have been building up inside this house, the biggest house in town. Then one morning the brother woke up and looked out the window. There was the suitcase, the same one he had delivered to the kidnappers with the money, on the front lawn. The house was on a kind of hill on the outskirts of town and the lawn sloped down to the road. Adele and I used to go sledding down the hill in the winter. The suitcase was sitting upright midway between the road and the house. The whole family came out and stood around the suitcase. The cops arrived. Then the brother said, 'I'm going to open it.' He lowered the suitcase on its side and unfastened the lid. There was a blanket inside the suitcase and wrapped in its folds was the arm of my friend Adele. The kidnappers had chopped off her arm. They never found the rest of her body."

"And the kidnappers," Joseph asked, "what happened to them?"

"The cops checked the suitcase for prints. It was a dumb idea to leave the suitcase. Hubris, really, since they already had the money."

"But at least the family knew that she was dead," I said. "It was better than waiting."

"So they found them," Joseph said.

"They found them," Madeline said. "They found them, moreorless. Once the cops had a clean set of prints to work with it was easy. They caught one of the kidnappers in Boston trying to board a plane to New Zealand and he gave the cops the addresses of his accomplices, a couple who lived in the next town over from where I lived, and where Adele lived, and who were furious at Adele's family. A lot of people hated Adele's family. People perceived them as being greedy. Of feeling superior to their neighbors because they had more money than anyone else. They had investments. They drove Japanese and German-make cars. Everyone else in town drove used American cars, cars with dented fenders, two hundred thousand miles under the hood. Rebuilt engines. Adele's family had a new fleet every few years. They didn't flaunt their wealth but they didn't try to hide it.

"Finally the real story of the kidnapping came out. It had to do with Adele's brother and the daughter of the couple. He had gotten her pregnant, she had an abortion, her parents found out. They found out after the fact. The girl's parents went crazy. The son of the richest family in town knocks up their daughter. On top of it all, they're against abortion. The type who protest outside abortion clinics. Real fanatics. They practically disowned their own daughter when she told them she was pregnant and didn't keep the baby. Adele's brother, this guy named Bobby, could sleep with anyone he wanted. Why did he have to choose their daughter? Bobby had decided to take a year off before going to college. He had a job in the family lumber business and too much time on his hands. He could pay his way into any college he wanted, regardless of his high school grades. His father had gone to Yale. I was only ten but I overheard stories about Bobby. My parents always changed the subject when I came into the room. There were some things they didn't want me to hear. Sex among sixteen year olds was out of the question. They didn't realize that all the kids in school talked about it nonstop. Adele, despite her family background, was well-liked by most of the kids. We didn't care much if her parents drove fancy cars, or we cared for the wrong reasons—we all wished our parents had that much money. We felt bad after she died. We knew the daughter of the kidnappers as well. Eventually she was sent to live with relatives outside Boston. Some of the kids had older sisters whom Bobby had seduced. It was like he had systematically fucked every girl in town over fifteen. He's dead now, or so I heard. He was in a car with some girl and it was hit by a truck. This was a few years later, after he eventually went to Yale, like his father. It was while he was an undergraduate that he was killed in a crash.

"The actual kidnapping wasn't hard. They waited for

her outside school. There were three of them involved. They were doing it for the money and to get back at Adele's brother. They waited outside the school every day. Sometimes one of the servants drove Adele home. Sometimes she lingered outside the school with her friends. I wasn't her best friend, but I had been in her house a few times. Every birthday. Sometimes she'd invite me and some other girls over after school. Or on rainy Saturday afternoons. She was a pretty girl with freckles and braids.

"They waited until the day she walked home alone. It was a ten-block walk from the school to her home, down tree-lined streets that were mostly empty in the middle of the day. They took her in broad daylight, swept down on her, the two men scooping her up into the backseat of the car while the woman drove. Anyone could have seen this happen—someone staring out the window of a nearby house—but if anyone did they kept it a secret. They drove to the deserted trailer. They called Adele's parents and demanded the money. They had no idea what to do with Adele. They tied her hands with rope, pasted masking tape over her mouth, and covered her eyes with a cloth. They dumped her in the back room of the trailer and locked the door. The room was empty except for a mattress on the floor. They decided not to give her any food, to let her starve, at least until the money arrived. The only person who showed any compassion was the woman who would sneak Adele bits of chocolate. She would untie the cloth around her mouth and kiss the girl, probing her chapped lips with her tongue. She would moisten the sides of her face with her tongue and rub the girl's legs and thighs.

"There were so many different versions of the story. It was Pete, the guy who was trying to escape to New Zealand, who told the police everything. How they drowned her by holding her head underwater in the bathtub and then hacked her body into pieces and tossed them in the river. Everything except an arm."

"That's a fucked up story," Joseph said. "Do you want another drink?'"

"I don't believe a word of it," Scott said.

"Every word is true. You think I lie about everything?"

"I don't know you that well," he said.

"You've known me longer than anyone. You know more about me than anyone."

"I don't know anything about you. Like if I knew you well I'd know whether you wanted another drink or you wanted to go home. This is what people who know each other well can tell about the other person."

"Guess then," Madeline said. She took his hand between her hands and placed it on her knee.

"Another drink," he said.

"You see. You think you don't know me, but you do. You can read my mind better than anyone."

ROMANCE

My mother once told me that my father's father used to swim in the East River when he was a kid. This was the early days of the century that is just ending. My father was born in 1930. My grandfather, who was born in Lithuania, was fifty when he became a father for the first time. My grandmother, who is still alive, was twenty-one. My grandmother, Evelyn, lives in a small town outside Buffalo, within walking distance of Lake Erie, with my father's younger brother Alvin, his wife and three children. When my father was alive I used to accompany him and my mother upstate once or twice a year, usually for Thanksgiving or Passover. We used to take the train, nine hours each way, more than enough time to read a book from start to finish. I remember observing my parents, both of them sleeping in the seats facing me, my mother's skirt inching up her thighs as she shifted positions, my father snoring heavily into the immaculate white pillowcase which the train provided, a book of music open on his lap.

Since my father died I haven't seen my grandmother once. I haven't even spoken to her on the phone. She still sends me a check for twenty-five dollars on my birthday and I respond with a note saying how much I miss her and how I hope to visit her. I'd like to think there was some truth in what I was telling her. What I know is that my mother has no interest in making the trip and I can't imagine going alone.

I never met my father's father. He died in prison. He was an accountant who spoke perfect English, staying up late at night studying the language of the country where he would eventually die, sleeping no more than four hours a night for most of his adult life, his child-bride waking in the middle of the night to an empty bed, and frequently an empty apartment. My grandfather Jake died a long time before I was born but I've seen a photograph of him and his wife, his arm draped over her shoulders, her head—framed by billowing curls of golden hair— pressed against his ribcage. She was at least a foot shorter so it was hard to avoid noticing the inequality of the embrace or that she was holding onto him so tightly. Most people who met them assumed he was her father. They would test people's reactions by being overly affectionate in public places.

"Let's fool around," he would say. They might be sitting on the grass in Central Park or riding the subway. Even holding hands aroused attention. She was twenty but looked younger; he could have passed for sixty, especially when he grew a beard.

It wasn't long after my own father was born that my grandfather went to jail for embezzling money from the corporation that had hired him to keep track of its profits and losses. He took a little money at a time and stashed it away in a shoe box in his closet. He was hoping if he was overly discreet that no one would notice. He had been hired to make sure that no one was cheating the company, and he cheated them himself. He cheated his employers out of their profits but never spent the money on himself.

This isn't true. Jake loved young women. It was his vice, though he wouldn't have called it that. He was addicted to women who were less than half his age, younger even than my grandmother. His relationships with these young women was his true vocation. There were two women, both in their late teens, Marlene and Estelle, whose rent he paid with the money he embezzled. He would use the money to buy clothing and jewelry for his girlfriends. And there was yet a third young woman, an adolescent who if anything looked younger than her age, who still lived with her parents and whom he provided for without ever becoming her lover. Presumably he was content seeing her dressed up in the clothing she purchased with his money. The girl's parents were too poor to question the motives of their daughter's patron. Maybe once a week my grandfather and the teenage girl went for a walk through the city, or had lunch together in a restaurant uptown, or sat on a bench in Central Park feeding the pigeons.

What the stolen money did was give him access to these women who would otherwise be the main characters in a fantasy world that was forbidden. The notion that life involved nothing more than endless feats of endurance and a will of steel to fight off the temptations of the flesh and seven days a week of hard work at a job he hated was abhorrent to him. The fact that he had married someone thirty years younger than himself had already made him an object of scorn by most of the members of his family, so he had nothing to lose by having even younger girlfriends. His family believed the key to success was never to stray beyond the rigid guidelines of morality which appeared to them as if written in stone as they made their awkward entrance into the new world. Adhering to this code assured them of a path up an imaginary ladder to an imaginary heaven of material wealth. The fact that this ladder of possibility existed was the reason they had come to this country to begin with. They felt privileged. As immigrants, they felt it was necessary to fit in, to conform; the worst thing you could do was call undue attention to yourself, to become a freak in the eyes of the people whose acceptance you craved. And that's what they thought of my grandfather—a freak!—when he appeared at the dinner with his young wife.

My grandfather Jake didn't mind being estranged from his family. He didn't care that they gossiped about him behind his back or that they stopped including him in their weekend gatherings. He didn't mind being alone, never felt lonely or nostalgic. Every spare moment when he wasn't working he spent with his wife or one of his girlfriends. He knew that the scorn of his relatives was fueled by jealousy. He couldn't understand why people would want to limit their circle of friends to their immediate family. His brothers and sisters, all of whom were married, spent their weekends and holidays together. Every potential spouse had to suffer an elaborate screening process before they were accepted and approved by the other members of the family. My grandfather, on the other hand, married his wife at City Hall, in the company of his only male friend and Evelyn's older sister Elizabeth. It was only after the marriage that he introduced his wife to his brothers and sisters. The last thing he wanted was to be trapped inside this xenophobic world.

He had done nothing to coerce Evelyn into marrying him. Her own father had died when she was an infant and she had been brought up in a household dominated by women. If he served as a surrogate father figure for her, so be it. She was a virgin when they met, but not because she wanted to be. The young men her own age were too diffident for her taste, refused to touch her when she wanted them to, seemed to be debating in their minds whether it was the right thing to do. When she met my grandfather she sensed instinctively the advantages of being with an experienced lover and made it clear to him that he could do what he wanted to her, that she was not like the prudish young women who talked about sex as if it was an obligation. It was Jake's forwardness that attracted her, his way of touching her arm or caressing her cheek when they talked, the physicality of his presence. She sensed that they felt similarly; that the only important thing was the willingness to give pleasure to someone else. She wasn't quite sure how to please another person but she wanted to learn. She sensed that my grandfather was the perfect teacher.

There were worse reasons to marry someone. There was no reason why my grandfather should deny himself the pleasures of a young wife. Or any pleasure at all. The disapproval of his family meant nothing to him. He was going to live his life based on the principal that what other people thought about him wasn't important. He had had his share of struggle, of suffering. He had fallen in love for the first time when he was younger but the woman, his classmate in the college in Lithuania they both attended, had rejected him—had said no to him—had told him she loved someone else. They had known each other in Lithuania and they had arrived in New York with their families at almost the same time. He had asked her to marry him and she had looked at him as if he was crazy but he had continued to love her from a distance, even when she married and had children. He would stand outside the expensive townhouse that her wealthy husband had bought—it was in the East 20s, near Gramercy Park—and watch their shadows embracing on the other side of the curtains. He had contemplated suicide at the idea that he would have to live out the rest of his life without the love of this particular person. He had thought of drowning himself, loading his pockets with stones and leaping off a pier into the East River. Of putting a bullet into his head.

When he met Evelyn he realized that he had been living a life of denial, estranged from his own self as much as he later became from his family. Now, he thought, it's my turn to live my life as I want. A voracious appetite for everything was not a sign of weakness. The rest of his family was devoted to the idea that curbing one's appetite was the key to success. He had read Nietzsche. A leather bound set of Nietzsche's collected writings, in German, was on the top shelf of the living room bookcase in my parents' apartment. He had learned from Nietzsche that to deny yourself what you wanted was a true crime. That the kind of morality his family worshipped was like a pill which you took to kill your desires, your instincts. Excess, as far as he was concerned, was healthier than asceticism. It was what he told Evelyn, his future wife, on the day they met.

I know all this about my grandfather because he wrote the story of his life when he was in prison. My father found the notebooks in his prison cell after he died. He dated each entry in the margin and it appeared that he wrote every day up until the time he became sick. Sometimes he wrote about the present—the reality of his life in prison—but most of the entries concerned the past. There were more than twenty notebooks, more than a thousand pages, each one covered from top to bottom with my grandfather's handwriting. My grandmother visited him every Sunday at Sing Sing, the prison in the town of Ossining, a two hour train ride from the city. She would supply him with the notebooks and the pens and the nineteenth century Russian novels which he would read when he wasn't writing or sleeping. Once a month Adele would take Oliver, my father, and Alvin, my father's younger brother, to see their father behind the wire netting that separated prisoner from visitor.

What we learned from my grandfather's writing was that my grandmother knew everything about her husband's secret life, his obsession with young women, that their relationship was based on truth telling and openness, and that Adele was preoccupied with her own life as well, and that this involved picking up men on the street and in bars and having sex for a few hours or a few minutes in a hotel room or an apartment or on warm nights on the grass in some nearby park. My grandfather described his wife's sexual encounters alongside his own. It was what they talked about when she visited on Sunday.

Insatiable. That was the word my grandfather used to describe his wife's sexual appetite. "The only person I know who is more insatiable than me." It was what they shared, what held them together, even more than the two children.

None of his young women friends visited him in prison. They had never really loved him, but he didn't blame them for their lack of gratitude. He hadn't asked them for love. He had wanted simply to be admitted into their presence and the only way he could make that happen was by giving them money. Sex was part of it, but rarely a necessity. Sometimes he was content just to look at them in their new clothes. He and Evelyn had sex together almost every night. No matter how many other men she was sleeping with, she never rejected him.

RALPH

For awhile we slept in separate beds. She was only sixteen and I was almost fifty. What do you expect? When we went to restaurants people assumed we were father and daughter. Little do they know, I thought, as I closed the menu and looked into the bored eyes of the waiter. "My name is Ralph," he said, "and I'm your waiter tonight." Melaine took a sip of water and stared at the waiter: "What do you recommend?" Later that night, for the first time, she crawled into bed with me. Her excuse was that she didn't want to be alone and my bed was big enough for both of us to sleep without touching. Ralph, the waiter, sat at the window in his furnished room, looking out at the night, wondering what he would do if he won the lottery. Every week, with his hard-earned money, with the money he earned from tips, he bought ten lottery tickets, but never won a dime. She came into bed with me and we both fell asleep but in the morning it was different. Something happens in the morning when people wake up in the same bed. Ralph once had a girlfriend, and her name was Sal. No, that isn't it. Her name was Devereaux. She had some French blood and she liked to dance. It was only after they broke up that

Ralph dropped out of college and became a waiter. There's something to be said for walking around naked in front of another person. I watched Melaine as she walked to the bathroom. She was tall and very thin and she walked with her shoulders hunched over. "I'd like the scallops," I said to Ralph and he said, "Excellent choice." Of course it couldn't go on forever but for awhile we couldn't stop touching one another, and not only in the morning. I knew the day would come when she wouldn't return home, when she would call to say she was late. I knew that eventually she would meet someone her own age. The last thing she wanted was to take care of an old man and she knew if we stayed together that would be her fate. I was getting old while she would be young for a long time. It was pointless to waste her youth on me. Ralph learned from a mutual friend that his former girlfriend Devereaux was getting married. He took a train to the town where the ceremony was going to take place. He planned to shoot both his girlfriend and her husband, but when she started down the aisle, on the arm of her father, all he could do was hide his face in his hands and weep. It was then that his baldheaded brother Lorenzo appeared, with a hardboiled egg on a silver tray. "Eat," he ordered, but Ralph wasn't hungry.

WE LIVE

We live according to rules that no one knows about but ourselves. We defy nature, in a way, by exerting pressure on areas of the skin that would draw blood to the surface, around the neck and throat area. My friend Marissa has to keep her neck covered at all times for fear that strangers would think she was being abused. Whenever she met someone for the first time she always turned off the lights before undressing so her new lover wasn't confused by her scars. They're in a room with no windows, a kind of bunker, and Marissa is standing against one wall smoking while the man she just met uncorks a bottle of wine. The room is filled with the odor of domestic animals. She wants to bury her face into the dead leaves that fall one by one onto the sidewalk. Her hair is combed over one eye. The next day, she promises herself, if she survives the night, she'll cut it all off. But the man, reading her mind, says: "Let's cut it off now." He takes a pair of garden shears from the back of the medicine cabinet. "How are your teeth?" he asks. Marissa remembers everything we taught each other, all those days back in her apartment after school, and in the local movie theaters on Saturday afternoons.

But it was confusing, especially the part about walking the walk and talking the talk, that didn't make sense in real life. Just the thought of talking and walking and smoking, all at the same time, seemed too much to ask. But when he lifted the pair of pliers and told her to open her mouth she figured it was easier to do what he asked than try to think of escaping. She remembered that the back door led to an alley surrounded by gates and she imagined what it felt like to be impaled on the spikes as she climbed over. Then she remembered the knock out drops I had given her before she left the house. "Don't forget to call," I said, kissing her on the forehead, "if you're going to be home late." She diverted his attention and poured the powder into his drink and in a minute he was writhing on the floor, a thick gel oozing out of the corner of his mouth. "Leave," Marissa thought to herself, as if she was a police sergeant talking to one of her underlings. They were at the scene of a crime and it was time to go home. She guided herself from room to room until she reached the front door. Then she was out in the open again, where everything mattered.

LOST TIME

The train was delayed, but when it finally entered the station, and after I found a seat near a window and hoisted my suitcase onto the rack, I noticed that the woman sitting across the aisle was a person I had known in high school. We had even gone out a few times, and she had let me kiss her good night on the steps of the house where she lived with her parents. I remember the smell of jasmine when I went to bite the flesh on the side of her neck, and the way she started wheezing as a sign of contentment, like a distant siren in the night. So I dozed off, planning to talk to her when I woke up, but when I opened my eyes she was gone, along with my suitcase. In her place, there was an elderly German, Herr Schwager, who told me he was a doctor, a neurologist to be exact, and that he was going to a conference at the Waldorf in New York. He told me that he and his wife had recently separated after being married for thirty years. "I've met someone new," he said. "How can I resist?" I wanted to ask him how his wife felt about all this, but another part of me wanted to congratulate him on his good fortune. He was the type of person who followed his tangents into dark alleyways, so there was no coming back to the initial topic. It was like listening to water running from a rusty faucet. It was like opening a well that had dried up years before, or a mine that had been boarded up since the turn of the last century. Once he started talking he didn't stop. The phrase "bottomless pit" comes to mind.

It seemed like she was everywhere, everywhere I looked. I had taken a train five hundred miles to meet her in the lobby of a hotel, but she never appeared. And now she was on the train, she was waiting in the station when the train pulled in, she was standing outside my apartment building when I got out of the cab, she was even waiting in the kitchen of my apartment, wearing just an apron. I could smell the bacon from the other end of the hall. "Why don't you take off your shoes, dinner will be ready in a minute, did you have a nice day?" She sounded pre-programmed, like a TV commentator, and I almost expected her to recite the five day forecast, what to expect in the days ahead. I could smell the jasmine, and then I could hear her voice from the distant past: "You can leave marks on my neck," she was saying, "I don't care." We were on the steps of her house, the private home where she lived with her parents. Our kisses seemed to last forever. I sometimes think her name is Jasmine, but obviously I'm confusing her with someone else. Whenever I smell jasmine, drink jasmine tea, I think of her. So that when she contacted me recently, and told me her address, and that I should visit her if I was ever traveling through town, I jumped at the chance. Coincidentally, I had a conference later that month in the midwestern city where she lived. She called back immediately and said how excited she was about seeing me again.

The first time I went to a therapist I was forty years old. My wife and I were breaking up—it was her idea, though we both agreed that living together had become intolerable. I'm the type of person who likes to keep things going past the time they should end. I've done this with other relationships as well but the stakes were much higher with my wife. We had a daughter who was only eight when we broke up. I moved from our apartment in Manhattan to an apartment in Brooklyn and my daughter spent half the week with me. But I wasn't happy. I couldn't sleep, for one thing, and eventually my doctor wrote me a prescription for valium, which was still in fashion in those days. Sometimes I would return home from my job at two in the afternoon—I was a professor in the same college that I teach in today—and get into bed. I wouldn't just take a nap but I'd take off all my clothing and disappear under the blankets and sheets. It was on one of the days when my daughter was sleeping over at her mother's and I didn't have anything to do. I had spent the last eight years involved in some form of daily childcare and I couldn't get used to not having somewhere to go, someone to pick up. You're free, I said to myself, and I knew I should take advantage of this time—go to the movies in mid-afternoon, something I liked to do when I was in college, or to a museum—but I couldn't.

So I decided to go to a therapist. Her name was Mrs. Z. I couldn't pay much money. I think she was on a list of therapists who saw patients on a sliding scale. And that someone probably recommended her. Her office was in a brownstone in the East 70s, near Central Park. I thought that going to a woman doctor was probably a good idea.

I've always had better rapport with women than with men. But for some reason I felt inhibited around her. It suddenly occurred to me that one might actually be smarter than one's therapist. I wanted to talk about sex, for instance, but I couldn't. I wanted to talk about how angry I became sometimes and how I wanted to be more in control of the way I expressed my feelings. Especially my anger. She seemed to think that expressing anger was a good thing. There was something about the way I expressed anger—I tried to explain this to her, but she didn't get it—that made the whole situation a lot worse. Once I arrived for an appointment, at the scheduled time, sat in the waiting room for half an hour, but Mrs. Z never showed up. This was before the days of cellphones and e-mails. So I left. A week later I saw her at our scheduled time and she asked me how I felt when I was waiting for her to come, when I realized that she wasn't going to come? I told her that I assumed she had a good reason for not showing up—that some emergency had prevented her from coming or that she was stuck in traffic. You didn't feel angry at me? she wanted to know. She didn't understand why I didn't come into the office absolutely furious. On the contrary, I was absolutely not furious. But part of me was beginning to feel furious at the idea that she was testing me. It occurred to me that she wanted to see if I'd feel angry. A few weeks later, when I told her about some fight I had with my wife, a kind of repetition of a fight we'd had before, she looked at me and said: "You want to make me cry, don't you?" I had no idea what she meant—the last thing I wanted to do was make her cry. A few weeks later I canceled my next appointment and stopped seeing her.

There are three or four women sitting alone at separate tables when I enter the hotel bar. They all look up at me, as if on cue. I wonder if they were planted there by the owners of the hotel to pick up men like myself—single, traveling alone, bored, disappointed. All of the above or none of the above—after awhile, it doesn't matter. One of the women, in a short pink dress, sits down besides me and orders a daiquiri. The waiter, whose name is Alfredo, winks at me, and points to the glass on the tablecloth in front of me. "Can I bring you another?" The woman introduces herself, her name is Phaedra, and she comes from Crete, a place I've never been. After fifteen minutes it seems we have almost nothing in common, but it doesn't deter us from returning to my room. "Can I run a bath?" Give it time, be patient, and something happens that you don't expect. I knelt at the side of the tub and massaged her stomach with an old cloth, just as one of my aunts,

Frieda—my mother's sister—used to do when I slept over at her house. She would come into the bathroom and kneel at the foot of my tub. At first I was embarrassed. I was ten years old, but I had an erection almost not-stop. "Does this feel good?" she said. She had taken my penis between her hands and in a few moments the semen began to spurt on her face. In similar manner, I leaned over the tub and caressed Phaedra's breasts. She took my hand and placed it between her legs. One night, when I slept over at my aunt's house, she came into my room as I was going to bed. "Are you awake?" she asked. She was wearing a long white nightgown which she lifted over her shoulders. Then she took my whole hand and placed it inside her, one finger at a time. So it seems that Phaedra and Frieda were the same person, or that they became confused in my mind as I rubbed the woman's shoulders with a towel and watched, as she lifted her arms, and piled her hair on top of her head and held it in place like a turban. I led her to the window of the bedroom where all the lights of the city were blinking in the distance like Chinese lanterns, like fire flies, like SOS signals, like the tips of a million cigarettes, at the darkest hour of the night, on the shortest day of the year, in the beginning of yet another century of recorded time, vanishing forever.

I'm waiting on the corner of Houston and Crosby, in Manhattan, for my high school girlfriend to show up. She called me on my cellphone only a half-hour before to tell me that she's going to be a few minutes late. I stare at the billboard sign above Houston Street. A young man with no shirt is lying on top of a woman who appears not to be wearing any clothing at all. The man is wearing jeans. The sign is an advertisement for jeans. You can see the woman's face, the tops of her breasts, and her long legs.

"Is that you?" I said. She leaned forward and kissed me on one cheek, and then another, and then she took my arm. "I know a restaurant," she said, "it isn't far." We tried to remember the last time we saw each other. I said, "The times I remember most are the sleigh rides," and she laughed. We were both living in the Bronx at the time, within walking distance, and one night, in the dead of winter, we went sleigh riding on the hills behind the house where she lived with her parents. She only had one sleigh. I was on bottom, she was on top. We held on for dear life. The sparks were flying from the blades. We couldn't stop laughing. There was no traffic, of course. Afterwards we walked back up the hill and she made hot chocolate and I stretched out on the couch with my head in her lap. It was not the last time we saw each other, but definitely the most vivid, more so even than the afternoons we spent in her house, when she would let me open her blouse and touch her breasts. "We have to make up for lost time," she said, as she lifted her glass of white wine in the form of a toast—to ourselves, our glittering past, all the moments leading up to this one.

"We were children then," she said, shaking her head. I didn't want to ask her what she had been doing since we last saw each other, graduation day twenty years ago, but of course that was what I wanted most to ask, what I wanted her to tell me, everything she had done, every person she had slept with, it could go on forever, or at least all night, and I would reciprocate by telling her everything that had happened to me, and it would end up resembling a long novel, one soliloquy after another, before we passed out in the hotel room where she was staying, both of us lying on top of the bed with our clothes on. We would have to wait till the next morning to summon the energy to be lovers once again. We could order room service, including a whole pot of coffee for each of us, and stay in bed all day, watching the local news reports, and exclaiming over and over again, until our voices became hoarse, how weird it was to see one another again, until it seemed we were like the uninvited guests who had worn our their welcome at a private party near a swimming pool. The host and hostess were eyeing us warily as we stuffed our pockets with *hors d'oeuvres* and meat sandwiches and I could see a security guard in a blue blazer heading in our direction. All I wanted to do was take off my clothes and dive into the pool where a young woman in a turquoise bathing suit, who reminded me of my first wife, was standing on her toes batting a beach ball high into the air.

WITHOUT SPEAKING

He liked to watch the way her face changed when they were in bed. The way her lips trembled as if she was on the verge of saying something—but she never did. She had a scar in the corner of her bottom lip and some of her lower front teeth were stained and crooked. She wore a silver ring in the shape of a snake around the middle finger of her right hand.Sometimes he tried to imagine what she would look like when she was older, as old as his mother had been when she died, but he couldn't. She told him she was thirty-five but he didn't believe her. He didn't want to believe her. When they were in bed together, with her ash blonde hair spread out on the pillow, she resembled a young girl, someone he had known in high school. If he wanted to, he could close his eyes and pretend he was in bed with someone else.

Once, in the dark, soon after they first met, she had cried out when they were having sex. But in recent months, and for reasons he didn't understand, she no longer made a sound. He had the sense that she was grimacing in the dark, waiting for it to be over. He was embarrassed to ask her whether she felt satisfied; if she didn't, he assumed she would say something that would make it better. She would tell him what she wanted him to do. The only way he could know otherwise was if he could read her mind. It was possible for him to get into her mind when they were having sex. He could tell what she was thinking, or so he imagined.

Both of them had been with other people in their lives but never for very long. The longest he had ever lived with another person was five years when he was in his thirties. Then it had ended. A few years later he fell in love with someone else, but she was married. They had a secret affair, her husband eventually found out, and it had ended, she had chosen her husband over him. He had held onto his love for this person for a long time, but now it was gone.

She, on the other hand, had been married twice. Once when she was seventeen, but that had lasted only a year. And then when she was older, but for not much longer. She told him that she had trouble sharing the same space with anyone. That it made her crazy to be around another person for too long a time. She didn't have to say this, he could read it in her eyes. She had circles under her eyes and the corners of her mouth curved downward, more out of resignation than unhappiness. Her eyes were small and angry, she was hiding her anger behind her eyes. He knew what she was thinking by the expression on her face.

Her eyes were closed and he was leaning over her, as always, with his weight on top of her, and she wasn't saying anything.

He rolled over onto his back so that she was on top of him and for a change her eyes were wide open. She was concentrating on the moment in a way he had never seen before. She was steadying herself on top of him and then leaning backwards, balancing herself with her hands. He could no longer see her eyes, or the expression on her face. Her thought was out there, in the space between them, like a blanket of molecules or a cloud. It was up to him to translate what she was thinking into a kind of music, like the cars going by on the street or the rain falling against the windows. The springs of the bed creaking under their weight.

He could hear the music of her thoughts when he was looking directly at her, it was loud and clear and he had to turn down the volume, he was hearing too much, and the sounds, like two people talking at the same time, were overlapping—he couldn't hear one thing clearly, or another. The different sounds were competing with each other for his attention like radios on a beach. When one song ended another began almost immediately. He could tell how tired she was from balancing herself on top of him while all he had to do was lie on his back and do nothing. He had the feeling she probably hated him for not giving her more pleasure.

He thought of himself in competition with her first and second husbands, neither of whom he had met. He had seen their photographs and it wasn't hard to imagine her in bed with them. Then she would be on top and crying out as the man moved beneath her. She would be expressing her pleasure without holding back.

She had been so young then she didn't care if any of the neighbors knew that she was having sex. She was only seventeen and the man she was with, whom she eventually married, was ten years older. A man who had slept with many women, who didn't care about anything except his own pleasure. The walls of the apartment building were like cardboard and everyone could hear everything. The walls of the room literally shook as she grabbed at his hair and cried out. She could imagine all her neighbors lying awake listening to her and Carlos, the friend of her brother who had seduced her on their first date, just as she listened to the people downstairs having sex late at night and the people down the hall when they were fighting with each other and throwing things.

This older man was her first lover but being with him wasn't as painful as she had imagined. All her friends had described "the searing pain" that happened when you had sex for the first time, as if "a branding iron was being held against your skin," and one of them had told her she thought she was going to die the pain was so unbearable. She was the last of her group of friends to have sex with anyone. Some of her friends had begun having sex when they were twelve or thirteen and here she was still a virgin at seventeen.

He could imagine her body when she was that young and in bed with someone else. Her arms were thin and she wore silver bracelets around her wrists. He could hear her cry out as the man named Carlos—the man in the photograph—climbed on top of her.

It had not always been this way. At one point in their life together, in the months after they first met, they were always laughing. He remembered that time wistfully, when they hardly knew each other. They were in the back of a cab, coming home from a party, and she rested her head on his shoulder so he could smell her perfume and when he put his hand on her knee she didn't push him away.

Another time, a week later—it was only the second time they had seen one another—she arrived at his apartment directly after work and they went to bed immediately. After they had sex she fell asleep and he watched her lips moving but he couldn't hear what she was saying. He put his ear very close to her mouth but all he could hear were fragments of sounds that reminded him of a foreign language, possibly Chinese, where each word means something different depending on how you say it. As I said before, it wasn't necessary for them to say anything. He liked to think he had the power to read her mind.

The first time they had sex was the time she came to his apartment after work. They were planning to go out to dinner together but it didn't happen. As soon as she arrived in his apartment she began taking off her clothes and it was just a matter of time, a few minutes, before they were in bed together. First she sat on a chair in the kitchen while he hovered over her. It was the first time she had been to his apartment but she wasn't looking around like a housing inspector in search of violations or to check on whether he was overly neat or slovenly. She didn't say something like "show me around" when she entered the apartment. She had gone right up to him. She had been thinking about him all day. She didn't have to say she was thinking about him, he could tell.

She was wearing a silver chain around her ankle, a slave bracelet, he noticed this when she was in the chair, and he leaned forward and she began undressing him. He could see the moisture in the corners of her eyes. Her eyes were hazel, he noticed, just like his. This was only the second time they had ever met. The first time was when he had taken her home in the cab after the party. He didn't approach her in any aggressive way or try to coerce her into having sex. It was she who had called him as she was leaving work. A half hour later she was lying naked across his bed.

He had been tempted, when she first entered the apartment, to say something like "do you want anything?" or "do you want a drink?" If he had known earlier she was coming over he would have bought a bottle of wine. All he had, as it turned out, was a bottle of vodka left over from a party he'd given a few weeks before. So it was pointless to offer her anything since there was not that much to offer and he was relieved when she stepped towards him and he closed the door behind her and she drew him towards her, lifting her knee between his legs, that the last thing on her mind was something to drink or eat, even though she had suggested over the phone they go out to dinner. He assumed they would eat later, but it never happened. She was napping, though it was only about eight o'clock in the evening, enough time to go out for food if that's what she wanted. Or they could call up the restaurant around the corner and have someone deliver it.

He had no idea why he was thinking about food. Nothing was important except the fact that she was there. That she had called him up and had come to his apartment. She was there and he was on top of her but she was making no sound. It was late November and it had been dark for hours. The room was dark and there was heat coming up through the pipes. He could hear the heat murmuring just like always. There were some winters when the people who occupied the building had to complain to the landlord about the lack of heat. While she was napping he pulled the covers over her body until all he could see was her mouth, her forehead, and her blonde hair spread out on the pillow behind her. He had been working at home all day so he felt less tired than she was. And her presence in the apartment excited him. He didn't want to leave her alone in the room. He had the feeling that if she woke up and he wasn't there she wouldn't know where she was. He sometimes had that feeling when he slept in a strange place.

Once he woke up in a hotel room in Los Angeles and there was a woman he didn't know sleeping beside him. He had gotten drunk the night before and couldn't remember what had happened. The woman told him her name was Cindy and they had met at a party. Now it all came back to him. He had been called to Los Angeles to work on a screenplay that someone else had written. He had spent most of his week in Los Angeles holed up in his hotel room working on the script. He was almost finished and the night before had been his reward to himself.

He had gone to a party, not necessarily to meet anyone, but to see what happened when he let down his guard. Someone must have introduced them, he couldn't remember who. All he could remember was that the party was at a pool and that there were many naked young women jumping into the water. They would swim around for a few minutes and splash one another as if they were in a commercial. And then they would get out and spread their towels on the side of the pool. They would rub suntan lotion into each other's shoulders and lie on their stomachs. Most of the men at the party were middle-aged like himself. They stood around watching the girls and drinking campari's. He had the feeling that the girls had been hired by the host of the party to entertain the men and that Cindy had been one of these girls, though he couldn't remember who had introduced them or anything else about the night. He didn't remember Cindy's name until she told him in the morning. He had the feeling that she was used to waking up in the morning next to men who didn't remember her name. Her skin was very white and seemed to have been poured over the bones of her face. Cindy wanted to have sex with him in the morning but he was too tired, which wasn't exactly true. She looked at him with disgust and slammed the door on her way out.

It was evident, almost immediately, that they had many things in common. The movies, for one thing. He couldn't imagine, since this was his profession, being with someone who didn't like watching movies. Almost everyone likes movies so it wasn't exactly a coincidence that they both liked the same thing. It would have probably been more surprising if she said she didn't like movies. But he could tell immediately that she was serious about her interest in movies, that she wasn't telling him she liked movies because she thought it would impress him.

She told him that when she was in college in Michigan she had been the film critic for the college newspaper. *The Beagle* or *The Eagle*, she couldn't remember which. It was also clear that she preferred foreign movies to Hollywood movies. She knew he worked in Hollywood so she was tentative when she said this but all he could do was shake his head.

"I couldn't agree with you more," he said.

They got down to specifics. Foreign movies was a big subject. There were French movies, which were her first love, especially the movies of the early nineteen sixties, the so-called "Nouvelle Vogue," the movies of people like Francois Truffaut, who had died in his early fifties but had made his best movies when he was a young man, movies like *400 Blows, Shoot the Piano Player,* and *Jules and Jim.* Then there was Jean-Luc Godard who was still alive and couldn't even find a distributor for his most recent movies. She had seen them all, while he had to admit that he had only seen the early movies by Godard like *Breathless, Alphaville* and *Une Femme est Une Femme.*

He wasn't a big fan of the movies of Godard but he didn't tell her this. Not only did she know the names of Godard's movies but she knew the actors and actresses who had appeared in each one, she knew the dates in which the movies had been made, and she could refer to specific scenes. He was impressed by her depth of knowledge but he didn't feel threatened. He saw her as someone who could teach him things he didn't know. He liked the idea that she knew more than he did. Later she told him that some men were put off by her seriousness. That when she told these men she liked foreign films they looked at her as if she was cross-eyed.

They were sitting opposite each other in a restaurant in the West Village talking about movies—they had known each other for about a month at this time—when she reached across the table, took his hand, and began to suck longingly on one of his fingers. She had taken his whole finger into her mouth, gently, then another finger, not caring if anyone at any of the other tables or any of the waiters or waitresses saw what she was doing. She stared at him while she did this and her eyelids quivered a little. He had the feeling she could look like a movie star if she wanted. One of the reasons he liked being with her was because she was always doing unexpected things. One minute they were innocently talking about movies in a fancy Italian restaurant and now all he could think of doing was paying the check and getting into a cab and going back to his apartment and having sex with her on the living room floor. He had lost interest in the food on his plate and in the conversation about movies. She took one finger after another into her mouth. The moment resembled a jewel in its clarity, the kind of jewel that contained colors inside it, and in which you could see your own reflection. At the same time he felt like he was trapped in a house that was on fire. He didn't want the moment to end but he knew if it continued he might die.

There were movies and sex (this goes without saying) and there was music as well. For most people having these things in common would be more than enough. It gave them something to talk about all the time. They spent more time watching movies at home than they did in the theater. Each of them had favorite movies that the other one hadn't seen.

One of the first times she came to his apartment she had checked out his CD collection, remarking how similar it was to her own. She stood next to the rack of CDs and every few seconds she said "I have this one too." There were the complete recordings of the piano music of Erik Satie, for instance, and five different versions of Rachmaninoff's Third Piano Concerto. There were the complete symphonies of Mahler, the piano sonatas of Beethoven. His favorite jazz musician was the pianist Bill Evans, but he also had a number of records by Wayne Shorter and Art Tatum. He admitted to her that Evans was his favorite jazz musician and that he had once studied jazz piano but had given it up because he didn't have time to practice. He told her that he had had a piano in a previous apartment but that he had sold it before moving. He had been playing a record by Bill Evans the night she first came over. They had only met once before. The first time they saw one another—the night they shared a cab and she rested her head on his shoulder—they had exchanged phone numbers. The second time was the time she called him from work. He had been home all day, drinking coffee and working on a new screenplay. Not a rewrite of someone else's screenplay but an original.

He made his living by rewriting other people's work and he had saved enough money to buy his own apartment if he wanted. But he was lazy about looking for a new place and he was comfortable in his rent-controlled dump. Compared to what other people were paying, his rent was next to nothing. The idea of looking for a new apartment as a single person didn't appeal to him. What was the point? The last thing he ever imagined was that he would get involved with someone again.

He was listening to a solo recording by Bill Evans when she rang the doorbell downstairs. It had taken her fifteen minutes to get from her job to his apartment. He closed the door behind her and she came towards him. He could hear Bill Evans playing in the background as she sat in a chair in the kitchen and he leaned over her, her hands on the buckle of his belt.

At one point in the middle of the night she woke up and asked him to give her directions to the bathroom in the dark and when he asked her if she wanted anything to drink she said "a glass of water." So he got up naked and walked to the kitchen, since he wanted some water too. He looked at the clock on the kitchen wall. It was three-fifteen in the morning. He had fallen asleep next to her but he hadn't been asleep for long. He thought he heard his cat Leopold purring in the foyer near the front door but then he realized that Leopold had died six months before and that he had been meaning to get a new cat. He had had Leopold for over fifteen years, for as long as he had been in this apartment. It occurred to him that she might be allergic to cats and he reminded himself to ask her about animals when they woke up. He drank one glass of water in the kitchen and then poured another glass for her. The apartment contained one bedroom, a living room—where he worked—and a kitchen.

She didn't say thank you when he handed her the glass of water but she sat up, wrapping the blanket around her, and held the glass between her knees.

"I'm sorry I fell asleep," she said. "I hadn't planned to stay over."

She had told him, a few hours earlier, that she had to go home, but then she had fallen back to sleep. He didn't know why she would want to go home. It was Friday night and she didn't have to go to work the next day. Or did she? He wasn't clear about her job. They hadn't talked very much. The previous time they had seen one another they had talked about movies. And books.

Books was another subject they had in common. It wasn't just that they read books but that they had read many of the same books. She worked, as far as he could tell, as an editor for a publishing company, and her life revolved around books, or so he assumed. They had been introduced at a party by a mutual friend, a movie producer named Melissa, but he hadn't spoken to this person since the night they met. All the other guests around the dinner table were interested in his experiences in Hollywood. He was sitting between Melissa and another woman, who was she? Someone had introduced them earlier but he had forgotten her name. He was aware that she was watching him closely as he told his stories but he wondered whether she was really listening. There was nothing furtive about the way she was looking at him. It was more like she was scanning his face, memorizing every feature, every pore on his skin. That she was evaluating him according to some agenda that wasn't clear, not even to herself. At one point they chatted briefly—she made a comment about his ring, the one with the black onyx stone that the woman he had been in love with in the past had given him, the married woman who had been too frightened to leave her husband. He remembered later that when they were talking he had been thinking what it might be like to touch her and that he had the feeling that if he put his hand under her skirt under the table and put his fingers inside her she wouldn't have pushed him away. When it was time to leave they realized that they lived in the same neighborhood and that it would make sense to share a cab. It was in the backseat of the cab that she rested her head on his shoulder and before she got out they exchanged phone numbers. Six days later he received the call in the late afternoon asking if he wanted to go to dinner.

"I'll be there in fifteen minutes," she had said.

Six days elapsed between the time she came over and the next time they saw one another. This time they actually went out for dinner. They met in a restaurant on West 13th Street that she said she liked.

She joked: "If we met at your place again, who knows what would happen?"

He wanted to tell her that he had missed her during the week and that he had been tempted to call even though she had asked him not to. She had made it clear that she would be the one who would call him about getting together. The last thing she said to him before she left the apartment was that she'd call him at the end of the week. She had bent towards him and offered him her cheek and he could smell persimmon on her skin. He saw the small piercings in her ears—she had taken off the silver loops that she had worn the night before. He had bathed in her scent which was everywhere—in his bed, on his skin— and which would follow her down the stairs and into the street where people would turn their heads as she walked by, and the drivers of cars would hit the brakes at the sight of her so that the car behind the car that stopped would plow into one of the other cars causing a traffic tie-up from the Holland Tunnel to the George Washington Bridge. It was more likely that no one would notice her at all. She was wearing the same clothing she had worn the night before and which she had tossed on the floor as he led her into the bedroom. She was wearing a short charcoal skirt and a white round-neck blouse and she had tied back her blonde hair with a green ribbon. She still wore the simple silver band around her ankle.

Every time the phone rang he hoped that it was her. It was hard not to think about her constantly and replay what had happened. It made him excited and distracted to remember what had happened when she came through the door. He had thought they would go out to dinner and that afterwards he would walk her home. Possibly they would kiss on the street outside her apartment. During the years he had been living alone he had played out a scenario over and over again in his head. Someone he barely knows arrives at the door of his apartment and without speaking begins taking off her clothes. Usually he fantasized about someone he saw on the street or in a bar or one of the actresses on one of the sets of the movies that he worked on—though in most cases the writer wasn't welcome on the set—or one of the many women who showed up at the parties he attended, both in Los Angeles and New York, anyone of whom might have gone home with him when they learned the names of the movies he had written or co-written in the hope that if they had sex together he might introduce her to the director of one of the movies or the head of one of the studios and in this way further her career. It wasn't unusual, and not only in Hollywood, for someone to sleep with someone else for this reason. In his fantasy, of course, the woman was kneeling on the floor in front of him. Submissiveness was the key to his fantasy, since he was a submissive person as well, and it was only in his fantasy world that the woman was more submissive than he was.

What he wanted in life was to be told what to do. What he wanted was not to have to do anything. What frightened him most was the thought that the woman wasn't interested in him. In order for him to feel that he wouldn't be rejected the woman had to make the first move. He had never taken the initiative with anyone—not since he was younger and all the women he met rejected him. What he loved most was the idea of not having to say anything, of not having to seduce anyone. When she arrived at his apartment for the first time it was as if she was following the tracks of his desire, through a veldt of misunderstandings and false conclusions, until finally— after years of broken promises—she was standing in the hallway, she had come to his door. She had come because she wanted to. There was no need to talk about why she was there.

He was working at home these days and at nights he liked to shut off his computer and go out with his friends but sometimes he preferred to stay home and read. Or watch one of the hundreds of movies in his collection of DVDs and videos. This week, especially, he didn't mind being alone. He had a hard time concentrating when he was reading and often he would find himself stuck on the same page, on the same paragraph, the same sentence. He would start reading and then he would look up and stare into space and remember how he had rolled over when they were having sex and she had climbed on top of him. Neither of them had said "roll over"—they had just done it, as one person. He didn't like to think he was staying home in the hope she would call but he had to admit that that's what he was doing. His friends would call him up and invite him to a party or an art opening or the preview of a movie he knew he would hate and he would make some excuse, "I'm tired," or "I'm still working." Most of his friends were people he had known for a long time. They were almost all part of couples and often, when they all got together, he was the odd person out. Everyone he knew had a mate except him. Or were between mates. He hadn't had a serious relationship for at least ten years, or a person he could call "my mate." It was hard, at this point, to even define what "serious" meant. All his friends had women friends who were single and they were constantly creating occasions for them to meet. Usually small dinner parties where the host and hostess arranged it so they would sit side by side. Once or twice he felt attracted to the person and they would go out to dinner and occasionally they would even go to bed together, but never more than once.

He didn't understand why she didn't want him to call but he realized that it wasn't his business. He had no right to feel that anything she did was his business. She had slept over on a Friday and the next morning he would have liked to take her out to breakfast and possibly spend the day in bed together but she wouldn't even allow him to make her coffee. She was dressed and ready to leave and it wasn't even 8 A.M. She apologized for falling asleep so early. She said, "I'll call you in a few days," and kissed him goodbye as they stood at the door.

There are people who live alone who prefer their own company. People who are happy to close the door on the outside world. But he wasn't one of them. It occurred to him, years ago, that he hated being alone. It was *intolerable*—that was the word he used when he thought about it. He had many friends, both male and female, and over the years he would confide in one or the other about the misery of being by himself. When he was younger he had often imagined himself in the future as a person with a family. He made enough money as a screenwriter to support a family, to buy an apartment in the city and a house in the country, to send his children to college. His parents weren't wealthy people but he had been an only child and when they died whatever money they had saved went to him. But that money had been irrelevant; by the time his parents died, a year apart, he was already making huge sums of money rewriting other people's screenplays. He even had a book of his own short stories published and for many years he tried, without success, to write a novel. The publisher of his stories had given him an advance to write a novel but after three years of trying he had to give back the money. He was tired of telling people he was working on a novel when he knew he couldn't do it. He had decided, anyway, that he would prefer writing screenplays. That was his real talent. Twice a year he was called to Hollywood to work on a script. Often a script went through numerous drafts and each of those drafts was written by a different writer. There were maybe five or six writers who were in demand to rewrite scripts and he was one of them. He had been working on a script of his own for years. The screenplay he was writing was legendary in screenwriting circles but he never showed it to anyone. He was frightened that someone would steal his idea.

The restaurant wasn't crowded, it was six in the evening. Most people in New York ate out later—often nine or ten.

At six most of the waiters and waitresses stand around bored. They stand outside smoking cigarettes waiting for customers. A young Japanese woman in a kimono and a sour-faced middle-aged Japanese man in black pants and a white shirt brought them water and saki and miso soup. The food came too fast and there was little time to talk. As soon as they finished the soup the waitress came by and took their bowls. They began to feel rushed, as if there was a line waiting outside the restaurant and people wanted their table. At one point her foot touched his leg under the table and she smiled at him and apologized but then she did it again.

There was a lot to talk about. All he had to do was ask a question and it would open up a door that would lead to a room that would open yet another door to another room. This endless hallway was a hackneyed metaphor for life itself. And yet every question was a kind of trigger that led to something else. If he said: What's your job like? she would tell him everything related to that subject. So that the next time they met he could ask her something about what she had said and she would be overjoyed that he had actually listened the first time. In this way there would be some kind of continuity from conversation to conversation. In this way they would get to know each other, at least up to a point.

And if they talked on the phone more frequently they would keep each other up to date about the other people in their lives whom neither of them had met as well as the work they were doing and how they spent the time when they were apart. Since in the beginning they were mostly apart. There was the dinner party where she stared at him and asked about his ring and then afterwards they took a cab back to the neighborhood where they both lived, each in their separate apartments, and then there was the second time when she came to his apartment and they spent the night together, and almost a month had passed between the first time and the time they were meeting again in the restaurant, with more than a week in between the first and second times, and then another week between the second and third times. Not quite a month but it seemed longer, endless. There was an immediate gap to fill, what had happened to them during the week, but the real gap was the entirety of both of their lives, from beginning to end. It was a bottomless pit. It didn't matter if there were snakes writhing at the bottom. What he wanted to know was everything—not drop by drop, as in a torture chamber, but like a deluge, all at once.

Yet all the time he listened to her talk over dinner he realized that none of it was necessary. That the only important thing was where it would end. He had lifted her dress or she was kneeling on the floor or she was raking her nails along his back or he had put his whole hand inside her and she was crying out. Literally screaming. Or they had turned over again, in unison, and she was on top with her hair falling in his face. It was all he could think about when she talked to him over dinner about her job, about the books she had acquired, or the books that an agent had sent her, every day a different agent sent a different book. Or about the long lunch she had with the new writer—"What an asshole!"—whose book her company had just acquired. She told him the names of all these people. She told him the names of the people she worked with. And even though all he could think about was what would happen when she returned to his apartment, he could still follow everything she said. He even remembered the names of her coworkers and the writers whose work she edited (some of whom he had heard of before but none of whom he had ever read), and after every few sentences, when she lifted her cup of saki to her lips, he would ask a question that in some way related to what she had said. The purpose of the question was to make her keep talking. He had to admit that some of what she said wasn't very interesting. Some of it. So much of what anyone said was only vaguely interesting. For his part, all he wanted to say was how much he wanted to go back to the apartment, how much he wished dinner was over.

"Shall we leave?"

The unsmiling waitress brought them the check. He took a credit card out of his wallet and handed it to her.

"I can pay half," the woman said.

She reached in her pocketbook for her wallet but he held up his hand.

"Let me do it," he said.

"Are you sure?" she said. "Next time I'll make dinner."

They walked up Seventh Avenue in the chill October air, past the Village Vanguard where he had once heard Bill Evans play, past St. Vincent's Hospital where he had once gone to the emergency room when Leopold the cat scratched his lower lip. She took his hand as they crossed

Fourteenth Street, standing just off the curb as the traffic came at them, and he thought that it was something a parent would do before crossing a crowded street, but that he didn't feel like her parent, despite the age difference, which was not really that much.

They held hands all the way back to the apartment building on Sixteenth Street and then he disengaged his fingers so he could open the front door with his key. In the elevator she stood very close to him and put her hand on the buttons of his jacket and opened them one by one. It occurred to him that she was thinking the same thing he was, that it had been a waste of time going to dinner, that they would have plenty of time in the future to eat and talk. What was there to talk about anyway? For a whole week he had waited for her to call so he could hear the sound of her voice. They had been in the restaurant for less than an hour but they had hardly spoken to one another. They each drank two cups of saki, but he didn't feel drunk. It was the way she had taken his hand that excited him, that made him feel lightheaded. He was no longer worrying that nothing was going to happen. He had worried all week that she would never call him and now that they had met he was worried they would go home to their separate apartments.

"Don't turn on the light," she said, when he closed the door behind him. The apartment was completely dark. He thought he heard Leopold whining in the corner. They were leaning up against the sink kissing and she put her hand down the front of his pants. He felt like an idiot for thinking she didn't want to have sex with him. She was on the floor in front of him, on her knees, just the way he imagined, and this time she pulled him down on top of her and lifted her skirt.

They were lying in bed smoking cigarettes. The first time they met one another, at the dinner party, she had rolled her own cigarettes, but now she was smoking Gitanes. In a blue box. She took out a cigarette, passed him the box, and then lit both of them. He had spent the last thirty years of his life trying to quit smoking. Sometimes he went for months at a time without a cigarette and then suddenly he was at a party, everyone around him was smoking, and he couldn't resist. And then he would start again, first only a few cigarettes a day. In a week or two he was up to a pack a day, sometimes more. Then he would start coughing uncontrollably before falling asleep and he would vow never to smoke again. Or he would notice that the people he was meeting, especially the women, were shrinking from him when he started talking, as if they couldn't bear the smell of smoke on his breath. It was only when he wasn't smoking that he was aware of the smell of smoke on other people. He made excuses for himself most often when he was working on a script. It was hard to imagine writing without fueling his body on cigarettes and coffee, especially when he was holed up in a hotel room in Los Angeles. He knew that he would have to stop smoking some time but he wasn't ready yet.

She put her finger to his lips as a signal that he should stop talking. He was telling her about the time he decided to drive from Los Angeles to New York by way of Canada. It was an old story, but he hadn't told it to anyone in a long time.

It was early in the morning in the middle of winter and still dark out. They were in her apartment now. They had gone out to a restaurant for dinner the night before because she had to work late and there had been no time to go shopping or prepare food. It was the first time he had ever been in her apartment.

He had left his house at six o'clock and walked east across 12th Street until he reached First Avenue. Then south along First until he came to Fourth Street where he turned east again . He walked past the Village View projects, many of the windows already alive with Christmas lights. He walked past a school with gated windows that looked like a prison. He had never lived in this neighborhood but he had visited it frequently. He had gone to parties here. He had gone to clubs to hear music in the days before the neighborhood had become trendy.

It was early December and the days were getting shorter.

He located her name on the panel in the inner lobby and pressed the buzzer.

And now it was the next morning. He was telling her about his dream and how it connected to something he had really done, the epic car trip from Los Angeles to New York by way of Canada. It was just a few minutes before she would have to get out of bed, put on her clothing, and go to work. She put her finger on his lips and shook her head as a way of saying that it wasn't necessary to say anything.

"Later," she said, "you can tell me all about it later."

Then she was walking across the bedroom floor naked in the dark to the kitchen to heat water for coffee. He couldn't remember the last time anyone had brought him coffee in bed. Then after she left for work he walked home, following the same route he had taken the night before, up Fourth Street to First—past the entrance to the school, past the Village View Projects, past the Strand Bookstore on the corner of 12th Street and Broadway which wasn't even open yet and where he would sometimes browse when he had nothing better to do. He had the distinct impression that he was walking one step slower than everyone else—all these people with dejected expressions on their faces disappearing into subway tunnels on the way to jobs they hated. He was not usually out this early and it made him appreciate how lucky he was to be a person who worked at home, who had the luxury to move through the streets at his own pace. And if he didn't want to go home that was a possibility too. He could buy the newspaper and eat breakfast, linger over breakfast, and when he did get home he could take a nap or a shower. He could do what he wanted.

At first, when she put her finger on his lips, he felt insulted, like she wasn't interested in what he was saying. But while she was in the kitchen getting the coffee he realized that there was no reason why she or anyone should care about something that had happened to him over twenty years ago, not this morning, not this moment when it was still dark out, when it was still the year 2000 and beginning to snow. It had snowed all night in fact and the flakes were swirling in the first light. She had to get to work early this morning. She had set the alarm for six o'clock and it had awakened him from a dream and as he remembered the dream he remembered the story about Canada, about the car that had broken down in Vancouver, about the days he had spent in the motel in Vancouver waiting for the car to be fixed before he drove it across Canada at a hundred miles an hour. There was a highway that crossed Canada, from Vancouver to Toronto, and it was like a straight line, a road that never curved, and that road was in his dream somehow, as if he had been driving nonstop into a big starless abyss.

He was left with the dream and with the feeling that she had slighted him but he knew she was right. It was something he had done in the past, with other women. He had gone on about himself, not questioning whether they cared or not. He had treated them as if their only purpose in life was to listen to him talk.

There was his clothing folded over the back of a chair at the foot of the bed. She was in the bathroom getting dressed. He could hear the shower. He would shower when he returned home, after the walk back, still not clear when they would see each other again. What he wanted was to rush things, to make it be tonight, to suggest that they have dinner again tonight, this time she could sleep over at his place, it didn't matter where.

She was wearing a floral print blouse and a woolen skirt with tights and around her neck a string of beads that extended to her waist. She stood in front of the mirror in the bedroom and fingered the beads as she leaned forward and inspected herself. She acted like he wasn't there. This is how she acts, he thought, when she's alone. There was a radio playing in the distance from someone else's apartment but otherwise there was no sound. He sat on the edge of the bed, fully dressed, waiting for her to say: Do you want more coffee? Waiting for her to say: Are you ready, I have to go?

She was ready, but there was still time. She really didn't have to be at work so early. She had told him this just so he would leave the house. She had to be free of him, she couldn't stand being with him a moment longer. They had met earlier the previous evening, they had spent the night together. That was enough. She couldn't tell him how much she loved her mornings alone before leaving for work. It meant something not to feel you had to talk to someone else. That you had to take someone else's needs into consideration. The hour before she left for work in the morning was her best time. There was never a moment during the day when she could think her own thoughts. It would begin the moment she stepped onto the elevator in the midtown office building where she worked. There was bound to be one of her coworkers heading up to the twentieth floor. There was the look of recognition followed by desultory attempts at conversation until finally the elevator stopped and they were free of each other, free of the obligation to make small talk. Her entire day consisted of business related talk, gossip and small talk, and she was good at all of it.

She pushed him back onto the bed and fell on top of him laughing. It didn't matter whether she was late for work or not. Her hair fell over his eyes and she smiled at him with her eyes open as if she were seeing him for the first time. He put his hands on the small of her back and he opened his mouth as if to say something but it was no longer important. Nothing was important except the light coming on.

SELF-PORTRAIT, SAN FRANCISCO, 1971

I get up just like everyone else and I eat a day-old donut and drink a cup of coffee. You can buy two day-old donuts on the corner for fifteen cents. We're talking March 1971, if you want to know exactly. I'm living on Oak Street, in San Francisco, right across from The Panhandle, a half block from Golden Gate Park. I don't have much money, that's one thing, nor a job, so whatever money I do have has to last me a while. So every morning I go up to the donut shop on Haight Street, two blocks away, and buy two day-old glazed donuts for fifteen cents, and after I eat them I don't feel like eating for the rest of the day.

It all happens in a minute. The rest of the day fades away. I can still taste the donuts from forty years ago and the way I sat in the kitchen of my apartment and stared out the back window at the garden (I was on the bottom floor) and ate the donuts and drank some coffee, wondering if this would be the high point of my day, and what would happen next, how time would unfold, if I could only regroup, backtrack, cut my losses and move on. It was the only place to be, but before I could do anything I had to repeat all the mistakes of the past one more time till I got the picture, a print of me in front of a window smoking a cigarette and drinking coffee (I had already eaten the donuts) while the sun cut through the cloud cover and the cars went by on The Panhandle. Maybe later I'll go for a walk in the park (or not). I could have stayed in that apartment forever and life would have been different, but I didn't. It was a two bedroom apartment, a few minutes from the park. I could still be living there now, forty years later. It might have been perfect, going to the park everyday. I could have lived in my own little world. I could have gotten a job and stayed there forever. Anything's possible. The donuts left a taste in my mouth but I didn't brush my teeth. They killed my appetite. They tasted older than a day, like they'd been sitting around for a week, at least. I ate them anyway. I didn't know where my next meal was going to come from, as they say, except that I made it, on the stove in the kitchen, and ate it at the same table where I ate the donuts, looking out at the garden in the back. It didn't last long. It seemed like a long time passed, but maybe only a few weeks. Then I got a job. It was in some office doing some vague kind of work involving tenant-landlord relations. It was a full-time job, I went every day. It was down near City Hall Park and I sat in the park on my lunch hour, ate a sandwich and read. I made the sandwich before leaving the house. I had to take a bus down Haight Street to get there.

Things add up, all the moments, dot dash dot, and the final word on it all is that it really happened. Snapshot of a moment in time that someone preserves under glass. Me on the job, at the desk, bumming a smoke from a coworker because I couldn't afford my own, a Japanese guy who didn't seem to mind. At lunch I sat on a bench in City Hall Park, eating a sandwich and reading Zukofsky, who for some reason I chose as my companion, since I hardly talked to anyone else. It was important just to go on like that. There were people in the office who had worked there twenty years. One night I met someone, at a reading, who I had met somewhere before, and I stayed over at her house a few times, that really happened, and in her apartment there was a view of Golden Gate Bridge, and I could see San Francisco Bay when we woke up and drank coffee. I wasn't sure what I was doing, to say the least. It was hard for me to imagine getting involved with anyone for a while. I took my own council, just like I always do, so to speak. Everything was up for grabs, life itself, and everything that went with it. I'd already done a few things but most of it was up ahead. It was something I told myself every morning. There was time, I had time, I could change everything. I didn't want to harm anyone. I wanted to be clear about what I was doing. I didn't want any secret motives. There was someone else out there, whom I hadn't met yet, waiting in the wings. I could have lived there forever, by myself, maybe. There was room for someone to move in, that's why I took the apartment, and everything could just go on. I was there only a few months and then I moved back up the coast to Stinson Beach. It was like an in between place before everything else happened. But it was important, that little moment in time. I learned how to breathe again. It was all I could do.

Lewis Warsh is the author of over thirty volumes of poetry, fiction and autobiography. He is coeditor of *The Angel Hair Anthology* and editor and publisher of United Artists Books. His fiction and poetry have appeared in numerous anthologies, including *The Best American Poetry* (1997, 2002, 2003) . He is recipient of grants from the National Endowment for the Arts, New York Foundation for the Arts, and The Fund for Poetry. He has also received an Editor's Fellowship Award from the Coordinating Council of Literary Magazines, and the James Shestack prize from *The American Poetry Review. Mimeo Mimeo* #7 (2012) featured his poetry, fiction and collages, and a bibliography of his work as an editor and publisher. He has taught at Naropa University, The Poetry Project, SUNY Albany, and Long Island University (Brooklyn) where he was founding director of the MFA program in creative writing (2007-13) and where he currently teaches. *Alien Abduction,* a new book of poems, is forthcoming from Ugly Duckling Presse in 2015.

9 780923 389932